JULES WAKE

Despite early ambitions, my path to being a published novelist took a diversion when after reading English at the University of East Anglia, I ended up in the glamorous and deeply shallow world of PR, and I spent a number of years honing my fictional writing skills on press releases.

In my head I'm a winning contestant on Strictly Come Dancing, a competitive skydiver and a domestic goddess. Unfortunately in reality I can't dance, or sky dive and dust bunnies gather in every corner of my house but in my fun, romantic comedy, my heroines can be anything they want.

From Italy With Love

JULES WAKE

Harper*Impulse* an imprint of
HarperCollins*Publishers* Ltd
1 London Bridge Street
London SE1 9GF

www.harpercollins.co.uk

A Paperback Original 2015

First published in Great Britain in ebook format by Harper*Impulse* 2015

A catalogue record for this book is
available from the British Library

ISBN: 9780008126346

This novel is entirely a work of fiction.
The names, characters and incidents portrayed in it are
the work of the author's imagination. Any resemblance to
actual persons, living or dead, events or localities is
entirely coincidental.

Automatically produced by Atomik ePublisher from Easypress

Printed and bound in Great Britain

For Nicola & Ian Walker, friends, steadfast & true.

Chapter 1

The minute Lauren saw the girl dressed in brilliant fuchsia, teetering along on mile-high heels, a fascinator bobbing in her hair like an exotic bird of paradise, she knew she'd got it wrong. Not just wrong – horribly, horribly wrong.

She liked this navy blue suit and until that moment had liked it a lot. Some might say it was serviceable, but they were just mean. It was smart, fitted well and she felt OK in it.

At the same time she realised her loose interpretation of Uncle Miles' edict, 'Don't wear black,' was way off the mark and that perhaps she should have paid more attention to the 'wear your glad rags' element of the instruction.

Huddling closer to Robert, equally conservative in dark jacket and trousers, did little to reassure her, as another girl exposing an awful lot of pert cleavage passed them, her stilettos crunching into the gravelled drive up to the chapel. Out of the corner of her eye, Laurie caught Robert's nipple radar go on high alert, even though he tried to look disapproving. Maybe she should have warned him about today. Not that it would have helped much. You had to have known Uncle Miles to appreciate his ... what? Excesses? Eccentricities? Ebullience? She swallowed hard, unable to believe she wouldn't hear his loud, imperative voice down the phone or see the impatient scrawl that covered his prolific postcards again.

'Bloody hell,' Robert breathed.

She looked up. Oh boy, had she ever got it wrong.

Flanking the chapel door were two beautiful blondes in full red and yellow leather cat-suits, very Flash Gordon, with zips slashed open to the navel, handing out Order of Service sheets printed on scarlet, no, make that Ferrari-red, card in the same shade as their glossy nails and pouty, shiny lips.

Taking one with a limp smile, she tugged at Robert's sleeve, ignoring his dazed look and pulling him inside with her. Could anyone really be struck dumb? It looked as if he might have been.

Inside, the high-beamed room echoed with chatter and the wooden pews were filled with colour, like an aviary of brightly-plumed birds.

Coming down the aisle, she felt like a decrepit Mini Metro at the Goodwood Festival of Speed.

'Where do you want to sit?' whispered Robert, indicating the pews with a sweep of his hand, nearly all of which were occupied but not full.

Perceptively perhaps, he didn't include the front two rows, where the more outlandish of the hats had taken roost. They belonged to Uncle Miles' coterie of ex-wives, all of whom were happily exchanging conversation and air kisses. Robert didn't know about them either. She closed her eyes for a second; what had she been thinking bringing him along with her? Pulling a face, she took a breath and focused on the four women in the first two rows of pews.

As family she couldn't skulk at the back but neither could she join them. They were too damn scary, although to be completely fair, they'd always been kind to her. The third row would do nicely.

'Mind if we sit here?' she asked the solitary figure sitting in the next pew.

'No, you're good.' He barely glanced at her before turning away but she caught a flash of blue eyes and unshaven cheeks. Despite the scruffiness of his jeans, he was definitely one of the beautiful people. She could bet he'd worn the casual linen shirt in that shade of turquoise knowing it emphasised the brilliant green of his eyes, and that the stubble was deliberate.

'Thanks,' she snapped, a stubborn lick of anger flaring as she glared at him.

He turned back to her, surprise and bafflement on his face.

Shame gnawed at her conscience. Now who was being small-minded? You shouldn't dislike someone just because they were too good-looking. Sighing she gave him a tight smile. She really needed to rein in that King Edward-sized chip on her shoulder.

Dipping her head, she sat down and studied Robert's polished black brogues. They contrasted with the worn, leather cowboy boots on her left.

'So, do you know *any* of these people?' asked Robert in a hushed, awed voice.

Did he have to make it sound such an impossibility? She looked around at the other mourners surreptitiously, looking for any familiar faces. That was a laugh. Laurie had only been looking for one face in particular, feeling slightly sick and praying she wouldn't come.

'Just my aunts,' she nodded at the four women talking in the pews ahead.

'Aunts?' Robert's eyebrows shot up like startled caterpillars. He looked at them again, studying each in turn with more attention now.

'Step-aunts, really. Uncle Miles married a few times.' She chose to deliberately misunderstand him.

'Those are your aunts?'

She nodded and gave him a bright non-committal smile. Livia could only just have turned thirty-five and Penny and Janine, at this side of fifty had been a good thirty-four years younger than her uncle.

'Yes. Uncle Miles was ...' she faltered not wanting to say anything more.

3

'A philanderer?' asked Robert, his tone sympathetic.

'No, no.' How did you explain Miles? Complicated, selfish, generous, opinionated, kind, slightly mad. 'He enjoyed being married but he liked women too.' She lifted her shoulders in a Gallic shrug, trying to explain something that couldn't be summed up in a few trite sentences.

'So how did he know all these people?' whispered Robert. 'I thought I saw Liz Hurley near the back.' His mouth curled as if that was a total impossibility. 'Don't you know anyone here?'

Guilt pinched at her. She hadn't seen Miles for nearly a year. Now he was dead, none of the reasons for putting off seeing him seemed like good ones. Too shy, too cowardly, too stubborn.

There was a flurry of activity and then suddenly at the front of the church, the vicar appeared. Although robed in black with a white collar looking every inch the traditional cleric, his eyes held a mischievous twinkle as if he'd been briefed by Miles as to exactly how this funeral should go.

The chapel quieted and then organ music began to swell as the back doors opened and the coffin flanked by four pall bearers all dressed in drivers' overalls and helmets came down the aisle.

Robert shot her an incredulous look and dug her in the ribs but she stared straight ahead, trying to pretend to be as blasé as the rest of the congregation – which didn't seem to find anything amiss.

The music soared, triumphant and vibrato, up to the high rafters. It sounded familiar but unfamiliar and it took Laurie a moment or two to place the tune. Oh my God. He hadn't. She glanced at the vicar beaming beatifically at the gathered congregation and bit back a giggle as the notes continued to rise in volume and reverberate with drama.

He had. She bit her lip hard, cheeks tense, trying to hold back the laughter, containing a snigger in her belly and making a funny sob noise.

Robert squeezed her hand, mistaking it for an expression of grief.

Sucking in a breath of air, she tried to get her equilibrium back and stared straight ahead at the stained glass window above the vicar's head. The procession bearing the coffin passed on her left and she held herself rigid not daring to look. Her diaphragm ached as she tried to hold everything in.

The stifled snort from her right did the damage and she made the mistake of turning just enough to register the man next to her valiantly swallowing and eyes fixed, his shoulders shaking.

This was awful, any moment now she was going to burst out laughing. She let out a wheeze, trying desperately to hold onto the rising hysteria but it was no good, another snort escaped. Tears were starting to leak down her face and any moment now she was going to start …

Her neighbour was no better, his puffed-up cheeks and tightly pressed lips told her he was as desperate to hold back the mirth as she. They caught each other's eyes and both let a snort escape.

As the notes of the organ rose again, building to the chorus, she felt something pressed into her left hand and looked down. A handkerchief, stark against his tanned hand, was being pushed into her palm. Gratefully she shook it out and held it up to her nose, covering most of her face, just in time to stifle the giggles that erupted.

She blew her nose loudly praying it looked like she was crying.

Recovering slightly she nodded her thanks to him. He winked and despite the solemnity of the occasion, she grinned at him.

When he smiled back, revealing perfect white teeth brilliant against swarthy skin and several day old bristles, one eyebrow quirking in amusement, adrenaline hit her, socking her straight in the chest. Desire shot downwards arrowing between her thighs while her nipples, the miserable traitors, leapt to attention. Horrified, she burrowed her flaming face in the hanky again and concentrated on the music.

Only Uncle Miles would have chosen *Bat Out of Hell* to kick off his funeral.

Cam only just managed to get himself under control. Laughing uproariously, even at Miles' funeral wasn't the done thing, although it was better than weeping. He was going to miss the old bugger.

The colourful card had felt more like a wedding invite, with its required dress code. It looked as if everyone else had followed Miles' instructions apart from the girl next to him. If the dull navy blue suit was the best she could do, her life was seriously missing the sense of fun Miles had indicated with his invitation to wear your glad rags. She was definitely missing the glad. Her connection to Miles had to be distant. Although at least she had a sense of humour.

Across the aisle Tania waved and smiled enthusiastically, her mouth a slash of scarlet against brilliant white teeth. He grinned back. It had been a while but she looked stunning, as always. The white dress showed off her opulent figure, cleavage to the fore and her dark hair cascaded artfully down one shoulder. He knew exactly how long it took her to achieve that, oh-so, casual placing and the softness of its touch. Was it Marbella or St Tropez the last time he'd seen her? He couldn't remember exactly. He had a memory of sultry Mediterranean heat and the scent of pines and the sea.

It would be nice to catch up with her at the wake. See how she was doing. Not bad from the look of things. Her skin still held the golden hue of the sun and her hand was linked proprietarily through the arm of a tall, blonde guy in a smart suit which shrieked designer. No, Tania was doing just fine. The guy looked much more her type, suitable in every way. With a self-deprecating twist of his mouth he looked down at his jeans, the material just about to give way across his left knee. Old and comfortable, he couldn't remember buying them. Absently he picked at the worn fabric before looking at Tania. Like most of the women he dated, she'd done her best to smarten him up.

'See you later, Cam,' she mouthed across the way. With an answering nod, he turned to scan the rest of the congregation. The wives were all gathered at the front. How the hell Miles managed it, he didn't know. Cam couldn't manage a civil conversation with his own ex-wife, Sylvie. Thank God they'd not overcomplicated things with children. Although neither had Miles; he'd had four wives, each successively younger than the last, remained friends with each of them and they all seemed to be friends too. They'd probably organised today, no – make that followed Miles' instructions together.

The old sod seemed to have planned every last detail. Cam could remember to the minute where he was when he heard that Miles had gone into the hospice. A terrible stilted phone conversation with Miles' friend Ron. No one knew, it seemed. Everyone had assumed he was leading his normal nomadic existence, flitting between Monte Carlo and Barcelona, Le Mans and Rome. No one realised that the wily old so-and-so had gone to ground and holed up at home.

Cam couldn't decide if knowing, or not knowing, his friend was dying was a good or a bad thing. Not saying goodbye in person ached. But it saved a lot of awkwardness. And wasn't he just the coward? Truth was, he couldn't have coped with a goodbye, any more than Miles. Christ the two of them would have got pissed, maudlin and then pissed again. No, maybe it was a good thing he'd not known.

The funeral progressed at a cracking pace, just the way Miles had planned, although the eulogy done by all of the ex-wives took a little time. Each one of them found it hard to get their words out. Their obvious grief said as much about Miles as the words. Finally the last hymn was sung.

With a reluctant, half-hearted smile at the curtains which closed on the coffin, Cam left the church and headed into the sunlit graveyard. At least someone was smiling down on him.

Outside there were plenty of people milling about and he could have spoken to any number but was drawn to Eric and his wife Norah. Of all the congregation they looked the most sombre and, he noticed, quite frail. Eric had been with Miles for as long as he could remember. He and Norah had lived in the housekeeper's quarters. She ran the house and Eric the garages, looking after the cars, tuning them up, doing oil changes and replacing spark plugs with the skill and dedication of a transplant surgeon.

He needn't worry what would happen to them – Miles would do right by them. Eric's job had been an act of charity for the last ten years. His rheumatic fingers did their best to polish the chrome and the minute he'd retired for the night, a young lad from the village came in and finished the job off properly under Cam's strict supervision.

Norah's eyes were red-rimmed but she dabbed at them with a heavily scented linen and lace handkerchief. He could smell the lavender from several feet away, reminding him that he'd just lost his one and only handkerchief.

'Cameron, young man. Well that was a fine service.' Eric pumped his hand.

Norah sniffed but her wrinkled eyes held a little glint. 'Mm, old devil. Always liked his own way.'

Cam grinned. 'And did he get it?'

She huffed. 'Yes, bless his generous soul. Told us a while back that he'd leave me and Eric the Old Wainwright cottage on the east side of the estate.'

'Thought he might.'

'For all his funny foibles,' Norah gave a scathing glance towards one of the leather clad ushers, 'he was a good man. Few strange ideas but there's nowt so queer.'

'Quite a few coming back to the big house,' observed Eric tipping his head to one side watching the crowd spilling out of the chapel. 'Just like old times.'

Cam followed his gaze trying to duck the punch of sadness at the sight of so many gathered, a testament to how popular and well-loved Miles had been. They'd all crowd into the salon at Merryview where no doubt an unorthodox but meaty and filling buffet would have been laid on. A ribbon of excitement fluttered in his chest tinged with shame. He knew once he got to the house the lure of the old stable block would be impossible to resist. Although there was nothing official, no paperwork, no exchange of ownership, Miles wouldn't have made the promise idly. A curl of satisfaction unfurled in his belly warming him. He could probably pick up the keys today.

'Well that was the weirdest funeral I've ever been to,' exhaled Robert as soon as they stepped out of the church and into the privacy of the shade of the cedars outside.

His mouth wrinkled in a line of displeasure. 'And I can't believe you did that.'

She sighed. Neither could she.

Meatloaf's song had not been written for the organ – that was for sure. Certainly an interesting interpretation. The guy beside them had thought so too, although if he hadn't started laughing first, she could have held out a bit longer.

'I don't think anyone else realised,' he eyed her sombrely, 'and they say grief does funny things to people.' He gave her a swift pat on the shoulder. 'It's over now. We won't stay too long at the wake. I suppose we have to go, though I'm not sure it matters.' He gave a disapproving look around at the people who were all talking a storm.

She followed his gaze, the two of them tucked away in the shadows away from the main event. For a moment it was like staring down a tunnel at another world, one she was long divorced from. An echo of a former life. Gaudily clad women danced and flitted here, there and everywhere resembling brilliant butterflies. They all seemed to know each other and had no inhibitions greeting and kissing with grace and ease, several times on either cheek, as if sliding into a dance and knowing all the moves – two kisses, three kisses, even four kisses. Everyone seemed instinctively to know the rules. Knowing her, she'd get it wrong and end up in an awkward embrace with a misplaced kiss right on the smacker.

She huddled closer to Robert.

'We don't have to go, if you don't want to, although it would look a bit odd. You seem to be his only living blood relative … here.' His mouth turned downwards in blatant disapproval. 'You'd have thought your mother would have made the effort for her own brother.'

Laurie hugged his arm to her, grateful for his support and ignored a twinge of irritation. Although she felt relieved her mother hadn't turned up; Robert had never met her.

Across the crematorium, she caught sight of her fellow conspirator. The sun glinted down on his dark glossy hair, firing up chestnut highlights but his attractiveness was enhanced by the memory of the laughter lines crinkling around those deep blue eyes as he'd tried to hold back his amusement. He scanned the crowd, but his gaze skipped right past her before he returned his attention to the older couple standing with him, bending his head and listening intently.

'Wow.' Robert voiced his astonishment as he steered through a pair of imposing gate posts and pulled up in front of the house, the circular driveway already ten deep in cars.

As Laurie looked up at the house, Merryview, a breath caught in her throat and without warning tears welled up. A shocking pull of homesickness tugged at her. If only Miles had told her he was dying. She wouldn't have stayed away. For a moment she gazed at the house, taking in the sun glinting in the leaded windows and the lichen-stained roof skimming the windows of the upper floor. It felt as if she'd come home. Her eyes traced the progress of the branches of wisteria, tracking across the east side of the house, framing the lower windows.

'You never said your Uncle was rolling in it.' The words were loaded with accusation as if the information had been deliberately withheld.

She shrugged. 'I suppose.' She'd spent so much time here when she was younger, it hadn't occurred to her to talk about the size of the house.

He glanced at her, his eyes suddenly intent. 'Do you think there'll be a reading of the will?'

Robert's question surprised her.

'Do they still do that sort of thing? I thought it was just in books and films.'

'Would make sense, if all the family is gathered together at one time.'

'Knowing Miles, he would have told them all already.'

'Them? What about you? You're a blood relative.'

Laurie swatted a fly away from her face with an irritable wave. 'I've got no expectation from Miles, I haven't seen him for …' Guilt stabbed her. She should have seen him. All the excuses in the world didn't justify her absence.

'What did he do? Apart from constantly sending those crappy postcards.'

A good question and Laurie couldn't help but smile. What didn't he do? Dilettante, bon viveur, raconteur. He'd played a bit of cricket for England, done some commentary, raced fast cars, and collected expensive wine and classic cars. She had no idea how he'd come by his money but he'd certainly known how to spend it.

'Wheeling and dealing,' she laughed, repeating Miles' words. Only now did she get it. He'd meant it quite literally.

Robert's mouth wrinkled in displeasure. For a brief disloyal moment, it reminded her of a prune. Unfair; he just liked things to be clear-cut and precise. He didn't do riddles. Regret pinched at her. He probably wouldn't have got on terribly well with Uncle Miles.

'He bought and sold classic cars. He would take commissions from wealthy people to go and find a specific classic car. You know … the last Ferrari designed by Enzo.'

Robert looked even blanker. Of course he did.

'Enzo as in Enzo Ferrari.'

She'd forgotten she even knew that. Like pinpricks of light through dark cloth, snippets of knowledge lit up her memory. Dots suddenly joined in ever-expanding memories. Facts she'd forgotten she knew. How could she have forgotten how much time she'd spent here in the holidays as a child? During the battleground of her parents' divorce this had been her second home.

'Oh,' Robert sounded distant. 'Do you want to lead the way?'

Stepping over the threshold was like snagging the trip wire of a booby trap, and a thousand more memories exploded in her head. In some ways nothing had changed in the huge airy entrance hall. Dappled sunlight still poured through the bank of leaded windows, just as it had every summer when she'd come to stay. The wicker baskets filled with piles of traditional green Hunter wellies; a size in there for everyone. The solid dark oak staircase looked as formidable as ever, the burgundy patterned carpet snaking down the middle held in place by brass stair-rods. The sight of the stack of Racing Posts, so high an avalanche was surely imminent, brought memories tumbling, stirring a lump in her throat almost choking her.

For a moment she could hear the sound of hooves thundering down on turf. York Races, just down the road. She'd forgotten that. The memory crystalized in her mind bringing with it the smell of horses, the crowd roaring on their favourite and the magpie chatter of touts shouting their odds. For a moment she faltered, as if caught between two worlds and then became aware of her surroundings.

An impassive waiter guarded the entrance to the grand hall, balancing a tray of wines, champagne in tall flutes, white in cut crystal and red in glass balloon goblets.

At least she could guarantee the quality of the wine today. When was the last time she'd tasted decent wine? Taking a glass from the waiter, she motioned to Robert to join her. He was still taking in the hall.

'Are you sure you want that? It's a big glass. Drinking at lunch time? Is that wise?'

'Probably not but what the hell … it'll be good. I guarantee it.'

'Really?'

'Definitely. Miles knew a thing or two about wine. Taste it.' She took a deep sniff, poking her nose right into the glass and then swirled the wine around.

Robert pulled a face, making it quite clear he thought she was being pretentious, and took a tentative sip. His brows drew together and begrudgingly he said, 'Very nice.'

'Chateau Lafite. '64.' She had no idea how she knew that but she just did and although she didn't mean to sound smug, she couldn't help the small flicker of pride that she knew what it was.

''64 eh? Yeah right, Laurie. More like Tesco's finest.'

'No, it is.'

A sceptical expression crossed his face. 'What do you know about wine?' he scoffed.

Her brief moment of confidence faded for a second before reasserting itself. 'It was Miles' favourite.'

'Ah, so you don't know for sure. You're just guessing.'

She faltered; maybe she was. See, that's what showing off did for you. It had been a long time. It probably wasn't the '64, although she did think it was Chateau Lafite. She took another healthy slurp, savouring the gorgeous rich berry flavour. Definitely had that distinctive earthiness to it.

'She's right, actually.' The deep, gravelled voice belonged to Mr Handsome from the church. The brief wink he shot her as he lifted a glass from the tray turned her stomach inside out. Blood rushed to her face and she prayed she wasn't blushing. Just those movie-star good looks – they were overwhelming, that was all. With an ironic toast he took a cheerful glug and disappeared into the crowded room beyond.

As he walked off her eyes were drawn to his long lean figure, his butt outlined in well-fitting denim.

'Tosser,' said Robert, shaking his head. 'Bet he knows even less about wine than you do. Come on, I hope there's some food to soak it up.' He put his arm across her shoulders and steered her into the crowded room.

She'd definitely drunk more wine than was sensible on an empty stomach but she hadn't been able to help herself and even now the third glass slipped down far too nicely. It had been lovely catching up with Penny, Livia and Janine and sharing lots of happy memories which she'd completely buried. Robert kept flashing her questioning looks across the room, as if she'd turned into some raving alcoholic, but luckily he'd been cornered by Norah pressing more sausage rolls on him.

She smiled to herself, taking another sip of the Lafite. Sophisticated in the wine department, yes, but Uncle Miles had had a decided preference for proper man food. His rants on vegetarians were as legendary as his views on eating salad, which he likened to committing food crime. She could imagine he'd been quite specific about today's menu, judging from the sideboard running the length of the dining room loaded with plates of good old-fashioned Cornish pasties, the pastry glistening with egg glaze, pork pies sliced to reveal solid pink insides and flaky sausage rolls, crisp enough to scatter dust motes of crumbs in the air.

The assembled glitzy gathering certainly seemed to be enjoying themselves from the sound of the animated buzz of chatter and laughter rippling through the room. Very Uncle Miles. Of course he'd want everyone to be happy. It seemed a lifetime ago that she'd stayed here, taking up residence every school holiday until that awful summer her mother left Dad. Then everything had changed. Dad wouldn't let her come and stay anymore. He blamed Miles for encouraging her mother to hanker after this kind of lifestyle and for allowing her to meet the man she ran off with. Rather unfair, thought Laurie, as Dad knew as well as anyone what his wife was like. Laurie blamed Miles for something far worse.

Overwhelmed by the bleakness of her memories, a sense of panic rose up. Without saying anything to Robert, who thankfully was engrossed in conversation with another couple, she let instinct guide her toward the door, weaving between the maze of outstretched hands bearing glasses and plates.

Instead of turning left out of the salon to the nearest downstairs loo, a rather grand commode affair, she turned right and crossed the hallway passing the staircase and keeping a careful eye on her wine so as not to spill a precious drop. She'd forgotten the treat of a truly delicious wine.

Tempted as she was to slip up the wide flat stairs, she walked past ignoring the impulse to check the polish on the banisters. Once, long ago, she'd helped to clean and polish the wood – by sliding down them on a towel. Uncle Miles believed in multi-tasking long before it had become a universal catch phrase.

She crossed the hallway, skirting the kitchen and ignoring the enticing smells of hot food. The sound of her footsteps on the flagstone floor was overpowered by the clatter of cutlery and the slamming of oven doors. Ducking through a series of wooden doorways, she passed the pantry, the laundry room and the mud room. The final door led out into the brick paved courtyard, the herringbone pattern embellished with vivid green moss.

Despite the balmy air, to her relief, there was no one out here. It would've been easy to stay there taking deep steady breaths to push away the hangover of emotion but instead she was drawn to the stable block.

The stables had been renovated with care to ensure that the essence of the house was retained. The wooden beams were still in place and the brickwork old, but huge, plate glass, modern windows replaced the draughty stable doors and the roof had been insulated to keep out the damp and the cold. High-tech security guarded the contents which replaced the old horse-power with the new – the engine. The key pad next to the heavy wooden door was a more recent model than she remembered.

It wouldn't be the end of the world if she didn't go inside, she could still press her nose up against the windows and peer inside.

Before she could get any closer she realised there was someone inside, a shadow moving with furtive purpose. The dark shape skimmed through the cars, their smooth aerodynamic shapes collected in the gloom, like a pod of exotic whales. The Aston Martin, a Rolls Royce Phantom, the Ferraris, a Lamborghini, she ticked off those she remembered. Her Uncle's passion. The shadow stopped close to the plate glass at the end of the gallery, reaching up to the cupboard that she knew housed all the car keys. A beam of light pierced the dark like a lighthouse with a brief flash and then it clicked out as the shadow leaned into the cupboard and then withdrew again.

The figure then moved back to one of the cars in the garage, circling an area, stopping periodically as if weighing something up like an art critic in a gallery. Laurie frowned and took a thoughtful sip of wine. If the person in there was supposed to be in there, why hadn't they put on the lights? Should she raise the alarm? The collection was extremely valuable. But then whoever it was clearly knew the access and alarm codes.

Hamstrung by indecision, she stepped back into the shrubbery which skirted the stables. She watched for what seemed like ages but the shadow, the height of which suggested male, stayed in the same part of the garage. It was difficult to see but as her eyes adjusted she could just make out a reverent hand being run over the bonnet of the car he'd appeared to have staked out. The car door was opened and whoever it was hunched down and eased into the drivers' seat, leaving the door open.

Who was in there and what were they up to? At the very moment she'd decided to slink back to the house, the man got out of the car, threw up his head and strode back through the other cars. Even without the ambient light that cast a quick strobe across his face Laurie recognised his silhouette, the mane of long curls, the broad shoulders and his loose limbed walk. As he carefully closed the door behind him, she heard the chink of keys as she watched him weigh them up in his hand before slipping them into his pocket.

With nowhere to hide, she backed into the shadow and bumped into one of the wisteria branches trailing across the wall; there was an eggshell crack of fragile glass and she froze. A few shards of the handsome balloon tinkled on the floor leaving her holding the stem and the fractured glass. The tall shadow paused briefly and looked her way. She held her breath, her heart suddenly pounding. It felt so fierce that she could almost imagine he could hear it. Stupidly she closed her eyes as if shutting out his image might make her invisible. A mistake because then all she could focus on was the soft crunch of footsteps on the brick-paved ground and for a horrible moment she thought he was heading towards her. A pause. And then silence. If he could see her now, she'd look really weird with her eyes squeezed tightly shut but then if she opened them, she'd have to face him. Feeling more stupid and awkward than she ever had in her life, she kept her eyes shut. Just as the silence threatened to swallow her up, she heard his steps retreating as he turned back towards the house.

Catching a breath, her relieved sigh puffed out into the night air. It would have been so embarrassing to be caught. And why couldn't she have just called out hello? What a nice evening? Isn't it hot inside? Instead she'd acted like a complete idiot and made it look as if she were spying on him, like a horrid suspicious family member. People behaved badly when inheritance and money was at stake. She hated that he might think she was mercenary enough to worry about such things. Her mouth twisted, she knew all about probate and the murky things families thought when they believed they were owed something.

Of course if he knew her, he'd have known she had no claim on Miles nor wanted anything from him, except perhaps for one last postcard. The incredibly valuable collection of cars and the properties scattered across the world would belong to her aunts now or once probate had been sorted. Miles was fair though, no doubt he'd sorted everything out to everyone's satisfaction.

'Enjoying the wine?'

The voice interrupted her reverie and she stared up at him, her cheeks turning pink. She'd just managed to snag a new full glass of the Lafite, abandoning the broken one out of sight in the laundry room on her way back in. Had he heard that tell-tale tinkle of glass? Did he know it was her? Was he about to challenge her on it?

He lifted an eyebrow while she struggled to think and speak before finally managing a squeaked, 'Yes'.

If only she could have come up with something wittier or clever to say. Ever since she'd followed him back indoors, her eyes kept straying towards him. The vibrant coloured shirt stood out in the room; it was impossible not to notice him. He seemed to know everyone and the women all seemed to know him. He'd charmed his way around the room.

For a moment he held up his glass, tilting the wine in it in consideration. Any minute now he was going to say something. Her stomach clenched with nerves.

'So how did you know it was Miles' favourite wine?' he asked with a flirtatious smile toying around his mouth. She almost sagged with relief.

His default expression, no doubt. Definitely a ladies' man. Although why not with those looks? No one with any sense would take him seriously. Love them and leave them was written all over him.

'Why shouldn't I?' Her words came more sharply than she intended. 'You knew?' She gave him, an uncharacteristically challenging look. Something surged in her blood, heady power buoyed up by nothing more than Dutch courage.

In response, the smile blossomed into a knowing grin as he gave her an unhurried look up and down, a leisurely perusal that tugged at her.

She gulped. He was good. And she was not his type. He knew

that as well as she did. And he certainly hadn't looked at her like that in the church.

Her eyes must have signalled something because he looked surprised and then intrigued for a second. He took a step back and this time studied her more carefully.

And she blushed … again.

'Hi,' the overly-loud voice cut through her stupor, 'I'm Robert Evans. Lauren's boyfriend.' He thrust out his hand towards the other man.

'Cameron, Cameron Matthews.' His eyes glittered with mischief. 'No one's boyfriend.'

The heat of the room or maybe it was the wine started to catch up with her, a flush suffused her face and she rocked, feeling dizzy.

'So,' Cameron's gaze took both of them in, 'how do you know Miles?' He looked at Robert's suit and then down to the shiny polished brogues. 'His accountant?' He nodded at Laurie, 'Wine broker?'

She didn't think Robert realised he was being insulted but she'd underestimated him.

'No, family.' Robert informed him.

The wine must have really got to her because she felt unexpectedly embarrassed at his pompous tone and aggrieved he'd applied the term to himself.

Cameron Matthews looked surprised.

'I'm Laurie, Miles' niece.'

'Laurie?' His voice went up in question. Disbelief etched across his face as he stepped back and said, 'You're Laurie. Aw shit.'

She flushed at the vehemence in his tone and watched as he turned on his heel and stomped out of the room, parting the crowd and leaving everyone staring their way with hushed voices.

'Rude bastard,' said Robert. 'What the hell was that about?'

'I have no idea.'

Chapter 2

'You happy to close up?' asked Gemma, the other librarian, as if it was an unusual occurrence. Leighton Buzzard Library had been dead for the last half hour.

Laurie nodded. Thank God, today was almost over. From the moment the alarm clock had gone off this morning, set for exactly 6.30 a.m. so Robert had time to make both packed lunches before he caught the train into London, she'd found herself checking the clock almost hourly. The damn long-hand seemed to be on a go-slow. The day just wasn't right. She couldn't put a finger on what was wrong. It just felt wrong. And as for what 'it' was, she had no bloody clue.

Served her right for drinking all that wine yesterday. Her spirits had been well and truly dampened. Alcohol did that, didn't it? And she wasn't used to it. Drinking more in one afternoon than you did in an entire month was bound to have an effect.

She stacked the last of the books on the trolley. Oh stuff it, just this once sorting the thrillers from the romance and Sci-Fi could wait until morning. In fact Gemma could do it. Time she pulled rank, she was the senior librarian, after all and Gemma needed reminding that librarians are well-read, not well-informed on celebrity gossip. And didn't that make Laurie sound a dried-up old stick. Part of her wondered whether maybe Gemma had got it right; the magazines seemed to be a stronger draw than books in the library these days. Other people's lifestyles proving more exciting than their own. Even Gemma's life seemed a lot more exciting than hers.

What was the matter with her today?

She had a job, a home of her own, a live-in boyfriend and her health. She was being ungrateful and stupid. Security, stability … you knew where you were with them. For a moment she wondered if she was trying to convince herself just a little too hard.

OK, so they didn't lead the most exciting life, her mouth turned down in disgust, they didn't lead an exciting life full stop, but then excitement wasn't all it was cracked up to be. Loads of people would kill for that type of security. She thought of her mother and then tried hard not to. She'd left Laurie's dad in her quest for excitement and had found fulfilment in fast cars, rich husbands, glitzy parties, designer clothes and visits to one exotic location after another. Quite what her mother had ever seen in Dad in the first place was a mystery. They were poles apart but he had clearly adored her at one point.

A tap on the window was an unwelcome reminder she should have switched out the lights and locked up.

'Hello dear, I know it's late but can I just …'

Laurie wasn't supposed to stay open after six. 'Go on, quickly.'

Mrs Wright slipped into the door and headed straight down to the crime section. 'You are a dear,' she called over her shoulder.

Laurie might as well start re-homing the books on the trolley.

Luckily Mrs Wright found something straight away.

'Thanks love, you're a lifesaver.'

Laurie smiled. The widow inhaled books like other people took in air. Her taste in gruesome killers obviously provided the escape from killing loneliness.

Rattling around on your own in a house when someone had died was so hard.

The ring of her mobile coincided with the click of the door

when Mrs Wright finally left. Robert.

'Hi.'

'Hi, you still at work?'

'Just leaving. I'll be a while. I'll heat up that shepherd's pie for you when I get back.'

'I'm already home. Actually, I thought I'd take you out to dinner.' Robert sounded very pleased with himself.

'Why, have you had a promotion or something?'

'Does there have to be a reason? I just thought you might like to be spoilt for a change.'

'That would be lovely. Thank you. I'm on my way.' If she got a wiggle on she could just catch the next bus.

See, she was just being a miserable old harpy. She had nothing to moan about. Her life was pretty good.

It wasn't supposed to happen this way. Not that she did know how it was supposed to happen but this felt pedestrian, as if she'd been short-changed.

The candle on the table danced, casting shadows on the red damask tablecloth as Robert pushed the box across the table towards her.

Her heart sank, leaden to the very pit of her stomach. The waiter loitering with a bottle of champagne looked on expectant.

'I know we said that we were fine as we are but ...' he shrugged, 'we don't have to have a big wedding. That would be a waste of money. I thought we could be spontaneous ... just book the registry office next week. They've got a slot on Monday at lunch time. How romantic would that be? Spur of the moment!'

Robert's face lit up with the thought. With a quiver of disappointment, she realised he felt genuinely excited by the idea.

Smiling took effort – she could feel the tautness of every muscle in her face. Robert had pushed the box right across the table, to sit centre stage in her place-setting like a dainty dish she needed to tuck into.

It sat there like an unexploded bomb that she was expected to diffuse. She didn't dare look at him, but she could tell, as he leant forward, his body language shouting eagerly, that he wanted her to open the box.

Her hands shook as she lifted them above the table.

'Aw … you don't need to be nervous. It's not the Rockefeller. Just a token really. We don't need to waste our money on symbols. We know what's important.'

Of course he was right. Having values. Being loyal. Maintaining integrity. Honesty. Unselfishness. They were the important things. Real love was based on friendship, stability and trust, not giddy emotion. She pushed away the thought of her mother, currently madly in love with husband number three.

Her fingers touched the box and she opened it. The ring, an emerald with a diamond chip on either side, was pretty. Really pretty. A lovely engagement ring and only a miserable, ungrateful, shallow cow would have even thought they would have preferred a sapphire.

She looked up at Robert. He beamed.

'Like it?'

'It's … lovely.'

Even as she blinked back tears, one escaped making a lonely trail down her cheek.

'So, what do you say? Monday?' He grinned hopefully, mistaking her tears for something else.

Numb, she stared at him. 'Monday? What, this Monday?' Frantically she tried to think was she was doing on Monday.

'Yeah. Twelve-fifteen.' He pulled the crinkly 'great-isn't-it' face, as if chivvying along her enthusiasm.

'But … but I've got work.'

'Come on, Laurie. They won't notice if you take an extra half an hour … and if they do, just tell them where you've been. That lot will think it's so romantic … just like one of those Mills & Boons.'

'I … I … This is all so …' She sounded even more clichéd

23

than him.

'Not really.' Robert had that let's be reasonable face on now, 'We've been living together for a while now. It's the next logical step isn't it? We're not getting any younger. We've got a house. We've no mortgage. We've both got steady jobs. Why not?'

She frowned. Actually, her house and her 'no mortgage'.

They'd not been going out that long when Robert moved in pointing out it didn't make sense paying bills on two separate homes. He'd been such a rock when her dad died so unexpectedly, leaving her so stricken and lonely she was incapable of deciding anything.

A nagging headache gnawed her right temple as she stared down at the ring. She didn't like green, never ever wore it. Her school uniform had been bottle green, enough to put anyone off.

This wasn't what she'd thought getting engaged would be like.

Was she crazy? Most girls dreamed of this! A steady, reliable man who didn't watch endless football, didn't spend money foolishly, did his share of the cooking and was a dab hand with the washing machine. Even came to Sainsbury's every Friday with her. Dependable, reliable, trustworthy.

Someone who wouldn't up and leave her behind.

So it wasn't the most romantic of proposals, but they weren't like that were they? She'd had a few serious boyfriends over the years and Robert was the only one she'd lived with but still she couldn't quite bring herself to say yes. This didn't feel right but how could she articulate it without upsetting him? As excuses went it was pretty rubbish.

'I … I don't know Robert. It doesn't feel right. The timing. Maybe because Uncle Miles …'

It was as good an excuse as any. Death in the family.

Robert gave her one of his tender smiles reaching for her hand. 'Poor Laurie. I do understand.'

Had she ever noticed before how his lips looked slightly crooked when he did that? 'I thought this might help. Losing family, it's

24

hard but we can start our own family. You and me. Have children. Our own little unit.'

Children! Plural. Was he serious? They'd never even discussed it. Having babies was big and grown up. Even though she'd just turned thirty and the old biological clock should be ticking, you had to be really, really sure before you had children. Before you had one, let alone two. If you split up … she deliberately shut out the memories. She wasn't prepared to go there. It was a long time ago and she was over it. All grown up now … well nearly. Just not grown up enough for children. Did she even want any? Adults did so many terrible things to children.

No, she wasn't ready and on a purely practical note – she glanced at Robert – what if they ended up with his nose? Long and a bit bulbous on the end.

Horrified by the unexpected thought, she stared at him. Where had that come from and when had she turned into such a cow? It was time to get a grip and stop being an idiot. She was nothing like her mother. This was just a silly, minor panic-attack.

Squeezing his hand, she took the ring out of the box, offering it to him. As he slid it onto her finger, he pulled her hand up to his lips and kissed each finger one by one very gently, his lips whispering across each knuckle.

It was a lovely gesture, even the waiter looked misty-eyed. Pushing her shoulders back, she ignored the small leaden lump nestling in her stomach and gave Robert a brilliant smile and asked, 'Are you going to pour me a glass of champagne then?'

'Stop it, that's ticklish,' she scrunched her neck up to her ear to try and stop Robert's kisses.

They stumbled through the front door and he pulled her to him. 'Bed, Mrs Evans-to-be?'

Mrs Evans! That was his mother, domineering, opinionated and disapproving of Laurie. Oh God, she'd be family!

His hands made a quick cold foray up under her shirt.

'Oooh,' she squeaked, pushing them away before they could hit their target. 'You're freezing.'

'Let's go upstairs and warm them up,' he suggested rubbing his hands together, waggling his eyebrows lasciviously.

She fended him off again and pushed herself off the wall towards the kitchen. Everything seemed a bit wobbly. Lovely wobbly from the champagne. And not so lovely wobbly. Something nagged at her. Worry that she'd not done the right thing. The wine was discombobulating her brain, a whole bottle of champagne on a week night wasn't conducive to straight-thinking, she needed to sink a few glasses of water otherwise her head would be in serious trouble in the morning.

Robert had already disappeared halfway up the stairs.

Staggering into the kitchen, she yanked open the kitchen cupboard and pulled out a pint glass, filled it to the brim and forced herself to drink the whole lot.

The room swam around and the lights bounced off the kettle which seemed to be moving up and down by itself. The evening had disappeared into a big blur, although she could feel the ring encircling her middle finger. Too big for her engagement finger, but Robert had wanted her to wear it. Guilt warred with confusion. Had she really agreed to get married on Monday?

It seemed so sudden and so out of character for Robert.

The dizziness increased and clutching a second pint of water to her chest she slumped into one of the wooden chairs at the scarred table. The fruit bowl in the middle was empty of fruit as always but there was a white envelope propped in it.

Miss L Browne. A proper letter. You didn't get those very often these days.

From the wrinkled back of the re-sealable envelope she guessed with slight irritation, Robert had already opened it.

Peeling the letter out of the envelope, she looked at the smart headed paper. Solicitors. Sadness misted over her like a rain cloud bearing drizzle. Uncle Miles.

Dear Miss Browne
Further to your uncle's recent death, we would be grateful if
you could call Mr R Leversedge to arrange a convenient
appointment to discuss the contents of Mr Miles Walford-
Cook's last will and testament.

She turned the letter over, as if expecting something on the back of it, like a clue as to why she'd been summoned. A nagging thought hovered at the back of her brain, like smoke curling out of reach.

She had no expectation from Uncle Miles. He had all his ex-wives to look after. Besides he was cross with her. Her mouth crumpled and she shut her eyes. Had been cross with her. Was probably still cross with her. Fancifully she glanced upwards. Yes, definitely would still be cross.

With a sudden smile, she thought of his irate face, faded gingery eyebrows scrunched up over rheumy eyes that still had the power to intimidate most people. Now she understood why he'd been so blinking stubborn. Regret lanced through her and her breath hitched. If only he'd told her he was dying.

Stupid old bugger. With a hurried swipe, she rubbed the tear from her face. And now it all made sense. Not so much his sudden desire that she go visit her mother, which of course had fallen on deaf ears, but his guilty admission.

Laurie let out a small mirthless laugh. She thought his guilt completely misplaced but hadn't been able to reassure him. He'd probably left her some small bequest. It would be nice to have a keepsake from him. But she certainly didn't expect or deserve anything else. Despite what he thought, it hadn't been his fault.

If anything she owed him; he'd offered a haven every holiday when home was too unbearable before her parents finally called time on their battlefield of a marriage. After that the visits to her uncle and Merryview had stopped. It had been awkward, Dad refusing to see his former best friend, his ex-wife's brother and Laurie hadn't liked to leave Dad on his own. Hadn't she also felt

Miles could have done more to stop his sister misbehaving?

As she tapped the letter against her hand wondering what it might be, the kitchen spotlights sparkled in the stones on her new ring. And insight as sharp as the refraction of the light, struck home.

She looked down at the letter, the envelope and then back at the ring. And then frowned at herself for even thinking it.

Chapter 3

She'd thought the solicitors would be more impressive than this. Leather chairs, old wooden desks and book shelves lined with tomes. Instead the desk was birch veneer, she suspected 2009 Ikea, as were the bucket chairs in front of the desk. The bookcase in the corner sagged under the weight of haphazard mottled-grey box files, papers bursting from them, looking like an untidy sentry in the corner.

An Olympic logo of coffee rings in varying shades of brown marked the top of the desk which was empty, apart from the phone and an outsize pad of paper.

Mr Leversedge blended in perfectly, a shambolic figure with hair standing in tufts and glasses perched on his nose that were slightly skewwhiff.

He smiled gently at Laurie inviting her to take a seat.

'Thank you for coming all this way. Was your journey good?'

'Yes, fine. Easy really. Train to Euston, walk to Kings Cross and train to York.'

'I'm glad and I appreciate you coming. I am sorry for your loss.' For a moment he looked bleak. 'I'll miss your uncle, he was one of a kind.'

'Did you know him well?' asked Laurie, partly out of politeness but also slightly puzzled.

'We both enjoyed a beer and a game of chequers at The Anchor once a month.'

Then it clicked. 'Ron; you're Ron.'

'That's right!' He looked delighted.

'I remember him slipping off on a Sunday evening saying he was off for a pint, always used to say he needed some "man-time" away from the ladies.' She smiled at the memory. Much as Miles had loved women, he'd disappear every now and then with a slightly apologetic air, to do 'man things'.

'Lovely to meet you, Lauren. He talked about you a lot ... especially in recent months.'

'Really?' her face crumpled. 'I feel so bad that I didn't see him.' She swallowed hard and looked down at her lap. 'I was ... should ... we'd sort of fallen out. And now it seems so stupid but ...'

Ron leant forward and patted her hand. 'Do you want to know something?'

She lifted her head, finding his understanding tone comforting and met the warm, steady gaze of his faded blue eyes. It was easy to imagine him and her uncle setting the world to rights. Ron had the same slight air of curiosity about the world, eyes alight and dancing. She wondered if they'd shared a tailor; Ron's eccentric scruffiness bore a marked resemblance to Miles' slapdash dress sense.

'He was tickled by your stubbornness. Said it showed character.'

Laurie sighed. 'Not really. I was refusing to go and see my mother. He wanted me to visit her.'

'And he understood exactly why you didn't want to. Miles was under no illusions about Celeste, your mother. Unfortunately he did feel very responsible.'

Laurie rolled her eyes. They'd had that argument several times over. 'Well he wasn't. I know Dad blamed him but I didn't. My mother obviously had her reasons.'

Ron shook his head. 'It was still a terrible thing to do. Sorry dear, that's a view I shared with Miles, and he felt he put the idea

30

into her head.'

Just thinking about the decision her mother had made, even all these years on, made her want to double over with the punch of pain she associated with that rejection.

'My mother came to that conclusion all by herself.' Laurie hated the bitterness that crept into her voice. She was grown up now, it didn't matter anymore.

Guilt twisted in her gut. Miles had kept his illness to himself and she'd had no idea how bad he was until he was admitted to the hospice. On her visit there, he'd barely been able to talk to her. Now it made sense; he didn't want her to be totally alone, he wanted her to connect with her last remaining family – especially with Dad dying only two years ago.

She clamped her lips together but it was no use, the lump in her throat overwhelmed her and the tears pooled and slid down her face.

Ron pushed a box of tissues towards her. His still watchfulness, gentle smile and the lack of inane platitudes felt soothing. Blowing her nose she finally managed to quash her emotions. 'Sorry, I … it was so unexpected. I had no idea he was so ill.'

'That's the way he wanted it, I'm afraid.' He gave a rueful smile. 'And you know Miles; nearly always got his own way.'

She nodded. Which was exactly why none of his marriages worked out. Despite his incredible generosity and garrulous personality, Miles had the attention span and self-awareness of a toddler. Some might say he was totally self-centred – but they would be mean and small-minded. He simply did what he wanted, when he wanted. Eventually the wives got fed up with him disappearing on a whim to track down a car he'd got a sniff of, the impromptu parties and the bringing home of waifs and strays from all over the world.

'However it did allow him to put his affairs in order and I'm pleased to say that he was particularly keen to ensure you were left with something of true meaning. He thought about this very carefully.' Ron's eyes twinkled as he pulled out an A4 folder. 'Very carefully.' He looked at his watch. 'We need to get through a fair amount before Mr Matthews arrives.'

'Mr Matthews?'

Laurie sat up straighter, a prickling sensation easing down her spine.

If Miles wasn't already dead, Cam would have been tempted to strangle the old bugger. He shook his head and carried on pacing outside the closed door. Something was up.

Being summoned was one thing, he expected that, the bankers' draft was ready and waiting and maybe he'd been a bit premature about taking the keys already but the money was all there, his intentions were good. But being invited to meet Laurie … that was something else. Laurie, who just happened to be female. When Miles had asked him to look out for his sister's child, Laurie, Cam had assumed it was a boy, not a young woman. Knowing the old man's predilection for drama, Cam should have thought twice about making any promises. Miles was a bloody liability. And Ron was no better, playing along. He was supposed to be the responsible one. Cam pictured them devising their Machiavellian plans over their chequers games and despite his concern about what they might have cooked up between them, a rueful smile lit his mouth. He would have promised Miles anything.

'Ah Cam, you're here.'

Ron appeared from behind the door. 'Come along in.'

The niece was already there. She looked paler than she had at the funeral, her face set in grim lines. She shot him an unfriendly look. It made him feel a lot better. He had no idea why he was here but he didn't want to get involved. She clearly didn't want him to be there either.

'I've asked you both here to relay the terms of Miles' will. Perhaps you'd both like to take a seat, as the terms are …' he paused and his eyebrows quirked with suppressed glee, 'somewhat unorthodox.'

'However, they are legal and Miles went to considerable lengths to ensure that all the terms are enforceable.' He pulled out a file from his briefcase and slipped on a pair of bifocals.

It took a while for Ron to cut to the nitty-gritty and while he went through legalese, Cam spent the time studying Laurie.

Her light, brownish hair had been scraped back into a severe ponytail which wouldn't have done anyone any favours but on her emphasised her pale narrow face and high cheekbones. She had good bone structure, he'd give her that, but she'd not bothered to do much with what she'd been given.

He couldn't tell whether it was her posture or the appalling cut of the same cheap suit as at the funeral that made her look like a navy blue sack of King Edwards. The jacket was square and the sleeves too short, so that her stick-thin wrists stuck out like a scarecrow's.

Then he realised she'd caught him staring and was now scowling at him.

Good.

'And now to the details …'

Both of them turned to face Ron, who took a deep breath and sat up a little straighter, as if preparing to go into battle and held the will a little higher like a protective shield.

Cam felt a warning twinge in his gut.

'To my niece I leave the Ferrari GT250 …' he didn't hear the rest. 'There's a letter for you.' Ron pushed a bulky white envelope towards Laurie which she took with a shaky hand.

An involuntary indignant hiss whistled out of his mouth. Fuck, shit and bollocks. No. That couldn't be right. Cold washed through him, an icy tidal wave of horror.

He caught a glimpse of startled blue eyes as she shot a look at him.

Ron peered over his glasses, a clear rebuke in his expression.

Cam responded with a furious stare, mind racing with the

ramifications, his teeth gritted as he fought against disbelief. Shit. What the hell? This wasn't the deal. Miles had agreed the fucking price.

'If I may continue?'

Cam nodded tightly, his hands clenched on the edge of the seat. He'd dreamed of owning that car since the first day he'd driven with Miles down to Goodwood.

'On the proviso that she takes it across Europe to Maranello within the next three weeks. Only on successful completion of the journey to a prescribed route, will the car be hers and at that point and that point only can she sell the car.'

Fury burned in Cam's chest.

'What?' Laurie shook her head. 'I don't understand.'

Of course she bloody didn't. Because it didn't make any fucking sense.

Ron smiled gently. 'Your uncle has left you one of his classic cars.'

Cam snorted loudly. One of … only the cream of the crop.

'But you have to take it to Italy before it's yours.' He looked at his watch, as if emphasizing the time constraint. 'But … you will need to leave within the next ten days.'

'But I … I can't.' She looked horrified.

Cam rolled his eyes cursing Miles. What the hell had the old bugger been thinking? This girl just didn't have the guts and she certainly didn't bloody deserve the car. It wasn't as if she'd have any interest in it; she hadn't earned it. Not like him.

She caught him and gave him a steely glance before lifting her chin and turning away. 'What if I don't want to do it? What am I going to do with a car like that?'

Cam shot her a look. Was she stupid? This was the classic Ferrari, Enzo's last design. Possibly, no make that definitely, the finest Ferrari ever made. People would kill to own it.

'Once you've completed the trip the car is yours to sell.'

She wrinkled her face.

'But I don't want to do the trip. I've got a job. Responsibilities.

I can't just up and go.'

'Then it's quite simple my dear. You forfeit the car and it goes to someone else.'

'What, him?' She indicated Cam with her thumb.

Suddenly relieved, he relaxed. Tension seeping out of his shoulders. Obviously that was why he was here. An easy transaction and he didn't even have to pay for it.

Ron held the moment, like a ringmaster holding court in a circus, a small smile playing around his mouth.

'No.'

Cam sat bolt upright.

'Your mother.'

Lauren's face hardened. 'Over my dead body,' she spat. 'If that's the case I'll drive it to Timbuk-bloody-tu.' Her eyes narrowed for a second.

'You don't need to go that far.' Ron's eyes twinkled as if pleased to see her sudden anger. 'There's a very clear route with places and people Miles wanted you to visit. He planned it all out, with accommodation along the way. As soon as you agree your departure date, I will make all the necessary arrangements.'

'How will you know I've done what he wanted?' Her chin had lifted in mutiny and Cam allowed himself a brief smile which was short lived. She had to succeed and complete the trip in order for him to buy the car from her. Bloody hell. Miles didn't make it easy.

'You have to send a postcard from each of the places specified.' Ron pointed to a map of Europe behind him; a blue highlighter had been used to outline a route from Calais to Italy. 'Fifteen in total. One from each town, which I've marked with a red drawing pin.' He grinned happily like an overgrown house elf and Cam wanted to weep. House elves came in books you read to your shiny-eyed innocent nephews.

Furious, Cam gave a disparaging look towards the map and its meandering route through France and the mountains of Switzerland and Italy. 'So what the hell am I here for?'

Ron grinned at him. 'Miles felt Laurie might need a co-driver.'

Might need? Bloody hell! What was that supposed to mean? He was just supposed to accompany Miles' niece out of the sheer goodness of his heart. In a car that Miles had damn well promised him. Except now he thought about it, what exactly had Miles promised? He recalled the exact words. A guaranteed price for the car once it went on sale. The wily bastard.

Ron pushed another one of the white envelopes towards him. 'You'll be recompensed, of course.'

'I don't want his money,' growled Cam. Money was no bloody good. How was that going to help him? Fuck. He almost put his head in his hands. How could Miles do this to him? A leaden lump settled in his stomach at the thought of phoning Nick and the way the conversation would pan out.

'Hi, Mate. You know that Ferrari I promised as the highlight of our classic car festival. Well I lied; it's not mine after all. And all that sponsorship money we've secured to make the festival happen, is all going to vanish in smoke, leaving you with huge debts because you've underwritten everything against a loan on your home. Both of our reputations are going to be down the pan.' Nick would go ape. Cam closed his eyes; his mother would kill him.

What was Miles thinking?

The white envelope mocked him. It felt like an insult. Miles knew damned well Cam would honour his promise to look after his niece, even if the conniving old coot had conned him somewhat by deliberately letting him think that Laurie was a small boy.

Truth was, he would have done just about anything for Miles. Despite the age difference, friendship had blossomed the day they met over the bonnet of a rather neat little Aston Martin. Cam had been the winner in that skirmish, outbidding Miles by several thousand to acquire the car for one of his clients. Miles had promptly taken the client and Cam out to lunch and done a deal to sell the client an E-type Jag for twice as much.

Ron's eyes narrowed and for a moment Cam saw the steely determination that made the solicitor a worthy representative of Miles. He picked up the envelope and pocketed it with a glare at Ron. The solicitor simply smiled.

Chapter 4

Her hands shook so hard the key barely hit the lock. Tears filled her eyes … again. The brass letterbox had done it.

Over the years how many postcards often starting with the imperative, Niece, you must see this place, dropped through the door? Miles loved his postcards.

Although they wound her dad up, each one made her smile. Even in the last few years when Miles was supposedly slowing down, the postcards had never let up. Random in their frequency, there was never a place too small or insignificant for him to stop and pick one up. She'd had cards from the Empire State Building in New York, the Bellagio in Las Vegas, the Great Orme in Llandudno and Arthur's Seat in Edinburgh. Today Miles' familiar, impatient scrawl, addressing her in his usual bossy fashion, brought piercing regret. No more postcards. Ever.

No more anything. She wouldn't even argue against the terms of the will. Miles knew her too well. Knew that she wouldn't deny him his last wish. Frowning hard, she gritted her jaw. Duty. She'd always been good at that. She'd stuck by her dad's side, despite Miles' repeated invitations to visit. Dad liked to blame Miles for the break-up of his marriage, not wanting to admit that it was probably inevitable that Celeste would leave him. He never really got over it. For him it had been a grand passion, love at first sight.

At least on his part. With ten years apart, he had tried to be the sensible one, holding her at arm's length, which had made the spoiled, wilful eighteen year old Celeste all the more determined to marry him.

Damn. The note. She'd leave it in the plastic bag in the hall along with the envelope that Ron had handed over. It felt too raw to share with anyone. Anyone? She meant Robert. Who else was there? And what would he say?

His car was already in the drive. Squaring her shoulders, she went inside.

And there he was already, twitching with anticipation.

'So? Did he leave you anything?'

She nodded. Well that was the truth. He had definitely left her something.

'What?'

She bit her lip. 'It's complicated.'

Robert frowned, 'How so?'

Shrugging out of her coat, she took her time hanging it up. 'Let me get us a cup of tea.'

'So you got nothing then?' Robert sounded sulky.

She faced him. 'Like I said, it's complicated. Come in the kitchen, sit down and I'll tell you.'

Holding the mug of steaming tea as if it were some kind of talisman, she decided it was best just to spit it out and see where the conversation went.

'Uncle Miles has left me one of his cars.'

'Oh,' Robert looked crestfallen. 'Is that all?' Then he rounded on her, irritation lining his face. 'But that's ridiculous? You don't drive.'

Her fingers strayed to her eyebrow, and she rubbed the bone there back and forth.

'I know,' she sighed thinking of the provisional driving licence still tucked in her drawer. Renewed faithfully for the last six years but yet to be upgraded. Booking a proper driving test was still … she couldn't do it. She would get round to it … one day, when the memories of her dad's first massive heart attack on the driveway of the test centre faded.

'So why leave you a bloody car?'

For a moment she stared bemused at him, but then he hadn't had much to do with Miles and had only been to the house on the day of the funeral.

She wanted to smile but worried Robert would take it the wrong way. The whole will was so typical of Miles and if she were totally honest, deep down inside, a tiny almost invisible speck of her was ever so slightly amused and intrigued by the idea of driving a high performance sports car as recognisable as a Ferrari across Europe. Something most people would never expect dull old Laurie Browne to do.

His shoulders sagged and his face twisted in disgust. 'Bummer. Thought you might get something decent … with you being a blood relative …'

'So who gets the house?' he demanded, a trace of belligerence tinging his voice. 'That must be worth a fortune … at least 4 mill current market value. Especially with that amount of land.'

What amount of land? Laurie stared at him.

'Forty acres! Can you imagine? You could flog half of it and still have loads. And it's all prime development land.' He laughed bitterly. 'Don't tell me, all the ex-wives cleaned him out. Bet he was in debt up to his eyeballs. All flash no cash. I suspected as much. I should have known it was too good to be true when you got the letter. Good job we aren't planning a fancy wedding.'

Laurie gripped her tea mug wondering if it might shatter if she held it any harder. She felt as fragile as the china under her fingers. Grief warred with anger but all she could summon was utter weariness. No wonder he'd been so understanding when she'd finally explained she wanted more than a quickie ceremony at lunch time at the registry office.

'Ron didn't say anything about the house. I've no idea what's happening to that. I don't know what will happen to it. He just talked about my bequest.'

'Bequest. Is that what they're calling it now? Hardly a bequest, leaving you his old car. Sorry Laurie, love. You've been left with a right old lemon. Not even that generous is it; not like he's using it now. Don't suppose he left you the money to tax and insure it. So what kind of car? It's not as if you even drive. I suppose we could flog it, get a bit of money for it.'

Laurie shook her head, a half-smile hovering on her lips at the thought of the 'old car'. 'Actually, it's one of his classic cars.' Miles had loved that car. 'I helped him track it down.' Despite being gadget mad, her uncle wasn't actually very good at using them and she'd helped him research and find the Benelli family who'd been the last known owners of that particular model.

Robert looked even more disappointed. 'You're kidding. That's a white elephant then. You won't be able to keep it.'

Uncharacteristic temper flashed and Laurie bristled. 'Why not?'

'Don't be daft. What for?'

He laid a hand over hers as if to soften the words but she found the gesture patronising and overbearing. 'It'd be a complete money pit for one thing. Will cost a fortune to run. God only knows what it would cost to insure and can you imagine the repair bills? We couldn't afford to run it. Besides it's probably worth something, if we sell it.'

Funny how things went so quickly from you to we.

'Thing is …' She heard her voice, it sounded cool and brittle, 'the condition of the will is that I'm not allowed to sell it—'

'What?' Robert slammed down his mug and tea splashed across the table. 'I bloody hope he's left you something for the upkeep then. That's crap. What a bloody cheek.' His voice tailed off as he stared angrily at her.

She returned his gaze, her chin lifting and her eyes narrowing. Controlled fury pounded, shocking her. Losing your temper was something other people did. Other people who let emotion rule without thinking of the consequences or taking responsibility for

41

the fallout. Taking a deep breath, she calmed herself. 'If you'd let me finish,' she said slowly, feeling the control slipping back into place, 'I can explain.'

Folding his arms, Robert leant back in his chair raising one eyebrow. She refused to be cowed by the deliberately patronising stance he'd adopted and waited a moment or two, holding his gaze until he dropped his arms.

'Sorry,' he said sulkily.

'I *can* sell the car—'

'I just thought you said you couldn't.'

His face reminded her of an unhappy toddler complete with sulky lower lip.

'Make up your mind.'

'I can sell it …'she paused. In Ron's office she'd wondered how he'd take it, now uncharacteristically she no longer cared, 'once I've been to Italy in it first.'

'What?'

'Miles wanted the car to have one last outing back to its birthplace.'

'So the old boy was bonkers then.'

'No!' She sighed. How did you explain Miles to someone like Robert who was as conventional as they came? Sitting in his winged leather chair offering her cigars and port, teaching her to taste wine, change spark plugs and polish chrome. 'Just a bit sentimental about his cars … and this one was his favourite.'

Robert shook his head and leaned onto the table. 'And how was he expecting that to happen? We'd have to take a couple of days off work. Use up our holiday allowance.'

Make a change from decorating then, she thought, tracing the track of the wood grain on the table in front of her.

'You don't expect me to drop everything to do that do you? You know what it's like at work at the moment.'

'No of course not,' said Laurie, gnawing at her lip, she knew how difficult things were at the office at the moment. Poor Robert hated his boss, who'd pretty much slept her way to promotion, leap-frogging him, and now took all the credit for the work he did.

She leaned forward and touched his hand. She still had to tell him the worst bit.

Robert shook his head in disgust. 'What was your uncle thinking? You can't even drive to Dunstable let alone across Europe.'

Laurie felt the blush of temper staining her cheeks and fought again to tamp it back.

'Whatever. It's still a ridiculous idea. Those old cars drink petrol. It'll cost an absolute fortune. Cost more in petrol than we'd get selling it. And think of the practicalities. We'd have to pay for hotels, food, the ferry crossing. What if it breaks down?'

Like she hadn't been thinking that ever since Mr Leversedge had been through the exact conditions that went with her inheritance. It was scaring the crap out of her. The practicalities …

Robert shook his head. 'No, it's out of the question. It wouldn't be worth it. I mean, at most, what's this car going to be worth? A couple of grand.'

She shrugged. 'I've no idea but that's not the point.'

'Well enlighten me, what is the point?'

She was sure he didn't mean it to sound quite so disparaging when he adopted that low, superior tone.

'Uncle Miles asked me to do it. He was good to me when I was younger.'

'Good to you? That sounds dodgy.'

'Robert!' she said snatching her hand away. 'Before my parents split up it was hell at home; it was a miracle we had a single plate left in the place. Going to Miles' house got me away from all that during the school holidays.'

Robert shrugged. He thought her childhood odd but then he'd come from a respectable, normal family with parents who'd celebrated their silver wedding anniversary, two point two children, a dog and a cat. It sounded perfect. And anyone accusing Mr and Mrs Evans of occasionally seeming a little dull were just uncharitable. There was a lot to be said for creating a stable home life for your children.

'He wants me to take his favourite car on one last journey across Europe to its original home in Italy. He said he didn't trust anyone else to do it.'

'He didn't trust anyone else?' Robert shouted with laughter. 'That's a joke. What a heap of sentimental crap.'

'It's not …' Laurie began hotly.

'Although a couple of thousand in the bank, now that would be nice … we'd have to do some sums,' his eyes scrunched in thought, 'but if we drove all day, stayed in cheap motels we could probably make a profit.'

There was that 'we' again.

'There are conditions.' She interrupted. 'I don't just have to … get the car to Italy …' The wince on her face must have finally communicated to him that not everything was that straightforward.

'You have to go somewhere else too?' He'd sobered now. 'Sounds like a con to me? I might have known it would be too good to be true.'

'Nothing like that, it's just that I have to … take a certain route and complete it within a—'

'What do you mean a 'certain' route?' Robert frowned.

'I have to visit certain places on the way and …' she had his attention now, she dropped her voice, 'it's got to be done within three weeks.'

'But that's impossible!' He began to pace the tiny kitchen, three strides and then back again. 'There's no way I can get that additional time off work.' He wheeled again, another three paces. 'Even if I explained to Gavin …. And you said they were looking to make redundancies at the library. You can kiss your job goodbye if you decide to go gallivanting off across Europe.'

Like she hadn't been thinking that ever since Ron had spelled out the full terms of the complex will.

Laurie worried for the lino as he span on his heel and paced the length of the room … and she still hadn't explained about Cameron Matthews.

He wheeled to face her. 'You'll have to contest the will. That's it. He was clearly barking. It's totally unreasonable to expect us to drive a car across Europe. That's ridiculous. And frankly quite weird. Controlling from the grave. I don't like it at all. I'm sure no one in their right mind is going to enforce it.'

'I'm pretty sure that Miles had it all worked out,' her voice dropped as she remembered how ill he'd been the last time she'd seen him. 'In fact …' she stopped, struggling to find the right words, 'he … organised … er … a mechanic to … go along too.'

'And this mechanic would just do it for … what? Love? Fresh air?' Robert shook his head at her naivety.

He had a point. 'I'm not sure … I think he's being paid for it. I know it all sounds strange but Uncle Miles had lots of time to think it all through and Ron, Mr Leversedge, the solicitor helped him draft the will. I don't think it can be contested.'

Robert lapsed into thought, his mouth twisting this way and that as if ruminating every angle.

After several minutes, he huffed out a sigh. 'Hmph, I'm not very happy about it, but you're probably right. He's got us over a barrel but for that money it's worth doing, I guess. You'll have to do it on your own. At least if you've got this mechanic chappie coming along, if you break down or anything you won't get ripped off.

'There's no point me giving up my job. It's not like yours brings in much, so if we have to sacrifice that in the short term for the bigger gain, it's a gamble worth taking … they might always take you back on or you could get an office job somewhere round here.'

'But …' She loved her job and he hated his. What about what she wanted?

'And you'd be happy me going on my own in a car worth thousands?' asked Laurie, wanting him to say it was out of the question and he would have to give up his job to come with her.

'Don't take that tone. Of course I'm not happy. The pension

45

at the library is a good one. And with the cuts you might have got a payoff. I wonder if there's any chance they might give you a sabbatical or offer you voluntary redundancy.'

She closed her eyes. The library was the only job she'd ever known; the thought of giving it up made her feel quite panicky. Leaving Leighton Buzzard made her feel sick. Once she was old enough to stop the obligatory trips to France to see her mother, she hadn't been out of England for the last twelve years.

She thought of the envelope Ron had given her. And that wasn't even the half of the problem.

Chapter 5

Cam gritted his teeth and gave the wheel nut another half turn. His shoulder ached like a bitch and he was cooking but he'd keep his T shirt on. He'd kept his promise and sorted Kerry's car out today. He'd feel easier about her making the trip to Birmingham to see her Mum. Bald tyres were an accident waiting to happen. And it was him that had pointed it out to her. Damn fool thing to do, as he then ended up offering to buy the new tyre and fit it for her. The last thing he needed was to encourage her.

That should do it. Rolling his aching shoulder he hauled himself to his feet and wiped his grimy hands down his jeans. Despite breaking his shoulder over five years ago, it still hurt like a bitch every now and then.

From inside the house that butted up next to his, he could hear Josh, Kerry's three-year-old revving up with an unhappy, I need food and sleep cry. No wonder she looked so tired all the time. It had to be hard work raising Josh alone.

But there was a difference between being neighbourly and playing Daddy, and despite the signals she'd been sending his way, he had no intention of signing up for that gig. Thank God for Josh's return from playgroup; the cleavage on display was most definitely for his benefit. He liked Kerry well enough, but a guy like him wasn't the answer. He wasn't the settling down type …

well not anymore. He'd tried it once and look what a disaster that had been. He'd made himself and Sylvie, his ex-wife, miserable. Kerry needed someone who would stick around.

He shoved the spanner into the tool box and gently pumped the jack to bring the aging Nissan back to earth. At least he could help her out with a spot of mechanical engineering from time to time. And didn't that just sound like one heck of a euphemism?

But it wasn't lack of sex that made him feel irritable and scratchy, although it had been a while. Maybe scratching that itch might help. There were any number of women he could hook up with, a lot more sophisticated and less needy than young Kerry. Maybe he should make a few calls, anything to put off the one call he was going to have to make. Damn Miles. What the hell had he been playing at?

Cam gave a rueful grimace, tempted to pull out the white envelope which was still folded in four and rammed in the back pocket of his jeans. The contents had offered some relief but he wasn't home and dry by a long shot. He'd debated all week whether to phone Nick and forewarn him that the deal might not be a definite but he was loath to do that just yet. Miles had tied things up neatly. Cam had to ensure that Laurie completed the journey across Europe to the Ferrari factory in Maranello. If he did that, he got first dibs on buying the car at the price they'd agreed. All well and good as long as she made it all the way to Maranello. Piece of cake … provided she sold. Although that was pretty much a foregone conclusion but he needed to make damn sure. Closing the tool box, he gave the new tyre a quick kick. He hoped Kerry would gracefully accept the tyre and not want to pay him.

A slow grin crossed his face. That was what he needed to do with Laurie. Make her overcome with gratitude and totally reliant on him to get her across Europe. So much so, that she would see how impractical it was to even consider keeping a car that kept breaking down, needed so much maintenance, was cold and draughty, and horribly expensive. There'd be no harm in charming her along the way, just to make sure she couldn't say no to him at the end of the trip. The relationship with the boyfriend looked a pretty joyless affair. He was a bit of a knob – some male attention would probably be quite welcome. Cam was sure that despite the shaky meeting at the solicitors, he could turn things around – after all they'd had that shared moment of empathy in the church. She obviously had a bit of a sense of humour.

So maybe his intentions were less than honourable but what had Miles intended the outcome to be, if not for Cam to have the car in the end?

Tucking the jack away in the boot, he slammed down the door and pressed the automatic lock. On cue at the sound of the beep, Kerry appeared in the doorway, a tear-stained Josh at her hip.

'You've finished,' she beamed at him. 'Can I feed you as a thank you? I've got a lasagne on the go and there's plenty there.'

The right thing would have been to say no but a suitable excuse evaded him. Besides, this might be a good opportunity to talk to her and make it clear that he wasn't in the market for any sort of relationship. Or he could show her what a real bastard he was and decline. Looking at her hopeful expression, he opened his arms to the boy.

'Hand him over and I'll keep him occupied while you do what you need to.' He might be a bastard but he wasn't cruel with it and the poor kid looked like she could do with a second pair of hands. There were still a couple of hours before his appointment to meet Miles' niece.

With a grateful smile, she complied and led the way into the house.

Josh shoved a sticky hand into Cam's hair, as he took him. 'Come on fella, let's give your ma a break.' He went into the lounge to find the big box of toy cars. Within minutes he had the little boy in fits of giggles as he showed him how to race the cars, taking them on two wheels, running them up his arms, crashing them, complete with sound effects.

Hell, life was so much easier at this level. Could Miles have made his will more damn convoluted? Cagey devil.

'Lunch's ready. Sorry I haven't got any beer or anything.' Kerry shrugged apologetically. For a moment he thought about nipping next door to grab one from his own fridge. A cold lager would slip down a treat, but then it might change the tone of the meal.

'I can't stay too long. I've got an appointment and then I'm going to be going away for a couple of weeks, so I need to start sorting things out.'

'Is it a job?'

'Yeah, sort of.' Cam pulled a face.

'Doesn't sound like you're too keen?'

Frankly, he'd rather get married again. 'It's one of those jobs where there's no pay off until you get to the end of the trip. Kind of puts all sorts of obligations on you. I prefer jobs where I agree the fee up front, do the job, get paid and everyone's happy.'

'Can't you say no? I mean …' She coloured up. 'Well, you're organising this big festival, I heard you'd got all the sponsorship in place. Do you need the money?'

He grinned, unembarrassed. 'No secrets living in this village.'

Except she didn't know that all the sponsorship was based on the Ferrari being the centre piece of the show. That it was the car that would elevate the event into a serious contender and attract the enthusiasts. If only he hadn't got his brother involved. If he lost everything there was only him. He could make ends meet. If Nick lost his home … it would be all his fault.

The call of racing had long ceased for him but he had an affinity with cars. Eric liked to say that Cam could make engines sing and while he wasn't sure about the romantic sentiment, he knew he was damn good with a rock solid rep which counted. Money was money. He only lived in the poky one up, one down because he hadn't done anything about finding a proper place to live since the divorce.

'So,' she persisted, taking a moment to redirect Josh's spoon of mashed potato which was being waved in the air. 'Why don't you say no?'

Because he couldn't. He needed that car and he'd made a promise to Miles. He said he'd look after Laurie. End of story.

The house looked exactly the same as it had on the day of the funeral. For some reason he'd expected it to look faded and dusty, as if it had been mothballed. He lifted the heavy knocker and to his surprise Eric opened the door.

'Ah Cam, good to see you.' Eric ushered him in, just like old times, and the smell of roasting chicken drifted up the hall.

Cam shook the older man's hand.

'Still here? I thought you'd been pensioned off with the cottage.'

'So did we, so did we. Turns out Miles had other ideas. Will asked us to stay on and run the big house for a couple of months. Cottage is ours to do with what we like but he wanted the house kept up.'

And it had been. Norah's diligence meant it looked exactly as if Miles might stroll in any second.

Cam shook his head in wonderment. Typical Miles, no doubt leaving the place ticking over just in case anyone called by not realising he'd passed on. The house had always been open to all. You never knew who'd be visiting. Miles had an eclectic set of friends and acquaintances including wine merchants, wine growers, sommeliers from renowned restaurants, the racing set. Even his extended family of ex-wives and their new husbands, offspring and other relatives were equally welcome.

'Norah has set tea up in the drawing room. Miss Laurie should be here soon. Taking her for a test drive, Ron says. And you're going to go with her across Europe. You take care of her.'

Cam wasn't sure whether Eric referred to the car or Laurie.

'I've got the keys for the garage block for you; you know the codes.' Eric handed over the slim set of keys. 'You know where all the keys are kept in the cupboard. Which car are you taking out?'

Cam felt the car keys weighing heavily in his pocket. So much for presumption. That night he'd been so sure the Ferrari was his. He clenched the garage keys in his hand for a moment. Some people would kill for these. What was going to happen to the rest of the car collection? The Ferrari had been accounted for, but what about the others? Nothing had been said about them or the house. He'd always thought that despite Miles' oft-aired view that cars had been designed to be driven, he might one day turn the place into a museum like Beaulieu.

Christ, if he was happy to put the best car of the lot into the hands of a complete amateur, he hadn't changed his philosophy much.

Hopefully she wouldn't wreck the engine. At least if he agreed to going along he could teach her to drive the damn thing properly … or, a slow smile slid across his face. Of course he could put her off driving it for good today. Frighten her a little. That would save the engine and ensure she sold the car. Miles' will and its conditions had been prescriptive to say the least but as far as he could see, and he'd read it carefully to check, there was nothing in it that said specifically *she* had to *drive* the car. Maybe it was the legal jargon but the phrase relating to the car said Laurie had to take the car across Europe.

All he had to do was show her what a difficult car it was to drive. And how much damage you could do if you didn't do it right.

It wasn't as if it was all that underhand – after all, if he wanted to be a real bastard, he could play any number of dirty tricks. Get lost along the route … miss out a place or two. Ensure she missed a couple of postcards. Make the journey twice as long as it needed to be. Get her to give up en-route.

He couldn't do that. He'd made a promise to Miles but that didn't mean he couldn't make Laurie face up to the huge impracticalities of owning and driving a high performance sports car. He suspected that she would be surprised by just how fast it could go. She'd probably never been in anything with an engine bigger than one point four litres. He smiled again. Today he'd take her out in the Ferrari, scare the shit out of her … and then, his mouth twisted wryly, he'd do the right thing. Sometimes he just hated that nagging conscience. He'd offer to drive it across Italy for her and show her along the way the realities and difficulties involved with owning and driving a classic car. She had to sell the car to him. There was no alternative.

Pleased with his plan, he swung down the corridor, keen to reach the stable block and reacquaint himself with the Ferrari.

Even if she hadn't known where to go, the signature growl of the engine would have guided her. Like the roar of a dragon about to strike, the noise vibrated around the courtyard. Her skin reacted, goose bumps erupting, and she stood upright, the air reverberating around her.

The sound brought back memories with a punch so hard it almost felled her. Tears pricked her eyes.

Cam was reversing the silver Ferrari out into the courtyard. He scowled at her through the open window. 'You're early.'

She shrugged. She'd had second, third and fourth thoughts about coming at all. When she'd phoned Ron to accept the terms of the will, he'd immediately suggested she travel up to York and meet up with Cam to sort things out. A test drive had not been on her agenda. Although, she told herself sternly, what had she imagined? She could just rock up at the garage at Merryview, get the keys and set off down to the Channel Tunnel?

Even though it made perfect sense, it still pissed her off that Cam had taken the initiative.

'Are you coming or not?'

'Not,' she scowled back.

He ignored her, leaned over and opened the passenger door.

Through the open door, she could see the red leather seat, the dash. Cam looked at her, challenge in his eyes.

If she stayed put she'd just look stupid.

The engine roared, as if impatient at being kept waiting and the sound howled around the courtyard, bouncing over the diamond pane windows and the honey brick walls. The car, a streak of silver, shimmered before her as her eyes blurred.

Belatedly remembering a promise to Robert, she took her phone from her bag and took a quick picture.

She stepped forward to get into the passenger seat which was on the right hand side. Of course the car was a left hand drive. It hadn't occurred to her that it would be. Awkwardly she lowered herself into the car, one leg having to stretch right over into the footwell to get down into the low slung seat. Folding your legs in at the right angle took some doing. Like a dying swan she sank into the seat dragging the other leg behind her. There was no way of doing it elegantly. Not that it was anything she'd ever aspired to. No doubt Mother could get in and out of a car like this with perfect grace.

'Nicely done,' chuckled Cam. 'Don't worry, it just takes practice.'

She shot him a dark look.

'I've been busy acquiring other skills.'

He raised one eyebrow.

She blushed furiously and looked down at her phone.

'So exactly which Ferrari is this? I've forgotten.'

Cam raised a cynical disbelieving eyebrow.

She didn't care what he thought. She had known once.

'The GT250 California Spyder, probably Enzo's finest design.'

At the reverence in his tone, she looked up from the text she was sending Robert. Uncle Miles had been like that about his cars. She pinged off the text to Robert, glad that she was now able to tell him the model of the car that she'd sort of inherited. It made it sound a little less pie in the sky and more real.

'Seatbelt on?' asked Cam.

She nodded and was surprised when he leant over to give a tug to double check. Did he not trust her to manage that much?

When he released the clutch, the car shot forward and she could feel the barely contained acceleration which matched the pace of her racing heart. She took in the interior. Basic and dated, it looked very little like the modern interiors of cars she was used to. It was noisy and she could feel the hum of the engine under her feet and the gentle vibrato of its song radiating through the body of the car. The well-worn leather of the seat seemed too smooth beneath her bottom and she kept slipping down and banging her knees on the dash.

There seemed to be more to the outside of the car than the inside, with very little room to stretch. Although the noisy rumble of the engine didn't preclude conversation, it certainly didn't encourage it, and she kept silent as they drove down the drive and out onto a country lane. Being so low enhanced the feeling of speed as the hedgerows sped past in a blur of brown and green, but even so, she was surprised by how fast Cam was going. He obviously knew the roads well.

Deciding she wouldn't give him the satisfaction of asking where they were going, she stared down at her knees, trying to ignore her speeding pulse. After a minute her stomach protested, nausea roiling and she had to give in and look out of the window.

They were going faster now and she was having trouble keeping her balance in the seat as they roared around bends and twisted along the country road. A tractor loomed ahead of them, trundling along at snail speed. Gripping her seat, she tensed and held her breath.

Cam shot her a disdainful look, dropped back a gear and zoomed around it in a move that threw her back into the seat with the force of a rocket blasting off. She let out a startled squeak as the car pulled in front of the tractor but refused to give Cam the satisfaction of voicing her fear. Instead she turned her head and looked out of the passenger window. Anyone would have been unnerved. There was no need for him to look at her as if she was some dumb hick who'd never sat in a Ferrari before. Gritting her teeth she tried to hold back the stirring of temper. No matter how hard she tensed her jaw she could feel it simmering in her veins.

The car's engine slowed and she heard the thrum as Cam changed down through the gears. She'd been so busy concentrating on keeping her emotion in check, she'd not noticed where they were. Now she looked up, she recognised it immediately.

The car faced a long straight track of tarmac, stretching out into the distance.

'Your turn.' Cam turned his head and gave her a smile which didn't get anywhere near his eyes. It reminded her of a shark measuring up its prey.

'Don't worry, this is a private track. The perfect place for you to learn how to drive this beauty. It's extremely difficult and you will find it very different to driving anything else. It needs a very light touch in some ways but firm handling in others.' He gave her a stern look. 'You need to be confident. Best to start here where there's nothing to hit.' His perfunctory smile and patronising driving instructor tone pricked her. 'We can start slow here, have a couple of lessons and get you used to it. It's not the sort of car for a novice I'm afraid … but let's see how you get on.'

With a smooth grace that belied those long jean-clad legs he uncoiled himself from the driver's seat, leaving the engine idling. Laurie scowled. He bloody would. Scrambling out of her own seat and slamming the door, she went round the back of the car to where he stood holding the driver's door for her. He took her elbow to guide her in, calloused palms grazed her skin as his larger hand cradled her arm making her conscious of how tall and broad he was. The gesture, old fashioned and courteous, gave her a sudden pang. For all his brusqueness, he was a gentleman. Not something she was used to at all.

Mutinously she glared at him, even more cross that he'd managed to make her feel like a gauche teenager.

As soon as she sat down, she arranged her seat to suit her, checked the mirror on the dashboard and ignoring him, looked down the track.

One mile. A smooth circuit. Privately owned, once an airfield but abandoned long ago in favour of a newer, shinier one closer to the town.

Rubber burns scarred the surface, veering off left and right, the harsh punctuation marks of cars put through their paces. Her nose twitched as if she could still smell burning rubber and the memory of the pistol shot of a blown tyre hit her along with a punch of adrenaline. The wash of unexpected and lost memories surfacing so suddenly left her dazed.

Stuff Cameron bloody patronising Matthews. She pulled the car door closed and before he could get to the passenger side, she depressed the tiny clutch, and pushed the gear stick into first, forgetting how different the gearbox felt to modern cars. It distracted her for a moment and then her muscle memory rescued her and anticipating the kick, she flicked her foot off the clutch and pressed the accelerator.

The car leapt forward and the acceleration fired up through her. In the mirror she caught sight of Cam's surprised face. She allowed a brief smile to cross her face and focused on driving. She knew that all her attention would be needed, like hanging onto a bucking bronco. The steering wheel seemed huge, its span larger than anything she'd driven … for a while. Now she was in the driving seat she knew exactly where the speedometer was.

It was just like riding a bike, well nearly. The speedo in front of her, the revs. Oil, water and fuel gauges lined along to right on the minimalist dashboard. She knew what she was doing. OK, not quite. It had been a long time, but the memory of things she didn't know she'd forgotten rose up like flotsam on the surface. It all came back to her. Her skills were definitely ropey. Hanging onto the steering wheel, she focused, trying to remember all the things that Miles had told her, sitting exactly where Cam had been sitting.

'*Steer into the corners. Keep your speed up. Don't brake.*' She could hear his voice, the commands clear and bright in her head.

Riding the adrenaline driving through her system, she hit the clutch, rammed the car into second, and braced herself for the leap forward as the car speeded up and then in no time the transition into third. It wasn't smooth, it was spiky, inelegant and not worthy of the car but the heady response of the accelerator beguiled her. Reckless, she accelerated, unable to resist the siren call of speed, pulsing in time with her heartbeat. Under her foot, she could feel the power trembling ready to answer her call; she depressed the pedal watching the speedometer needle leap forward. Outside the track shimmered and blurred as she concentrated on steering a straight course. Even this felt familiar; although she hadn't been on the track for ten years, she knew it like the lines on her hand. With a wry smile she gave into the devil rising in her blood. Served Cam right for being so patronising. Feeling the car buck as she hit seventy, she pushed on still to reach eighty.

'Oh for fuck's sake,' said Cam as she pulled away without him. Shaking his head, he folded his arms and waited for her to bunny hop to a halt the first time she tried to change gear. If you weren't used to driving vintage cars they were very different to modern ones. She'd find the clutch very tricky. He steeled himself to hear the whine of the engine when she messed it up but surprisingly she wasn't doing too badly. The car picked up speed. She'd probably got up into third. Not bad. Better than he would have expected and she was holding it steady, going all of thirty. She had no idea what the car was capable of but that was OK, he'd soon show her. In hindsight he should have done a couple of circuits before handing over to her. Now she'd tootle round the track in third and come back all pleased with herself. Damn he'd missed an opportunity to show her the car needed healthy respect.

Then his ears pricked up as the engine note changed and he heard the growl as the revs increased. Bloody hell.

'Slow down. Slow down.' He took a sharp breath. Shit, she was speeding up. Christ, right at the wrong time. Half way down the straight. And still accelerating. She couldn't take the bend at that speed. He started forward unable to take his eyes off the car, a macabre compulsion, knowing that any moment she'd hit the bend, lose control of the car and come flying off and then plough straight into the wall there. Fuck, fuck, fuck. Breathing heavily he willed her to slow down. For God's sake, please.

Miles would never forgive him if he killed his niece on her first outing.

But even as he prayed, he heard the whine of the engine. Sweet Jesus. Thank you. The car flew into the bend but held the road. She must have dropped down to third. Sheer luck rather than judgement. Thank God. She'd probably scared the shit out of herself. Wait til he got hold of her; he'd bloody kill her. What the hell did she think she was playing at? Did she have any idea how bloody rare this car was?

What the … he stared as she began to speed up again out of the bend. This time the acceleration was even faster and she came roaring down the straight. With mounting fury, he watched as she came up to the new bend and this time took it even faster than the last. Stepping out onto the track, he waved to her to stop. When she was three hundred metres away, he realised she had no intention of stopping and he shot back. The car zipped past leaving him doused in a trail of exhaust fumes.

He stared down the track after her, his mouth firming into a line. Where the hell had she learned to drive like that?

Here of course. Miles had owned this track for years. He shook his head at his own stupidity. She'd probably learned to drive on this track. While some more practice was certainly needed, he could see that she'd been well taught. *Duh!* Of course she'd been taught well, she was Miles' niece but why the hell hadn't the old bugger said anything?

With a mirthless laugh, he shoved his hands in his pocket. She might have said something, although he'd been so wrapped up in his own preconceptions, he'd not exactly given her a chance. You had to give it to her, she had balls. Not that he wouldn't be reading the riot act. Taking risks like that in a strange car. An inexperienced driver. Anything could have happened. She didn't know the car. It was stupid. Crazy. Dangerous. Gave a massive adrenaline rush like no other … and he should know. He also knew how easy it was to miscalculate and how frail the human body was in a high speed crash. Stupid, stupid, stupid. This time as the little car came back into view, he stepped out into the track making it clear he expected her to stop.

Chapter 6

As she brought the car to a stop, she could see Cam was in a towering fury. Suddenly her bravado evaporated, the adrenaline surging through her veins catapulted to an abrupt stop and she gulped. He yanked open the car door and hauled her out to face him, his eyes blazing. Standing on shaky legs, all she could manage was to stare up at him, completely mute. Her heart still pounded and the last vestiges of euphoria sizzled in her nerve endings. That had been something else.

'What the fuck do you think you were playing at?' He ground the words out as if through gritted teeth.

Reality crashed in and the enormity of what she'd just done hit her. 'I knew what I was doing,' she muttered. Oh God, she sounded just like a sulky teenager.

Cam annoyingly quirked one eyebrow as if to say, 'Who are you kidding?' He shook his head.

When that first bend came up a lot quicker than she remembered, she thought her heart might just burst out of her chest. Fighting to get the car into third had taken all her wits and strength but she wasn't going to admit it to Cam. The look on his face the first time she'd passed him had been worth it. Sheer surprise. Served him right. Just because she didn't mix with the jet set, didn't mean she was some numpty dullard beneath his notice. The second lap of the track had been pure heaven though and she couldn't regret it.

She'd braced herself for him to shout but he seemed to have got himself under control.

'Well, you might think you know what you're doing,' his stern expression made it clear, he didn't think so, 'but you can't drive like that on public roads. There are a lot of other things to think about instead of showing off. And don't forget it's a left hand drive.'

Damn. He was right. She was going to have to back-track like mad. It was perfectly legal to drive with a provisional licence on a private road but not on a public road. She'd let herself get carried away. The magic of the car. See, that's what happened when you let yourself be ruled by emotion. She didn't want to risk driving. She'd been planning to play the girly-I-can't-drive-a-car-like-that card.

'Sorry, you're right. It was irresponsible.' She tried to strike a humble note even though she wanted to stick out her tongue at him. 'I hadn't thought. It would be very different with other cars around.'

'Yes, if you hit something else that would be very bad news.' Cam looked very serious. 'Cars like this aren't built like modern cars; even a minor bump can cause a huge amount of damage. And if you're not used to left hand drive, it's difficult to orientate yourself.'

Her face fell. She hadn't thought of that either. Of course the car would probably crumple like a tin can. No, no driving for her. It wasn't like you could get spare parts for a car like this. All the better reason for him to drive.

'Cam …?'

'Yes?'

'Perhaps it would be better if you did most of the driving and I just did little bits on the quiet bits. I mean it doesn't say anything, as far as I can see … I'll check with Ron … but there's nothing to say I have to drive, is there?'

An odd expression crossed Cam's face. Almost like relief – or was that triumph?

'Sounds good to me. These high performance cars do take quite a bit of getting used to, and trying to drive on the other side of the road and coping with French drivers, not to mention the Italians, will make it even harder. I think that's a good call.' He sounded impossibly pompous and she gave him a curious look. It was not at all like the devil-may-care attitude she'd glimpsed before.

He was right though. Disappointment flared, once she'd got used to the feel of the clutch and the accelerator, the responsiveness of the car had dazzled her, that burst of speed, the handling. But it was for the best, she couldn't possibly take her test before they had to leave and there was no way she'd admit to Mr Super-sophisticated that she didn't have a full driving-licence. She gave the low slung bonnet a longing look. Shame, driving it had been something else.

Robert appeared in the hallway as soon as she opened the front door.

'How was it? How did you get on?'

Laurie grinned, pleased to see his enthusiasm. She'd half expected him to be a bit sulky. 'It was great. I surprised myself. It's a difficult car to drive …'

'You drove it! I thought he was driving—'

'Don't worry,' she put a hand out to placate him, 'it was on private land. Uncle Miles owns a disused track. I drove it there.'

'Well I don't see why you bothered. It's not as if you can drive it anyway.'

'That's the thing; I'd forgotten I …' There probably wasn't any point explaining to Robert that her uncle had taught her to drive at the age of thirteen and that until she was fifteen she'd been a regular at the track. She knew he would be horrified.

'Anyway Cam's agreed to do the driving.'

'What all the way to Italy?' Robert looked sceptical

She nodded.

His mouth turned down. 'That's great then, isn't it?'

'What do you mean?'

'Well he's hardly doing it out of the goodness of his heart is he? So your uncle must have paid him. How much I wonder?' Then he brightened. 'I suppose it will be worth it when you get to Italy.'

'Yes.' She stepped past him into the kitchen. No sign of food on the go yet.

'That's brilliant.' Robert scooped her up in his arms and swung her around. 'You're amazing, you know that.' He kissed her soundly and then deepened the kiss, his tongue diving into her mouth.

His sudden enthusiasm and the unexpected amorous lunge of his hand down her shirt and into her bra confused her. To put it bluntly he'd always been a lights off, in bed only type of guy and much as she might have occasionally wished for a bit more spontaneity, this didn't feel right.

With his other arm he pulled her against him.

'Oh Laurie, I love you so much,' he moaned, nuzzling her neck. 'I'm going to miss you so much.'

'Robert,' she tried to push him away but he was kissing her mouth again and pushing his groin against her with such insistence that she suddenly found herself with her back against the draining board.

'I love you …' He kissed her full on the lips again, eyes focused and bright. 'Let's get married. I know the registry office idea threw you … but with you going away … let's just do it. Life's too short. I hate the idea of you being so far away from me. I need to know you'll come back to me. Mrs Evans.' He held her face in his hand, his fingers biting just a bit too hard into her jaw.

The intensity of his gaze, full beam, stirred anxiety rather than joy. This should have been romantic, incredibly romantic … it wasn't.

'What's wrong, Robert?'

'Nothing. It's just you not wanting to get married knocked me.

I couldn't bear to lose you.'

'Don't be silly.' She smiled to take the sting out of the words but he was being completely ridiculous. In their time together he'd never had a particularly romantic bent. They just weren't that sort of couple. Why now? And why was he spouting about 'losing' her? It was ridiculously melodramatic.

'If you really want all the bells and whistles, we can do that when you get back. Renewal of vows. The important bit is us, you and me, promising to each other. A declaration, private, just the two of us.' Robert's earnest gaze bored into her. She felt saliva collecting in her mouth, her jaw tense, aching.

She closed her eyes trying to distance herself from him. The last thing she wanted to do was hurt his feelings. What a contrary bitch she was. After such an impassioned, desperate declaration. And that was the clincher. Desperate.

The word rang in her head. Desperate. Why was he suddenly so desperate? In eighteen months, he'd never shown any interest in getting married. She'd broached the subject six months ago, and despite the possible tax breaks, he'd been quite sure there wasn't much point.

'Honestly Robert, don't be so daft.' She pushed past him and opened the fridge. 'Fancy an omelette for tea?' Not waiting for his answer, she carried on, 'Besides, it's only a couple of weeks.' She shook her head refusing to give into irritation. He'd got some bee in his bonnet but she wasn't going to let it cause an argument.

She didn't do arguments or confrontation.

'Laurie, darling … don't you want to marry me?'

He was pouting, looking ludicrous and she had no idea what to do.

The easiest thing would have been to say, don't be silly … of course I do, but she couldn't bring herself to say the words instead she said, 'Don't be ridiculous.'

'Well why won't you then?'

'Why won't I what?' She stalled, taking a pack of eggs from

the fridge.

'Marry me.' Robert looked entreatingly at her and guilt curdled in the bottom of her stomach. Why the hell didn't she just say yes? For an easy life? But she couldn't bring herself to.

'But Robert, six months ago, you didn't want to.'

'I never said that.' His mouth snapped shut in a mutinous line.

'Yes you did. We talked about it.'

'No we didn't.'

'We did. You said the only point was possible tax breaks.'

'So you don't want to marry me.'

'I didn't say that.' Tamping down her exasperation, she cracked the eggs smartly on the edge of a Pyrex bowl, pushing the empty shells to one side.

'Well you don't exactly seem to be champing at the bit.' With a sudden movement, he smashed his fist into one of the half shells crushing it.

Realising she needed to tread carefully, she decided to change tack. 'It's not that … it's just the timing.'

'What's wrong with the timing? I'd have thought with another death in the family, you'd want the security of another income. If I wasn't around you'd be completely on your own.'

Laurie closed her eyes, a feeling of unbearable sadness descending from nowhere. Everything he said had a horrible logic about it. Was that all it was about? Not being on her own? They made a good solid couple. Sensible.

And today she'd tasted something else. Not sensible. For a moment she'd glimpsed a different world, experienced a surge of exhilaration and felt a moment of soaring freedom.

Chapter 7

She didn't need the ring of the doorbell to tell her that Cam had arrived. The low grumble outside announced that it was time to leave.

For some reason his punctuality surprised her. Robert lived his life to the second, a slave to perfect timing. She'd assumed Cam would be either very early or very late.

With a last glance around the kitchen, she picked up her bag and hurried for the door. Her fingers toyed with her engagement ring. It would be mean and petty to dump it on the hall table. Reducing herself to Robert's level. It didn't feel right leaving without saying a proper goodbye but he'd left her no choice. Leaving her ring would have made a symbolic statement which would hurt him. A bit of distance now was probably exactly what they needed. The row about not getting married was utterly stupid and for him to carry it on and refuse to talk to her was even more stupid.

Crossing quickly to the front door, she yanked it open. She didn't want Cam wondering if she'd chickened out or to see the indecision lurking on her face. She had to go, for Miles and … Robert had to understand.

She crossed her fingers, hoping she was doing the right thing.

Forty-eight hours had lapsed since Robert issued his final ultimatum and he hadn't uttered a word to her. She hated going away without settling things between them but when he'd gone ahead and booked an appointment at the registry office, despite everything she'd said, it had made her dig her heels in. She felt bruised and exhausted. Having spent the last two nights on her own in the double bed in the master bedroom, with Robert in the spare room and pointedly refusing to speak to her as they played do-si-do around the kitchen, it was a huge relief to get out of the house and away.

As soon as she opened the door, the car's low level rumble buzzed through her making her legs turn to jelly as the enormity of the adventure hit her. For a moment she wanted nothing more than to turn back into the dark hallway of home, beg Robert's forgiveness, call the head librarian and say she was cancelling her very short-notice holiday and didn't want to be considered for voluntary redundancy after all. Then the dragon's roar of the engine pulled at her, as enticing as a siren call and as she stepped into the summer sunshine, excitement shimmered with the promise of something wonderful.

In the tiny garden, dancing delphiniums, phlox and lupins nodded their heads in unison, urging her on as if all the elements had conspired to send her off.

Cam met her half-way down the path.

'Morning. Let me take that for you.' He looked beyond her expectantly at the door. 'Is this everything?' he asked, an odd look crossing his face. If she'd had to guess she'd have said it was disappointment.

She nodded feeling disconcerted. Didn't men prefer to travel light?

In response he snatched up her bag and then with a sigh he touched her elbow as if to guide her toward the car which waited at the gate, the silver bodywork gleaming in the sunlight. 'I'll take these as well.' He took her jacket and an ancient beige cardigan she'd grabbed at the last minute. She gave a reluctant smile. Despite his odd demeanour, he had good manners and being looked after felt rather nice.

Bugger, just his luck, the first female of his acquaintance who didn't need an entire wardrobe at their disposal. He'd deliberately avoided talking to her about luggage. A hard shell case was hopeless, you needed something that would squash into the tiny luggage areas. Whether by luck or by judgement, she'd got it right. No, judgement, she was one of life's sensible girls and about as low maintenance as they came … and he was an expert. Sylvie had never travelled light; she couldn't leave the house without packing half the contents of the bathroom cabinet in her handbag. The size of Laurie's bag wouldn't have contained Sylvie's accessories, let alone a week's worth of clothes.

It messed plan A up though. She was supposed to have a great big suitcase full of clothes which he would have made her unpack and repack into a much smaller bag right there on the doorstep, accompanied with constant reminders that they had to get on the road otherwise they'd miss their train. The idea was that with his interference, she'd make decisions in such haste that she'd end up with all the wrong sorts of clothes for the trip.

At least he'd snaffled her cardigan and coat, he thought with a wry grin, as they went with her bag into the boot. She might live to regret handing them over quite so easily.

'Good bag choice,' he lied, flashing a smile, hoping it might loosen her up. This was going to be a long journey and it was going to be damn uncomfortable for the first leg. He ignored the twinge of guilt as he looked at her short-sleeved T shirt. Crossing his fingers behind his back, he hoped she was one of life's stoics otherwise he was in for a lot of earache. He didn't have her down as a sulker. In fact he didn't have her down for anything. She seemed incredibly self-contained, distant and buttoned-up. Nothing emotion-wise leaked from her face. Even her mouth measured out in a straight line of neutrality, neither disapproving nor approving.

The rare view of the carefree girl on the race track had vanished again as if he'd imagined it. She inclined her head but still didn't say much. He sighed loud enough to make the point. Her handbag suddenly seemed to command all her attention, and he watched as she touched her passport, and smoothed a bunch of papers.

'You happy for me to drive the first leg. Get us to the tunnel?'

She nodded and he wondered at the flash of relief crossing her face. She didn't need to worry; her driving rated well above competent. Hell, she knew how to handle a car. Amusement flooded anew through him. Who'd have thought it? Although she'd scared the shit out of him at the time!

'Not got any more surprises for me?' he asked with a wry smile, thinking of what he'd got in store for her.

Her eyes widened. 'No. Why?'

She sounded nervy again, with that tone of almost guilt.

'Just wanted to check you weren't going to pull any more stunts like the last one.'

She shook her head, her ponytail whipping out quickly, reminding him of a dog shaking itself dry.

'Got everything?' he asked firing up the ignition.

For a moment he saw her hands grip together around the bag, as if clutching a lifebelt.

'Yes,' her chin lifted as if she'd come to a decision. 'Let's go.'

For the first couple of miles he concentrated on the road and had to go at a relatively steady place. In the heavy sweater he felt too warm but he sat it out, knowing that as soon as they hit the faster road, he'd be grateful for it.

Once they joined the M25 and started to pick up speed, nipping along in the fast lane, the temperature began to drop inside the car. Out of the corner of his eye, he saw Laurie shrink into her seat as if trying to escape the chilly breeze that was leaking through the nearly closed windows.

'Sorry, the windows don't fit as well as they do in a modern car,' he shouted over the shrill whine of the wind that filtered through the small gap. 'Should have forewarned you,' he lied. Before he'd set off that morning he'd deliberately tampered with the windows, opening them just a few millimetres so that they would let the air whistle in to make the journey as uncomfortably draughty and noisy as possible. Now they were cruising along at seventy, the full effect had made itself felt.

'You OK?' he yelled, cheerfully mindful of the goose bumps appearing on her arms.

'Fine.'

He smiled to himself and then focused on the road, nipping into the outside lane and starting to pick up speed. At eighty the whistling was horrible and starting to hurt his ears, but no pain no gain. For the next twenty minutes he needed to keep his wits about him. The M25 was a pig at the best of times, with a tendency to back up with no notice and invariably you got some pillock spotting the badge and deciding to take you on.

It was only when he realised how cold his hands were that he risked a glance at Laurie. Unfortunately the effect of the cold on Laurie's body had made itself very apparent and her nipples on her small rounded breasts were suddenly very prominent. Like a magnet they drew his gaze and Laurie glanced round and caught him in the act. With a florid blush staining her cheeks, she crossed her arms and determinedly looked out of the window.

He swallowed hard. Shit the last thing he'd meant to do was embarrass her.

'Do you want me to stop? So you can get a jumper or something?'

'No,' she muttered, her head still turned away from him.

He felt a complete arse but despite that, now that he'd registered the peaked nipples, he couldn't seem to help himself keep checking her profile.

Letting her freeze was one thing, humiliating her was another.

'Do you want to see if you can do something with the windows, sometimes the mechanism works loose during the journey. You might be able to wind it up a bit.' The lies sounded lame to his own ears.

She gave him a sharp glance and with quick neat fingers, wound the old fashioned lever. The glass slid smoothly into place with a sharp clean move, immediately quenching the awful whistling and the cold wind.

Watching the road, he didn't need to turn to her to see her steady gaze on him; he could damn well feel it boring into him.

'Funny that. Do you think your side might have "worked loose" too?'

He wound his window up feeling like a chastened schoolboy. OK, so that hadn't gone so well, but they had a long way to go and he still had plan C.

Hopefully without talking and no music, Laurie would quickly get bored and realise that ownership of this car was quite different to the comfort and ease she was used to.

An hour into the journey, he realised that although she seemed quiet and contemplative, she'd relaxed a little. Like a student determined to learn everything she could, she watched the gear changes and studied the flow of the traffic around them. He smiled at her concentration. She looked like a rapt robin, her head bobbing up and down, her lower lip caught between her teeth as she took everything in.

The bing of her mobile coincided with them mounting the incline of the Dartford Bridge. The fingers on the hand holding the phone whitened, as she read whatever the message said and he heard her breath hiss out. He waited, sliding into the middle lane, still aware of all the traffic around them, expectant of some moan or complaint. Except that was totally unfair. So far, despite having some cause, she hadn't moaned or complained once and despite him not talking, she seemed quite capable of holding her own counsel.

Clearly something was going on with the texts, it was the fourth she'd received since they set off and her face had become increasingly grim but she'd not said a word. Not like his ex-wife who liked to share every nuance of emotion and feeling, and had expected the same in response.

He winced at the memories. The constant emotional barrage had pushed him further and further back like a snail retreating into its shell for safety. He didn't want his emotions picked over constantly but she'd taken it as failure and the more he retreated the more she needed him to 'talk to her'.

Something had clearly upset Laurie but she seemed content to keep it to herself. Or was that him failing 'to empathise' which Sylvie had accused him of on a regular basis.

'You OK?' he asked.

'Yeah, fine.' She turned her head and looked out of the passenger window. He was getting a little fed up with looking at the back of her ponytail all the time. On the edge of his vision, he could see she lifted her chin and held the tension in the tendons in her neck. Remembering how it felt when Sylvie had persisted, he took her at her word and focused on the traffic.

Cam obviously hadn't spent much time on public transport. Half her teenage years had been spent travelling on rickety old buses which invariably broke down half way to Milton Keynes. If he thought a bit of a draught bothered her, it just went to show how different they were. No doubt the sort of women he was used to would catch a chill or need to be wrapped up in furs. She curled her lip as much in disgust with herself, if she wasn't careful she'd turn into a right old curmudgeon. Staring out of the window, she watched the grey choppy waves of the Thames below the bridge. They matched her mood, scratchy and unsettled. Not angry, not sad ... just antsy. She hated feeling like this. Only a few weeks ago everything had been fine. Normal.

Robert's text had her clenching her fists under her thighs, hidden from Cam. The last thing she wanted to do was air her dirty laundry.

I take it you've gone then. I might not be here when you get back. Hope you're happy now.

Of course she wasn't happy. Upsetting him hadn't been her intention but it would have been wrong to get married, to rush it now. Not when it didn't feel right.

Ironically, his childish text pushed aside the guilt that had been mounting ever since she closed the front door, firming her resolve. She'd started this journey; she was going to finish it, with or without Robert's approval.

Arriving at the Channel Tunnel was disappointing. She'd envisioned a yawning black hole that was clearly visible for miles, a scary looking challenge, not for the faint-hearted, which brought up images of Stargate, The Hobbit and Dr Who. Instead it was all horribly pedestrian, the most boring train station on the planet immortalised in industrialised concrete.

The only vaguely exotic thing was the paper hanger with the letter G which was propped on top of the dashboard.

As they drew into a parking space in the busiest section of the car park, Cam turned to her. 'Both of us can't leave the car at the same time. We'll have to take it in turns to go in. Unless you need the loo, I'll go and get us a drink. Tea or Coffee?'

'I'm fine. Tea, please, milk and one sugar.'

He got out of the car and then leaned back in to call across, 'You might want to get out and stretch your legs, but stay by the car. You don't want some little oik scratching it or anything.'

Twisting in her seat, she did feel a little stiff and it would be good to get out in the sunshine. After Cam's little refrigeration stunt, she could do with warming up. Unwinding herself from the seat, she got out and found herself with an audience. In the few short minutes they'd been there, the car had drawn an interested couple of by-standers. They stared at her and then at the car and she smiled stiffly back at them. It felt a bit like showing off to be standing right beside it, as if to say, look at me and my car. Shifting, she looked down at the floor, wishing she'd grabbed her handbag. She could have pretended to be texting or something.

A woman came up right next to her, and without saying a word, pushed her way between Laurie and the car and put her hand on the bonnet. Too surprised to say anything, Laurie took a step back and watched in amazement as the woman's boyfriend calmly took a couple of shots of the woman with his phone.

'Nice car,' he tossed at her as he draped his arm across the woman's shoulders and they walked off.

'Mind if I take a picture?' asked another man. Smartly dressed in a suit in his mid-forties, he looked as if he were on his way to a meeting.

'No, its fine,' she said before adding tartly, 'At least you asked.'

'Sorry, Ferraris are a passion. It's a 250 isn't it?'

She nodded, grateful he hadn't asked anything more complicated. If he started asking anything petrol-heady, she wouldn't have a clue. She'd occasionally seen Top Gear and knew that car enthusiasts could get quite technical and while she'd absorbed some of that stuff around Uncle Miles, it had been a very long time ago.

'Mind if I look inside?' Another man stepped forward.

She looked over towards the entrances of the services. Where was Cam? How long did it take to get a couple of drinks?

'No, fine,' she said. Like a flood, the five or six people who had been hanging about all pushed forward and started peering inside the window.

'So what's max speed?'

'How fast have you taken it?'

Peppered with sudden questions, she froze. 'I er … don't know.'

Under the disapproving gaze of assorted men and one woman, she might as well have announced she murdered puppies as a hobby.

They began talking among themselves, making suppositions and guesses about the possible performance of the car. Laurie stepped back and let them get on with it, stealing another anxious look towards the services. What had happened to Cam?

Ten minutes later he finally appeared, sauntering across the car park with a lazy stroll that irritated the hell out of her, which was ridiculous because he couldn't have known that leaving her with the car was tantamount to throwing her to the wolves. Could he?

'Everything all right?' he asked with a cheery grin. He handed her the tea. 'There you go. It's probably cooled down enough to drink. I had to get a few supplies.' He indicated several bags of Jelly Babies tucked under his arm.

'Thank you,' she bit out, determined not to give in and ask what had kept him for so long. She took a tentative sip. Bloody hell, it was lukewarm. Through narrowed eyes she stared at him but he looked totally unconcerned sipping his own coffee, one hand shoved in his jeans pocket. He looked just too comfortable, too innocent and too damn pleased with himself.

'I'm going to the loo,' she snapped but might as well been talking to herself, the sod was already chatting to the gathered car enthusiasts.

With long quick strides she crossed the car park, went inside the services and hurried into the ladies'. Once locked into a cubicle she leaned against the door, glad of the privacy. She looked at her watch. She should be in Leighton Buzzard. At work in the library. Sitting at the front desk. Organising the piles of books waiting to be replaced on shelves. Gemma slouched in a chair reading out the latest ridiculous gossip on Cheryl Cole or Kim Kardashian from Heat magazine. A tiny sob escaped her and she screwed up her eyes. Bloody Miles and his stupid ideas. Getting the time off had meant she'd had to agree to put in for voluntary redundancy. She might not even have a job to go back to. And at this rate, she wouldn't have a fiancé to go back to either.

And since when had crying helped. Impatient with herself she took a deep breath. Woman or mouse? She just needed to get on with it. Taking a quick wee, she hurried out of the loos.

Compared to the way she felt, everyone else around her seemed in a festive mood. Women in pretty pastels applying lipstick in the mirrors, checking passports in their bags, and children darting underfoot from sinks to dryers. In front of her a little girl in a white broderie anglais dress was dancing up and down on the spot, her plaits swinging and not quite getting her hands in the stream of hot air, clearly driving her exasperated mother demented.

'Daisy! Stand still. Look this lady wants to dry her hands too.'

The little girl giggled and gave Laurie a gappy grin.

'Sorry,' the woman beamed not sounding the least bit apologetic, 'she's just excited about going on holiday.'

'We're going to France,' said the little girl, placing great emphasis on the word 'France' her eyes wide with wonder, as if it was the greatest adventure ever. 'To the seaside. And I'm going to swim every day. Daddy says I can have ice cream every day.'

'I'm going to France too,' said Laurie, her spirits suddenly lifting.

Returning to the car, she found a couple of people talking enthusiastically to Cam. She loitered on the edge watching him in conversation with a man and his young son. A minute later, the bonnet had been opened and they crowded round the uncovered engine, like trainee doctors around a patient with Cam as the consultant.

'Wow, is that …'

'Would you look …?'

'How many …'

The babble of questions merged into one, she had absolutely no idea what they were talking about. Not so, Cam. Answering each question, she could see him smiling and laughing, engaging with each of them, lifting the boy up to take a better look.

For a minute she watched him as they all nodded respectfully, hanging on his every word. He answered each question with equal consideration, whether talking to the small boy and gently removing his sticky fingers from the bodywork, a pair of awkward spotty teenagers who were bursting with enthusiasm or the annoyingly know-it-all man who kept chipping in and contradicting the answers Cam gave.

At that moment, Cam looked up, and over the tops of heads of his adoring crowd, caught her eye. He turned his head, pointed to some spark plug or something and then turned back to her and threw her a big grin followed by a quick conspiratorial wink and a roll of his eyes.

Standing in the direct beam of that infectious smile made her feel as if the sun had suddenly come out. With a few quick words he seemed to disperse the small group. He slammed the bonnet shut and beckoned her over.

'Sorry folks. Show's over. We're all headed to Italy.'

The quick, careless use of 'all' suddenly charmed her. It sounded like she, Cam and the car were a team.

Coming towards her, he winked again and opened the passenger door for her, pressing the tatty beige cardigan into her hands with a look of mute apology as she lowered herself into the car. He must have retrieved it from the boot while she was in the Ladies'. With a gentlemanly flourish he shut the passenger door, waved goodbye to the last of the people and got into the car.

With a roar the engine burst into life as he switched on the ignition. He turned to her. 'Ready then. France here we come.'

'As ready as I'll ever be,' she said crossing her fingers beneath her legs on the seat. This was it, no turning back. France. She looked around at the familiar English countryside. 'Do we get ice cream every day?' she asked with a sudden chuckle.

Cam's eyes twinkled in response. 'If you want … but don't you dare spill any on the seats.'

With that he thrust the car into gear and they meandered their way down the tarmac jungle through lanes and traffic lights until all of a sudden they were driving down a ramp to the waiting train.

'Up or down?' asked Cam.

'What?'

78

'It's a game I always play; you have to predict whether we'll be on the upper or lower deck of the train. Loser buys the first ice cream.'

'I didn't even know there was an upstairs and a downstairs.' Fascinated, she stared at the long metallic carriages. They looked functional and robust, although that was probably as well given they were going under the sea, which was a pretty daunting thought.

After thirty-five minutes cocooned in a carriage along with two other cars, having rocked their way under the channel, suddenly they were dropping back down the ramp and emerging into weak French sunshine. Without any further ado they were on the motorway and Laurie couldn't believe how easy it all was. Or that the first ice cream would be on Cam.

It always took a little while to get back into the swing of driving on the other side of the road but after an hour he could relax. Miles had picked an interesting route. Scenic, meandering and long. First official port of call was a small French seaside town. Thankfully Laurie didn't seem inclined to chat. At first he'd been worried by her quietness, concerned that she was bored and sulky, just like Sylvie used to be on long journeys but with her head swinging this way and that, it was clear she was drinking in the scenery, alert to all the continental differences in the landscape.

Thank God for sat nav these days, when you didn't have to rely on anyone in the passenger seat to navigate for you, although he had a feeling Laurie would be quite competent. There was an understated air of calm about her, as if she could weather difficulties like a stately ship gliding through. Of course you could easily mistake that calm for indifference, lack of emotion or inability to empathise. Cam prided himself on being a good judge of character but Laurie left him confused.

The desolate lost look on her face when he came back to the car with the hot drinks had made him feel horribly guilty. He should have been gentler with her. There was plenty of time en route to emphasise how impractical the car was, this morning he'd underestimated how she might be feeling. From what he'd gathered from Ron since the reading of the will, she was a home bird who had yet to fly the nest. He couldn't imagine her and the boyfriend did much travelling.

And didn't they always say you could catch more flies with honey? Plan A and B hadn't exactly panned out that well. Maybe he should focus on befriending her. Getting her on side. If she liked him enough, she'd find it hard to refuse selling the car to him.

From her silence, he sensed she was enjoying the journey.

'You OK? Want to stop or anything?'

She shook her head.

'You will say … if you need a loo break? Coffee? Tea? Jelly babies?'

'Jelly Babies?' her mouth curved into an unexpectedly sweet smile as if she was charmed by the thought.

He shrugged, feeling the beginnings of a blush start to ride his cheeks. 'Personal weakness.'

She grinned, sudden and naughty. 'I kind of like that … the wicked pirate with a secret weakness for sugar.'

The unexpected pixie smile punched him in the gut and he gripped the wheel tighter.

'Pirate?' He risked a quick glance at her.

'It's not a compliment.' The sudden return of her starchy tone was belied by dimple in her cheek. If he wasn't mistaken she was trying hard not to smile again.

'I didn't think it was.' He shot her a grin, determined to keep the sea change going. 'I've been called a lot of things … but not a pirate.' He paused. 'At least not to my face.'

Vivid pink fired along her cheekbone. 'Sorry I didn't meant to …'

'No offence taken. So any idea on why Miles chose this route? It's not exactly beginner's material. Do you know about the Stelvio

Pass?'

What the hell was Miles thinking including that little challenge? Not for the faint-hearted. Or even the crassly stupid. He knew people who had died on that section of road.

Laurie shrugged. 'Should I have heard of it?'

'No, not unless you're a bit of a petrol-head. It's the road down across the Swiss-Italian border, one of the steepest, most difficult drives in Europe. Forty-eight consecutive hair pin bends. It's tough. Although this is a short wheel base which makes it easier to manoeuvre. Hell on the bumps on the road though.

'And not for an inexperienced driver in a high performance car. With all those twists and turns, you need to know what you're doing.' He shuddered. 'If you misjudge one of the corners, hit the barrier and go over the edge …' It didn't bear thinking about.

'Perhaps I'll leave that one to you then,' said Laurie. She tapped the white A4 envelope on her knee. 'Uncle Miles liked to shake things up … he sent me postcards all the time. I think he wanted me to see some of the places he talked about.

'Honfleur always sounded so pretty. Just the name sounds lovely … don't you …' her voice trailed off.

He felt a pang for her sudden self-consciousness.

'Onfleeeuuur,' he said emphasizing the French pronunciation. 'You're right, it does have quite a ring about it.'

She shot him a suspicious look as if he were taking the piss.

'Funny, isn't it,' he kept his gaze straight ahead, 'most place names are suitable … they fit the place. Or do you think it's just because we associate those places with the name?'

'I prefer the former. Honfleur sounds pretty. I suppose it's because I know fleur is French for flower. It sounds as if the name is something flower and I know from the postcards Miles sent, it is a pretty place. Have you been before?'

'A couple of times.'

'Sorry I should have asked before. What exactly do you do? We kind of got foisted on each other but I never really understood

81

… did you work for my uncle?'

'We were business partners …' he winced, 'sorry, that sounds a bit dodgy.'

She gave him a sympathetic look. 'I don't think Miles would associate with a crook.'

'Thanks … I think. I worked with Miles. Originally, we were rivals, seeking out cars on commission. With the internet, a lot of the research could be done online but as he got older, even though he didn't want to, he realised he had to relinquish the driving to someone else.'

Hadn't stopped him dishing out plenty of instructions though, thought Cam with a rueful grin.

'He approached me … and the rest is history. I regularly drive … drove … across Europe to evaluate cars, persuade owners to sell … that sort of thing …'

'What about his cars, the ones back at the house … this one? Did he buy them to sell originally?'

Cam laughed, thinking of Miles. In some ways he'd been a brilliant business man, understanding the desire people held to obtain the cars of their dreams, in others he'd been a hopeless romantic, unable to part with his favourites. And wasn't that the pot calling the kettle black? He was no better when it came to the Ferrari. He clutched the steering wheel beneath his palms. Only a couple more weeks and it would be his, as long as Laurie completed Miles' challenge. No difficult conversations with Nick or the bank.

Managing her was going to be a bit trickier than he'd first thought. From the dowdy clothes and Ron's description of a homebody, he'd assumed she'd be a bit of a pushover and follow his instructions. In fact she was damn prickly, easy to offend and quick to assume the worst, especially of him. What would she think if he showed her the letter Miles had written which was currently tucked in his bag? A couple of times he'd caught a flash of steel in the cool blue eyes and she certainly wasn't as buttoned-up and reserved beneath the surface as he'd first assumed.

'Miles was a whizz at matching cars with potential owners' bank balances and in many instances, their overdrafts, but quite often he couldn't bear to part with them. Luckily sometimes he was able to persuade punters to buy a completely different car to the one we'd been asked to track down.'

'Handy,' she observed.

'There are two types of car buyers, enthusiasts and aficionados. The latter can be persuaded …' he shook his head, 'the aficionados … never.'

'Let me guess, you and Miles fall into the "never" category.'

'That's right … which is why Miles ended up with a stable full of cars.'

'How about you? How many do you have then?'

He stilled; dangerous ground. 'I don't … yet.' He waited, expecting more questions.

With a complete lack of curiosity, she simply nodded her head. 'Fair enough. So how long do you think it will take us to get there?'

'Not long at all. Fifteen, twenty minutes. Although Honfleur is not great for this baby. Too many cobbled streets. Plays havoc with the suspension.'

As the car ate up the road heading south to Honfleur, they chatted, if not like old friends, an awful lot like new friends treading carefully towards a friendship.

'So do you know what he had in store for us?' Cam motioned towards the envelope clutched to her chest like a shield.

'I know the route,' she worried her lip with her teeth, 'and the places we have to visit.' The protective hunch of her shoulders over the envelope made him wonder what demons she was expecting to face along the way.

Looked like it could be an interesting journey.

Chapter 8

Driving with Cam turned out to be surprisingly relaxing and she couldn't help comparing him to Robert. Their whole approach differed. Robert crouched over the steering wheel like a turtle peering out of its shell, clutching the steering wheel in a death grip, making any passenger tense up in accord.

With his hand resting negligently on the gear stick, the other lazily controlling the steering wheel, Cam exhibited a nonchalance that immediately calmed her although it hinted at a level of sophistication that unnerved her.

Her thoughts went back to the funeral, Cam jewel-bright among the women, whose smart clothes and immaculate grooming reminded her of her mother. He fitted in that world. No doubt her mother would approve of him. And today she wasn't going to think about her mother. Comfort had been sacrificed for performance, no doubt about that, but the roar of the engine vibrating through her pulsed along with her heartbeat. Low to the ground, every bump and jolt in the road translated straight to her bottom but for some reason she rather liked it. It made her feel in tune with the car.

With a sudden smile, she sat back and gave into the feeling of excitement that tripped, as fast as the car, along her veins and when they stopped for lunch in the pretty town of Honfleur, she felt pumped and charged as well as slightly romantic and foolish but in the brilliant sunshine of the picture-perfect street, she allowed herself to give in to the fantasy. She was on holiday, away from the everyday routine, with a man whom she'd probably never see again after this week.

It was a relief to stretch and stand tall and despite the stiffness in her joints, the envious glances as she and Cam peeled themselves out of what she thought of as a tiny cockpit, gave her a buzz. It disconcerted her. Earlier today those glances had made her feel horribly awkward. Was it because they were in France now?

'Coffee?' asked Cam, pushing his shoulders back and rolling them. Tall and broad, it must have been uncomfortable for him, driving in the cramped space but then as his shirt lifted revealing a smooth abdomen and an arrow of hair pointing downwards beneath his jeans, all thoughts of his discomfort vanished. Her mouth went dry. Totally inappropriate and uncharacteristic curiosity consumed her. What would it feel like to touch that sexy stomach? Hastily she looked away as a blush fired up her whole body, racing its way along her pulse points. It had to be the heat of the day making her feel hot and bothered. She didn't do sexy or lust after people. That happened in books, not real life. Even so the brief flash of skin reminded her of some of the racier front covers in the library. Cam could easily have modelled for any of them.

Hoping he hadn't read any of her thoughts, she grabbed her bag. 'I'm gasping for a Coke.'

He lifted one eyebrow in a way that instantly made her feel he could see right through her. 'Plenty of places to choose from,' he inclined his head indicating the cobbled street ahead, brimming with parasols and outside tables.

Lovely as they were, all of the cafés seemed to exhibit hugely overpriced and expensive menus outside. She winced. Thank goodness Ron had given her a bit of a float for the journey. She hadn't counted how many Euros were in the envelope but there was enough for quite a few drinks.

Now, looking at the price of Coca Cola, an overblown amount of Euros which translated into nearly a fiver in English money, she hoped it would be enough.

Despite pressing Ron for details on how much Cam was being paid, the wily solicitor had said it was Cam's business and up to him to share with her if he chose. Fair enough except, what she really needed to know was whether he was being paid enough to share the expenses or whether she should pay them. Her last month's salary from the library would only go so far. According to the itinerary drawn up by Miles, Ron would make the reservations in advance to the necessary hotels en route. She hadn't thought to ask him if they were budget hotels. But she had his phone number to text if their dates changed.

She glanced at Cam as they sat outside under a large canvas parasol watching the world go by. Although he dressed with casual ease, in faded jeans and a crisp cotton shirt, with a sweater flung over his shoulders, the watch he wore was clearly an expensive one. Even she'd heard of Breitling. The leather travel bag in the boot was well-worn but again of high quality, the sort you saw in Sunday supplements and wondered who could afford to spend that much on a bag.

He exuded an air of being well-travelled and from seeing him in action at the funeral, he was plenty experienced with women, hardly surprising with his good looks. He'd probably had women flocking round him since the day he hit manhood.

Everything about him shouted sophistication, so she was surprised to find what restful company he was. He seemed happy to sip his coffee and keep conversation to the minimum. Although there was a chance that that was because he found her boring.

Her mother would have been looking round constantly, her eyes roving for something more interesting, newer, shinier, brighter. Commenting on the clothes, the looks of other women, comparing the quality of the coffee to some other top notch café; name and place dropping.

Holding the tiny demitasse cup, white china brilliant against his tawny, dark skin and the movie-star, startling green eyes, he looked like an A- list celebrity.

She traced the voluptuous lines of the Coke bottle ... reluctant to break the silence.

In fact he'd been so accommodating, she felt she owed it to him to discuss the route.

'I take it you do know where we're going.'

The tentative question drew a slow smile from Cam.

'I know as much in as I know the proposed route but that's pretty much it.' He ticked points off on his fingers. 'There are certain places we have to send cards from. Miles arranged with Ron to book or arrange appropriate accommodation along the way which is fairly crucial to ensure the demands of the insurance policy are fulfilled,' he paused. 'Unfortunately with a baby that rare you can't just leave it overnight on the street. So we need to stick to schedule ... but the precise details are in your hands.' He nodded at the envelope she'd placed on the table.

How could he be so uncurious about the route? He made it all sound so simple.

'Don't you worry about it?'

'Worry?' Cam looked horribly amused as he slipped on his sunglasses. 'What about?'

She stared at him. Where did she start? The anxiety in her head was like an overstuffed teddy bear threatening to burst its seams, the kapok already threading its way out between the stitches.

'I trust Miles ... he wouldn't have made any leg of the journey too long.'

She sighed. If only it were that simple. They had hotels to stay in, meals to negotiate. What happened when they arrived at a hotel? What if it were too expensive? Would their rooms be near each other? Would they have dinner together or would he want to go off and do his own thing? Would he feel obliged to eat with her? Keep her company? And what about breakfast?

'Erm … you know when we get to the hotel this evening?'

Cam turned towards her, giving her full attention but behind the sunglasses it was impossible to discern his expression. It added to her anxiety. 'Well it was just … I … don't expect you to … you know …' She sipped her drink to calm her nerves.

Over the dark aviators, she saw his brows lift and his mouth quirk.

'Are you offering to sleep with me?' he asked, a smile playing around his lips. 'Or just share a room?'

The Coke sputtered past her lips, spraying the tablecloth. 'Neither. I've got a boyf … fiancé remember.'

'Oh,' he tipped his head on one side, studying her with consideration. 'So that's the only thing stopping you?'

Her face flamed. When he put it like that? If she didn't have Robert, would she? Clothed, he was a pretty fine specimen. Imagining him naked made her feel decidedly warm.

Pretending that her face wasn't beet red, she thrust her chin up. 'What I meant was that I don't expect you to feel obliged to spend your free time with me. So if we're staying in a hotel, I don't expect you have to dinner with me … or breakfast. We don't even have to have coffee together when we stop.'

'You do remember you're not my boss?' Cam leaned further back in his chair, his face inscrutable apart from the dimple appearing just left of his mouth.

She flushed again, hating the thought that she'd come over sounding as if she was. Even at work being the boss didn't sit comfortably.

She focused on the dimple. It was entirely too cute and didn't suit him at all. Dimples said nice, warm and friendly. Cam had danger written all over him. The kind of danger that made women shiver. Especially women that had read far too many romantic novels.

'You've got a tendency to worry, haven't you,' he drawled, hooking one arm over the back of the chair as if he had the whole

88

afternoon to while away in the shady corner spot. 'Its early days … why don't you just kick back, go with the flow. See what happens.'

The nonchalant shrug of his shoulders made her feel gauche and stupid and especially vulnerable sitting there in the brilliant sunshine with nothing to hide behind.

She itched to rip his bloody sunglasses off him and find out whether he was laughing at her or not. Go with the flow did not come into the equation. She had a route, a set number of days and a mission to achieve.

'I've no idea what might happen, that's why I'm trying to set some ground rules now.' She tried to tilt her chin like some worldly sophisticate. Probably looked like an escaped giraffe.

'Ground rules?' Again his mouth tilted in amusement.

Battling irritation that she was providing such excellent sport for him, she ploughed on. 'Yes, so that we both know exactly where we are.' Even to her ears it sounded prissy and horribly earnest.

'Honey, we're in Honfleur, Northern France with a journey of 1300 kilometres miles to go. I'd have said that we have a pretty good idea of where we are. We also know we're going to Maranello, so that gives us an equally good idea of where we're going. What happens in between can be considered an adventure.

'If you stress about what will be, what might happen before we even get there, you won't leave yourself any time to enjoy the moment and make the most of the opportunity. You're won't ever get the chance to drive one of these little ladies again.'

'I'm not stressing—'

'—You're doing a very good impersonation of it then.'

'I'm not,' she gritted her teeth, feeling the tell-tale flush of embarrassment which always arrived when she lied badly. 'OK, I am. This is all … a bit overwhelming. I don't stay in hotels, never go abroad for holidays and don't normally dr—' she stopped herself just in time, 'dr … dress … dress up in the evenings.'

'No one's asking you to do that.' The quirky smile was back. 'Lauren, it's a road trip. Take each day as it comes. We're in no hurry, why don't you enjoy yourself? Enjoy the sunshine, the countryside, and the car. I'll even let you drive if you want to.' He raised his sunglasses and gave her a playful wink.

'Yeah right,' she quipped back, unable to resist his charm. One thing she'd sussed about him already was that he was as besotted by the car as Uncle Miles had been.

Just as well he didn't know that she shouldn't drive the car, hopefully she'd get away with it for the whole journey.

She watched a couple stroll past the café; the man looked a little like Cam and the woman with him was stunning. 'Are you married?' she asked as the couple kissed and sauntered over to study the menu at the next café.

His mouth quirked at one side in pretended amusement and he tracked her gaze.

'No … not anymore.'

Loathe to pry, she didn't ask any more but unprompted he carried on. 'I was married. To Sylvie. We got married far too young. And I didn't get along with her mother.'

He didn't seem old now. 'How old were you?'

'Twenty-two. Young and stupid. We were divorced by the time I was twenty-six.'

'Ouch' said Laurie sympathetically.

'It wasn't great. I could have handled it better … When Sylvie met me, I was working for the Jordan race team. Lots of money, lots of travel. She liked the trappings … more than she liked me as it turned out.

'I went solo, set up my own freelance business. She hated it, the insecurity of it, never knowing where the next pay check was coming from.'

'I can relate to that,' said Laurie. She and Robert budgeted to the penny each month knowing exactly what they had to spend. 'Although, didn't she work?' Laurie couldn't imagine not working, or not having your own financial security.

'Not once she met me. To be fair she gave up work to travel with me, otherwise I'd have barely seen her. That was the first mistake.'

'And the second?' asked Laurie intrigued.

'Second, third, fourth, fifth etcetera, etcetera, etcetera.' He shook his head. 'We might have made a go of it … if her mother hadn't got involved. Every time we had a row and Sylvie didn't get what she wanted, she'd be straight on the phone to her mother, who instead of telling her to grow up, be a wife and get on with it, would sympathise and agree with her what a bastard I was.'

'Were you?' asked Laurie. She couldn't imagine sharing anything that personal with either of her parents.

Cam looked off into the distance, his shoulders drooping slightly. 'Yeah … I probably was some days. She was fragile, needy. I was too immature and not the right man for her. I could have been kinder,' he pulled a face, 'should have been kinder. I regret that now. But she's OK now … she ran off with a rich contact of mine,' he laughed with self-deprecation, 'I sold him a Ferrari and he got my wife. She's probably a million times happier with him.

'So how did you meet Robert? And how long have you been engaged?'

The abrupt change of subject made it clear he was done with talking about his ex-wife.

'We met in the library, where I work. He came in, we got chatting.' She shrugged. It sounded so dull.

'So how long have you been together?'

'Just over two years.'

'And when did he pop the question? He didn't introduce you as his fiancé at the funeral.'

For some reason she suddenly felt defensive. 'A couple of weeks ago.'

'Interesting timing,' observed Cam with a devilish glint of mischief.

'What's that supposed to mean?' Laurie didn't like the tone of his voice, even if her own thoughts had occasionally meandered down the same track. What was responsible for Robert's sudden and ardent proposal?

'Nothing. I'm being old fashioned. In the olden days, people used to wait a suitable period of mourning, that's all.' He shrugged.

'My dad died nearly two years ago and then Miles. Robert felt I might like the security of being married.'

'What about your mother?'

Laurie snorted. 'She's not exactly the maternal type.'

Cam held her gaze. 'When was the last time you saw her?'

Laurie shrugged. 'Can't remember,' she lied. 'Shall we get the bill?'

With some discreet signal, he managed to summon a waitress who locked onto them and headed their way like an Exocet missile fixed on its target.

'Good afternoon m'sieur, would you like to pay the bill?' Her husky voice and fractured French accent brought an appreciative glance from Cam. Laurie felt like an oversized English sheepdog next to the elegant young woman. Why was it so many French women looked like they might be related to Audrey Tautou? And there was Cam responding with his charming smile. Any minute he'd be doing that cheesy kissing her fingers, he was so busy fawning over her.

'Yes please ...' he glanced at the badge above her breast. 'Monique.'

To Lauren's jaundiced eye, the name badge had been placed with flirtatious aforethought, deliberately to draw the eye to the perky cleavage on display and Cam was definitely availing himself of a good long look at the creamy flesh tastefully bared.

'Are you 'ere on 'oliday?' she asked with a winsome smile. 'Staying in Honfleur?' The way she said it was full of sexy French promise that had Lauren wincing at her own earlier whimsical attempts.

'Sadly not, just passing through.' Cam's regretful smile was charmingly done.

'Zat is a shame,' the French girl murmured. 'It is a ver pretty place.'

'Maybe another time,' responded Cam.

Monique blushed and her cheeks dimpled.

Laurie pointedly ignored their pigeon English conversation and focused on tapping out a text she knew she'd never send to Robert, but it made her look busy and indifferent. Cam was a free agent; it was nothing to her who he flirted with, but it would have been nice if he didn't do it quite so blatantly in front of her.

'Are you ready, Laurie?' His matter of fact tone was very different to the softer one he'd used talking to Monique. Not that it mattered one jot.

The second leg of the journey started well enough with Laurie determined to be cool but friendly to Cam. He'd opened up briefly to her and they were on a long journey together; they needed to get along but she also needed to remember he wasn't above exercising his undeniable charm when it suited him. Somewhere just north of their destination they got caught in a horrible traffic jam which left Cam anxiously checking the temperature gauge.

Ironically the heating had to go on full blast as he was worried the engine might overheat which meant that she definitely didn't need the cardigan or the fleece she'd made sure she kept with her. By the time they arrived at their first hotel it was late and Laurie felt dishevelled, hot and sticky and Cam's white linen shirt stuck to his back, his curls damp around his forehead.

Feeling like a tramp who had no place in the richly appointed foyer, she approached the check-in desk, furtively looking for a room rate list but it was the sort of discreet establishment which didn't believe in such things.

A receptionist with a neat bun, a pristine white shirt and a big floppy black scarf looked up and immediately fired a thousand kilowatt smile in Cam's direction as if Laurie didn't exist.

'Bonjour Monsieur, Madame. How can I help you?'

'We'd like some rooms, s'il vous plait,' Cam responded with a ready smile, dropping his bag at his feet. 'Preferably with a long cool shower and a beer.' He undid a button and fanned himself, exposing more of the strong column of his neck. The receptionist gave him a very interested look. He leaned towards her and in a husky voice said, 'It's been a very long day.'

Laurie gave him a suspicious glance. What did he mean by that? Had her company been that onerous?

'I am sure we can provide everything you need, Monsieur.' Something glimmered in her eyes and her body language suddenly suggested a whole lot more. Her back straightened, her boobs went out and her voice dropped an octave.

Like a horse to water, Cam leaned on the desk, his tanned forearms resting on the surface, looking completely at home. She tilted her head towards him. 'We pride ourselves on our excellent service.'

'I'm sure you do.'

Laurie wanted to kick him hard on the ankle.

'Do you have reservations, monsieur?'

'We have rooms booked,' Laurie snapped, irritated that she should even care. Cam was such a player. He'd flirt with anything. Resolutely she refused to look at him, even though she could feel his gaze suddenly boring into her.

The receptionist looked momentarily startled and then her ultra-professional mask smoothed back into place. 'Names please.'

'Miss Browne and Mr Matthews.' She sounded shrewish but she refused to care.

'Room 101 and 102. I'll get your keys. Please could you fill these in?'

She disappeared.

'What the hell was that about?' asked Cam.

'"I'm sure we can provide everything you need, M'sieur"' retorted Laurie. 'I'll just bet she can. All part of the service, M'sieur.'

Before Cam could respond, the receptionist returned with two large keys with large gold tassels on them. Laurie took one, feeling the weight. Sumptuous like everything else. It all felt very expensive.

'I'm afraid the restaurant is fully booked this evening, but you can order room service if you would like to eat with us.'

Laurie turned to Cam, suddenly unsure. Normally when she and Robert stayed in a B and B they'd go out for a McDonalds or something. Room service had never been an option before.

'Go ahead, Laurie.' Although Cam's face seemed impassive, Laurie knew she'd offended him. 'I need to get out for a run.' He rolled his neck, pushing his shoulders back and she heard a slight click.

He picked up the keys, handed her one and thanked the receptionist in a burst of fluent French to which she responded with several rapid fire sentences before wishing him *bonne nuit* with another flirtatious smile.

Laurie let out an irritated huff.

Cam glared and strode ahead, leading the way towards the rooms. She could see him rubbing his shoulder and hurried to catch up with him. Crimping his six foot frame into the driver's seat for so many hours must be hard work. Was that why he was suddenly in such a bad mood?

It also explained why the route Miles had planned was so strung out.

Cam thrust the key to room 102 into her hand.

'I'll say good night. Breakfast is at 7.30. Which is what the young lady at the desk was just telling me. Probably best to get a head start before the day gets too warm. And just for the record, I was being friendly.'

He let himself into the room next door and slammed it, without giving her chance to draw breath.

She stared at the closed door, her teeth tugging at her lip. Talk about making a prat of herself. He was right. Just looking at that gorgeous face gave her the tingles, how could she complain if another woman thought so too? It wasn't as if Cam sought the attention. Again she remembered him at the funeral. He'd been charming, attentive and friendly to the many women that sought his company but if she were totally honest, he had been nothing more than polite.

Damn and now she was going to have to apologise to Cam. She looked at the firmly closed door. Probably best to wait until the morning.

Besides she had humble pie eating to do with Robert first. He always came around eventually; it just took a certain amount of grovelling. Unsurprisingly the home phone went unanswered. When her own voice kicked in on the answer machine, she hung up, there was no point leaving a message. Robert would be there but refusing to answer. She tried his mobile. It rang twice and then was cut off.

She texted him.

First leg completed. All going well. Love Lx

Her room service meal, a simple Tuna Nicoise overpowered by strong dark black olives and an odd chemical taste, added to her overriding sense of disappointment.

She felt cheated. She'd finally decided to commit to the big adventure and this dull but expensive room felt commonplace. She could have been anywhere. Having wandered around the room and tried to sit and read, she found the silence too overpowering. The plastic, double-glazed units of the window made it feel as if she was hermetically sealed off from the world, there was no sense of noise or smell or temperature. It felt unreal and disconnected.

Where was Cam? Had he come back from his run? Probably in the shower by now.

And that was so not an appropriate thought.

She pushed the tray of half eaten salad outside her door and headed for bed, setting her mobile as an alarm. Sitting in a car all day doing nothing was exhausting.

Having nervously practised her apology, she sat down at the breakfast table where Cam was half way through a croissant.

'About last night, I'm sorry. You were quite right. I was unfair. I shouldn't have …' Her words dried up at his amused smirk.

'Laurie, I was tired and grumpy. You rubbed me up the wrong way. Let's just forget about it. Now, we've got a couple of easy days of driving, is there anywhere you fancy going?'

And that was that. She kept peeking at him when he wasn't looking to check that he really was OK, but he seemed perfectly happy as he discussed possible routes to get them to their next destination.

Over the next two days they headed south to Le Mans and then east to Orleans and Laurie successfully managed to avoid driving. Not that it was that hard, Cam clearly relished driving the Ferrari and the journeys to Miles' prescribed destinations were relatively short hops.

She felt slightly self-conscious at first when writing the postcards to Ron. It wasn't as if she knew him that well but somehow it felt mean not writing something more personal. He'd clearly been a great friend of her uncle and she could remember what a lift she'd got each time she received one of his postcards.

In Le Mans she selected a card of the view of the town from the river featuring the old stone buildings with their round turrets. On the postcard from Honfleur, she'd commented how pretty the place was, she could hardly do the same on this one. Instead she mentioned how well the journey was going and how much interest the car elicited wherever they went.

In Orleans she chose a picture of the Cathedral and told Ron how Joan of Arc, the Maid of Orleans, dominated the city. She also thanked him for making all the arrangements. To her huge relief, Ron had organised payment for their accommodation in advance which meant she could relax.

She also found that spending hours on end with Cam in the car wasn't too bad. During one leg, he insisted they went out of their way to take in the glorious Cathedral at Rouen after she mentioned how much she'd enjoyed Ken Follett's *Pillars of the Earth*.

To her surprise he was an avid reader, although their taste differed enormously. He loved Lee Childs and Mark Thorne thrillers but unlike Robert didn't disdain her love of historical novels and romance.

Talking in the car wasn't that easy over the pulse of the engine but the glorious June weather encouraged them to make frequent stops, which Cam insisted were necessary to ensure the car didn't overheat. In every one of the small villages and towns he insisted on driving around to check out where the local mechanics were, just in case they might break down on the next leg. At each stop he would open up the bonnet and um and ah like an anxious mother over the engine. Laurie had no idea what he was looking at but didn't for a minute think it was because he was really worried about the car. He just liked gloating over its superior engine.

After the third town, where Cam spent several hours fussing at one of the garages but not appearing to do much but chat to the owners, she decided that rather than waste the time in a boring wait she should make the most of being there. She took to abandoning Cam and wandering off to visit bustling markets, local galleries and tiny churches.

For lunch they would buy fresh French bread and local cheese. Having not been abroad since she was a child, the choice of different foods amazed her as did the busy markets and the variety of local architecture. Listening to the chatter of French around her made her old life seem a million miles away, instead of just a couple of day's drive.

Cam was easy company and despite the punctuation of regular texts from an increasingly maudlin Robert, she realised as they left the hotel in Orleans, she was really enjoying herself.

Today's text from Robert was pitiful and she was starting to get quite cross with him.

We would have been married for five days by now.

Replying to them took so much energy. She'd tried to phone but Robert never answered. Instead she sent diplomatic responses but she couldn't bring herself to say 'forgive me'.

I'm sorry I hurt your feelings. X

From the thick wooded hillside of the Loire Valley, the spires of a fairy tale-inspired castle rose. All the perfect chateau lacked was flying ramparts from the round pointed turrets. Laurie took in a deep breath as she stared at the crenelated towers outlined against the skyline and tugged at her ponytail, curling the ends of her hair around her wrist, over and over. Tension skimmed along her nerves like a tightrope walker.

New people. Friends of Miles'. He'd asked them to call in. No hotel was booked; they'd been offered hospitality at the chateau. She thought back to the glittery, smart women at his funeral and felt a fraud arriving in this gorgeous shiny monster, dressed in comfy Next jeans and an oversized grey T shirt.

The Comte and Comtesse. She could picture the Comtesse already. Immaculate in some black dress with hair in a chic perfect bob. Laurie wanted nothing more than to slink on to the nearby town and find a hotel. Surely a postcard from the town was enough.

'You'll be fine.' Cam's voice penetrated her thoughts. 'Stop worrying about what they're going to think of you. They might be nervous about meeting you.'

'What? Why would they be nervous of me?'

He shrugged. 'Exactly. And they'd probably be equally horrified at the prospect of you being nervous about meeting them. They're good friends of Miles', looking forward to meeting his kin.'

She pulled a face and poked her tongue out at his smug expression. 'I hate it when you do that.'

'Do what?'

'Be sensible and reasonable.'
'It's a talent.'
'Hmph,' snorted Laurie, tossing her ponytail.

Chapter 9

'Lovely isn't it?' asked Cam pulling over to the side of the road on the edge of the valley.

'Bet it was hard work building it into the hill like that.'

Her observation drew a chuckle from Cam. 'No romance in you, is there? Ever practical. Needs must in those days, I guess. Pretty good defensive position. No one's going to sneak up on you, not with sentries posted on each of those towers. Probably had archers ready and waiting as well as boiling oil to pour over the ramparts.'

She gave him a sudden amused grin. 'I hate to disappoint you but it's not that old.'

'Whatcha mean?'

'Mid Victorian. Gothic reproduction principally.' You had a lot of time to read in a library. She knew all sorts of miscellaneous facts and this wasn't the real deal. 'Made to look medieval.'

Cam looked suspicious as if she were teasing him.

'The Chateau was considerably enhanced in the 1890's by the Beaulieu family who inherited the land by default and came by their money from tobacco rather than wine.' Where had that knowledge popped up from? Not the library, for sure. And there was more. It filled her head like an old song she'd heard on the radio and could remember every single word. 'Rumour has it that the owner murdered his brothers so he wouldn't have to share his inheritance.'

'Have you swallowed the guide book or something?'

'It just popped into my head. I think Miles told me during a tasting … I can't remember where we were.' She had a vague memory of being in some kind of wine cellar.

'How old would you have been?'

'Probably about fourteen but I remember it, because the wine was possibly the best I've ever tasted in my life.'

'Nice age to start learning to have a discerning palate.'

'You're joking! It was disastrous. Spoilt me for anything ever since. I got used to the expensive stuff. Once I ordered a glass of red wine in a pub. Nearly spat it out all over the bar. Robert thought I was being pretentious.'

'Were you?'

'No, I've got used to the cheap stuff … but I can still taste a good one.' She smiled at the memory, 'Like at Miles' funeral.'

He grinned at her. 'Well, as its on Miles' itinerary, let's find out if your palate is still as discerning? Are you up for a tasting before we go and introduce ourselves to the Comte?'

Unbidden, rich berry flavours filled her head and for a moment the memory of taste blocked out everything else. Heady scents and tannins spreading across her tongue, she could almost smell and taste them still, the memory was so strong and vibrant. A sense of exhilaration and freedom filled her, as she realised that there was nothing to stop her saying yes. No obligations, no other person to consider, no place to be, no time constraints. The concept suddenly seemed as big as the universe.

For a moment it was as if she were weightless and could float away without anything anchoring her to earth. The headiness of the thought terrified her. She needed direction, purpose, duty. Duty? Where had that come from? She'd been bound by duty for so long, it had become another layer of her. Was that habit? Or conscience?

'Earth to Laurie?'

She stared at him, feeling a little dazed at the sudden insight to her world. A chink of light that had thrown several things into sharp relief. As if she'd walked into a dim room from the bright sunshine and then things gradually became clearer again. It was as if she'd been in the dark for a long time.

The road wound up the side of the hill over a small bridge crossing the river and then up through a gentle slope. On either side of the single track road row upon row of vines stretched, neatly trimmed in uniform lines, with rose bushes in full bloom, marking the end of the rows like full stops.

Another memory popped into her head. Roses? She remembered their sweet fragrance and skipping along the rows of vines which had then been taller than her, the flat green canopy of freshly trimmed leaves above. The roses she knew were more than decorative. They were there to show any signs of disease. The rose would be affected first and the viticulturist could do something about it in time.

The details, the knowledge was all there, buried in her head but popping to the surface with remarkable ease at the sight of the flowers and the terraces of vines. The more she tried to remember why or how she knew these things, the further they seemed to recede in her head until she convinced herself that it all must have come from some TV programme a long time ago.

'Bonjour Madam.' With an elegant practiced move that seemed completely natural, the Comte took Laurie's fingers, brought her hand up to his lips, and brushed her knuckles with them. He turned to Cam. 'Sir. Welcome to the Chateau de La Miroir.' He looked out towards the car. 'We've been expecting you. Miles was a regular visitor here and promised he would send his niece back again. I am so sorry for your loss. He will be greatly missed, especially here at the Chateau. He was a gentleman, non?' His eyes twinkled and he raised his eyebrows as if Miles had been no such thing.

'Thank you,' murmured Laurie, feeling wrong footed and

disconcerted by something he'd said, but she couldn't define it. She wished Miles' notes had included a little more detail.

The Frenchman studied her for a second, his head on one side and waited and then he smiled, the mischievous twinkle back again. 'Ah, you do not remember me, do you? You were only a little girl at the time. You came here the first time with your parents. You were all legs and pigtails, running here and there, always asking questions. Wanting to know how everything worked. I am Philippe.'

She stared. 'Really, I er … er.' She didn't want to offend him by not remembering but she hadn't got a clue and he'd said the first time. She didn't remember her parents ever being together, let alone being somewhere with them as a family. If you'd asked her, she would have sworn blind that they'd never been on holiday together. Surely she would have remembered something like that? And the second visit which was implied.

In fact she had no recollection of them ever all living in the house she shared with Dad. The time after her mother buggered off was clear in her mind. Shared meals with Dad. Holidays in Weymouth. Going to work with him for work experience at the insurance offices. Him coming to parents' evenings at school. Loads of things. Her mother had a new glamorous life, an important wealthy husband and lots of parties to go to; she didn't want an unappealing fourteen year old with braces and greasy hair messing things up.

The Comte's laugh penetrated her ugly thoughts as he took her elbow to guide her in through the huge oak gothic door into the cool stone winery. 'No worries Laurie. You are here now and we are delighted to have you back. I hope that you will stay with us at the Chateau this evening. My wife and son will be very pleased to see you again, although perhaps my son won't remember you either. You are the same age. Marie was a big fan of Miles. He always brought British presents and outrageous compliments.'

'I … er …' wide-eyed, she looked at Cam.

He was no help.

'Are you … sure … it …'

'No, no I insist. Absolutement.'

With that he turned and held a hand out to Cam, 'Excusez-moi, you must be Monsieur Matthews. Delighted to meet you. Miles always spoke highly of you,' the twinkle was back, 'although he was less complimentary about your palate.'

Cam grinned back. 'That's being polite; bet he said I was a philistine when it came to wine.'

Philippe nodded. 'Something along those lines, although he also said you did appreciate fine things in life once they'd been brought to your attention.' Laurie caught a faint undertone in the words but Cam seemed unperturbed.

Philippe smiled smoothly again. 'I hope during and after dinner we can educate that palate a little more.'

Cam shrugged. 'I'm not one to turn down a decent bottle of wine.'

Laurie thought back to the funeral and gave him a rebuking look. He knew enough about wine to appreciate the good stuff.

'Would you like to drive around to the house? Jean will show you where to park the car and we can show you to your rooms.'

Laurie turned pink. 'Are you sure you don't mind putting us up?' It seemed a terrible imposition; after all they were complete strangers, even if he did seem very friendly. She couldn't remember the last time she'd stayed in anyone's home, apart from Miles' and there she knew the routine, the layout of the house.

Panic hovered. What if she made a fool of herself?

'Nonsense. The rooms are ready. We would not hear of it.' He shook his head vehemently. 'Non, non, non. Come.'

Laurie exchanged a glance with Cam. He was no bloody help at all, he just shrugged his shoulders in that laconic fashion of his. She frowned at him, pulling a clear help-me-out here face.

He just laughed. 'I'll take the car round to the Chateau, why don't you walk up with Philippe?'

He hauled the bags out of the tiny boot. Not a bad place to stay for the night. He'd stayed in far worse and perhaps better. Although it was probably best to wait and see what lay beyond the doors. Too many times he'd seen places that shouted grandeur and wealth but it was nothing more than a façade and inside the shell revealed the dent that inheritance taxes and maintaining the ancient structure had made on the pockets of the families. Although from the general upkeep of the place and the awards that filled the winery walls and Miles' patronage, he had a feeling that Chateau de La Miroir was more than making ends meet.

And how many more surprises did Miles have up his sleeve along the route? Not that he was complaining. He was happy to go with the flow but not Laurie. She was a prickly thing. Difficult to read. Sylvie would have jumped at the chance to stay in a fairy princess castle like this place. For him, the biggest bonus was not having to worry about garaging the car. He'd had his suspicions that part of this job, as he still thought of it, was to baby-sit the car and that some nights he'd be kipping in the bucket seat.

Laurie had managed to confound most of his plans. The car had been running like a dream which had thwarted the attempt to reinforce the idea that it was terribly temperamental and difficult to maintain. The additional efforts to ramp up incipient anxiety had also failed miserably. She'd quickly bored with hanging around endlessly at the local garages and had gone off on little sight-seeing tours, if anything returning looking happier as if reassured by the provincial ordinariness of the towns they'd passed thorough. To be honest he was sick of passing the time of day with the car-struck mechanics of northern France.

Looked like he was going to have to fall back on making her like him enough that not selling the car to him wasn't an option, which now he was getting to know her, wasn't that much of a hardship.

A young man opened the double glass doors at the top of a flight of stone steps elegantly bound by wrought iron tracery.

'Bonjour, I'm Jean.' He looked around questioningly.

'Laurie's walking up with your father.' The likeness between the young man and the older man was marked.

'Bon. Entrez. Have you had a good journey?' He looked with longing at the car.

'How could I not driving this beauty? Want to take a closer look?'

They exchanged conspiratorial grins and within minutes Jean was in the driver's seat.

By the time Laurie and Philippe appeared, their heads together deep in conversation, he hadn't even made it into the house.

Philippe's eyes rolled at the sight of his son with his head under the bonnet of the Ferrari but then within several short strides he joined him. All three men had their heads stuffed under the bonnet of the car.

Laurie wanted to be impatient with them but their boyish enthusiasm over the glories of the engine and car intrigued her. She was starting to see what so enthralled them.

When had that itch to place her palms on the steering wheel become so insistent? She suspected she was already half in love with the car. Sitting as a passenger today had been sheer pleasure heightened by Cam's competent and careful handling of the mighty engine. No, scrub that ... careful sounded cautious and that wasn't true, they'd hit 120km on the fine straight, country roads.

She had to remind herself it was just a car. An old car at that.

The sleepy, sexy eyes of the headlights on the long slow hood held her gaze as if challenging her. OK, not just any old car.

A Ferrari. How many people could say that they owned a Ferrari? Her heart did a funny little skip. What would those boys at school say? All the people that had left Leighton and moved on? Laurie the librarian, owner of a Ferrari. She rather liked that.

Her eyes ran over the sleek lines. It was rather beautiful. She should be driving it, not leaving it to Cam. This was a once in a lifetime opportunity. And she ought to make the most of it, especially as coming had upset Robert and probably cost her a job. She looked longingly at the car. What were the chances of them being stopped by the police? Or asked for her licence? Her palms itched. No, she needed to be sensible. Let Cam drive.

Suddenly she wasn't sure she'd be able to. Until now she'd been fighting the desire to drive, in denial. Going along for the ride. Happy in the passenger seat. Just like always, a little voice pointed out. Laurie bit her lip and quashed the unwelcome observation.

In irritation she cleared her throat and all three heads popped up in surprise like a trio of meerkats. She smiled meekly. 'Er …'

'Sorry, come.' Philippe held out his arm, motioning her to lead the way into the Chateau.

The inside was cool but brilliantly bright, the high ceiling white with light, diamond-sharp, refracting from the mirrors that covered the main wall from top to bottom. Remembrance flooded back and, entranced, Laurie stepped forward, her gaze captured by the largest gilt framed mirror over the white marble carved fireplace and ornate mantelpiece.

'The hall of mirrors,' she murmured turning on the spot to look at the various mirrors all over the walls. She thought she'd dreamt this place, or imagined it from the pages of a fairy tale. An image of a smiling girl filled her head. Her. Here in this hall. Running up the stairs, coming down for dinner pretending to be a French aristocrat in a huge dress, catching sight of herself in each of the framed mirrors, like windows lining the stairs' outside wall.

As she turned her head, she caught sight of herself. Pain lanced and she turned away from her reflection. Where had that laughing, without-a-care-in-the-world girl gone?

'Must take some getting used to,' observed Cam, looking acutely uncomfortable.

The two French men exchanged rueful smiles. 'An ancestor's idea of sorting the wheat from the chaff,' explained Philippe. 'His first wife was incredibly vain and put looks above everything. She surrounded herself by equally vain people who adored her for her beauty but none of them could chastise her. Her vanity led her to purchase a stallion which she couldn't control but she looked good upon. She fell and broke her neck on her very first outing, leaving her children motherless. The Comte was determined that if he married again he wouldn't marry a vain woman, so he filled the hall with mirrors to judge the reaction of the women that stayed here. Those that admired themselves or looked at themselves in more than three mirrors were deemed too vain.'

The story held a certain resonance, Laurie reflected bitterly. An abject lesson in the perils of vanity. As a young teen she'd looked in every mirror on the way down. How things had changed since then. Now she only owned one dress, which Ron had suggested rather forcefully that she pack. It was black, easy to wash and fitted OK.

Cam walked downstairs, doing up the buttons of a clean shirt as he went. He'd stayed in many far more impressive rooms over the years but this one, with its selection of old hardback books on the shelves, mismatched but very fluffy towels and an ancient wardrobe held up on one side by a stone brick, charmed him.

After being scrunched up in the car, his legs needed a good stretch and the grounds of the Chateau were extensive. He had of course checked on the car, making sure the oil levels and tyre pressure were still OK, but that was basic. Despite his fussing in front of Laurie, he knew the car was in tip-top condition. It had been looked after with as much care as a thoroughbred racehorse, but she didn't need to know that. Tomorrow he'd have another stab at unsettling her and introduce the idea of a funny knocking noise which might be indicative of a problem with the head gasket. Of course if that went they could be held up for days.

The gardens around the house were immaculate but he had little appreciation for the perfection of box hedges, gravelled paths or artfully placed fountains. Instead he paced on to the more wild patch of woodland beyond and followed a path that led up the slope. After the growl of the engine all day, he welcomed the peace and serenity of the woods in the late afternoon. He was used to being part of a two man team, either driving or navigating. This was his life and getting away on his own for part of the day was also his antidote to being in such close proximity all day with someone else.

Being in the car with Laurie was different though. In the past he and his co-driver would have shared a common aim – to win a race or to reach a destination, either way they'd be rewarded with glory or financially. Without being mercenary, this was how he'd made his living.

He hadn't been entirely honest with her. Was there any point telling her the truth? It would make her even more uncomfortable about expenses and things. Miles' will had been complicated enough with more twists and turns than the Stelvio Pass itself.

It had obviously been important to him. Cam did wonder at Laurie's naivety. Did she know he wasn't being paid for the trip? Hadn't she ever heard the expression, 'no such thing as a free lunch'?

Now they'd started the journey, it felt as if he'd missed the opportunity to tell her that Miles had promised him first refusal on the car. Pig-headedness, really. Her attitude that he was some sort of international playboy had irked him and if he'd told her that Miles had promised him first dibs on the car at an advantageous rate, it would have further reinforced her negative feelings towards him. He really needed her to like him so that she would feel well-disposed to selling the car to him.

He didn't like admitting it but he didn't like being viewed with suspicion. So his marriage to Sylvie hadn't ended well but he wasn't a bad person. He'd never led anyone on without being totally honest with them. Except not telling Laurie about the deal Miles had made on the price of the car wasn't exactly honest.

When he finally returned to the mirrored hallway of the Chateau, it was almost dinner time. A long corridor led the way and he listened to see if it would give up a clue as to where he might find his hosts. A murmur of voices came from one of the rooms

110

along with the clink and chink of cutlery and plates. Someone laying a table?

A movement at the top of the stairs caught his eye and there was Laurie looking pensive, hovering indecisively on the top step. She hadn't seen him. He watched, seeing her make up her mind and take the first step. The shapeless black dress she'd changed into hung loose, doing nothing for her, completely disguising any shape she might have. The hem stopped well below her knees, hanging like droopy bunting. Having spent several hours in close proximity in the car, all he knew was that her legs were long. You'd never have guessed; the dress seemed to cut them off at the worst possible point. Shapely calves and neat ankles had been flattened out by flat ugly, black sandals.

For the first time, she'd left her soft honey hair down rather than having it in the harsh ponytail which emphasised her slightly sticky out ears. It fell in waves, making her look quite different. Much gentler and more approachable. For a brief moment, he found himself wondering what the rest of her looked like under the ill-fitting dress. Slim definitely. Her arms were slender, almost too slender, the wrists looked tiny and there were no unsightly bulges in the dress. It just hung, square, hiding her frame. What were her breasts like? An image of those pert nipples came back to him. And where the hell had that thought come from? What would she feel like if he held her to him?

She came down the steps as if facing a firing squad, her face averted from the mirrors. He felt a pang at her obvious discomfort and wanted to reassure her.

Damn, charming her was one thing but he couldn't get involved. It wasn't down to him to look after her. He didn't like the direction his thoughts were taking. She might well be an attractive woman with a lot of unrealised potential but he had to have that Ferrari and not let any feelings side-track him. Nice as she was, he had to remember Laurie was a means to an end – besides she wasn't his kind of woman. She'd want too much. Commitment for a start, being sensible, planning things, doing the right thing. He thought of his ex-wife and could almost hear her voice thick with disapproval. She'd never been one to hold back on her opinion of other women's dress sense.

The slap of Laurie's sandals on the marble white stairs broke his reverie and he stepped forward. Her gaze met his and he almost laughed when she lifted her chin and held it with a regal tilt all the way down. Maybe she didn't need looking after as much as he'd thought.

She reached the bottom and stayed on the last step gripping the ornate iron banister, as if psyching herself up to abandon the security of the banister and step, to find out just how deep the swimming pool was going to be.

Then again, maybe she knew already.

Chapter 10

Crossing the floor in six rapid strides, he held out his arm for her to link hers through.

'Allow me.' She looked up, with a brief flash of gratitude which she quickly doused, as if giving too much away. 'Your hair looks lovely.' Deliberately, he let his gaze rove over her waves.

'Thank you, I think.' She raised one cynical eyebrow. 'I think that's called damning with faint praise.'

'Would you rather I lied? That dress is hideous, where the hell did you get it from?'

'I can see why you're such a hit with the ladies,' her mouth turned downwards but her blue eyes danced with mischief.

'Sorry that was ungallant of me and most ladies would have slapped me across the face. I apologise.'

She shrugged. 'I'm not very good with clothes. At least I own a dress.'

'Mmm.' It looked more like a recycled bin liner. 'I was only insulting the dress, I'm sure that underneath ...' Aw, hell where was he going with that one?

Taking pity on him she took his arm and urged him forward. A delicate rose scent reached his nose, old-fashioned and yet eternal; he might have guessed that would be her choice.

Her stride matched his as they went down the hallway towards the salon as directed by Philippe.

'Ah Laurie, Cam. This is Marie, my wife.'

A woman hopped up beside him from the ornate sofa, upholstered in watered silk. She barely met Philippe's shoulders. With unabashed curiosity her dark eyes studied Laurie, her head tilted to one side like a delicate ballerina, looking her up and down.

Although he'd done exactly the same, only minutes before, he immediately stood closer to Laurie. Marie's face dimpled as a friendly smile spread across it and she stepped forward and put both hands on Laurie's shoulders, kissing her on either cheek.

'Welcome, *cherie*. I think you have the look of your mother.'

Laurie stiffened.

Then Marie gave a wicked smile and only Cam noticed the quick dart of her eyes to Laurie's lumpy black dress. 'But perhaps not her personality.'

He looked at Laurie's face. Her polite expression didn't alter, despite the implied criticism of her mother. What was the story there? Laurie spoke warmly of her father but had yet to mention a word about her mother. Their itinerary took in a visit to the mother's home on the other side of France but almost like the elephant in the room, neither of them had so much as mentioned it. How did she feel about her mother?

'Thank you for having me, it's very kind of you.' Laurie's stilted words were brushed aside by the Comtesse, who immediately led her to the ornate marble mantelpiece covered in silver photo frames.

'Not at all. Miles was a very dear friend.' Her expressive eyes filled with tears but her smile held as she pointed to a picture of him sandwiched between her and her husband. 'We owe a huge debt of gratitude to him. Without his help all those years ago … we would have to have sold the Chateau.'

'So, we should drink a toast to Miles,' said Philippe, putting his arm around his wife, a tear visible in his eyes too.

A moment later, he crossed the light airy salon to a table settled in a window alcove and deftly removed the foil from a bottle of wine. In perfect synchrony, Marie joined him to sort out five crystal wine glasses.

Laurie reminded Cam of a stork, standing on one leg and then the other, then crossing her legs and uncrossing them. She was clearly uncomfortable with the emotion running high and at being the centre of attention. Funny how he'd only been on the road with her for twenty-four hours but he was already picking up on the nuances of her personality.

Philippe poured them all generous glasses of rich ruby red wine. With a chink they all murmured. 'To Miles.'

'May he rest in peace,' Philippe added, trying to look solemn. 'But I doubt it. Wherever he is, he'll be stirring things up. He did so love to meddle, interfere and get involved.'

'And we are very grateful for that,' interjected Marie, scolding Philippe. 'He took our wine and made sure lots of important people tasted it, he created the demand for it and we sell out every year now. How many vineyards can say that in this day and age?'

Cam took an idle sip of the wine and was almost knocked sideways by the intensity of flavour. This was not your ordinary vintage. While he wasn't an expert, he'd tasted enough of the good stuff at Miles' place to know that this was a seriously good wine. He glanced at Laurie to see if her palate was as finely-tuned as she'd intimated at Miles' funeral. Her eyes were closed and there was a dreamy smile on her face. The most expressive he'd ever seen on her.

'The 1997,' she pronounced opening her eyes, looking surprised by her knowledge.

'Splendid. I thought you might have forgotten. Miles trained you well.'

'I … er …' she shrugged. 'I've no idea how I know. I just do.' Her brow wrinkled in confusion.

'A type of muscle memory. When you came here, you were fourteen. We tasted our way through fifty wines. You had an amazing recall of flavours even then.'

'Did I?' She had no memory of being able to taste wine. Although she knew what she liked and it had always been a bit of a party piece that she could identify wine varieties. Not that she went to many events where that sort of wine was served. In fact it caused more embarrassment. On one occasion Robert had won a meal at a posh restaurant and she'd ordered the wine. When it came it wasn't what she'd ordered and to Robert's absolute mortification, she'd asked to see the bottle beneath the napkin wrapped around the neck. To the wine waiter's chagrin, it was indeed an inferior bottle.

Marie clapped her hands. 'You did, you did. I think we should have a cellar visit after dinner. Don't you think Philippe? We could get the '96 out … and the 2001 and …'

Laurie looked alarmed. 'It's OK, I don't want to …'

'An excellent idea.' Philippe beamed. 'Yes, yes. Jean, go and tell Albert to set up the cellar room for a tasting.'

Laurie turned worried eyes towards Cam. He winked at her.

Already Marie was sweeping Philippe out towards the dining room, keen to move things along.

'Don't look so panicky,' Cam whispered as they followed behind. 'They're loving this. They obviously adored Miles …'

'Yes, Miles. Not me. He was interesting, funny …' Her mouth twisted in self-deprecation.

'And …? Just be yourself.'

'Easy for you to say that.' She tossed her head and rolled her eyes. 'Why?'

'Come on. You mean you didn't catch a glimpse of yourself in all those mirrors. Mr Sex-on-legs. I'm so gorgeous I can—'

The horrified look on her face as she came to an abrupt halt amused him more than the words.

'I think … although I'm not precisely sure … I might be flattered, although I don't think you meant to compliment me.' He thought of his earlier clumsy compliment to her.

Pausing, he dug his hands deep in his jeans pockets and cocked his head to one side. 'Sex-on-legs, hmm.'

Her face fired up with a delicious blush.

'Or maybe you did,' he teased.

Her eyes widened and she stared at him.

The innocent, unambiguous gaze hit him, and a sudden unexpected bolt of lust shot through him, tightening his groin.

For the first time in his life he'd stepped into unfamiliar territory and he didn't have a clue what to do. Instinct told him that kissing her now would be a seriously big mistake. It would reinforce everything she thought about him and he really needed her to like him.

With Marie's vivacity, Philippe's charm and Jean's cheerful conversation, dinner was a lively affair and Laurie found herself able to relax, fascinated by the obvious and open affection between them. It also stopped her thinking … no she was not going to dwell on it … not even going to …

She sighed. Stealing a look at Cam, talking torques and tyres to Jean, she couldn't help her eyes being drawn to his lips or remember the tingle when she thought he might kiss her. Get a grip. He probably kissed girls all the time. It meant nothing; time to stop thinking about what it might feel like … a hesitant touch … soft skin … the speed of her pulse and the touch-light to desire.

She wanted to clamp right down on *that* thought. Ignore the glow between her legs.

Novelty. Hormones. Normal bodily response. That's all. She'd never been kissed by anyone other than Robert for years, it meant nothing. And Robert. So they'd had a row. If only she'd managed to speak to him before she left. Sort things out. He'd decided to play silly buggers, not answering his phone or responding to her calls and messages. Typical Robert, being stubborn and childish. He'd come around eventually … after she'd apologised at least ten times.

'Laurie?'

'Sorry?'

'I was just asking if you'd like coffee or shall we go down to the cellars now? You might need a chale,' Marie looked to her husband for the word and spoke to him in quick fire French.

'Wrap or a cardigan,' translated Philippe with a smile. 'It's quite cool down there.'

Laurie caught Cam's eye. Wrap? Cardigan? All she had was an old fleece or the tatty beige cardigan, which would make her look like a bag lady next to the impossibly elegant Comtesse.

'Marie, do you have something Laurie might borrow?' Cam leaned across the table, shaking his head. 'I'm afraid I was very strict with her baggage allowance.' He flashed her another of those self-deprecating grins.

'But of course. Sorry.' Marie jumped up and as she hurried from the room called to Philippe, 'Make sure you do not buy one of these silly little cars.'

Laurie snorted at the outraged expressions on the men's faces.

'Sacrilege,' murmured Cam and his host's head nodded vehemently in agreement.

Laurie narrowed her eyes, undecided as to whether she liked his intervention. For sure, he'd saved face for her but he'd assumed she had nothing suitable. The most galling thing was that he'd assumed correctly. Shooting a glare at him, she stiffened her shoulders. He'd obviously hung around too many high maintenance women.

Even without his friendship with Miles, Cam had been lucky enough to mingle in the sort of circles that made fine wine a priority. He might not know much about the subject, and to be honest really wasn't that interested, he liked the taste and could appreciate good wines but that was as far as it went.

Philippe's enthusiasm and passion made him a generous host as he kept producing top notch bottle after bottle. What fascinated Cam the most was Laurie. He couldn't take his eyes off her. It was like seeing a different person.

Philippe had set up six bottles each with a set of short stemmed long bodied glasses around them. He talked through each one, inviting them to taste them, to compare and discuss. Cam tuned out, sipping from the one glass, focusing on Laurie.

Her approach reminded him of a racing driver, the moment before he climbed into the driver's seat. She took each glass, her forehead furrowed, swirling the wine and holding it up to the light to watch the legs, as Philippe had described the viaduct loops of liquid that formed. Then with eyes squeezed shut, she took a deep sniff at the top of the glass, a faint smile playing around her lips as she inhaled.

Then she tasted. He saw the pleasure on her face, the blissful expression and the catch of her hand against her heart as she savoured the flavours. Watching her became addictive.

He became observer, as she steadily worked through the wines, chatting with Philippe and Jean. Suddenly animated, her hands talked; the slender fingers expressive and balletic.

Her whole body, in shadow, appeared more graceful as she moved from bottle to bottle. Cam edged closer to hear what she was saying.

She'd reached the final table and judging from Philippe and Jean's bated breath, they were anxious to find out what she thought of this one.

Taking her time, she twisted the glass in her hand, her wrist held high. Cam's eyes followed the movement, her fingers firm on the stem. Her mouth parted with anticipation. For a moment, she looked totally uninhibited. She closed her eyes and as she tasted the wine, she let out a low moan of sheer pleasure, her throat bobbing as she swallowed.

Cam had to turn away. Would she look like that in the throes of sex? An image of her beneath him stole his breath as a punch of lust slammed into him.

Unnerved, he grasped the glass in his hand and knocked back

119

the entire contents in one shocked mouthful. What the hell was wrong with him? Laurie was not his type. Plus she was engaged. Plus she was not the sort to indulge in affairs, long or short. Plus, he kind of liked her. Plus sleeping with her would definitely muddy the waters for the rest of the trip. Four good reasons not to go there. Not one of them was having any effect on the erection pressing uncomfortably against the zip of his jeans.

Chapter 11

The next morning as they drove away, they received a handsome send-off which included several bottles of Chateau Miroir wedged into every spare bit of space in the boot. Laurie's head throbbed from over-indulgence, not a full blown hangover, but the evening's tasting had been rich beyond compare. Her senses were still reeling from the assault of fine wine on her taste buds.

As they approached the car neither said a word. She watched as Cam dug the keys out of the tight back pocket of his jeans and her gaze lingered a little longer on the view. Robert never wore jeans and if he did, he wouldn't fill them out quite the way Cam did. The taut denim outlined his butt rather nicely and drew attention to the long lean thighs that were going to be a hand's touch away from hers for the rest of the day. Her mouth went dry. He wore his jeans in an unselfconsciously masculine way. All man. A stab of guilt made her look hard down at the ground. Robert was more of a chinos man and there was nothing wrong with that.

Not looking where she was going she collided with Cam. He smelt fresh with citrus undertones. Last night's almost-kiss came back to her. How tempting it would be to lean over and run her lips along his lightly-stubbled jawline. Lust coiled in her stomach, snaking downwards between her thighs.

With a squeak she let out a whimper of surprise and prayed

he wasn't a mind reader.

'You all right?' asked Cam.

'Bumped my nose,' she hedged quickly.

The blue eyes honed in on her nose. 'Daydreaming? I was just about to hand the keys over … now I'm not so sure.' His eyes glinted with humour.

She could feel a blush lighting up her cheekbones and felt the accompanying hot flush sizzle through her. Ducking her head down, she ignored his outstretched hands. 'I'm not driving,' she growled and stomped around to the passenger side.

He took a step back and held up his hands. 'OK.'

She felt she should apologise but instead tried to open the door with shaking fingers. It was locked and she had to wait for Cam to get in and lean over from the driver's seat to unlock the other door. There was no central locking when this car was made.

As they headed down the hill, her face cooled and she managed to get her equilibrium back.

She waved the postcard Philippe had kindly given her. A variety were sold in the Chateau's tasting room and shop and this one depicted the Chateau and vineyards in early morning sunshine, doused in dew.

'I need to stop in the village to post this. I need a stamp.'

'No worries,' Cam glanced at her, 'they'll have a tabac. You might as well get quite a few. How many more postcards do you have to send in?'

Laurie pulled open the file and studied the route Ron had outlined on an A3 Sheet photocopy of Europe. They were now about to double-back on themselves heading up to Paris. She'd already sent the cards from Calais, Honfleur, Le Mans and Orleans.

'Two from Paris, both sides of the river? Troyes, Chaumont, Bresancon, Basel, Zurich, Monstein, Bormio and Maranello.'

'Miles certainly chose a convoluted route, some of it I get the reasoning …'

'There's reasoning,' sighed Laurie gritting her teeth. She was

122

not looking forward to going to Bresancon.

Cam glanced at her, but in typical Cam fashion didn't ask. He had an uncanny knack of knowing when not to push it. Unlike Robert, who still hadn't called, although she'd received another text.

Kitchen tap leaking, we need a plumber. Your house, your call.

The idiot had included the plumber's number.

The tabac was easy to spot in the small village which seem to consist of one road, straddled by a few shops and houses on either side. In no time they were heading north east towards Paris. They stopped for lunch at a pretty roadside café which looked promising due to the large numbers in the car park. Laurie caused great offence with her order for well-done steak and fries, while he received a gracious nod from the waiter when he selected the Moules Marinières.

It left them plenty of time to get to Paris, although he checked his watch; he didn't want to get caught up on the Peripherique. It was hell at the best of times, let alone in rush hour.

As the sun rose in the sky, the afternoon got hotter and hotter. He rolled down his window, trying to get some air into the car. The heat didn't seem to bother Laurie, she looked perfectly happy in her ubiquitous uniform of baggy T shirt and jeans.

For some reason, the road seemed much harder work; all these bends made his stomach roll uneasily and as he took another curve in the road, he felt quite nauseous.

Behind them a Citroen tooted furiously and then with a burst of speed as soon as they were on a straight stretch, veered round them.

'Bloody idiot. What's his problem?'

'Are you OK, Cam?' asked Laurie and out of the corner of his eye he could see her peering anxiously at him. His eyes felt too heavy to look at her properly.

'Yeah, fine, why?' The words came out listless and heavy.

'Well I just wondered why you'd dropped right back to 50 km on this road.'

'Do you want to drive?' he snapped, trying to overcome the rising queasiness in his stomach.

'No, you're fine.' She turned her head and stared out of the window, a sign he now knew meant she was pissed off. Not that she ever said it.

He felt the car roll into another corner. 'Jesus,' he muttered as his stomach protested violently, cramping hard. He'd never been carsick in his life. This road really did take the biscuit. He winced as his stomach griped again and took his foot off the accelerator. The car stuttered, the engine whining in protest. Shit, he hadn't changed down a gear. What gear was he in?

An exasperated sigh came from the passenger seat.

'Try sitting in this seat, lady, before you start huffing and puffing at me,' he growled.

'Cam, you've slowed down to 20 miles per hour here.'

A flash of cold hit him, followed by a flush of heat that brought sweat beading onto his forehead. He could feel it rolling down his cheek.

In the distance, he heard her ask again, 'Are you OK?' Her voice almost disappeared against the background buzz. Waves of nausea rode him and he felt his jaws tighten, almost locking.

'Cam,' she shouted as they veered towards the grass verge. 'Stop the car. Stop the car.'

He did just that, pulling over still in fourth. With an angry sputter, the engine protested and promptly stalled.

'Sor—' even as he tried to say the word, he was fumbling with the door handle.

He had it open. And almost fell out. He staggered on jelly-like legs towards a verdant hedge and then, as if sucked into a cyclone, he felt his whole system buck. He had no control over the vomit that forced itself up like a tsunami, as wave after wave of cramping pain hit his stomach. Unable to manage his legs any longer, he sank to his knees as once again his stomach heaved, forcing everything upwards. Sour acid swirled in his mouth, his nostrils and then his stomach relented, relaxing. He took a deep breath, sucking in the air, realising he was breathless. No sooner had he reflated his lungs, his stomach clenched again bringing with it another wave of nausea.

He threw up again. And again.

Shuddering with weakness, he gave up the attempt to stay upright and keeled over to the right, away from the pool of vomit, praying fervently that there was nothing left to bring up. His stomach still cramped, painfully and his mouth tasted like shit.

'Cam,' her diffident voice drifted in to his head but he could barely grasp it.

'Here.' He felt her lift his head and prop it up as a water bottle touched his lips. 'Just swill your mouth out. Don't swallow.' He felt something cool wipe his forehead but his lids were too heavy to open, he just wanted to lay there and die. The bottle nudged his lips, insistent and annoying. He tried to push it away but someone gripped his wrist with a strength he couldn't beat. Water trickled between his dry lips but he could hardly bring himself to do a thing. The cool fresh taste eased around his mouth and he grunted and in response, the hands holding his head in a vice-like grip, turned him so that mercifully the water spilled out again. His body felt limp and boneless. And there was the bottle again. Water again. Couldn't they just leave him alone? Leave him to die. If only he could just sink into the ground.

'Cam,' the voice came again. 'Cam.'

He felt ineffectual hands prodding him, pulling him, felt his foot twist uncomfortably. He managed to open one eye but all he could see was the grass and a woman's shoe. A very ugly black sandal.

Merciful oblivion swamped him.

Cam lay face down on the grass verge, huddled in a crescent shape that was almost foetal. She was conscious of the buzz of bees in the nearby hedgerow and the scream of a bird in the sky but little else. No other cars for sure. No signs of nearby civilisation, a tractor, church bells. Nothing had passed since they'd pulled over.

Sweat soaked his forehead and the neck of his T-shirt was wringing. He'd passed out cold. Glancing back towards the car, she measured the distance. She could probably drag him that far but loading him into the awkward, low seats was another matter. She pulled ineffectually at his shoulders hoping he might stir, but he was a dead weight and clearly out for the count.

Scanning the road ahead, she couldn't see anything – no handy farmhouse or farmer tilling a nearby field. Even her mobile phone was useless.

She looked down at his grey face.

Well no one was coming to come along and rescue them, and she didn't have France's answer to the AA on her. First of all she had to get him into the car. She'd seen a tarpaulin in the boot. That would do the trick. Using it like a blanket, she shunted Cam's limp body left and right until she managed to get him onto it. Then relying on its smooth underside she pulled and dragged him right up to the passenger door. Although the low slung seat meant she didn't have to physically lift him too high into the car, it was still going to be impossible for her to get him in by himself.

'Wake up Cam. You've got to wake up.' She patted his cheek gently, forcing the water bottle between his lips.

With a splutter and angry push of hands, he roused briefly.

'Cam,' she said firmly. 'You have to help me.' Blearily he opened one eye as she grasped him under the shoulders and heaved him towards the car. Although he roused enough to take heaviness out of his limbs, it was tough going. With a combination of pushing and shoving his immobile form, somehow she managed to get him into the seat. Buckling a seat belt around the leaden body took just another five minutes.

She sat back on her heels, perspiration running down her face.

She'd done it. Got him in, although it had taken the best part of an hour. Just achieving that milestone made her feel she'd accomplished a mountain climb in one day. That was just the start. She refused to think about anything else. One step at a time.

With him in the passenger seat, that left only one place for her to sit. She slid into the driver's seat, gingerly placing her hands on the steering wheel. She glanced over at Cam and then back at all the dials on the dashboard. Olio, Acqua, Benzina. She looked around. The road was empty. No one to see her bunny hopping down the road. It was all very well on the private track with no one to see and no other road users or obstacles but now she was driving on the other side of the road in a strange place. God help her.

She looked again at Cam's slumped form in the seat beside her. Grey in the face with a listless pulse in his jawline. He really didn't look well.

Step by step. The sat nav was already programmed to reach the hotel, complete with valet parking, which had been arranged by Miles. The logical thing would be to head for Paris and get the hotel to call a doctor as soon as they arrived. She could drive … it was only if she got stopped she'd have some explaining to do … and even then they might not ask for her driving licence. And if they did, would the French police know it was only a provisional licence?

Anyway, any idiot could see it was an emergency. Cam's colour now matched putty with a greenish sheen to his waxy skin.

Her hands trembled. Swallowing hard, she grasped the keys and turned them sharply in the ignition. A low groan from Cam killed any further indecision. She jumped slightly as the engine roared into life, the vibration erupting under her seat.

I can do this, I can do this, she told herself, gripping the steering wheel hard. Taking a deep breath, she tried hard to remember her driving lessons and Miles' instructions. Clutch in, handbrake off, ease clutch up.

Like a spring-loaded catapult the clutch shot up, her foot slipped off and the car hopped forwarded like a demented kangaroo and then promptly stalled with an outraged whine.

Shit, this thing was alive. She looked down at the pedals with a little more respect. OK, gently did it. For all her bravado on the test track, being on a real road was a thousand times scarier. Then, she'd been running on adrenaline and pride.

Starting the engine again, this time she was ready for the clutch and quickly pushed the gear stick up into first; it felt jerky as if it might jump back at any second, then gingerly but firmly let the clutch lift. To her delight the car began to move forward and kept going until she found herself on the other side of the road. Shit. Steering. She'd forgotten about that as well. Grasping the wheel, she ended up over-steering and almost finished up on the verge and then realised she had no idea what side of the road she should be on.

And while she had to contend with all that, the protesting whine of the engine told her she should have been thinking about moving up a gear. Fighting against the tight gear box, she missed second, shoved the car into fourth and it shuddered to a virtual halt. Quickly she rectified it and the car jolted again.

She shot a glance at Cam, who flopped forward. Oh Christ. She gritted her teeth, grasped the gear stick and speeding up to get into third.

Cam had slipped back into the seat and while he didn't look comfortable, he didn't look uncomfortable.

At least he couldn't see how badly she was driving, although it was starting to come together. There. That felt better already. Checking all the dials in front of her she was able to work out that she was only doing thirty-five kmph. Why did it seem so much faster?

She decided to stick at her current pace. This felt OK.

Gradually her speed increased and she was able to start taking in the road signs and directions. Everything pointed to Paris, maybe it was best to press on there.

Any further indecision was killed by the need to concentrate on driving. The speed limit signs heralded a settlement up ahead but as she drove into the outskirts she quickly realised that it was a tiny town with very little to recommend it. Dithering for a moment, she looked up and down the street. No sign of a hotel. Cam hadn't stirred for the last fifteen minutes and while he still looked grey and groaned periodically, he seemed to be asleep. And the sat nav lady was still urging her on.

Sod it, she'd carry on.

Although her shoulders were rigid with tension and her neck cramped from leaning forward too hard, once she'd got used to it the driving wasn't so bad. In fact she barely acknowledged the traffic around her; she was too busy concentrating on driving. Although it had been ages since she'd driven a car out on a road and her hands shook unsteadily, she did take secret satisfaction every time she managed a gear change. There were a few false starts and the gears crunched horribly as she didn't quite get her foot off the clutch in time and every time she glanced at Cam, she was a tiny bit glad he remained unconscious.

Driving the Peripherique was every bit as bad as she'd heard. The M25 to the power of ten complete with French drama and general craziness. Cars zipped this way and that, making her head spin as she tried to keep an eye on the traffic in both wing mirrors and rear-view mirror.

For an hour she gripped the steering wheel as if it were her shield as she battled her way through the onslaught of traffic. Fighting to keep the car in a low gear, she feinted the gear stick like a sword as she alternated between first and second.

When the sat nav finally bleated, 'destination in 500 metres', she let out a huge sigh and took the final turning off the main road.

Halfway down the street, she spotted the hotel and almost slumped in her seat with relief. Mission accomplished. Her hands ached from hanging onto the steering wheel so hard and her bottom felt like it had been welded into the seat. How on earth did Cam manage? He was a hell of a lot of taller than her and yet he hadn't once complained about the cramped conditions. Now she knew why they took such regular breaks.

She pulled up outside the hotel and let out a relieved breath. Made it. The last half hour had been hair-raising and most definitely grey-making. Now she'd arrived, she felt a quiet sense of satisfaction, not that Cam had any idea of what she'd just been through. Her thighs were shaking and her pulse racing

She sat for a moment, waiting for some energy to propel her legs to get out of the car and surveyed the entrance of the hotel. A huge canopy swung out over the road to scoop in visiting cars and a small set of steps unfolded towards the car.

Cam was still sound asleep or whatever he was. He looked dishevelled and travel worn. Would the immaculate doorman in his dark black and grey livery take pity on them and help Cam up to a room? Hopefully her schoolgirl French would be sufficient to explain that '*mon ami est mauvais*' so that the staff wouldn't assume he'd been on a drunken binge. Mixed expressions crossed the doorman's face, admiration for the car and concern at the passenger lolling sideways in his seat.

She mustered her best smile, wishing she had a French dictionary which would give her the correct word for food poisoning. All she could think of, was Mal de Mer. Perhaps if she said that and mimed eating food, she might get the message across.

'Bonjour, Monsieur.'

'Bonjour Mademoiselle. Bienvenue a L'Hotel du Leine.' The footman managed obsequious and impressed at the same time.

'Mon ami …' she pointed to Cam in the passenger seat. 'Il est mort.'

Chapter 12

'Mort!' the French-man's eyebrows shot up in excitable surprise. 'Mon Dieu.' He started and called to a colleague. 'Pierre, vien ici. Il est mort!'

As a crowd quickly gathered around the car, she quickly realised that her French vocabulary had failed her spectacularly.

Shit, mort! It meant dead, didn't it?

At least the car gave her some street cred.

'Non, non. Pardonez moi. Il est mal.' Everyone looked blankly at her. 'Mal de Mer?' She rubbed her tummy. Still more blank looks. Oh God, she was going to have to mime throwing up.

Closing her eyes, wishing she were anywhere else, she clutched her stomach and imitated retching.

The bloody doorman just stared at her and then at the crowd gathering around.

'Sick. Vomit?'

The footman finally grasped her meaning immediately, pointing from her to Cam.

'Il?'

'Oui.' She nodded, indicating Cam.

'Ah, je comprends.' He fired rapid French at the gathered crowds and everyone shot off in several directions seemingly randomly. They reconvened within seconds, organised and with purpose. A wheelchair accompanied by a lady with a big red rug was wheeled up to the passenger door. Two burly doormen pulled and dragged Cam out of the car into the chair, tucking the red blanket around him to keep him in place. Hastily she grabbed Cam's bag from the car and popped it onto his lap.

When the concierge appeared and held out a hand for the car keys, she dropped her bag on the pavement and complied without thinking.

'Don't worry I will take care of everything,' the concierge assured her. So she left her bag and the keys with him and followed the bizarre procession into the hotel lobby.

It was dark and cosy with sumptuous wallpaper in dark black flock lit with gold and silver. Very classy tart's boudoir in an art deco sort of way.

A male receptionist, standing ramrod straight, awaited them at the desk and watched the motley crew each step of the way as they came towards him. The expression on his face, turning up his nose and mouth suggested that she wasn't welcome and had better watch her step before he turned her away. His attitude irked her so much that she lifted her chin and went in prepared for battle.

'My companion has contracted a nasty case of food poisoning. I have a reservation here for me, my companion and my car.' She looked down her nose at him emphasising the words, 'my car.' In the mirror behind the manager, she could see the doorman frantically signing. The meaning was clear, 'you should see this car!'

She ignored what was going on behind her, held her head in a suitably haughty and regal position and waited for the manager to appreciate just what she was.

'The reservation was made in the name of Liversedge on behalf of my uncle, Miles T… she didn't even need to finish his name. The manager's jaw dropped in recognition and suddenly he was on the other side of the desk.

'Mais, certainment mademoiselle. Please accept our apologies. Follow me.' He snapped his fingers at the staff around. All fell neatly into place, either in support or back to their usual duties.

She was escorted to the lift, Cam, head lolling in the wheelchair a few feet behind.

'My companion is very ill. He needs a doctor. Please could you arrange for one to visit immediately?'

'Oui, certainly.'

'He has food poisoning. Shell-fish.' She kept up her imperious attitude, even though inside she'd started to flag. Being in a strange country, not speaking the language with a very sick man … not her idea of fun at all.

Looking at Cam's grey face, she felt sick herself. Did he need a doctor? At what point should she be worried? Should she get some medicine? Seek medical advice. All she knew about people who'd been sick was that they needed fluids but to avoid milk products and to introduce white foods very slowly like rice, plain chicken and plain white bread. She suspected that Cam was a long way off any of those things.

First things, get the doctor's verdict, she told herself as the lift went up. She was still accompanied by two footmen, pushing Cam's wheelchair in which he flopped listlessly like an old man. She wished he'd open his eyes. Just so that she'd know he was still in there and not as close to death as he looked.

With every bump and jolt of the wheelchair, she saw pain spasm across his face. At least it meant he was still conscious.

At last they were outside the room. She fumbled with the key and with relief opened the door to see a large double bed in front of her. If she could just get Cam into bed, then she'd feel a lot better.

Both footmen loitered in the door.

'Oh for goodness sake,' she muttered. Were they after a tip? What now? She sighed and took her handbag off her shoulder and dumped it on the coffee table. Crossing back to the bed, she peeled back the covers and waited, making it quite clear there would be no tips until Cam had been transferred from the wheel-chair into the bed.

The protracted vomiting had obviously left him spent, the minute his head hit the pillow he fell into a deep sleep. She looked at him breathing deeply and evenly. Out for the count. He looked grey and in the short space of time since they'd arrived, the lines on his face had deepened.

She glanced down at his clothes. The jeans were filthy, mainly mud from the grass verge he'd collapsed on and his usual white T shirt was exceptionally grubby. Oh God, she couldn't tuck him into the crisp white cotton sheets like that. The clothes were going to have to come off.

T shirt first, then she'd summon courage to do the bottom half. Needs must. Nurses did this sort of thing all the time.

Taking the bottom of the cotton hem, she lifted it and slid the front upwards, before sliding her hand under his back to pull up the bunched fabric. His arms weighed a ton but she managed to lift them over his head. He stirred and muttered, struggling against her slightly but was too weak to do much and didn't even manage to open his eyes.

Focusing on the T shirt and not on the gorgeous torso revealed, she bundled it into the hotel laundry bag. It would be pervy to look at a defenceless man. Wrong. Completely wrong. Robert would be … Robert wouldn't be anything because he wouldn't ever envisage her in this situation. She would never have envisaged herself in this situation.

Even though she knew she shouldn't but because she could, she gazed down at Cam's motionless body. Her mouth went dry. It had to be said she'd never imagined herself within touching distance of a body like this. He was like every fantasy man rolled into one, the stuff of movie stars. Dark hair dusted the golden skin of his lean chest before arrowing down, across the sharply defined muscles of his stomach, into the snug-fitting jeans.

Would he wake if she touched that expanse of skin? Or if she let her fingers smooth along the collar-bone? She'd never felt this stark bolt of desire before and couldn't help drinking the sight of him in. What would it be like to run her tongue around the flat dark nipples, teasing the light circle of dark hair? Trace her fingers over his ribs and then up over the firm pectorals, touching their firm, satin smoothness? Stroke her thumbs over the lean hip bones above the waistband of his jeans?

Heat flushed her skin and for a moment she felt light-headed, her fingers itching to touch. Instead she forced herself to consider the belt buckle of his jeans. She needed to finish undressing him and get him into that bed and covered up. Pronto.

With clumsy fingers she set to work on the belt and then not looking up at his face, she busied herself with the zip. Reaching round his waist to shimmy the jeans down his hips, it was impossible not to touch naked skin. He was cool and a little clammy, so she worked quickly sliding the jeans off his hips to reveal snug black briefs which she tried hard not to look at. Moving to his feet, she pulled off his socks and tugged the denim down.

He groaned and doubled over, his arm grasping his stomach. 'Cam?'

He groaned again but didn't answer.

She pulled the duvet around him and tucked him in. Grey pallor tinged his cheeks and damp curls clung to his clammy face.

Gingerly she perched on the edge of the bed for a minute studying the strong masculine jawline. He was all man that was for sure, his mouth with the fuller lower lip was a firm slash across his face, framed with bold cheekbones. And she should be ashamed of herself, the man was sick and here she was ogling him. What the hell was wrong with her?

Watching him sleeping wasn't going to get her very far. Hopefully reception would send a doctor up quite soon.

Leaving his side, she turned around and took in the room properly. It was more like a suite, with two sofas facing a coffee table and a very large flat screen TV. Walking over to the window, she discovered that the double French doors opened out onto a tiny balcony dominated by a brasserie table and two chairs.

Even the carpet beneath her feet seemed so much deeper than anything she'd ever seen. Keen to see everything, she checked out the bathroom and let out a sigh. Bathroom perfection – a walk in shower with a dozen different heads, two sinks, low lighting and a long low bath, complete with Jacuzzi jets.

At least she'd be comfortable while Cam was out for the count.

Itching to try the shower and wash away her travel grime, she started to strip off. Where was her bag?

Damn. Pulling her T shirt back on, she went back to the lounge area. Where was it? The concierge must have forgotten to bring it up.

Making up her mind, she lined the waste paper basket under the window with one of the hotel's laundry bags and placed it beside the bed. She also left a towel there and a brief note saying she'd be back soon, although looking at him, she doubted very much that he would be waking up for a while.

The concierge frowned haughtily as if she'd maligned his honour. 'Monsieur had the bag on his knee. That is the only bag I saw.'

'No, I had one. I left it with you when I gave you the keys for my car.'

'Where?'

'Outside, on the pavement. I put it on the pavement.' Nooo. She tugged at the necklace around her neck. Surely he'd picked it up. Her bag had all her clothes, clean knickers, toothbrush and the black dress. OK, that might not be such a great loss but she couldn't spend the rest of the trip in these jeans.

'Outside?'

'Oui.' Quite why she tried French, she wasn't sure. He seemed to be understanding her just fine. Unfortunately.

'Ze pavement?'

'Oui.'

'Non, I took the keys for the so beautiful car ...' A brief flash of horror crossed his face. 'Madam. Pardon.'

He rushed from behind the desk out through the lobby, down the stairs onto the busy pavement. Laurie followed a few steps behind to find him anxiously scanning the street this way and that.

He caught sight of her and lapsed into a torrent of passionate French punctuated by a steady stream of 'pardons'.

Breathe. It wasn't the end of the world. She could cope. Her passport, purse, money and Kindle were all in her handbag. Nothing was irreplaceable. She could buy more knickers, T-shirts and jeans.

Although perhaps she ought to let the concierge know, as his wild gesticulation and furious pace of French put her in mind of some bizarre combination of Fawlty Towers and Monty Python.

The manager was called, the under-concierge was called and the head receptionist. They convened in the lobby, where Laurie waited not understanding a word of the conversation.

She couldn't help feeling it wasn't anybody's fault, just a communication breakdown. It could be reasonably argued that she had abandoned the bag. It could also be argued that the concierge had taken one look at the car and forgotten everything else. Six of one and half a dozen of the other. Although how you translated that into French, she had no clue.

The upshot from the manager, who kept shooting daggers at the concierge, was that Laurie should claim on her travel insurance. The hotel was not responsible for luggage left outside the hotel, only for luggage left with the concierge within the hotel.

After all that had happened today, Laurie couldn't summon the energy to argue. Did she even have travel insurance? Best to check with Ron.

A quick call to the solicitor's office in England got her no further ahead as Ron was out. Leaving a message with Mrs Lacey, she explained the situation and asked him to call as soon as he got back.

The plus point from the fracas was that the manager hastily agreed to hurry the doctor up.

In the meantime she would have to rinse out her underwear

in the bathroom tonight and pray her knickers dried by morning.

The uber-chic pharmacy made her even more aware of her travel-weary, unwashed state. It seemed only to stock expensive face creams and perfume at first sight but then she realised the glossy walls hid cupboards full of well-packaged creams. The white-coated assistant that stepped forward was immaculately made up and just looking at her made Laurie feel grubby and under-dressed in her well-worn travelling clothes.

She blushed, wondering how bad she looked.

'Can I help you?' the French woman asked in perfect English. God, how did they do it? What was it that gave her nationality away? She looked down at her rumpled T shirt and shabby jeans and loose fitting ballet flats and then back at the woman's five denier hosiery, low-heeled glossy court shoes and snow white coat. Her thick brunette hair was caught neatly in a barrette; not a single stray hair had escaped.

'My friend is ill? He has food poisoning and the doctor suggested I get him some …' she read from the scrawled note the doctor had left her.

The woman waved her hand as if to dismiss any doctor's knowhow. 'How long has he been sick?'

'Since lunchtime.'

She then rattled off a series of questions about his condition, how long he'd been vomiting for before concluding with a friendly professional smile. 'Sleep is probably the best thing. It's the body's way of recuperating.'

Her English was as flawless as her advice. It was exactly the same as the doctor's.

'You should get him to drink some fluids. This is a special hydrating solution which will help.'

By the time Laurie had finished she had a carrier bag full of medical goodies and a fine selection of face creams, lotions and potions, most of which were free samples the pharmacist had pressed upon her when Laurie had told her about her missing luggage.

The language barrier had proved easily overcome and the pharmacist's detailed advice made her feel much better than the doctor, who had shrugged a lot. At least she could play nurse with a bit more confidence now.

As she made her way back to the hotel, she'd skirted a market buzzing busy with people carrying bulging string bags, zig-zagging from one side of the market to the other, chattering and pointing at all the delicious fresh produce.

Unable to resist the rich spicy scents wafting from a charcuterie stall, she halted her journey. Another five minutes wouldn't make so much difference and she was intrigued by the gourmet feast on display. From pale delicate meats, to rich blood red slices, the stall had the biggest selection of meats and pâtés she'd ever seen. May be she could buy some to have for supper. She'd already passed a bread stall which had called with its fresh baked scent and there was the cheese which looked wonderful, as well as all the fresh fruit and vegetables. The peaches, plump and fleshy, looked irresistible.

It was so different from schlepping around Sainsbury's. It would probably be a good idea to buy in supplies for the room, so she wouldn't have to leave Cam on his own again.

With bread, cheese and fruit and other goodies stashed in plastic bags, she suddenly realised another twenty minutes had elapsed. She really ought to get back.

To her relief and slight irritation, Cam was still sound asleep when she got back to the room which felt stuffy and dark after the sunshine and scents of the vibrant market.

She threw open the French doors to let in some fresh air and stepped out onto the miniscule balcony. The sound of the street below made her feel slightly less alone.

At least Cam hadn't been sick any more.

Conscious of the loss of her bag, she rinsed out her knickers, squeezing out as much moisture as she could. She put the shaving light on in the bathroom. If Cam woke and needed the bathroom it wouldn't be pitch dark in the room.

Settling down with her bread, cheese and wine, she suddenly remembered the bottles of wine Philippe had pressed upon them. There was one in Cam's bag.

Feeling incredibly decadent, she opened the bottle and poured herself a glass of the pale straw Sancerre. It was every bit as good as she remembered. And very moreish.

By eight o'clock she'd almost finished the bottle … in fact it seemed a terrible waste to leave that last bit, although when she poured it, it filled her glass to the brim.

Cam still hadn't woken. Several times during the evening she crossed to the bed to check he was still breathing. Whoops, the table leg caught her out. Had it always been there? The room span a bit but she managed the twenty steps. His colour looked better although his face suddenly seemed a bit blurry round the edges … or maybe that was her. In fact everything seemed a bit blurry.

The wine was very delicious though. Shame Cam didn't have two bottles in his bag.

Bag. She needed to replace her bag. Shopping. Where did one shop in Paris? Blurrily she remembered her Kindle Fire. The interweb. She could google 'where to shop in Paris when all your clothes have been nicked by some bastard'. For some reason the touchscreen seemed to have a mind of its own and she couldn't get the words typed in, in the right order. Abandoning the searches, she picked up the hotel magazine.

Personal shopping at Galeries Lafayette. Now that sounded good. Get someone else to do the donkey work. She didn't like shopping. Too complicated, too much choice and she'd never got the hang of knowing what suited her. That's what happened when you grew up with your dad and he didn't know anything about girls' clothes. This sounded the bees' bollocks.

Picking up the phone she called reception.

Chapter 13

When her eyelids began to droop, she glanced at the bed; it appeared to be moving slightly but it didn't seem to bother Cam. He'd barely moved and if it wasn't for her persistent checking … before the room started spinning … she could have been easily persuaded he was dead. Which was a good thing, as he wouldn't be aware of her in the bed with him. She giggled softly to herself. It was all right, she'd sleep in a dressing gown. That would be … thingy. The word eluded her. Although, come to think of it, he wouldn't know if she rifled through his bags and pinched one of his lovely white T shirts. The idea had merit. The thick heavy knot on the front of the dressing gown would be uncomfortable. Woozily, she unzipped his bag and removed one of the neatly folded T shirts.

While she was at it, she removed his wash bag and put it in the bathroom. For a moment she dithered in front of the mirror, her image swaying rather oddly. She really, really, really couldn't borrow his toothbrush but she could nick a bit of toothpaste. Rub it round her teeth with her fingers. What else did he have she might be able to borrow? The deodorant she'd help herself to in the morning.

Feeling very tired, she slid into the cool sheets, careful not to rock the mattress or disturb Cam.

She lay looking up at the ceiling, arms rigid by her side. In. Bed. With another man. Another man who wasn't Robert. Turning onto her side, she stared across at him. Apart from Robert she'd never shared a bed with any other man. Ought to make the most of it. She giggled softly to herself, aware that she really wasn't making much sense. He did have a delicious chest thought. Really quite yummy. Just an arm span away.

Cam shifted in his sleep, turning towards her, the sheet slipping down. She blinked, sudden awareness at his proximity, dousing her with sense. Her libido needed a good slap. Turning her back on him, she clicked out the light with a determined snap of her fingers.

Sleep took a long time coming but eventually her heightened awareness of another body in the bed dimmed and she fell asleep.

A long low groan startled her from sleep. Next to her in the dim light she could see Cam clutching his stomach, almost curled double.

Reaching out she grabbed his shoulder, he looked up, his face taut and white.

Quite how she knew, she had no clue, but she had to get him to the bathroom. Quickly she slid out of bed and rushed around to his side of the bed, pulling him towards the bathroom.

His breath came in pants as he stumbled after her.

'It's OK, Cam,' she led him through the door, the white sanitary ware glowing slightly from the low light cast by the shaving fixture and guided him to sit next to the toilet on the floor.

When she saw his finely chiselled abs spasm, she pushed his head towards the bowl, grateful for the shadows as the poor man retched again and again.

It seemed to last for ever, his body shaking with effort as his stomach once again tried to force its contents out. All the while, she soothed his hair back from his face, the curls damp and clammy.

Eventually he lay his forehead on the seat, breathing hard as if totally spent. Checking he was propped up, she stood and soaked one of the hand towels with warm water and filled a tooth glass with cold water.

'Here sip this, and spit it out, don't swallow it,' she murmured not sure if it was the best advice or not. As he did she wiped his face gently with the hand towels, slipping it around the back of his damp neck.

'Thanks,' he whispered hoarsely.

She eased him back, to prop him up against the bath again. His head lolled back. He looked exhausted. Unable to help herself she rubbed his shoulder.

He leaned towards her as if enjoying the comfort. She slipped her arm along to his other shoulder and he leaned into her, his head drooping down to rest on her chest. The long dark curls tickled slightly and she went to stroke them away, her fingers tangling in the soft hair and massaging his scalp. With a stuttered sigh, his body softened and he snuggled into her. Her heart filled and swelled at the sensation of giving comfort to Cam while he was so vulnerable. It made her want to take care of him. Mother him. She kept up the gentle caress of his hair, savouring the quiet moment in the dark. A lone tear slipped down her cheek. Had her mother ever held her like this? She couldn't remember. Dad, on the other hand, had been a whizz with Lucozade, books, back rubs and cuddles whenever she'd been poorly.

It seemed as if Cam was over the worst of it but she carried on holding him ignoring the coldness of the tiles biting into her bottom and legs stretched straight out in front of her. Cam seemed comfortable enough.

Blearily he lifted his head to look at her. 'Sylvie?' he asked sounding confused. 'No, Laurie.' His face was so close to hers she could see how hard he was finding it to focus and how his eyelids drooped.

'Yes, it's Laurie, and I think we need to get you back to bed.'

'Bed,' he slurred.

'Come on, you need to help me.'

Easing herself up, wincing at the stiffness in her limbs, she took both of his hands. It took all her strength to pull him to his feet.

'Laurie,' he muttered. 'Course it is.' He staggered as he finally lurched to his feet. 'Laurie.'

The minute she'd guided him to the bed, he flopped backwards and thankfully fell asleep almost instantly.

Someone had crushed his head between a couple of rocks and put his stomach through a mangle. With gut twisting painfully, he came to, his mouth crying out for moisture. His eyelids had been glued shut in the night and surely a cat had shat in his mouth and then added the rest of the litter tray. If this was dying, let it be over soon. He tried again to lift his eyelids and this time fuzzy light filtered through. A figure haloed by the light stood in front of him, it had to be an angel because of the softness and gentleness of the hands that held his head, and offered sips of water.

Water trickled around his mouth, removing the disgusting paste lining the roof. Just doing that much sapped his energy and he fell back again into the pillows. It was official, he wanted to die.

Soothing hands brushed his hair from his face where it had tangled in overgrown bristles. The unfamiliar bed was comfortable and cocooning and he'd have liked to burrow in forever but like the light on an alarm blinking, something bothered him. He should be doing something. It niggled at him exacerbating the pounding in his head.

A voice talked slowly and quietly to him but he couldn't place it. Those cool fingers were back, brushing his forehead, he wanted them to stay. When they lifted from his face, he groaned. They came back and he relaxed back into the mattress. His angel was right beside him.

'Cam?' The voice was unfamiliar and he fought to surface from the fug he'd sunk into. His eyes focused on a sweet, unadorned face. Just as you'd expect an angel. Not a scrap of make-up. He knew her but he didn't.

Cam had slept well and in the morning, his colour seemed a lot better. She wanted something to do, to take her out of the room. You could only lean over someone so many times to check their breathing before they woke up and caught you in the act.

With free Wi-Fi she'd toured Paris extensively on Cam's laptop. Seen all the places that she'd like to see in real life, all the while waiting for him to wake up.

The ticking clock intruded. Although it had to be faulty because every time she looked up at it, only another minute had passed. She tried playing a game in a bid to avoid looking at the time before a full ten minutes had elapsed.

Even a new book on her Kindle failed to hold her attention against the loud bullying tick of the clock. Finally she threw it down and gave Cam another baleful glare. Miles' itinerary had suggested a visit to the Musée Marmottan four doors down. It was no distance at all. Cam probably wouldn't even know she'd gone.

It wasn't as if she were his mother, friend or even girlfriend. And besides he might be embarrassed or just want to be left alone when he came to.

And damn, the clock still only said five past ten. Even if Cam woke up, he wasn't going anywhere and would probably welcome the peace and quiet. She'd just leave him a note, a bottle of water and to be on the safe side the trusty waste-paper basket come sick bucket.

Sunshine dappled the street, peering through an avenue of trees that lined either side of the road. As she left the shadow of the grand entrance of the hotel, the tightness in her chest, which seemed to have been a permanent presence for the last twenty-four hours, eased and she took a deep breath of air. It felt wonderful to be outside, even though the air wasn't that fresh, and you could hear the regular murmur of the Peripherique just a few streets away. Guiltily she cast a look upwards wondering if she should have left a window open for Cam.

145

The museum was literally a hop skip and jump away and according to Miles' notes housed a couple of Monet paintings. She'd visited an exhibition of Impressionist Painters in Sheffield at the age of twelve, and been fascinated by them ever since. Being so close was an opportunity not to be missed especially as she was on her own.

At the top of the stone steps, she stopped to admire the hallway, and opened up the envelope Ron had provided with money for expenses to pay her entrance. She withdrew a note ... €500! That was over £400 in English money. And there were ... rifling through as discreetly as she could, one, two ... twenty! Over €10,000 in €500 notes not to mention, a quantity of other denominations. Bloody hell! And she'd been worried about paying for meals and drinks. This was more than she could spend in a year.

Once her pulse had returned to normal, she tucked the envelope to the very bottom of her handbag and drifted out into a crowd. Safety in numbers, she figured. For a while she stuck with the group until side-tracked by a painting tucked in an alcove above an ornate table. Studying it for a second, she allowed herself to daydream about what the building might have been like in its day.

Eventually she came to a set of flat wide white steps, all sharp contemporary angles which contrasted starkly with the late nine-teenth century style of the rest of the building. As she descended the sounds became muted by the buzz of air conditioning units. The stairs turned a sharp corner and then opened out into a wide open brightly lit space.

She blinked in surprise and her heart soared in sudden delight. The room was filled with Monet canvasses. Huge vibrant splashes of colour filling the walls, displayed with little fuss or pretension.

For a moment all she could do was stand and smile. After a while she began to tour the room, taking time to study and absorb the beauty of each painting, standing as close as possible to the pictures, looking at the colours and brush strokes, occasionally stepping right back to see the pictures from a distance, where the colours merged to create the famous blurred images that contradictorily coalesced into a complete, concrete scene.

She came back over and over, to one picture. A water lily picture. The astonishing purples and blues held her captive. Sinking onto a bench, she stared. The colours were amazing. Just looking at it made her heart swell and she wanted to imprint its sheer beauty on her brain for ever.

Wouldn't it be wonderful if everything in life resonated with this much colour and magic. It took her back to that day at the gallery in Sheffield when the world had held so much promise and possibility.

When had her world become so grey and colourless? The piercing thought scored into her brain bringing with it physical pain at the recognition of its truth. What had happened to her? What had doused the promise and excitement of the future?

Another tourist bumped into her with a polite, 'pardon' rousing her from her reverie. 12.30 already. She needed to get back to Cam and check on him.

Leaving the museum with a reluctant half-glance back, she promised herself she'd come back. It wasn't as if Paris was that far away. She and Robert could come here for a long weekend. Although he wasn't usually a big fan of art galleries or museums.

Cam had changed position and now lay sprawled on his stomach. The bottle of water had been half drunk and his colour looked a lot better. He was even snoring slightly. That was a good sign, wasn't it? She had never really had to nurse anyone before. Her dad's first heart attack, the day she was due to take her driving test, had been an awful shock but he'd got better remarkably quickly. He'd returned to full fitness with relative ease which was why it was such a shock when ten years later, he had the massive heart attack that killed him.

Memories of the steadfast, bone-crushing loneliness she'd felt when he died shimmered and then quite suddenly lifted as a warmth burgeoned in her chest. That's all they were – just memories. She'd survived and now it felt as if a weight had been lifted. This morning had been thoroughly wonderful. Being on her own. She should visit more galleries when she got home. Go to London. The Tate Modern. The National Portrait Gallery. The Courtauld Institute. Live by herself.

Like a bubble bursting into a thousand shards of colour the thought crystallised in her head. Where had that come from? But wouldn't it be rather nice to live alone, have space and time to call your own? Robert moved in so soon after Dad died, she'd never really had chance to ride out the solitude of the empty house. Guilt hovered. Robert. She sighed. She hadn't even looked at her phone since yesterday morning. So much had happened.

Three missed calls from Robert. And two texts.

I'm sorry. I was a berk. Please forgive me. I love you. I miss you so much. When you get home, we'll plan a proper wedding.

Laurie immediately felt guilty because she was pretty sure she wasn't missing him but then she was away, doing different things. That was quite normal. At home he'd be in the usual routine without her, it was bound to be different. She should ring him and sort things out. He must feel bad, she'd never known him back down or apologise, not without considerable effort to please on her part.

The second text put the first in context.

Talked to Mum and she told me off. Said you were right, she'd be upset if she didn't get an invite. Call me. I love you.

There was a third text from an unknown number.

Don't forget your appointment with your personal shopper, Mandy at Galeries Lafayette at 2.30 p.m.

Chapter 14

Hell, she'd completely forgotten her impulsive call to reception last night. Too much Sancerre. It had seemed the most wonderful idea at the time. The perfect solution to her lost luggage problem. Gnawing at her lip, she checked her watch. With an hour to go it would be rude to cancel.

She glanced at Cam, still asleep. It wasn't as if he would miss her. Maybe she should go. After all she did need clothes, she couldn't keep pinching Cam's T-shirts. In fact she should buy him a couple.

If she'd known how swish Galeries Lafayette was inside, Laurie may not have summoned the courage to walk in, let alone seek out a personal shopper. The huge department store sparkled with jewelled light from the gorgeous overhead dome around which were balconied floors overlooking the ground floor. The effect was sumptuous and regal and slightly intimidating, which didn't help as Laurie didn't like being intimidated.

The air was redolent with a thousand perfumes which drifted upwards from the make-up concessions a long way below.

'Hi I'm Mandy.' The girl introduced herself once Laurie had found the correct department. 'You'll be an 8, I'm guessing,' she said prowling around Laurie, assessing her from every angle after Laurie explained what had happened to her bag. 'Which makes a

38 in France.' She clapped her hands together in seeming delight startling Laurie.

'No, I'm a ten. Sometimes a twelve.'

'UK 10, American 8, Italian 42 and German 36.' The American girl grinned, even without her clipped New York accent, her teeth would have given her nationality away. 'I'm an expert on dress sizes. And,' she lowered her voice, 'I don't get to dress many your size. Usually rich matrons with waistlines that have seen way too much rich living. I could have a lot of fun with you. You've got a great figure. In fact you're a natural clothes horse. Lovely slender neck. Nice shoulders. Not much of a waist but good slim hips and those legs, whoa girl. What size feet are you? 38? 39?'

A twinge of unease nudged her. Jeans. T shirts. Bra, knickers, socks. That's all she needed.

'UK 6, which I know is a 39.'

'Great. And colour palate? What are you looking for?'

Colour palate. What in hell's name was that? She shrugged. 'I'm not really sure. Look I just want something to travel in for the next few weeks. Capsule wardrobe. The boot of the car is tiny. I only had two pairs of jeans, some T shirts, fleeces and a dress. A pair of sandals and these.' She pointed to her purple Converse high tops, the trendiest thing she owned. They'd been left, brand new in their box, in the library and six months on no one had ever collected them. For the record, she had put £10 in the charity box for the local hospice. Thankfully they hadn't been in her bag but wedged in the boot of the car.

'Ooh, I love a challenge.' Mandy's beam grew wider, if that were humanly possible. In fact Laurie was starting to wonder if she was some kind of Pollyanna alien. Nothing seemed to faze this woman. 'You just leave it to me. With your colouring, there's lots to play with …' she sighed, a wrinkle appearing on her brow and Laurie immediately felt guilty. '… your hair is a gorgeous colour.'

Laurie could feel the 'but' hanging.

'… the style, really could use some work. It doesn't do you any favours. God I'd love to have hair like that.' She pushed her fingers through the ponytail, shaking it out. 'Thick, wavy.'

She danced behind Laurie, positioned her in the mirror and with quick light fingers, pulled each side of her hair up. 'Look. See. A few layers would lighten it up around your face. It's so heavy at the moment, it drags your face down. Bit like Morticia. Too severe. Would make it much more feminine and enhance your face. Hide your ears.' Mandy smiled sympathetically as she said it adding, 'You've got the most fab cheekbones.'

Her breezy, enthusiastic stream of chatter robbed her blunt comments of any offence.

'Hmm, I have a brilliant idea. You just wait here.'

Mandy darted off to a nearby counter and picked up a phone. Within seconds she was back with a mile-wide beam.

'Sorted, you are one lucky chick. Marc is free. He's almost never free. Top, top stylist here. Normally you have to wait months to see him.

'Then we'll get you into some decent clothes. I can tell you've had to borrow those jeans and that bra. Poor you. Good job someone lent you a decent T shirt. You look a mess but don't worry, Mandy's here.'

'What?' Laurie was starting to feel like Alice and that she'd fallen through a rabbit hole. It was probably too late to own up to the jeans and bra being her own. The T shirt of course was Cam's which she'd 'borrowed'.

'Marc will do your hair … and then,' Mandy beamed as if it were Christmas, 'when you come back here, we'll have … we are going to have so much fun. I'm thinking blues, perhaps coral.' Again she sized Laurie up, the dark raven eyes darting here and there, as if taking in every angle of Laurie's body.

'But—'

'Don't worry, don't thank me until you've seen what Marc's done. He's an absolute genius.'

'I—' She might as well be fighting a demolition ball, although it felt as if it had already hit her and she was like one of those cartoon characters plastered to the side of said ball, having to go where it took her.

'Come on, chop, chop.'

Laurie found herself propelled into the lift and minutes later, in a large leather chair in front of a mirror, with the diminutive Marc, lifting her hair this way and that, muttering to himself in French. On either side of him two girls with matching perfect bobs, hung on his every word, nodding like a pair of lapdogs. One had already combed her hair.

This had to stop, it didn't need cutting. She liked it fine the way it was. Neat, tidy and practical and she wasn't going to be bossed about by some prima donna, French hairdresser bounding about in tight leather trousers and a ridiculously low cut T shirt, showing off a very hairy chest. It was a bit Simon Cowell meets Napoleon.

'I just want a trim.' She enunciated the words to make it clear. 'Nothing else.'

Marc waved the two girls away, pulled up a nearby chair, swung his legs over it so the back faced him and rested his elbows casually on the top of the back.

'What's your name?' he asked, the effeminate voice vanishing.

'Laurie,' she answered puzzled by the instant change of his demeanour.

'You are the client. I'm here to do exactly what you want. This is your hair. No one should ever feel they are being forced. There is nothing worse than having a haircut you hate.' He smiled at her. Rich brown eyes, so large and limpid they really did remind her of a spaniel. 'I want every woman to leave my salon feeling a million dollars. If you say you want a trim, then that is what I will do.'

The earnest tone of his voice made her wonder if maybe she'd been a bit uptight and ridiculous as she sank into the soft buttery leather chair.

'If you want a new style, this I can do also. I am here to please you. Make women realise their true beauty and I tell you, Laurie, may I call you Laurie, your hair is very beautiful. Either way I will not let you leave here until you are completely happy. But in my heart of hearts, I would be doing you a disservice, if I were not to advise you with my professional heart, that your hair would suit you so much more with layers here,' he indicated the sides, 'and here. It would give your hair the bounce and life it deserves.'

Laurie looked at herself in the mirror. Her hair had been like this forever. Hair grew, didn't it?

'O… K … you can … cut it, but not too short.'

'Short,' said Marc in horror. 'Never. I will take a little bit,' he indicated with thumb and finger. 'But ah, the difference. You will love it. I promise you.' He jumped up, reverted back to pocket dynamo, and began barking orders and instructions to the two girls.

Laurie crossed her fingers under the long black gown. It would always grow.

'Wow, you look amazing.'

Laurie grinned, feeling sunshine in her heart. Her whole head felt lighter and she couldn't help the bounce in her walk which set her curls bobbing which she kept fluffing up with her fingers. Who knew what a difference a haircut could make! It could all go horribly wrong when she washed it the first time, but at this moment, she absolutely loved it. She'd never loved her hair before. It had just been there.

'Told you he was a genius,' smirked Mandy, as Laurie came to a standstill in the changing room. Genius didn't begin to describe him. When he'd finished she'd almost cried.

'Right. Selection of pants, bras, socks over there. Shoes here and separates here. I've lined up some outfits for you to try on and then we'll accessorize as we go.'

Outfits and accessories? Laurie caught a glimpse of her new hair in the mirror and barely recognised herself. It looked pretty and feminine, glossy and stylish the way that Miles' wives had always managed to look when she was a teenager. She thought of them at the funeral, chic in their gorgeous rainbow of colours … and her serviceable navy suit.

The rail in the changing room had very few items hanging on it. She'd expected Mandy to go to town and make the most of the sales opportunity by filling the changing room with a huge array of garments. Instead there were no more than ten hangers on the rail.

'First up, white linen trousers. Nice heavy linen which won't crease too much in the car, will keep their shape but will be lovely and cool. Teamed with this very pretty cornflower blue T. Three quarter lengths sleeves and a low scoop neck with buttons down.' Mandy gave a wicked grin. 'You can button it up as much as you like or team it up with a vest underneath with all the buttons undone. It's quite different.'

What made the blue T-shirt different was the price. Thirty-five euros for a T shirt. That was £30!

Even so, she did as Mandy bade and slipped off Cam's white t shirt. The minute she put the trousers and top on they felt as if they'd been made for her. The cornflower blue was the perfect colour and when Mandy looped a soft cotton scarf in whites, blues and lime greens around her neck, it transformed the simple outfit into something else. A pair of lime green ballet flats that Laurie would never have even looked at, let alone considered buying raised it to a whole new level. Then Mandy insisted she try on a pair of cream kitten heeled sling-backs which were quite simply the most divine pair of shoes she'd ever worn.

Staring at herself in the mirror, she could scarcely believe it was her. What a difference clothes could make. Maybe there'd been something in the shampoo Marc had used. She had no idea what the entire ensemble would cost … and sod it she really didn't care. She would take all of it, even the lime green pumps and the cream kitten heels. In fact, definitely the lime green pumps … just because she could.

'Right then, let's get started,' she said stripping off again.

Mandy knew her stuff and two hours and a pair of black Capri pants, linen trousers, shorts, three T shirts, a red cardigan, a lime green cardigan, several more scarves and two more pairs of shoes later, Laurie felt like hugging her. Shopping had never been so much fun or so reckless.

Mandy was so good that Laurie had already resolved to take everything.

'This is amazing.' She twirled in the mirror. 'I love it all.'

Although she did gulp slightly at the cost – €844, although as Mandy explained with cost per wear factored in and that figure divided by the number of outfit permutations, you were actually looking at only €38 per outfit. See, not that bad at all, besides, the sum barely made a dent in the pile of euros Ron had provided her with.

Mandy had also found her a basic stock of cotton underwear and plain T shirt bras, as well as two bra and pants sets, which definitely fell into the lingerie category. Tempted to dismiss them as being impractical, she couldn't help touch the satin and lace and was lost. She had to have them.

The final outfit was a lovely, slinky, red jersey dress which she wouldn't have looked at in a million years but Mandy insisted she try it on. It fitted like a second skin and flared out with every step she took. Incredibly pretty, it made her feel feminine and sexy. With black heels in softest suede, it looked fabulous and she knew she just had to have both.

After all who knew what this trip would throw at her. She felt prepared for anything with the haul of clothes and best of all, it would all fold down to virtually nothing and pack into the leather holdall, that she'd picked from the selection Mandy had thought-fully provided. Just like the one Cam owned.

Sipping black coffee on the fifth floor in one of her new outfits, Laurie felt as if she belonged among the smart Parisians. Who knew that trying on clothes could be so much fun? Although having a personal shopper was a little different from trying stuff on in Next. It was amazing the difference an expensive cut could make.

A brief foray into the make-up basement left her emerging blinking and feeling her brain had been scrambled. She'd splurged, and that was the only word for it, on Clarins mascara, Clinique eye-shadows and blushers and Yves St Laurent Touche Éclat, which she read about a million times but never even tried before. Mandy had tipped off the make-up lady on the Clarins' counter and she'd been expecting Laurie. She rounded up all the ladies on the different concessions, who pressed various freebies and samples into her hand. Yvette, the Clarins lady, had taught her to shade and shadow her face in natural colours, so that her make-up was barely there.

Once she got started, she couldn't seem to stop and when she left Galeries Lafayette, emerging into brilliant sunshine, Laurie wanted to giggle out loud. It was absurd but she felt taller. Everything looked brighter. Her walk bouncier. A man passing caught her eye and where once, she would have ducked her head, she caught his gaze full on and smiled, feeling the smile take hold deep down, spreading through her. He grinned back, making her smile broaden.

On impulse she turned and headed south towards the Seine and then stopped abruptly. She really ought to get back to Cam. She looked back at the way she'd come. There was so much of Paris to see. And she needed postcards from both sides of the river. And an ice cream. She looked at her watch. Four hours since she'd left him.

If she walked really quickly, the slightly longer route back wouldn't take that much more and she could cover quite a lot of ground. With a determined pace she set off. Stately buildings lined wide boulevards, so different from home with their attic dormer windows. Leighton Buzzard seemed a world away. So did Robert.

What would he make of her new clothes?

Quickly she turned a corner and caught a glimpse of the Eiffel

Tower. She'd love to visit the top. Maybe another time. She craned her neck to get the most of the view as she hurried along the pavement before stopping to buy a postcard for Ron. Maybe she should send one to Robert … or would that be rubbing salt in the wound?

She couldn't picture Robert in Paris any more than she could picture him liking her new clothes. They'd stand out in her wardrobe. The colours contrasting with the pre-dominance of navy blue and black, white and cream. She stopped. She couldn't picture Robert in her room any more. The idea of living on her own had really taken root.

She felt a numbness. What to do? She couldn't think about him now. It was cowardly but she tucked the thoughts away.

As if she'd conjured it up a beep on her phone alerted her to a text from him.

Love you. Hope you're enjoying the trip. Doing my Top Gear bit, so is this car a short wheel base or a long wheel base?

She shoved her phone back in her pocket. She'd answer later.

Birdsong and distant traffic greeted him and for a moment he thought he was in his own bed, except this was much more comfortable. At home he still had the lumpy mattress from the knackered old spare bed that he had taken from the house he'd shared with Sylvie – before she'd run away to someone who could provide for her properly; for her emotional needs.

He slumped back into the welcome embrace of the pillows. His head felt like a bowling ball and his neck ached like a bitch from trying to hold it up. What the hell had happened? How did he get here? Pieces began to filter back. Heat washed over him. Shit. Being violently ill on the side of the road. The pincer grip of cramps on his stomach. Lying down on the verge wanting to die? And that was literally the last he remembered. Had he imagined

157

Laurie's gentle hands, or her soft voice urging him to drink some water. From the corner of his eye, he could see a bottle of water on the nightstand beside him. Reaching out an arm as heavy as lead, he made a hesitant stab at picking it up and pulling it to his dry lips. He felt like shit. His stomach protested, curling up in tense awareness of the water he gulped down. Gradually the room around him came into focus. Standard hotel fare. Lamps on either side of the big double bed. Crisp white sheets. Functional furniture. An upholstered chair with matching curtains. Anonymity reigned supreme. He could have been anywhere in the world except, he remembered now, he was in France with Miles' niece.

He opened his eyes wider to scan the room. No sign of her. Was she in the bathroom? The door was open. He hauled himself out of bed realising he needed to pee.

'Laurie?' his voice rasped, husky from idleness. He tried again, 'Laurie.'

Rising to his feet took considerable effort. Hell he was weaker than he'd thought. The room span and he had to grab the bed to stop himself falling backwards onto it. For a moment he tried to summon up his energy. Nothing. He was running on empty. His limbs seemed to have become spaghetti since driving this morning. It was this morning they'd left Chateau Le Miroir, wasn't it? It felt a million years ago now.

The sunlight filtering through the half drawn curtains and the noises outside the windows suggested it was daytime. How long had he been here? A couple of hours? They'd stopped for lunch. It must be early evening. He had no idea. He had a vague recollection of Laurie's voice urging him to drink water. So where was she now?

Surely she wouldn't have abandoned him. The pile of empty sachets by the water caught his eye. Medicine? He picked one up and studied it. Of course. She was out getting additional supplies. He could imagine her. Face serious, intent on making herself understood in schoolgirl French.

He stood up and he felt the floor beneath his feet rock slightly.

The urge to pee had grown and with hesitant steps he crossed the huge divide of all of a metre and a half to the bathroom.

Having relieved himself, he stopped when he caught sight of himself in the mirror. Bloody hell. What day was it? No one looked this bad after a day's illness. Gaunt hollows underscored his cheekbones, at least a day of ragged stubble straggled across his chin and his skin was tinged with a zombie-like grey pallor. He looked like death had warmed him, abandoned the attempt and left him to rot.

No wonder he felt so crap. Getting into the shower was daunting but he hoped the pounding of water might energise him or at least lift this dull fug that had taken over his brain.

Standing under the spray took every bit of effort he'd been worried about and some more. Finally towelling himself dry, he sank onto the toilet seat, every limb aching. At least his brain felt a bit sharper. Sharp enough to realise that the last time he remembered, he'd been fully dressed. To get into the shower, he'd only needed to remove his briefs. The other thing he noticed was the solitary wash bag in the bathroom.

Looking round, he realised there was absolutely no sign of Laurie anywhere.

Duh! What an idiot, she'd hardly share a room with him?

Lifting the phone receiver and calling reception didn't provide the answer he'd expected. There was only one room booked in the name of Matthews or Browne. This one. So where the hell was she? Where was her stuff?

The room contained nothing of hers. Not a single item. Something contracted in his already tender stomach. Had she cut and run?

No. Not her. Where could she go without him? Laurie was too sensible to drive off without him. Not like Sylvie, who would have been quite capable of flouncing off in the car in a state of tear-stained high-emotion. Although she probably would have totalled it within half a mile. Maybe Laurie had chickened out completely? Fallen at the first hurdle, so gone home. The hotel reception could easily arrange airline tickets and transport to Charles De Gaulle for her.

He sank back into the bed barely able to hold his head up any longer and closed his eyes. Surely she hadn't gone home. He tried to focus on his thoughts. No, not her. Fighting to open his eyes again, an image of her lifting her chin in defiance, her eyes sparkling popped into his head. No, she wouldn't give up. Not without some kind of fight.

He lay there watching the clock tick as more and more permutations of what could have happened to her rattled through his head.

Chapter 15

By the time she crossed the foyer of the hotel, her feet ached and she'd swapped the bags from each hand so many times that the cord handles had rubbed sore patches but she still had a mile-wide grin on her face. During her walk back she'd seen the Eiffel Tower, whizzed through the Tuileries, blinking hard as the sunlight reflected harshly on the white gravel expanse and then trotted fast along the Seine, nearly keeping abreast with the glass domed tourist boats chugging past.

At reception, barely pausing for breath she ordered room service and asked for extra French bread. White food, uncooked and plain would be best for Cam in the coming days.

Crossing her fingers, knowing it was stupid, she headed towards the lift. If he wasn't awake by now, she had no idea what to do. What if he'd been sick again while she'd been out? Her heart lurched. Shit, she was a heartless cow, leaving him all this time.

Quickly and quietly she let herself into the hotel room and immediately noticed the tantalising fresh scent of lemon. That along with the dampness in the air suggested, much to her relief, a very recent shower. If he'd managed that, he had to be much better. If he'd still been asleep she wasn't sure what she'd have done.

She hurried into the bedroom to find him propped up against the pillows, his tanned bare chest in stark contrast with the white crisp cotton. Her mouth went dry as her eyes traced the dark hair on his chest disappearing down below the sheets. For a moment she felt a complete idiot as all she could do was stare.

'You're bet—' her words trailed off. Anger blazed in his green eyes as they sharpened on her. Her stomach went into freefall and she froze to the spot. It was the first time since she'd seen him at Miles' funeral that he'd shown any real emotion. She hadn't noticed until now that his manner had been distant and … plastic. Totally insincerely platitudinous.

'Where the hell have you been?' he growled tossing the sheets aside and rising to his feet.

She was obsessed. Fixated. His stomach, chest, legs and whoa … don't look. Her breath came out in a slight pant and she closed her eyes, praying he hadn't heard. God. He was quite simply … gorgeous, even now when he looked all mean and piratical.

She rocked on the spot, her tongue uselessly limp in her mouth, desperately trying to keep her eyes on his face.

'I've been worried sick about …' His eyes narrowed as they focused on the shopping bags in her hand. 'I might have bloody known. No point wasting valuable time in Paris. So where are you staying, George V?'

'What?' She stared at him.

'Well you clearly dumped me here … and then buggered off …'

'I stayed here,' she hated the whine in her voice, it sounded so defensive and she hadn't bloody done a thing wrong.

'Not in this hotel you didn't. I checked … because I was,' he stopped and scowled as he'd bitten his tongue, 'never mind. I checked with reception. They said this was the only room you'd booked.'

Even as he spat the words at her, she could see the worry etched in the taut lines around his eyes.

Guilt swamped her. Despite his temper, he swayed on the spot as if any moment he might pass out.

Damn. A clear sign that he still wasn't well. She crossed over and pushed him gently back on to the bed. 'That's right.' She waited as he sank back onto the bed. 'I could hardly abandon you in the state you were in.'

He raised a disbelieving eyebrow. 'So what changed? Looks like you've been off swanning about the shops all afternoon. Not exactly been Florence Nightingale.'

So he had no recollection of the long hours on the cold, tiled bathroom floor last night. Only the knock at the door stopped her hitting him over the head with one of the bags. Miserable bastard.

Turning on her heel, she span round, her nose as far in the air as possible to make her point and flounced off to let room service in.

The waiter brought with him the welcome smell of chicken. Her stomach gave an answering twinge reminding her she'd completely forgotten to eat.

He placed a large tray on one of the small tables in the room, fussed with napkins and cutlery and then finally left after she'd slipped a couple of Euros into his hand.

'I thought you might be ready for some food. You haven't eaten for thirty hours. You must be hungry. The pharmacist recommended chicken consommé; I guess it's the closest thing we know to chicken broth.'

She collected a bowl and spoon along with some French bread and took it to the bed-side. Cam's stomach growled in response.

'Thirty hours?' His eyes narrowed.

'It's Wednesday evening.' Laurie did her best not to sound smug as she held up the bowl. 'We got here yesterday afternoon.'

Cam's face went through a multitude of expressions as he took the spoon from her and only a saint could have resisted making it clear that he owed her, big time.

Laurie was no saint. 'You were ill nearly all of Tuesday night and asleep all day today. The pharmacist said you need to sleep.'

The consommé was exactly what he needed, although he only managed half of it. As she held the bowl, eating gave him time to think and also purged some of the fuzziness from his brain. Memories began to trickle through, fairly random and still leaving a number of blanks in places.

He remembered driving. Feeling ill. Really, really ill. Then being in a bathroom. Lying on a cold tile floor, his head resting on the loo seat. Laurie there, wrapping him in a towel. Feeling really ill, wanting-to-die type ill, with his stomach aching as if it had been scoured out by an industrial digger.

Laurie half dragging and supporting him to the bed. Tucking him in.

He closed his eyes. Shit. Talk about making a complete dick of himself.

Welcoming the softness of the pillow, he tried hard not to squirm with embarrassment. And he'd just bawled her out for shopping.

He'd been out for a day and a half. Christ, no wonder he felt so drained. Although the soup was refreshing most parts.

It was noticeable she didn't say a word as he ate; just nodded encouragement, watching impassively, as he spooned in each mouthful. Once he laid down the spoon in defeat, she didn't nag or try to persuade him to take some more. She simply took the bowl and laid it on the side and pushed the bottle of water nearer.

He closed his eyes, thankful for her restful manner, unable to find the energy to move. She pulled the covers up over his shoulders, soothed hair from his forehead with the gentle touch of a mother and then he felt her weight leave the bed. Laying there he listened, cutlery tapping china as she ate her own meal, the soft movements of her about the room and outside the coo of pigeons and distant traffic. He didn't fall asleep but remained conscious of her presence. At one point he heard the click of the side lamps.

She brought with her a sense of peace and it was easy to lie still drifting between sleep and unconsciousness. Although he felt lousy, he couldn't remember the last time he'd felt such a sense of contentment. He liked his own company and clearly she was happy in hers. She made no demands on him. Let him be.

When he did open his eyes he could see her, curled in a chair in a pool of light by the window, absorbed in her e-reader. Through half-open lids he watched as every now and then her eyes would cast his way as if to check on him. Something was different about her.

Although he felt dopey, sleep danced just out of reach but he felt happy to lie there thinking and trying to figure out what it was. It was only when the lights snapped off and he heard the run of water and the hiss of the shower, that it came to him. Something about the way she held her head, as if a weight had been lifted.

He almost came to with a start when he felt the bed beside him dip. It seemed such an un-Laurie like thing to do. He quickly changed his mind as he realised she was doing her best to keep as still as possible, moving with deliberately slow movements as she climbed into bed, slipping between the sheets next to him.

She'd been nothing but kindness to him and all he'd done was grumble at her.

'Laurie,' he whispered.

As she rolled over to face him, he caught the scent of lemon verbena, his own shower gel. The bathroom light was still on and he could see her face, her eyes wide and uncertain.

'Thanks for looking after me.' He reached out to give her arm a squeeze. 'Sorry I wasn't very grateful.'

'It's fine. I'm sorry you were worried. I had to go out …'

'Ssh, you don't have to explain. It was very kind of you to look after me but—'

'No, you don't understand.' A frown puckered her brow. 'My luggage got stolen. I had to go out and replace everything.' Her face lightened, a secretive smile playing at her lips.

'Everything?'

'Yes.'

'So that's why you've been pinching my shower gel,' he teased.

'Sorry,' she gave him an unapologetic smile, 'I didn't get round to replacing my toiletries.'

'God I hope you didn't replace that hideous black dress.'

'Cam!' Playfully she hit him, her arm arcing across his chest. 'That's really mean.'

Her quick grin belied her words.

'I said the dress was hideous, not you.' Without thinking he grabbed her arm and pressed his lips against her inner wrist in a kiss of apology against it. Her soft, satin skin smelt clean and fresh. A memory of last night, of her holding him, soothing him, flared.

He wanted to hold her, to reciprocate – if he was honest to feel that sense of safety and security again. Laurie's air of serenity and calm gave him a sense of being grounded. Giving into instinct he pulled her arm down to rest on his chest and placed his hand over it. 'Thank you for looking after me last night.'

'You remember?'

She stilled and tensed, he stroked her wrist.

He closed his eyes, the rhythmic motion of his own hand and the feel of her arm warm and heavy on his chest, lulling him to sleep.

Waking, she stretched cautiously, lifted her head and immediately realised that there was no one in the bed beside her. No sign of Cam. Phew. Just as well. That quiet gentle interlude just before he fell asleep last night had left her awake for hours. Being so close to his delicious half-naked body had sparked some odd dreams, heated and erotic. She felt confused with a low-grade sexual ache between her legs. What would it be like to sleep with him? He had a body to die for. She'd been a late starter which probably wasn't helped by the fact that her dad knew what young men were like and quite often scared them off. As a result she'd only ever slept with Robert. Cam had experience, it was written all over him.

She sank back into the pillow. Get a grip girl. Going down that route with Cam would be asking for trouble. She wasn't his sort. That girl at the funeral was. Glossy thoroughbreds like her were the sort Cam hung out with.

Biting her lip, she prayed Robert would never find out she'd shared a bed with Cam. Innocent as it was, she couldn't see him taking a particularly understanding view. What he didn't know wouldn't harm him.

Where was Cam? She listened but didn't hear anything. The room and bathroom were empty. Relaxing, she scooped up a pile of her new clothes and took everything into the spacious bathroom.

Taking her time, enjoying Cam's toiletries again and regretting forgetting to buy a toothbrush as she rubbed her fingers around her gums with his toothpaste, she took out her plain new underwear, by-passing the frilly lingerie. Then she caught sight of her own wistful face in the mirror. This was stupid. Why deny herself? She tossed the plain white bra aside and slipped on the satin and lace confection. It gave her bust an obvious new definition which she deliberately didn't admire in the mirror.

A door slammed and realising Cam was back, she finished dressing quickly and shot out of the bathroom. She didn't want Cam to think … what? That she was making too much effort.

'Breakfast,' said Cam as he strode towards the tall balcony windows without even glancing at her. 'Croissant and coffee. Pain au chocolat for you.'

She followed him out onto the sunny balcony to the table where he ripped open the baker's bags to reveal a glistening croissant.

'I'm absolutely st—' His double take lit a slow burn of satisfaction low in her stomach. 'Wow, you look …' he swallowed, and looked at her chest, '… undressed.'

'What?' she looked down. Shit she'd forgotten to finish buttoning the cornflower T shirt. Her cleavage, pushed up by the new dramatic enhancing boning, was on full display.

Her skin turned fiery red and she turned her back on him to do up the buttons.

'Sorry.'

'Don't apologise to me, babe.' His wicked grin set lights dancing in his eyes. 'I always appreciate a nice view.'

The 'babe' instantly reminded her how far out of his league she was. Ignoring his flirtatious tone, she sat down at the bistro table.

'I just bet you do,' she said sweetly.

'Nice colour, suits you … although I guess you know that already.'

'What's that supposed to mean? You really do need to work on your lines you know.'

'You mean you didn't choose that colour to bring out the blue in your eyes?'

'It does?' Was that some kind of back-handed compliment or a twisted insult?

'It does.' He nodded gravely, disconcerting her.

'Well thank you, I think. I didn't choose it, I …' Saying she'd had a personal shopper sounded awfully decadent and self-indulgent. 'Thanks for this,' she said quickly, nodding at her pain au chocolat. 'How are you feeling? Are you up to eating?' The view from the balcony kept her from looking directly into his face. No doubt he was still laughing at her.

'My stomach feels as if it's been scoured out by an industrial digger. I'm starving but nervous about what I eat. I'm not sure I should be drinking coffee but …' He took a tentative sip, and pulled a blissed out face. 'That's much better.'

'You need to eat plain, white food,' said Laurie. 'Something light.'

'Doesn't croissant count?' he asked reaching for one of flaky crescents.

She shrugged, 'I'm not sure but you haven't been sick for 24 hours, so I think you'll be ok.' The colour had come back into his face and he needed to eat something, although he probably felt a lot worse than he was letting on. The way he'd sunk into his chair so quickly suggested the short walk outside had tired him.

'So what time do you want to head off?'

'What? Today?' Had he looked in the mirror?

'We're due at the Chateaux Descourts in two days' time. If we don't go today, we'll need to do some straight driving. Toll roads. A to B driving. Boring as shit. And you always get guys trying to take you on.'

Panic unfurled in her stomach but she managed an impassive face as she toyed with the piece of chocolate poking from the end of her pastry. She'd almost forgotten the strict time schedule. Clearly, despite his illness, Cam hadn't. Sweet of him, given she was the one who would forfeit the car if she gave up en route.

'We can always ring and explain we'll be delayed.' She sounded every bit like the petulant teenager she felt. 'As long as we get to Maranello on time.'

'Won't your mother be expecting you – presumably Ron has been in touch with her?' Cam's voice was mild as if he was totally disinterested but she could tell by the alert watchfulness on his face he knew.

'I don't think you're well enough to drive today. You need to get some strength back. At the moment you look as if a five-year-old could pick a fight with you and win, with both hands tied behind his back.' And that was being kind.

'And you complain about my compliments.'

'It wasn't a compliment.'

'You could drive.' Cam said with resignation in his voice.

The lack of enthusiasm in the statement made her smile and she raised her eyebrows.

He shrugged. 'You managed to get me here.'

'Only because you were too out of it to watch my driving.'

'What if I promise not to make a single comment?'

'Is that possible?' her smile broke out at the pained expression on his face. Although it would probably be better with him compos mentis this time. Besides what were the chances of them being stopped? It wasn't as if there wasn't another adult who'd passed their test in the car. She could drive … it was just she didn't yet have that bit of paper that said she'd passed her test. 'Do you think you could manage it?'

'Probably not …' he gave one of his charming grins, 'but I'll try really hard.'

'Hmph.' Was that a dozen pigs she spotted flying over the Paris skyline? 'One word. Just one word and I'm out of that driving seat in a flash.'

'Scout's honour,'

'Like they'd let you in the Scouts,' she snorted, enjoying the devilish gleam in his eyes.

Chapter 16

'Want to carry on driving?' asked Cam as they left the roadside café they'd stopped in for lunch.

'Can you bear me to?'

He considered her for a moment before flashing the smile that made her insides flip.

'Actually you're not bad. A bit clutch-heavy sometimes … but not too bad.'

She elbowed him hard in the ribs. 'For a girl you're quite good.'

Coming from Cam that was high praise indeed especially given he didn't believe anyone could drive the car as well as he could.

Despite the death stare she levelled at him, he laughed. A joyful burst of light-heartedness which made her smile at him instead of issuing the challenge she wanted. Part of her itched to drive again despite the low-grade headache circling her brow but she shouldn't tempt fate any more than she already had.

As always the Ferrari had attracted attention. A man and his son were taking pictures as they approached. She smiled at the sight and a little bubble of pride filled her heart. Her car.

It took a lot of concentration and focus to drive the car. It needed handling. You couldn't just lapse into automatic. Driving the Peripherique in this morning's traffic had been challenging.

Cam seemed a lot better now, although his appetite still hadn't returned to full service and he'd refused Jelly Babies this morning. She'd seen to it he'd eaten a good bowl of onion soup and more crusty bread, surprising herself by how bossy she'd been with him and more at how he'd acquiesced. Another sign he wasn't firing on all cylinders.

'Do you feel up to it?' she asked, digging in her handbag for the keys, still in two minds as to whether to hand them over or not.

The laughter sobered. He nodded.

'It'll give you a break. You probably need one.' He put up a hand. 'And not because you're a girl, this baby takes a lot of work and you're not used to it. That's all.'

'Let you off then.' She gave into the headache and handed the keys over.

Watching him drive wasn't exactly a hardship.

He put the car in reverse and manoeuvred out of the side street. They wound through the small streets until they hit the main road out of town where they settled into a smooth pace.

Laurie sank back into the seat, relieved after all to take a rest. Under his command the ride was fast and smooth, but he had flair and drove with verve and the arrogant confidence that made her totally secure in his ability. She glanced at Cam's face; he seemed absorbed in the road. She really should tell him she didn't have a full licence.

'So, what's with the new haircut?'

The idle question surprised her. He hadn't acknowledged it before and she'd assumed he hadn't noticed it.

'I got talked into it,' she said firmly resisting the temptation to ask him if he liked it.

'Suits you,' observed Cam.

'Thanks.' As a compliment it was hardly fulsome.

'Mind you, anything on the last one was an improvement.'

Her head snapped round in time to see the dimple in his cheek fade. A sure sign of one those quick fire grins he used with such lethal effect.

'Your lines just don't get any better.'

'I was just being honest. Would you rather I lied?'

'No. I should be grateful that you don't use your lines on me.'

'Lines? What do you think I am? Some kind of playboy.'

She folded her arms.

He turned his head to look at her.

'Keep your eyes on the road. I don't want you totalling *my* car.'

'Seriously? You think I'm a … Really?'

His aggrieved tone didn't fool her. She sniggered. 'Cam, you're a ladies man. You were at a damn funeral and you had women lining up. "Oooh Cam, it's been such a long time. I missed you in Monte Carlo this year. Call me?"' The sugary voice she adopted made Cam's heavy brows arch.

'Tania's a friend. A good friend.'

'I'll bet.' She hated herself for sounding so snide. And being so petty. Cam's world meant that his friends were bound to be of that ilk – gorgeous, clad in designer clothes and worldly-wise. Just like her mother. She glanced at her watch.

'Jealous?'

'As if,' she snapped a little too quickly, regretting it as soon as she did. Now it sounded as if she were exactly that. 'I'm not in your league.' His top flight premier division status in the mating ranks definitely outweighed her third division position.

'True.' The bastard, he didn't have to be quite so unchivalrous nodding in agreement and for a moment she felt her fists curling. If he wasn't driving a couple of thousand pounds worth of metal she would have been sorely tempted to punch him.

Pointedly she looked out of the passenger window, turning as much of her back on him as was possible in the tiny space. It was a useful wake-up call. In another few hours she'd have to come face to face with the reality of it all. Meeting her mother. This was a helpful reminder.

'I've offended you?' Cam sounded surprised.

'Not at all.' Laurie said her words dripping with faux sweetness. 'You're just being honest. Clearly you outrank me by—'

'Laurie! Get rid of the chip for a moment, I meant if we were talking league tables, you are the better person. Jeez, you really don't have a very high opinion of me at all, do you?'

'Sorry,' she said, her voice small.

They travelled in silence for the next half hour until they pulled up outside a road-side café.

'Do you want me to drive for a while,' asked Laurie, conscious that he rolled his shoulders as they got up from the table and feeling she ought to make amends. 'I guess it can get quite uncomfortable for you after a while.'

'I'm fine. I'm used to doing this on my own.' His mouth curved into a smile, 'Although it's much nicer with company.' The green eyes twinkled as he turned that easy charm on her. Say one thing about him; he didn't bear a grudge, not like Robert, from whom there'd been another text this morning.

'I bet you say that to all the girls.' She pursed her lips.

'Only the really pretty ones.' He grinned, raised his eyebrows at her and hooking his thumbs in his pockets he sauntered off leaving her to admire the view from behind.

'Want an ice cream?' he called over his shoulder.

With his collar length hair blowing in the breeze, the loping stripes of the long lean legs and that altogether tight bum, he looked like some modern day knight ready to take on his next challenge.

And she had to stop this silly nonsense. This was a business partnership to get her to Maranello. He was not her romantic hero and never would be. She still had a fiancé waiting at home for her, if she wanted him. Robert's image came to her. Solid, dependable, reliable. Everything, she thought she'd wanted. Now she wasn't sure. He'd be home now, she could bet on it, washing the car on the drive, skimming the Saturday Mail, getting his kit ready for tomorrow's match, shopping at Sainsbury's and choosing the

Hot Pepperoni pizza because she was away. And still upset with her for not wanting to get married. How was he going to take it, if she announced she didn't want to live together anymore? She thought of this morning's text.

Missing you so much. Marry me? x

Lifting her hand, she rubbed at the band of tension across her forehead. That would be one uncomfortable conversation but she'd made up her mind. Robert would blow a gasket.

In technicolour hindsight they'd moved in together far too quickly. She'd been too lost in her grief to make any sensible decisions. Robert had just sort of taken over. It was her own fault, she'd let him.

Don't think about it. That was what she was going to do. Determined to push Robert to the back of her mind, she looked around. With her new haircut, new clothes and sense of lightness of being, she could almost imagine she was another person. Cam was leaning against the car waiting for her, holding two ice creams. She smiled. Behind him there was a patchwork of colour, the dark leafy green of the forest, the sandy walls of the town's medieval walls and the long length of bridge crossing the silver lights of the river where the sunlight danced upon the water. It felt like being on holiday, with the warmth of the sunshine on her hair, face and bare arms and the slight scent of pine from the trees lining the valley below. It was tempting to call Cam over and suggest they stay longer, finish their ice creams, buy a second coffee and sit on the low wall to take in the view and while away the rest of the day.

Half of her rebelled against this sudden whimsical desire to be spontaneous, pointing out it was nothing more than procrastination.

Her mouth firmed, lips tightening and she let out an exasperated sigh. Better to get this over with. If he wasn't already dead, she could quite happily have strangled Miles ... bloody meddling.

What had he hoped to achieve sending her on this detour? Surely he must have realised it was the equivalent of casting her into an emotional hell.

Watching the expressions contorting her face was quite fascinating. Since they'd got on the road this morning, Laurie looked like a fierce warrior, girding her loins ready to go into battle. Did she have any idea how expressive her face was? So often her face showed exactly what she thought. It had already mirrored the view that he was some womanizing dilettante, which he probably was if he analysed his love life in her terms. Thing was all those women were sophisticates who knew exactly what they were getting into. She was a curious mix, keeping everything in and not saying much about how she felt and then in another way, so unfettered in the way her emotions shone out of her eyes. Reading her was so easy.

Something had happened in Paris. She'd seemed to come to life. Last night, they'd stayed overnight in Troyes, where she'd been utterly entranced by its tall, medieval timber-framed town houses. Dinner together had been fun and ever so slightly flirty. Maintaining this fun, light companionship would be perfect, sealing a sort of friendship. Driving the car, she almost sizzled from the buzz she got from handling it along the wide country roads. It amused him watching her in the driving seat, her wide mouth curved in that slow secret smile and the upright posture, like a proud empress in front of her subjects, she adopted whenever she got behind the wheel.

Since they'd stopped for coffee today, it felt as the clock had been turned back. Something was definitely bugging her. Her mouth kept tightening as if in the grip of an unpleasant thought and she carried the strain in her jaw-line, noticeable in the slight angle in which it was thrust forward. Someone who hadn't sat next to her for forty-eight hours on the trot might not have noticed it, but he could feel the waves of tension radiating from her in the close quarters of the car.

The girl that had emerged during his sickness bout was retreating beneath the shell again. She even looked different. Her hair up in a sharp neat ponytail, not a single loose curl. The prickly hedgehog had its spines raised again.

As she slid behind the wheel, she slumped for a second, and he thought he saw her mouth curve downwards. He ignored his instinct not to say anything.

'Are you OK?'

She looked at him and he saw a bleakness in her eyes that he'd not seen before. It echoed some complication and yet she seemed so uncomplicated.

'No … Yes. I'm fine.' She shook her head and then as if stiffening her resolve, she sat up straight, rammed the key in the ignition and started the car up. As she revved the engine just a tad too much, he thought he heard her mutter.

'Let's do this.'

The two hour journey passed in silence. He studied maps, looking at where the next leg of the journey would take them before they headed up to Switzerland and then on to Italy, not wanting to intrude on whatever was eating Lauren. She drove with an increasingly grim twist to her mouth.

At last the sat nav indicated that it was time to pull off the main road and Laurie followed the unemotional instructions as the roads got smaller and smaller until they pulled up outside a gated entrance.

An intercom on the side of the gate pillar alerted someone to their presence and the large black gates swung open, eerily quiet as if pulled by invisible magical threads. Laurie paused the car at the threshold of the drive, her knuckles white.

He laid a hand on her hand gripping the gear stick and gave it a quick squeeze, hoping to offer some moral support. Whatever was bothering her, she didn't want to talk about it.

The drive took them right up to a courtyard area, off which led the wing of a small country house. The courtyard was packed with other cars, BMWs, Mercedes, Range Rovers as well as the odd Maserati and Lamborghini. He eyed the latter with interest, wondering if he might know anyone here. There was obviously quite a party gathered which was a shame because Laurie probably needed to spend some time with her mother. He was intrigued by her cool attitude and could only think it was nerves because she hadn't seen her in a while. It was odd that she hadn't come over for her brother's funeral.

Laurie parked with her usual economic efficiency.

'Nicely done,' he said.

She flashed him a quick grateful grin and for a moment they were comfortable with each other again. 'Sorry I'm a bit tense. I don't see my Mum or ...' she paused, 'very often.'

Something in the way she said it sparked a warning bell in his head piquing his curiosity. 'How often?'

She looked guarded for a moment. 'Once in the last three years. For lunch in London. Just after my dad died. I've never been here to this house or stayed with her.'

Trying to hide his surprise he said, 'Well Miles obviously thought it would be a good idea. Maybe it's time you saw her. She must miss you.' He couldn't think of a day that Sylvie hadn't been on the phone to her mother. His own mother never complained he didn't visit often enough, but she always made it clear when he did how delighted she was to see him.

'I doubt it.' She'd turned her head and was looking out of the passenger window. He couldn't gauge anything from her expression or her voice. It was as if a steam roller had been along to level away all trace of emotion, flattening it into nothing.

Finally she turned to face him. 'Weird huh?' she observed staring into his eyes as if trying to read his reaction. Hers broadcast guilt, defiance and sadness wrapped up in one confusing package. Laurie normally seemed so together, level-headed and normal. Now she seemed cowed.

As they got out of the car, he grabbed the bags from the boot and swung his free arm around her shoulder, pulling her head towards his and giving her quick brief kiss on top of her head. 'Let's do this.'

His hand snaked to the back of her head. 'And this.' With a quick tug he pulled the band from her ponytail, letting her new layered hair spill out of its tight confines. 'That's better, makes you look more relaxed and not about to storm the castle.'

There was the briefest pause and then she gave him a quick barely-there hug. 'Thanks Cam.'

She picked up the pace and marched to the door, her chin lifted again. He smiled, she still looked like she was storming a castle. You had to hand it to her, she had plenty of guts. Whatever challenge came up, she took it head on. She never shirked a duty or a chore. Honourable, honest. That was Laurie. Perfect for him. When it came to selling the car, everything told him she'd sell it to him. He really should tell her about the deal Miles had made with him but something held him back. At first he'd been nursing a grudge and it had irked him that she assumed he was being paid to take her across Europe, like some bloody mercenary. That wasn't him and she'd jumped to conclusions.

Now he understood her better, a woman with her own deep-seated principles and someone to admire. He needed to tell her about the terms of Miles' will and how he stood to benefit with regard to the Ferrari. As soon as they left here, he'd tell her.

He found himself studying her as she raised a hand to pull hard and decisively on the old fashioned bell pull beside the double wooden doors. Ramrod straight, she stood dead centre in the doorway holding her ground.

'Good afternoon.'

Good afternoon, I'm Lauren Browne, I'm here to see my mother.'

The black-suited butler quirked his eyebrow but it was the only sign that she'd discomfited him. 'Please come in, I will let Madame Harvieu know you are here.'

Chapter 17

'Lauren, darling, at last you're here.' Her mother came tap-tapping down the marble-tiled hall towards them, looking exactly like she had last time Laurie had seen her. Immaculately groomed in black trousers, heels, a silk blouse and that perfectly smooth youthful complexion highlighted with the barest touches of expensive make-up.

'Hi … Mum.' As her mother grasped her and kissed her, French style on both cheeks, Laurie wasn't quite sure where to put her arms. Hugging her mother seemed wrong.

'And look at you, don't you just look fabulous. You've finally learned a bit of dress sense.'

What did you say to that? Thank you?

'That colour suits you. It's so wonderful to see you, I can't imagine why it's been so long.'

Because you live the other side of France and I live in England, thought Laurie, grinding her teeth to hold the comment back. And you were always too busy. Not even here five minutes and she felt childish and resentful.

'Good journey? Looking after the car, I hope.' Her mother accompanied the words with a coy smile.

Laurie tensed. She hadn't forgotten that the car would be forfeited to her mother if she didn't reach the end of the journey.

How much did her mother know?

'The journey was fine thanks. How are you? How's Siena?'

'And Harry?' her mother added, her eyes narrowing.

'Sorry … and Harry.' Oh for God's sake she barely knew the man. She wished she had the guts to say what she really thought. Why did her mother persist in the idea that he was in any way relevant to her? Laurie wanted to know about Siena.

'Just pop your bags down there. Jackson will take them up to your room.' While she was saying this Laurie could see her mother giving her another once over and wished she'd stopped to put a bit of make up on and brush her hair. Even in her new clothes, with her new hairdo, she felt like a mongrel next to a pedigree.

'Laurie's obviously not going to introduce us. I'm her mother, Celeste.' Laurie wanted to punch something. How did her mother always do it? Make her feel wrong-footed.

'I'm so sorry Cam, how rude of me.' Laurie gave him her sweetest smile. 'I should have introduced you. Cam, this is my mother, Celeste Harvieu. Mum this is Cam.'

Her mother's nostrils flared, the only sign that Laurie's petty point-scoring had hit the target. Rising above Laurie's needling, she didn't ask him who he was but she obviously approved of his good looks because she greeted him with a satisfied, cat-licked-the-cream smile. 'Hello, Cam. Lovely to meet you. Welcome. Come through, we were just about to have tea.' She gestured down the hall to Cam and as he took the lead, she gave Lauren a knowing look.

'All man isn't he? Not what I'd have expected you to have in tow at all,' she murmured, eyeing Cam thoughtfully before shooting an assessing look at Lauren as if to say there must be more to you than meets the eye.

Lauren wanted to sink through the floor at her mother's blatant remarks. It was her own fault she guessed for not introducing him properly and there seemed little point correcting the assumption that Cam was her lover. It would lead to having to explain the situation, which she didn't want to go into. It was too personal.

She shared as little as possible with her mother, mainly because her mother wasn't that interested in her. Her attention span ran to nought percent of short.

To his credit, Cam's face remained impressively impassive in the wake of the undercurrent between the two women.

The large salon into which they were ushered immediately reminded Laurie of a stately home. Small, impractical period furniture was arranged around the focal point of the room, a cherub festooned onyx and marble mantelpiece. Laurie stepped forward gingerly feeling over-large and clumsy among the delicate furniture. She wasn't sure if she should sit on anything or just stand. Nothing in the room suggested it was ever used for anything other than show. Even the fine china tea service laid out on the coffee table looked too fragile to use. Cam's thumbs probably wouldn't even fit into the tiny cup handles.

'Do sit down. Now Cam, would you like a cup of tea or would you prefer something a bit stronger?'

'Tea's fine, thank you.'

'Laurie?'

'Yes, please.'

'Well you've timed your visit perfectly. We've got a full house at the moment.' She flashed a smile at Cameron. 'It's that time of year, we have so many visitors popping in on their way down to Cannes. It's lucky we had a spare room for you. Shame you weren't here last week. Georges Claudine was here with Elisabet Jennings ... you know the film director? She's his leading lady. And just last month we had Nick Faldo and Sam Torrance to dinner when Harry played in a pro-celebrity tournament.' She gave a light-hearted girlish laugh. 'Not of course that Harry's a proper celebrity or anything but you know ...'

With a change of tack like a hawk dropping on to its pray, she asked, 'So what is happening with the car? Mr Leversedge was rather circumspect.' Her face tautened in disapproval, making her cheekbones slightly shiny as if the skin was too tight over the bones.

'He's always been curt and rude. I've no idea what his problem is.'

'Really?' Laurie hammed up her surprised look. 'He's been an absolute sweetie to me.'

Celeste completely ignored the comment and poured herself another cup of tea. 'So? The car? All old misery guts would tell me was that you were driving it to Italy.' Laurie shot a quick look at Cam, wishing she'd forewarned him not to say anything about their real mission. She knew that the subject of Miles' legacy would be broached at some point but she was hoping that she could delay it as long as possible.

'Miles wanted it driven one last time across Europe and asked me to do it.'

'He always was a sentimental old fool. Harry will be livid. Putting more miles on the clock on a car as valuable as that. It's ludicrous.'

Laurie bristled. What business was it of Harry's?

'And where do you come in, Cam?'

'I'm … I'm a mechanic, I guess you'd say.'

'Oh.' Her eye's narrowed and she turned to Laurie with a worried frown. 'You do realise, Laurie, it's an extremely valuable car.'

Laurie smiled down into her tea at Cam's sudden overwhelming interest in his own drink. Laurie wanted to laugh – only it wasn't funny, it was embarrassing.

'He's being modest, he's not just a mechanic. He … he … well it's to do with classic cars.'

'Oh, one of Miles' protégées, why didn't you say? Did you know my brother? Which reminds me Laurie, how did the funeral go? I would have liked to have gone but it was Paris Fashion week and I just didn't think I could have fitted it all in.' She laughed girlishly again and said to Cameron, 'It's not as if Miles would have noticed.'

Cam's face was shuttered and Laurie could read very little from the polite mask he'd adopted.

'Were all the wives there? Bet they were wondering which one of them would get the house. Has the will gone to probate yet?

I've not heard anything yet and the solicitor was very cagey but then the post out here is shocking.' She stared hard at Laurie, her dark eyes suddenly beady and acquisitive. 'Or is that perhaps why you're here? Delivering messages ... from beyond the grave.'

Laurie felt cold for a moment. They'd not even been here half an hour.

'So who did get the house?'

'No one.'

'No one? Are you sure? Someone must have got it?' her mother's voice was shrill with dismay.

Laurie shrugged. 'No one knows about the house. It's tied up in some special trust that the solicitor is administering.'

'And what about the car?'

Laurie felt the blood rush to her face and her stomach coil in embarrassment. Damn this was the moment she'd have to fess up about the car; she shot a quick glance at Cam. His face was unreadable.

'I ... er ... don't know. The GT250 ...'

Her mother's head bobbed up, her face alight with avaricious interest.

The words faltered on her tongue '... will...' She looked at Cam.

'It's going to be sold after Laurie gets it to Maranello.'

Laurie could have kissed Cam for his handsome interjection. Although to be honest, kissing him would come easy ... and she didn't want to even start to go down that road.

Her mother put her cup down on its saucer with a loud chink. 'How odd? I thought it would stay in the family. It would have fitted beautifully in Harry's collection. A shame, but it will go for a huge amount. Harry says most Ferraris have quadrupled in value in the last few years.'

If Laurie hadn't been watching Cam's face at that moment, she probably wouldn't have noticed the way he froze and the guilty expression as his spoon clattered into his saucer.

'I wondered if Miles might have arranged to turn the house

into a museum with all the cars on display.'

'That is so typical of your uncle. He was such a romantic.' The way she said it, didn't suggest that was a good thing.

Interesting how Miles, her own brother, suddenly became 'your uncle.'

'Look how many times he got married … no fool like an old fool. Spent a fortune on them all. So there's no money left then? I thought he might leave some to the family at least. He's got no other blood relatives apart from us, well, and you. I'd have thought he might have left Siena something.

'After all your father didn't leave her anything. I still can't believe that. The house should have been shared between you and Siena.' Her mouth pursed, leaving heavy lines into which her bright lipstick was just starting to leach, the bitter twist to her mouth suggesting she also remembered Laurie refusing to sign on the dotted line. The ensuing lunch of high drama, emotional blackmail and wheedling coercion had left a hangover of guilt and disappointment that still had the power to make Laurie feel depressed even now. For a brief foolish few days, she'd honestly thought that her mother was coming over to see her to check she was OK after the death of her father. Invite her over to France; tell her she always had a home there.

Laurie closed her eyes. Surely she must have got over her disbelief by now. Please don't bring this up in front of Cam. But she did.

'Can you believe it? What kind of father does that?'

He'd leant forward, his eyes bright darting back and forth between her and her mother. 'Who's Siena?' he mouthed. Laurie shook her head slightly.

Her mother's lips pressed together in a tight firm line as if to shut out any possible unpleasantness.

'It's very disappointing about Miles. He did leave a proper will I take it. You have checked. Maybe I should have come back to oversee things.' She was talking more to herself than Laurie, brushing the knees of her smart black trousers, shaking her head the whole time.

'I may have my solicitor look into things. You know what it's like, as people get older. They get some funny notions.'

Laurie swallowed hard. Well her mother had hit the nail on the head there. What would she think if Laurie told her that she was here at the express instruction of her uncle?

'I think Miles knew what he was doing,' interrupted Cam. 'He had quite some time to prepare things. I'd say he had it all planned out quite neatly.'

'Oh.' Laurie's mother lapsed into silence and Laurie shot him a small grateful smile. Not many people managed in subduing her mother.

It didn't last for long though. 'Well, as soon as you've finished your tea, I'll have Jackson show you upstairs. And I'll have to leave you as there's so much to be done for this evening. The Rossiters are coming and we've got Count Rothman arriving along with Caroline Linklater, she's engaged to some Danish Prince ... or maybe its Swedish, I can't quite recall.' She paused and looked Laurie up and down. 'I don't suppose you brought anything with you to wear? You look about the same dress size as Siena. I'll see if there's something of hers that will do for you.

'We'll be serving champagne in the Blue Room from seven and then dinner in the dining room at about nine. If you need anything in the meantime do ask any of the staff. Right, I really must get on, there's so much to do. Quite a few people arrived yesterday and they're all out to lunch. They'll be back soon. I do adore having guests but it's hard work.'

She waved her hands in the air as if to demonstrate how busy she was. The immaculate nails in rose pink suggested that the hard work was done by others. 'Do excuse me. Finish your tea.'

With that she tip tapped out of the room, calling 'Jackson, Jackson.'

Laurie let a huge long sigh.

Cameron blinked slowly and took in a deep breath, checking

over his shoulder before he spoke. 'Well that was interesting? I take it Harry is … step-dad?'

'I wouldn't exactly call him that; I've only met him a couple of times. Whenever Mum was in London, I'd get the grand summons to lunch. He's her latest husband, number three. They've been married for about five years.'

'And how long have they lived here?'

'For about the same time. Harry's a Comte or something. It's his ancestral home. He's not really called Harry, it's just a nick-name for Harvieu.'

'So you grew up with …'

Her face dropped. 'My dad … for the last years of his life. I'll never know why he and Mum married in the first place.' This grand house was a million miles away from the tidy terrace house she lived in with Robert.

Cam watched her and she felt herself colour up. She'd managed to avoid mentioning Siena so far. Going into the whole story would be tedious and she didn't want his pity or his sympathy. Explaining it galled her particularly as she'd never had the gumption to say anything to her mother.

Suddenly she felt unutterably weary and wished she were back at home. Before all this had started. Before the funeral, before the will. When things with Robert were nice and simple. When her life had no twists and turns, just a straight road with no diversions. Bless him; she understood what Miles was trying to do. Show her what she was missing. Travel, glamour but she didn't need any of that. Perhaps this evening she could stay in her room and avoid her mother's glamorous party.

It was bound to be full of people she had nothing in common with and nothing to say to. The sort of people that Cam would slot right in with.

'You OK?' Cam's eyes were kind and they held her gaze. For a moment she was tempted to say no, I'm not, get me out of here. But that wouldn't be fair. It was bad enough that he had to

187

witness this and have to put up with twenty four hours of being here, without her unloading on him.

'Yeah, fine. Just mother-daughter stuff.'

He raised a cynical eyebrow which said that he didn't believe her for a second.

'I'll show you to your room.'

The boot-faced butler appeared in the doorway, reminding him of the last time he'd drunk tea from a cup and saucer. That was with Laurie too, back at Miles' house before all this began.

If he'd known what Miles was getting him into he might have turned this gig down. Now he'd arrived at Cinderella's enchanted castle and all the players were messed up. Laurie's mother had to be the most self-absorbed creature he'd ever come across. Many spoilt women had crossed his path but she took the biscuit.

This was all familiar, the money, the pretension, the social climbing and the name dropping – it went with the territory. For every genuine classic car enthusiast, there were ten trophy collectors, who wanted the fast cars along with the younger, tauter wives. Tonight's do would be like many he'd been to before, he might even know a few people. The circle of rich and richer was relatively small.

Poor Laurie, it was like watching a kitten stepping up to a lion and expecting it to play nice. He grimaced. No doubt it would fall to him to play the role of protector.

'Did he say room?' whispered Laurie, poking him in the back as he followed the upright back of the butler to the foot of the stairs. This staircase was very grand, splitting into two and then curving away along long balconies, bordered by ornate metalwork.

'No idea,' he muttered. God this trip was getting more and more farcical. Miles was probably laughing his socks off if he was looking down, although, Cam's mouth tightened, the old sod deserved to be in hell for putting him through this. All he wanted was a nice uncomplicated life and the Ferrari of his dreams. By the time he took possession of the beauty he was going to have bloody earned it.

A sudden skittering of heels came as a tall, slender, blonde young woman rushed down the marble tiled hall and slid to a coltish halt staring in surprise at both him and Laurie.

'You're here.' She blushed vividly. In turn Laurie had become rigid, her head frozen into place.

For a moment the two stared at each other, one all jerky movements and barely contained excitement, the other wary and trapped. The air buzzed with a strange tension. Cam couldn't figure it out at all.

'S-Siena?' Laurie managed and then stared at the other girl.

Siena, whoever she was, had rippling hair a much lighter shade than Laurie's, which fell to her waist, and a pretty face. She had that ultra-polished, accessorized-to-death sort of appearance that you saw in the ski resorts of Verbier and on the decks of yachts in St Tropez. Not Cam's type at all but one he was familiar with. Trust-fund rich kids who all looked and sounded the same and every one an understudy for Made in Chelsea.

'Yes,' the girl whispered.

'Siena!' A loud voice called from down the hallway. Celeste's peremptory tones had the girl looking anxiously back the way she'd come.

'Gotta go.' With a flash of perfect white teeth she darted away.

'Who the hell was that?' Cam asked irritably.

'My sister.'

Cam was ready to kill Jackson as he wound slowly up the stairs taking his sweet time. He was bursting to ask Laurie what the hell that was all about. He scanned his memory but no, he was pretty sure, she'd never once mentioned a sister.

No doubt the petite Barbie doll they'd just met was a half-sister or step sister which would explain their strained greeting.

Together he and Laurie walked down a plush carpeted corridor with lots of high wide-framed doors to either side, with him shooting questioning glances at her. Laurie refused to look at him and kept her head turned slightly away as if admiring the fresh flowers lining the tables along the endless corridors. With the many paintings and occasional bits of furniture just waiting to catch the unwary out, it would be easy to think you were in a hotel. This house had certainly been built for entertaining.

At the far end of the hall, Jackson stopped and held open a door for them.

Laurie went in first and he followed.

She stopped and sighed. 'We're not … do you have another room as well?'

Jackson looked uncomfortable for a moment, as if he wasn't used to getting things wrong.

'I'm terribly sorry Madam, but this is the only room available. The house is full. I could ask some of the gentleman if they might be willing to consider sharing.' He made it sound as if this would be a herculean task with an uncertain outcome.

She blushed.

Cam turned to the butler to ask if there was any other solution but Jackson had already turned and was disappearing fast back down the hall.

'Sorry,' Laurie screwed up her face. 'This is such a cliché. I can't believe my mother's made such a massive assumption about … well you know.'

Cam raised a cynical eyebrow, charmed momentarily by her gauche innocence. In a house like this, it was truly refreshing.

'Don't worry,' he said, 'we'll manage.' He gave her a quick grin. 'I trust you. You managed not to pounce on me last time.'

She glared at him, her chin lifted like a boxer ready to take on a fight. 'It really wasn't that hard.'

Her fight wasn't with him. Tension lined her forehead and he could bet there were lines crossing her palms where her fists had been clenched off and on for the last half hour.

'You OK?' he asked, wondering whether to give in to the urge to take her in his arms and rub the hunched shoulders.

The bleakness in her eyes as she said quietly, 'No,' almost floored him and he crossed the room and put his arms around her. Like a child she crumpled into them, sighing heavily. The muscles in her back had tied themselves into rigid knots which he automatically began to rub with rhythmic strokes in time with her soft breathing.

Words seemed useless because what could he possibly say? Laurie had been dealt a crap hand.

'So what's the story with Siena?' he asked, feeling those knots tense and the heave of her chest as she took in a deeper breath.

'When my parents split up, they divided the spoils in half. One sister each.' Laurie's dull monotone spoke of a depth of hurt. Shit and no wonder.

'Seriously?' He pulled back to look at her sad face.

She lifted her shoulders and looked away over his shoulder. He didn't need to imagine her pain – he could see it in her eyes. He pulled her towards him, cradling her against his chest.

The gentle knock on the door sounded again. The first had been so quiet he thought he'd imagined it. Laurie looked up at him and he gave her a comforting squeeze before releasing her to go and open the door.

Siena was back, her stance posed, as if she knew the doorway made a perfect frame but was also unsure. She stayed there for a few seconds as if poised for entrance. Cam thought it said a lot about her uncertainty.

'Hi, can I come in?' she asked her voice perky and confident.

Laurie nodded, shadows haunting her eyes.

Siena walked in to stand in front of Laurie, slightly taller, thanks to the five inch heels on her tiny feet. With her blue eyes outlined with perfect black eyeliner, sooty lashes and glossy lips, she made quite a contrast to her sister.

Cam felt uncomfortable watching the two sisters sizing each other up, this was one time they probably didn't need an audience

191

but then Siena was on home turf and Laurie was the outsider. The thought seared him as he realised her vulnerability and made him determined to stay unless she asked him to leave.

'I bet I've changed. Do you remember me?'

'A little,' said Laurie, finding it hard to relate this grown up glossy creature to the tiny blonde girl in red gingham school-dresses in old school photos of them both. To be truthful, all her memories of her sister came from photos and Dad had put most of them away because the image of Siena was too painful. Did Siena remember their Dad?

'Hmm, we don't look much like each other do we?'

She walked round her, her eyes looking her up and down.

What did you do when confronted by a sister you hadn't seen in ten years? Shake hands? Air kiss? Siena didn't seem to be fazed.

'Well, you know I'm Laurie.'

Siena's head lifted in surprise. 'I never thought of you as a Laurie. You've always been Lauren but you look more of a Laurie than a Lauren. More homely. Lauren sounds quite stately.'

What did you say to that?

With a wide smile which revealed American perfect cheerleader teeth, Siena stepped forward and graciously bestowed an air kiss on each of Laurie's cheeks.

Siena looked a million dollars or at least had had that much spent on her. Her blonde hair had been expertly highlighted to enhance its golden tones which glinted in the overhead light, her dress drew attention to her perfect cleavage, tiny waist and finished a few inches above the knee to show off amazingly long Bambi legs which were finished in high heeled golden gladiator-style sandals. Everything about her exuded wealth and polish.

'I always wondered what it would be like to have a sister. Nice to meet you at last …' She glanced over Laurie's shoulder, suddenly spotting Cam.

'Well hi.' Her voice lifted with sudden enthusiasm that had Laurie wanting to roll her eyes. Hello, obvious.

'Hi,' he stepped forward and formally put out his hand to shake hers. 'I'm Cameron.'

The deliberately formal use of his name made Laurie smile, a signal that he wasn't having any of it.

'Nice to meet you too.' Her eyes lingered on his.

She turned back to Laurie, her smile widening and her face softening.

'Sorry, to intrude. I just thought that, like, maybe you weren't expecting a party and that you might, like, not have the right stuff with you and that I could maybe help you get ready and maybe lend some stuff and … you know … maybe?' Suddenly she was a different person. Her words hit Laurie like a waterfall of worry, her eyes wide with uncertain anticipation.

Which just went to show how wrong you could be and what a bitch she was. That chip on her shoulder really did need some work. For all her polish, Siena was probably just as nervous and desperately trying to what … break the ice, make amends? It wasn't Siena's fault their mother had chosen her. If anything Laurie had been the elder, perhaps she should have made the effort to track Siena down. As her sister stood in front of her, looking so eager to please, Laurie felt guilty. She should have tried to see her sister. Being totally honest she'd also resented her sister for being the one Celeste chose, even though it was a horrible thing to admit.

After a while it had been easier for the two fractured families to keep apart, less emotional upheaval that way.

'It's lovely to meet you and yes that would be nice.' What the hell would she talk about to Siena? 'I've got a nice red dress and some black shoes, so if you have anything I could borrow or accessorize, that would be lovely.'

'We're, like, talking formal dinner wear. Black tie rather than white but still … a nice red dress … nah.' Siena shook her head vigorously. 'Don't worry I've got oodles of designer stuff. We'll have you sorted out in a trice and I,' Laurie almost expected her to puff out her chest, 'will transform you. You wait.' A wicked grin lit her face. 'I'm really, like, into fashion. I'm so going to give you a makeover.'

Laurie stared at her for a moment, this weird mixture of woman and girl. For all her gloss, she was a very young twenty-two.

'Well …' She turned helplessly to Cam, who was no help at all.

'I think that sounds like a great idea,' interjected Cam with a sly grin and wink at Laurie, 'give you a chance to catch up a bit. I'll be fine; I want to check my emails. You go ahead, Laurie.'

'Ooh, it'll be such fun,' squealed Siena, grabbing Laurie's hand, her earlier shyness suddenly vanishing. 'Come on, come with me.'

'But … I …'

'I can lend you everything. Come on we need to get started, we've only got three hours.' She lunged for Laurie's hand and dragged her out of the room, giving Cam a perky little wave.

'I'll bring Cinders back to you at seven. You won't believe your eyes.'

Three hours! Laurie's heart sank. God, what was she planning to do? Visions of the film Grease and the song Beauty School Drop Out filled her head, followed by the overwhelming image of a guinea pig in pink curlers.

Cam heaved a sigh as the door closed on the young whirlwind. He dreaded to think what that forceful young lady had in store for Laurie. Taking his wash bag through to the en-suite, he unloaded his shaving gear. Hopefully it wouldn't be too OTT but he had a horrible feeling that it would. Siena looked like she was of the more is more school. Although from the look of guilt on Laurie's face, he guessed she'd do anything to please her younger sister. He couldn't imagine him and Nick being separated like that. Wouldn't he have attempted to stay in touch? Who knew what went on in families?

He had to remember, he wasn't Laurie's keeper. He placed his toothbrush in the glass tumbler by the sink. He wasn't her anything. Although if it were down to him, he'd snatch her up, bundle her into the car and head far, far away from this place. Loathsome woman. Laurie probably wouldn't believe him but the woman had probably done her a favour leaving when she did, although separating the sisters had been unbelievably cruel for both the girls and their father. Tonight he'd stick close to her, protect her from the vultures and make sure her mother kept her claws to herself. He caught sight of his fierce expression in the mirror. Oh God, he was doing it again. Laurie didn't need rescuing. Don't get involved, he told his reflection. He should have learned by now. Look what a disaster things had turned out with Sylvie. He'd tried to rescue her. Look after her. But he couldn't stay the course. He wasn't cut out for it.

He had to stick to the plan. Get Laurie to Maranello. Buy the car and drive off into the sunset and never see her again. So why couldn't he shake this horrible vision of her in too much eye make-up, scarlet lipstick and big hair in a dress the wrong colour. And since when had he considered what the right colour was for her?

See, he was already turning into her big brother. Worrying about her. He shook his head. Been down that road before. He was not going to feel responsible for Laurie. She didn't need it and wouldn't thank him for it. Women didn't come more independent than her, steady job, own home and boyfriend waiting by the hearth. In a few days' time she'd go home, they'd get married, have kids, with a very nice nest egg courtesy of his bank manager, and this trip wouldn't even feature as any more than a blip in her memories.

In the meantime he would go down and check on the car, and a place like this was bound to have a billiard room or a library he could hole out in until it was time to collect Cinders. Give him chance to get the lie of the land, although the landscape was pretty familiar. The jet set didn't vary that much from country to country. They all fell into the usual stereotypes.

Coming out of the bedroom he headed down the stairs and went out to the garage block at the back of the house to find the Ferrari gleaming in the late afternoon sunlight. Soon it would be his. What a beauty. Driving her this far had been heaven sent, although now Laurie was getting more confident, he was getting less and less driving hours in. Good job she drove as well as she did or it would have been pure torture.

'Nice car,' a languid voice purred through a steam of cigarette smoke.

Cam looked up, taking in the scent and realising it had been years since he'd had or wanted a cigarette. The smoker pushed himself up from the nearby wall and came to stand beside Cam. 'Yours?'

'Sadly, no.'

Laurie had been very circumspect with her mother, so he was wary of giving anything away. Once again he got the horrible feeling that she was like a lamb among vultures.

'Worth a bit?'

Cam's eyes narrowed. The guy was like so many other spoilt trust-fund brats. You could tell just from the cut of their floppy hair and the casual grace that illustrated itself in the way they lounged everywhere. The car was worth a fortune but only an idiot would think about money when they looked at this masterpiece of engineering. The guy was a dickhead.

'Is that a question or an observation?'

'Both?'

Cam couldn't resist showing off even though he knew he shouldn't. Guys like this always irritated the hell out of him. 'It's probably worth more than double your trust fund.'

The boy man raised his eyebrows and sneered. 'I wouldn't be so sure of that if I were you.'

Chapter 18

Siena's room had more homely touches than the hotel-like bedroom and salon that Laurie had seen so far but it was still a far cry from her own teenage bedroom. There certainly wasn't a poster in sight and all the furniture matched. It would have been lovely except the floor was covered in clothes and the dressing table strewn with make-up. Wardrobes lined one wall from which spilled a rainbow of colours.

Siena clearly didn't understand the concept of tidiness.

With quick rapid movements, she cleared a high backed velvet seat by transferring the mountain of clothes onto the bed.

'Here, sit down,' she said to Laurie, her eyes alight with eagerness.

She promptly sat down on the bed uncaring of the clothes beneath her crossed legs, looking like a genie who'd just popped out of a lamp.

'So, is he your boyfriend then?' Siena leaned forward with avid interest as if she planned to learn everything she could about having a sister in the next three hours.

Laurie laughed at her earnest tone. 'Sorry, no we're just … friends.' She guessed that's what they were now.

Siena's face fell. 'He's delish. Don't you fancy him at all? '

Laurie laughed again, refusing to even consider the question properly. She'd seen Cam half-naked, been up close and personal to those gorgeous green eyes; he was completely delicious and also completely out of her league, but she had no intention of admitting that to her little sister who seemed to have a bit of a case of sister-worship going on.

'Go on, you must. He's like a film-star.'

'We're friends. I've got a boyfriend back home.'

'What's he like? Better looking than Cameron?'

Laurie pressed her lips together to stop the gurgle of amusement escaping. No one was better looking than Cameron. Having her sister think she was cool appealed. Rather than lie, she shrugged.

'How old is he? What's he called?'

'He's called Robert. He's thirty, and he works in computer sales.'

Siena's eyes widened. 'Wow. No trust fund then.' The grown up words were at odds with her youthful bounce.

''Fraid not. How about you? Do you have a boyfriend?'

'No, although Edouard's quite keen, but he's,' Siena gave an insouciant lift of her shoulders, 'a bit dull and can't ski to save his life.'

Laurie nodded gravely as if agreeing that that was a terribly important consideration in life.

'Maman would like me and Yves, his family own the estate that borders ours, to get together. I guess I probably will one day.'

That sounded sad but Siena seemed unperturbed by the thought.

'So are you at college? University?'

Siena's face clouded briefly. 'I thought I might like to go to fashion college but St Martins in London were a bit fussy. They wanted portfolios of work and baccalaureates or GCSE's and things. And they wanted you to be there all the time, which I thought was a bit strange. I mean you need a few weeks for Milan, Paris and London and then there's New York. How can you study fashion, if you don't go to all the shows?'

Laurie nodded, charmed by her sister's naivety. It seemed a fair point.

'And Maman said I would have missed the skiing season. There didn't seem much point. Where do you ski?'

'I don't.' Laurie tempered her answer with a smile, not wanting to embarrass her sister. 'I work and they're a bit sniffy about taking the whole skiing season off.'

'What a bore.' Siena bounced on the bed. 'Maman says you work in a library. That's very brave.'

Laurie frowned, trying to work out how on earth working in a library could possibly be seen as brave. What happened in libraries in France?

She had a sudden vision of herself guarding the front door of the library in Leighton Buzzard clad in armour with a sword drawn, carrying a large round shield.

'It must be very germy.'

'Germy?' Was that a French word?

'You know, all those people touching books and then you having to touch them.' Siena gave a gentle shudder.

'Right.' Laurie nodded, trying hard not to smile. Such a thing had never even occurred to her.

Suddenly Siena jumped up with a squeal. 'Look at the time.' She began rifling through the pile of clothes on the bed, before triumphantly pulling out a black bra. 'I knew it was here some-where.' She pulled it over her chest, patting herself and looking at herself in the mirror. 'Yep that's the right one.'

'Right, now tonight's quite formal. A few crown princes and minor royalty, possibly Mick, you know Jagger, Rolling Stones, and a captain of industry or two, they're always the dullest though. So I think we could emphasise your classic English rose beauty. Very Kate Winslet I think.'

The words were very grown up as if they were being repeated from a play or a film.

While saying this, Siena circled her. Then she leant forward scooped Laurie's hair up to reveal her neckline. 'Nice cut, where did you have this done? I'm getting a bit fed up with my hairdresser.'

Unable to resist it, Laurie casually answered as if she often flew to Paris just for a haircut, 'Marc at Galeries—

'Marc! My God, you're kidding. He's like, well it's impossible to get an appointment with him.' She pouted. 'Wait 'til I tell Maman.'

She sounded so put out, Laurie almost felt like apologising. Then like a butterfly flitting to the next plant, she was off again.

'My, you have lovely bone structure and you don't have my stupid nose.'

Laurie raised an eyebrow; the doll-like nose looked perfectly fine to her.

'It's too small. I look like an elf or something' She wrinkled the offending nose in disgust. 'No one takes you seriously if you look little and elfy.'

'Oh,' Laurie tried to digest all this information, but her head was starting to spin. Siena's mind did tend to leap about quite a lot.

'Nice place you've got,' said Laurie inanely, suddenly aware that she needed to make some conversation with her sister. 'So you live here … all the time?'

Siena eyes widened. 'Well of course, except when we're in the Paris apartment or at the ski lodge in Verbier. Where else would I live?'

Laurie shrugged. It seemed mean to say that some girls her age lived with friends and had jobs. Siena's pretty brow wrinkled in confusion and she shook her head. 'No, I live here with Maman and Harry. He's her latest husband. Very nice.'

Laurie bit back a surprised laugh. Siena made it sound so commonplace as if perhaps their mother changed her husband on a regular basis.

'Those jeans are awful. Where did you get them?' Siena changed gear with a startling turn of speed

'Next,' said Laurie, too shocked by her sister's forthright-ness to stand up to her rudeness. For some pig-headed reason she'd resisted putting on her lovely new white linen trousers this morning.

'Well they don't do you any favours. You've got quite good legs but the cut is all wrong for you. I always get my jeans from Diesel, I swear by their fit. We're the same shape – you should try them.' Her face lit up and she darted off, bringing to mind an erratic fairy.

Rummaging through a pile on the floor of the wardrobe, she pulled out a pair of denims waving them triumphantly like a trophy. 'Here. Try these on, while I find you a dress for tonight. I've got just the thing.'

'What? Now?'

'Yes.' Siena, began tugging enthusiastically at her zip.

'Whoa, I can manage.' Laurie pushed Siena's busy fingers away.

Siena winced, her big eyes shadowing. 'Sorry … I'm a bit … too…'

Laurie warmed to her sister. 'You're fine. But I can manage my own jeans. Honest.'

'Well hurry up then. I'm dying to see you in a decent pair of jeans. Honestly those ones are so—'

Laurie fixed her with a stern look.

'Sorry, big sister. You look all scary like that.' Siena giggled.

Laurie's heart turned to mush. Siena was trying to so hard to please her.

'Now shoes for tonight. What size are your feet?'

'Six … sometimes five and half.'

Siena looked crestfallen.

'No way. Are you sure?'

Laurie raised an eyebrow.

Siena giggled. 'Sorry. Damn, I'm only a five.' Then she brightened. 'It's OK, Maman's the right size. Be right back. You put those on.'

As she darted out of the room, Laurie took a breath. She felt exhausted. Siena was like a cheerful hummingbird, all action and colour.

She came back with a pile of boxes, stacked so high that all Laurie could see was her legs and a hand anchoring the top of

201

the pile. Her eyes widened as she spotted the words written on one of the boxes. She'd never even seen a pair of Jimmy Choos, let alone tried any on.

Two hours later she'd been rubbed, plucked, brushed and teased before Siena was finally happy enough with the result to let her take a look in the mirror. In that time, Laurie had completely fallen in love with her sister and was determined to ensure that she spent more time with her. Vivacious and generous, completely innocent, she was utterly spoilt but without a mean bone in her body. It was hard to believe that she'd grown up with Celeste or that she didn't remember Dad. He had loved her. Waves of pain rocked over Laurie as she thought of what he'd missed. Maybe that was why after the first few years he didn't try so hard. Celeste hadn't made visitation rights easy. It was easier to let go than feel the pain of loss all the time. As time went by it had been easy; just the two of them, her and Dad and in a way she'd liked it like that.

'Ta dah!' Siena allowed her to turn and look in the mirror. Laurie's eyes fixed on the anxious face of her sister bouncing up and down in the background in the reflection in the mirror. With a burst of love, she turned round and gave her sister a hug, feeling the tiny bones of her ribcage crunch as her sister returned the hug twice as hard. They stood like that for a minute.

'Thanks Siena. I've enjoyed this afternoon,' whispered Laurie.

'My pleasure, Sis,' beamed Siena. 'Now look what I've done.' She pushed her around to face the mirror.

The image stunned her. Siena had worked miracles. With clever shadowing and shading, she made her eyes look even bigger as well as smoky and sultry. Her cheekbones shone, dusted with highlighter which emphasised the shape of her face and her hair had been scooped up into some sort of up-do which then cascaded down at the back in a flurry of curls. She tossed her head from this side to that, entranced by the unfamiliar image.

Mandy had made her look better but Siena had exceeded that. Laurie could scarcely believe it was her in the mirror. For the first time ever that slight sense of inferiority lifted. A smile tilted her lips. Looking like this, she could certainly hold her own. She straightened and admired herself again.

'Wow,' she breathed not wanting to break the illusion that this glamorous creature was really her.

In her sister's borrowed dress, she looked beautiful. The designer sheath dress in midnight blue silk could have been made for her, it hugged every contour of her figure accentuating the length of her limbs and making her look long and lean. The neckline was far lower than she would have chosen but after a few furtive tugs trying to pull it a little higher over the deep V of her cleavage, she gave up. She pulled a wry face at herself in the mirror. It wasn't that bad really by current standards and there were bound to be women with far more exposed cleavage.

Laurie bit her lip. What would Cam think?

Nerves danced in the bottom of her stomach. He was used to well-groomed, glamorous women. Would he even notice? With a fierce pang, it hit her. She really wanted him to notice her.

Siena looked very very pleased with herself.

'Right, now it's my turn. I need to get ready.'

'Do you want me to stay and give you a hand?' asked Laurie, feeling a little more kinship with her sister. It was kind of Siena to have given up her time to make her look good and she hadn't even started getting ready herself yet.

Siena giggled. 'No, I've got this one. I'll see you later.'

Effectively dismissed, Laurie headed back to her own room, wondering if Cam would be in there.

The jeans tossed on one side of the bed, boxers on the floor and a pair of dark socks cast on the silk upholstered chair, suggested that he'd changed already. Did he have a dinner suit with him? She doubted it. Although with Cam, it didn't really matter what he wore.

In the bathroom, the mirror still had steam etched around

its borders, testament to the room's recent use. Lemon verbena permeated the still slightly damp air and a twinge of longing hit her stomach. L'Occitane shower gel. The one she'd used in Paris. Without thinking she crossed to the bottle and took a dreamy sniff. The familiarity of the smell reminded of her of how many hours they'd spent in such close proximity in the car.

Impatient with herself she pushed the bottle away. She just liked the smell. Clean, with a hint of citrus, fresh – she'd definitely have to buy some. Robert didn't go in for that sort of thing. An expensive con. Soap lasted much longer and did the same job for a fraction of the price.

Soap didn't smell this good though. No, she would buy herself some. Everyone could use a little spoiling now and then. She'd enjoyed her pampering session with Siena, even if many of the brand names of the vast array of cosmetics and hair products in gorgeous packaging had been unfamiliar. The designer names on the clothes had been very familiar, although that knowledge until now had all been gleaned from the pages of magazines. Gemma would be so impressed. Laurie had to admit – you got what you paid for. She couldn't bring herself to look again at the price tag on the Diesel jeans Siena had insisted she keep but they were lovely and Robert need never know just how much they cost. God he'd be horrified. And why did he have to keep intruding on her thoughts?

What would Cam think? He seemed so laid back. How much did he spend on his jeans? She couldn't imagine him worrying about it. If they fit, he'd buy them without worrying about the price tag or the designer tag.

That got her thinking. He did jeans a justice that was for sure. And she shouldn't be thinking like that but if ever a man was born to wear jeans, it was him. Her mouth went dry. Even with holes in the knees, he just looked so darned sexy.

And every other female on the planet thought so too.

At least tonight, thanks to Siena's handy work, she wouldn't look completely out of place next to him.

She was glad that Cam had agreed to come and knock for her when it was time to go down for the pre-dinner drinks. The formality of the instructions made her feel she was in a hotel rather than someone's home; even the hotel in Paris hadn't been this grand. She'd never seen quite so much gilt, satin and silk in one place before. The bed was piled high with watered silk cushions, and a plump satin appliquéd coverlet in pale blue which matched the blousy full length curtains with flounces and furbelows gracing the high sash windows. These were anchored to the walls as if they might fly away at any second with heavy brocade tie-backs cinching their middles.

As she pulled on her shoes, again borrowed, elegant dark blue satin with straps encrusted with tiny diamanté studs, the elegant heels sank into the fine velvet pile of the carpet leaving tiny spike footprints.

A stranger looked back at her from the mirror and she gave a mirthless smile. With her hair up and proper make-up for a change, she looked composed and elegant, almost as if she belonged here. She inclined her head, lifting her chin and assessing herself critically. Her jewellery was simple, a gold chain and small gold studs at her ears. Her long slim arms were unadorned but that simply drew attention to the stark, simplistic tailoring of the dress which did so much for her figure. She nodded pleased with what she saw. At least no one could see how much her stomach see-sawed and turned under the surface.

Meeting new people didn't faze her. Working in a library equipped you to deal with all sorts. She smiled, remembering some of the odder visitors she used to have to deal with. What worried her more was how many of the people present would know that she was the prodigal daughter. Did her mother ever talk about her? It wasn't as if Laurie ever talked about her or Siena.

Cam knocked at exactly five to seven and she opened the door.

The moisture dried in her mouth as it dropped open into a

surprised 'o'. She'd never seen him in anything so formal before. The black tuxedo jacket fit his broad shoulders to perfection and the crisp white studded shirt highlighted his tan. For once the stubble had gone, leaving his strong chin smooth and tempting and she could smell the aftershave he'd used. As the thoughts raced through her head, she felt herself swaying on the spot almost hypnotized by his appearance. She wanted to lean in and smell him, run a hand over that smooth masculine jawline. He'd robbed her of speech and her pulse rate shot up like a racehorse out of the blocks. She blinked at him and stood silent in the doorway just staring at him like a complete idiot.

Luckily he stared back, his eyes widening, the pupils darkening his iris. She registered his brief movement as he shifted on one foot and the duck of his Adam's apple as he swallowed.

A dart of satisfaction warmed her at the obvious appreciation in his sultry gaze, although it was also getting a tad embarrassing, no one had ever looked at her quite like that.

'You look nice,' she blurted out. An understatement if there ever was one.

Even the formal clothes couldn't tame the pirate and he gave her a distinctly predatory smile as he looked her up and down. 'And so do you. Very nice indeed.'

His smoky eyes were saying an awful lot more.

She blushed as her heart did that funny flippity flop in her chest. 'Shall we?' He held out his arm.

Looping her hand through his arm felt natural and she fell into step beside him wondering if he might be able to feel her hammering pulse through his jacket. Her fingers linked round smooth firm bicep.

'Thank you.'

He turned with a surprised expression. 'What for?'

'For coming to get me. Escorting me down.'

'All part of the service,' he smiled and for a moment she sobered, remembering why he was here.

The salon tinkled with light and laughter which they could hear as they approached. A huge chandelier sparkled from the ceiling, its crystals dancing with silver light. Lauren felt as if she was stepping onto a film set; none of it seemed quite real. The room was full of elegant, soignée people, immaculately groomed and presented. The men were to a man in identical black tuxedos and the women, all slim in beautifully smart dresses. Lauren was incredibly grateful for Siena's work; she felt the part on the outside, if not the inside.

Cam seemed to know the score because he steered her round to the far edge of the room where waiters were circulating with big silver trays of champagne in tall crystal flutes. With practiced ease, he snagged two glasses and presented one to her.

'To you, you look lovely and only I know you feel like a hen in a fox-house.'

She shot him a startled look in question. It was exactly how she felt but it was disappointing that her composed façade hadn't fooled him.

He leant forward and she felt his breath warm and soft on her neck making butterflies dance in her stomach. 'You were gripping my arm so hard I thought the blood-flow might stop any second and I'd have to have it amputated later,' he whispered in a teasing tone. 'You don't need to worry. You look … stunning is too commonplace … elegant, un-showy.'

'Oh,' she whispered back with an apologetic grin. 'Sorry, I'm a bit nervous.'

He scanned the crowd and nodded at someone across the room.

'Do you know him?' Laurie asked, her heart sinking, hoping that he wouldn't abandon her.

'Mmm.' Cam's voice was at odds with the impassive expression his face assumed. 'Can you see your mother anywhere?'

'Not yet.'

He smiled. 'It will be fine. We can leave whenever you like. Duty done. I'm not sure what Miles was playing at but he obviously had a reason for you coming here but it's up to you how long you

207

stay. As long as we pick up a postcard from the village and get it back to Ron, you're home and dry.'

She smiled in gratitude at his timely reminder. Of course she could but then she'd have to say goodbye already to Siena.

Her sister had been so keen to please this afternoon and they'd enjoyed real time together. It had been sweet of Siena to put all that effort into making Laurie look a million dollars. No one had ever made her feel that special before, prepared to pamper her, or go to all that trouble.

'Ah, Lauren. There you are.' Her mother appeared at her shoulder and then her expression turned coy. 'And Cam. Gosh just look at you, all gussied up. Don't you look rather wonderful?' A wistful expression crossed her face. 'Would you be a sweetie and grab me a glass of champagne?' She all but shoved him over towards the waiter on the other side the room.

'You're a dark horse.' Celeste observed, watching Cam saunter gracefully away. She sighed. 'Very handsome indeed; he reminds me of your father.'

Laurie rolled her eyes in disgust and to her horror realised her mother had caught her.

'I did love him very much once, you know.' Celeste's face had softened as she clutched at Laurie's arm.

Her petite hand felt warm against Laurie's skin. 'We were just all wrong for each other. No, I was all wrong for him. He knew. Yes lovely man, he knew. But would I be told?' Her fingers gripped more tightly. 'I thought love would be enough. At eighteen I had no clue. Greg,' her eyes misted for a second.

It was the first time Laurie had ever heard her speak of Dad with such fondness. 'He did love me. Enough to try and put me off. He was older and wiser but the more he tried the more I wanted to prove he was wrong.' Her mouth dipped down and she gave a mirthless unhappy laugh. 'And he was right, although I don't think being able to say 'I told you so,' gave him any pleasure. He was a good man.'

'So why did you leave him?' Urgency made Laurie's voice shrill and she glanced round hoping no one had heard.

'Because I wasn't a good woman.' Celeste looked thoughtful, her gaze distant as if lost in memories. Then her lips tightened as if in regret. 'Marrying for love isn't all it's cracked up to be. I wouldn't encourage any daughter of mine to marry for love. Especially when both parties can be incredibly stubborn.' Her voice was brittle, her eyes shadowed and for the first time it occurred to Laurie that maybe her mother's heart had been left a little bruised.

Laurie wondered if she was supposed to disagree at this point but couldn't bring herself to utter the words even as a platitude. Thankfully Cam returned at that moment.

'Here you go, Celeste.' His smile to Laurie was especially warm and she got the feeling he'd hurried so she wouldn't be left unprotected for too long. His fingers touched hers in a deliberate gesture as he handed the champagne to her mother with the other hand, a small lifeline as if to say, I'm here. She felt a surge of gratitude; this ordeal would have been a hundred times worse without him along.

'I was just saying to Laurie, you remind me of the girls' father.' Celeste was all coy and charming again, the brief moment of sincerity swept away in a second.

Laurie scowled at her mother.

Celeste let out a tinkling laugh, as if suddenly horribly aware she'd revealed too much of herself.

Lauren looked at her mother steadily as if daring her to carry on.

'Oh, you're not still bearing that little grudge. Honestly,' Laurie's mother smiled widely at Cam. 'When I left Greg, which was an incredibly difficult decision, I had to take Siena with me. You have to understand that coping with two children as a single parent … well,' she lifted her shoulders in a Gallic shrug, 'it was just impossible. And Laurie was at that difficult age.'

Laurie clenched her fingers into tight little balls hidden behind her thighs. A single parent shacked up with a multi-millionaire who paid for nannies and housekeepers, holidays across the world and apartments in three capital cities this side of the Atlantic alone.

'Besides, Siena was only young.'

And, thought Laurie, viciously, prettier, cuter and not so argumentative. She took a long gulp of champagne, almost emptying the glass.

'Siena thinks of Georges as her father. It was easier that way. I knew you'd be alright with your father.' Celeste pulled a sad face, which Laurie knew damn well was purely for Cam's benefit. 'It wasn't as if you weren't invited to see us *all* the time. He was so mean not letting you come to Barbados or on that trip to Lake Tahoe or for the summer in France.'

The same old justification had been trotted out many times before and Laurie knew there was absolutely no point explaining to her mother why she'd not been able to come but she was damned if she'd let Celeste get away with it in front of Cam.

'It was more to do with the fact that the summer you invited me to Barbados, I had GSCEs, the trip to Lake Tahoe coincided with my mock A-levels and the summer in France, I'd just started work. We only get four weeks holiday a year, sadly not three months.'

Celeste shook her perfect bob with an irritated toss of her head. 'The offer was always there. Your father was just being difficult. He could be so stubborn. Ah, here's Siena. Doesn't she look lovely?'

Laurie stared at her mother, wondering if she'd imagined the conversation just minutes earlier. Clearly her parents had loved each other for some brief impossible spell, although it was difficult to believe.

She turned to look at Siena, who was even more glossily fabulous than she had been earlier. Her dress, a waterfall of brilliant fuchsia silk, was far more showy and dramatic than Laurie's but then Laurie would never have had the confidence to carry the one shouldered style off. Siena's hair had now been scooped up into an elaborate style of curls and spirals captured by diamante clips, no – probably diamonds, which sparkled brilliantly in her blonde hair. Even her lustrous lipstick twinkled as if full of pearl dust.

Siena smiled, 'What do you think, Maman?' She spread her hands. 'Turn around Laurie, show Maman the full effect.'

'Another triumph, darling. You're getting very good at your little makeovers.' Celeste rolled her eyes good naturedly. 'And it makes a change from having to rescue the staff. Thank heavens. I do get fed up with having to retrieve my shoes from the servants.'

Disappointment flickered in Siena's eyes. Laurie leant forward and touched her hand.

'You did a fantastic job. I'm really grateful.'

'Pish, you've got good genes. Just takes a bit of time and effort.' Celeste's mouth narrowed.

Laurie lifted her glass and drained the rest of it in one.

'Oh look. There's Francois and Belle.' A happy smile settled on Siena's face as she reviewed the crowded room. 'I do love a party.' With a little wave of her hand, she glided off, diving into the fray. Her laugh rang out gaily as she was welcomed into a group of equally sparkling people.

Her mother smiled fondly after her and then turned to Laurie, the expression on her face suddenly chillier.

'You do look better, I'll say that. I ought to thank you for giving her something to do. Poor thing, she finds it dull here. There's more for her to do in Paris but Harry likes to be here for the summer.'

Laurie swallowed hard at the horrid lump that had just formed in her throat.

'Well I'm grateful for her time this afternoon. It was very kind of her.'

Her mother shrugged, 'I suppose.'

The lump slid down Laurie's throat and settled in her stomach.

'Now I must go and circulate. Enjoy yourselves.'

Laurie stared after her as she too disappeared into the crowd with a tinkling laugh.

'You OK?' asked Cam.

She nodded dully, feeling all kinds of fool. Had she just been a diversion for her sister?

211

'Let's grab you another drink? You might as well enjoy the champagne on the go.' Cam nodded at the black clad waiters circulating with trays of crystal glasses of bubbling white wine. 'If I'm not mistaken it looks like a Dom Perignon. Know anything about champagne?'

She shook her head which felt heavy. All her earlier elation had evaporated.

'Well you're about to find out. Come on.' He grabbed her hand and pulled her round the edge of the room.

Thank God for Cam; he had a knack of saying or doing the right thing at the right time. For someone who was supposedly so brusque and taciturn, he had an amazingly kind streak. Genuinely kind, she realised.

The champagne was definitely superior and Cam's determined conversation thawed out her feelings. She kept an eye open for Siena, but her sister was never still, darting from group to group, her smile brilliant and her laugh carefree.

'Do you know anyone?' He was so well-travelled, she couldn't believe he wouldn't.

'Know them, no. Know of some of them, yes. Usual hangers-on and freeloaders.' He pointed to a trio of loud and handsome young men. 'They hang around the racing circuit a lot. Fast cars and big trust funds.'

Gradually they began to integrate with some of the groups but it was only when Cam disappeared to go to the loo that she realised he hadn't left her side all evening. She smiled; he reminded her of an unruly Newfoundland dog, guiding her around the room.

For a moment she studied the gilded crowd.

'Madame.' A tall good looking man with floppy blonde hair falling over one eye stopped before her. 'I'm Christophe Baudelaire.' The heavily accented voice had a husky tinge to it and a lilt at the end of the sentence as if he expected her to know who he was. 'I know you from somewhere.' He looked deep into her eyes and took her hand.

Laurie had to press her lips hard together to stop a burst of laughter escaping. He took the cheese award for the night.

'I don't think so,' said Laurie ever so politely. 'I think I would have remembered.'

'I am sure we have, ma chère. How could anyone forget a beautiful woman like you?' His heavily accented voice should have been charming, but unfortunately all that Laurie could think was that what he'd just said was ridiculous.

But he didn't give up lightly. Now he stroked the inside of her wrist, treating her as if she was some femme fatale, when she was plain old Laurie Browne from Leighton Buzzard who'd scrubbed up rather well for one night only. Did he think it was supposed to be sensuous or seductive or something? It just made her feel weird.

'Cherie.' He leaned in and whispered in her ear, his breath warm. She squirmed.

'Ah there you are Laurie; I've been looking for you.' Cam's eyes bored into hers. She smiled, delighted to see him despite the disdain he showed in his eyes. He looked very disapproving as he glared down at Christophe. Surely he didn't think she'd been encouraging the younger man.

'Ah the chauffeur,' sniped the Frenchman, sliding an arm around Laurie's shoulder and leaning nonchalantly on her.

Cam raised an eyebrow.

'Oh, he's not really … I mean the car's mine … well sort of … '

Christophe lifted a playful eyebrow. 'You are the owner of the car! You must tell me all about it.'

Laurie raised her shoulders. 'Well …'

Cam glared at her and before she could say another word, wheeled around and disappeared into the crowd that parted as he approached.

'We're co-drivers really.' She stared after him. Surely he wasn't cross that he'd been mistaken for the hired help. Not a man of his experience and worldly sophistication. Ridiculous.

'So the car. It is yours? And how much would you sell it for?'

'Sell it?'

'Yes, it is a beautiful car but,' he shrugged, 'not a car ordinaire. It is a collector's car. You do not seem … the type.'

'Type?' Maybe because English clearly wasn't his first language or the champagne had gone to her head, but she found herself saying. 'Our acquaintance is hardly long-standing enough for you to know my type. I'm not sure quite how you've come about your conclusion.'

It took a few seconds for him to compute and translate the stilted phrases before charming confusion spread across his face. 'Please mademoiselle, I have been talking to your sister Siena.'

Laurie smiled, pleased that her instinct to dislike him had been correct. He'd lied, pretending he didn't know who she was. Genuinely a creep.

'She tells me you have a very boring life in England. A boring *bibliotech*. I can't imagine you would drive to work in such a car. This car is worth a lot of money. You wouldn't have to work at this boring job anymore. You could be like your sister.' He waved his glass at the opulent surroundings, still smiling like a circling vulture.

Laurie drained her glass in one sharp toss, the bubbles tingling her nose. 'I can't imagine you know anything.'

The pleased with himself smile faltered as her words penetrated. The boyish face crumpled in confusion, he obviously wasn't used to people saying no to him.

She stalked off. When had Siena said this to him? Her jaw locked as she gritted her teeth and fought against the black hole of disappointment and stupidity threatening to consume her. She couldn't and wouldn't believe that Siena would say anything that mean. He had twisted it in translation. How dare Christophe Baudelaire presume to know anything about her life? And how dare he assume that she was too ordinary to want to drive a car like that?

214

Vicious pride burst like a blood vessel in her heart leeching a bitchy satisfaction. The car was hers. And if he was the last person breathing, she wouldn't sell to him.

Grabbing another glass of champagne she headed out towards the double doors to the terrace beyond.

'Sorry to abandon you. It was that or punch the little shit.'

Looking to her left she saw Cam leaning on the balustrade, a long glass of golden lager in his hand. He'd dispensed with his jacket, undone his tie and now with his rumpled hair, looked much more him.

'I wish you had,' she said with a rueful smile.

'Why?' He straightened as if ready to defend her.

'Because he was a weasel. Wants to buy my car. Apparently it wouldn't suit my lifestyle.'

'A car like that doesn't suit anybody's lifestyle. It owns you.' Cam settled back against the balustrade. She went over to join him, staring out at the view.

'Celeste has a pretty nice lifestyle here,' she sighed. 'Imagine living here.' She sipped thoughtfully before gazing at the straw-coloured liquid with its fine columns of bubbles dancing to the surface. It was a very long way from home. 'No wonder she left Dad. This certainly beats a three bedroom terrace house, it would fit on this entire terrace.'

'What happened?'

'Dad was Uncle Miles' insurance broker, very good looking, steady and sensible. Miles said they were very in love to start with but once me and Siena came along, she got bored with the drudgery of it all compared to what her brother had. Fantastic lifestyle, glamorous, celebrity friends and Merryview. She started spending more and more time there. I was at school and Siena wasn't, so she would take Siena with her and then she met Georges there, he was the husband before Harvieu. Not quite as rich but richer than Dad.'

'So she ran off with him.'

215

'Yup.'

'How come you and Siena were split up?'

His bluntness punched into her. 'Normally people ask that in a much more roundabout way? Did you not want to live with your mother? Or something like that.'

'Remember, living dangerously is what I do,' he said with a charming smile.

His honesty after the artful twists and turns of conversation with Celeste was a welcome balm.

'Like I said I was already in school. Settled. Siena was small enough to be an accessory.'

'But surely your dad wanted both of you.'

'He did.' Laurie bit her lip. 'But Celeste gave him an ultimatum. One or none.'

'What?'

'She said if he didn't let her take Siena, she'd sue for custody for both of us. Poor Dad, he didn't know what was for the best. With me at school and Siena away so often with Celeste, in the end he decided Siena was so young she'd miss mum more than him. He was devastated though.'

'Poor Siena.'

'Poor Siena,' Laurie looked around at the opulent surroundings.

'Yeah. It must be pretty dull for her.'

'Dull?' she echoed disbelieving.

'There's not a lot to do. Fancy rooms and a big house aren't good company. It's all very formal. I can't imagine living here; it's more like a hotel. You couldn't put your feet on the sofa that's for sure. Miles from the nearest town, no neighbours. No wonder your sister is bored out of her brain. She lives in a gilded prison. This lot are a bunch of freeloaders. They'll move onto the next party after this.

'You would never have been happy if your mother had brought you to live here.'

In that moment, she hated Cam for his perception.

216

Like a child she wanted to shout, 'Yes I would,' and stamp her feet. Her jaw locked with tension, holding in the sheer fury that rocked through her. She didn't want his deadly accurate insight, or him overturning everything she'd hugged close for all these years.

Cam cupped her face in his hand. 'You could have come to see her at any time in all these years. You chose not to. Why not?' The brutality of his words belied the gentleness of his touch.

She flinched as his insight punched hard. Tears welled up but she wouldn't give him the satisfaction. How dare he? She clenched her fingers, feeling the joints strain.

She'd been so sure all these years. So utterly sure. She had had the rough end of the stick. Left behind. Her sister chosen instead of her. It had shaped her. Dictated the way she lived her life, measured out the parameters for her. She did the right thing. She didn't leave people. She didn't take risks.

And now, here was Cam, tearing all that away.

Without a second thought she tossed her champagne in his face.

Chapter 19

He still had the diplomatic touch then. Rather than follow her back into the thronging ballroom, he slipped down the terrace stairs and skirted the house towards the courtyard at the back. The Ferrari gleamed long and low in the moonlight. He felt in his pocket for the keys and let himself in. Stretching out in the leather seat, he gazed through the windscreen up at the moon. A clear night.

It was tempting to try and sleep here rather than return to the room but it would be best to wait for a few hours, let her settle and hopefully fall asleep before he went back. He regretted being so honest now but he could see there would never be any relationship between Laurie and her mother. He thought of his own. Slightly batty, constantly losing things, bossy and demanding, particularly when he didn't text more than once a week to let her know he was still alive. Not perfect, he grinned, in fact quite often bonkers, but he loved her and knew she loved him. Wasn't that what counted? Celeste would never love anyone but herself.

'Miles, Miles. What were you thinking, old mate?' He shook his head at his own fancifulness, waiting a moment for the old boy's reply. 'I know you were probably trying to mend fences ... but I think you just made things a whole lot worse.' He pushed his hair back from his face. What a God awful mess.

He had to hand it to Laurie – she handled most things.

Champagne in the face aside, there'd been no histrionics, just calm acceptance.

She was out of her depth here though. Celeste would sell her down the river as soon as look at her and Siena, while sweet enough, had nothing but her looks to recommend her. The gilding of the lily tonight had given Laurie added confidence. It was just a shame she didn't realise that this lot wouldn't recognise all the merits that she had in spades such as integrity, loyalty and duty.

The bedroom was in darkness when he returned but in the moonlight pouring through the tall windows, he could make out the shape of Laurie on the far right of the bed. He'd stayed out as long as he could, hoping she'd be deeply asleep when he came back. The house was full and with the low level ache his shoulder had acquired from driving the car, he was not going to mess about trying to find a sofa for the night. They were grown adults, besides they'd already shared a room and a bed. In fact if memory served she'd pretty much seen everything there was to see already.

He crept into the bathroom and stripped quickly, leaving on his briefs and grabbing a T shirt. Listening to her breathing, he could tell she wasn't asleep but trying hard to pretend to be. Best leave her be and pretend with her.

He slipped between the covers. The king-size bed was plenty big enough although he could feel the heat from her body where she'd warmed the bed. It brought back memories of when he'd been married. Coming home to a warm body had definitely been one of the perks. Not sex, but the quiet warmth in the middle of the night, the companionship of knowing someone else was there. With a surprised jolt he realised that while he didn't miss Sylvie, he did miss the companionship of being married. The pull of Laurie's warmth made him long for something he hadn't realised he needed.

Who was he kidding? He did not need that complication in life and certainly not with someone like Laurie. If ever there was a commitment babe who wanted to stay at home and hearth it was her.

She moved and he felt her body shift on the mattress. She wasn't asleep, he could tell. The pattern of her breathing just wasn't quite right. Not quite snuffly and unself-conscious enough. Despite everything he found himself wondering about how she was feeling. Christ, it had to be tough. Celeste had the warmth of an icicle and how did it feel to see your sister ensconced like a princess in a fairy castle when you'd been scrubbing the hearth back home for several years? Even if the hearth had the warmth of home. He got the feeling Laurie didn't quite see it like that.

Laurie sighed again. Her mind raced as she lay stiffly next to Cameron. He was probably asleep by now. Carefully she turned to the bedside table to check the time. Ten past three, only fifteen minutes since the last time she'd checked. She sighed again. It was as if she was chasing the elusive tendrils of sleep which were always one step ahead out of her grasp. A bit like her mother and sister. Bitterness washed through her mind, a bitterness that normally in the daylight hours she was able to push away. Here in the wee small hours, it overwhelmed her. What had she done so wrong that she had been left behind? For a small part of today, she'd felt like she fitted in but as the evening had worn on, the illusion had faded. An illusion she had let mesmerise her because she wanted it to be true. In her borrowed clothes and finery, she'd felt like a poor relation.

She sighed again at her stupidity and felt a silent self-pitying tear slide down her cheek. Sniffing, she wiped it impatiently away.

A warm hand nudged hers and then covered her fingers, the palm of his hand lying heavy across hers. 'Are you OK?'

She started. 'Sorry, did I wake you? She'd been trying so hard to keep still and not fidget.

'No … well, not really.' She could hear the amusement in his voice. 'So what's wrong? Why the heavy sighs?'

'Stupid thoughts really. Feeling sorry for myself. Sorry … I threw the champagne over you. I should have thrown it over that awful Christophe.'

'I forgive you for wasting damn good champagne and I'm sorry I upset you. That wasn't my intention.'

'I know. I'm sorry … it all just got …'

'Want to tell me about it?'

'Not really.' Now she wasn't really talking to Cam, just talking out loud. Being in the dark with him made it a lot easier to talk, almost as if the shadows swallowed her embarrassment.

'If I say it out loud … what I feel … it will show just how stupid I've been.' She was silent for a moment and then the words spilled out. 'I shouldn't have come here. What the hell was I thinking? I knew it would be like this. I knew I wouldn't fit in. That's why my mother didn't take me.' She was unsuccessful in swallowing the sudden sob that overwhelmed her.

'Hey,' Cam's warm arm slipped under her and pulled her to him.

Warm tears seeped down her face as his gentle move breached her dam. He'd shown more feeling towards her in two short weeks than her mother ever had. The realisation made her start to cry harder.

'My mother left me behind. She took Siena and why wouldn't she? And it's not Siena's fault that my mother loved her more. But it seems so unfair. She has all this and I don't fit. And I know its shallow and I shouldn't care. I stayed with Dad and I did the right thing … I know I did. I should feel morally superior. The better person. I know I am …' she sighed, 'but do you know what? It feels like crap. Like a stupid fairy tale cliché. Except I'm not that helpless and I'm not a victim, I shouldn't feel bad because … all this, it isn't important. It's frivolous, shallow … and I do … and I hate myself for caring about this crap.

'The worst thing is that I thought spending that time with Siena was special and I was getting to know her. Starting to build a relationship with her, but then it turns out she's so bored, she does that with everyone. Nothing to do with me, I'm a new guinea

221

pig one up from the servants.'

Cam laughed.

The bastard laughed out loud, although he gave her a squeeze so she could forgive him.

'Can you lay it on any thicker? Christ Laurie. Give yourself a break. You were dealt a lousy deal. Your mother's a cold fish. Calculating, totally self-absorbed. I think you probably had a lucky escape. At least you had your father. You built a proper relationship with him. You had Miles. Maybe you should be pitying Siena. Yes, maybe the makeover thing is her thing. What she does. But I think she enjoyed spending time with you. From what I saw she took a lot of time and trouble … you could have been dressed and made-up like a Barbie doll but actually, you looked like you. She'd either chosen incredibly well or she'd managed to find out quite a lot about what you like and feel comfortable with. You looked self-assured, comfortable *and* confident. Don't be so hard on yourself and on her. I think Siena has talent …'

Laurie snorted.

'No really … and she used it to great effect. Because she wanted to please you. She spent time with you, working out what made you tick, finding out about you. She must have done. Everything – the dress, the make-up, the hair … they were … they were you.'

'And what? You're some kind of fashion guru now?' Laurie laughed bitterly, although she recognised the truth in his words. Siena's own dress had been showy, jewel bright and perfect for her. Many of the outfits at the party had been too flashy and too obvious for Laurie's taste and yet Siena had managed to choose exactly the dress she would have chosen herself, had she had the money or time to find such a dress. Even the colour. And for all her forthright comments about the cut of her jeans, Siena hadn't tried to press anything revealing, brightly coloured, too short, too tight.

He laughed, 'You know what? I do know a thing or two about women's fashion … My time as an international playboy, remember. So yeah I do know what I'm talking about.'

222

Laurie lay back and thought about what he'd said and smiled in the darkness.

She turned. 'Thanks Cam,' she whispered and rolled onto her side to give him a quick kiss.

At the same moment he moved, his breath whispered in her hair and instinctively she tipped her head up. In the dark, she could just make out the shadow of his head.

She wasn't sure who kissed who first, but the tentative touch of his lips on hers sent her system into hyper-alert. Every nerve ending seemed to come alive, tingling with joy and sensation. She let out a tiny gasp as the feelings fizzing through her threatened to blow a fuse.

The gentle kissing carried on, Cam's hand shaping her face as those mobile lips explored her face. She sank back into the pillow under the delicious onslaught. Gentle, so gentle. See? Someone wanted her. She rose into the kiss, her tongue testing as it touched his lips. She felt him buck in surprise and then a growl as he deepened the kiss, his tongue teasing out hers. Excitement hissed in the pit of her stomach.

Her heart had charged off without her and there was a buzz from her stomach downwards causing an insistent ache between her legs.

When he pulled away, she felt bereft and blindly pulled him back to her, cringing inside at her neediness. He felt so right.

He pushed her gently away.

A pang pierced her heart. She couldn't take another rejection. Not now.

'Laurie,' he sighed as she held on to him. His head dipped again, coming back to nibble at her lips. She sank into the mattress, pulling him with her, determined to lose herself in him. The length of his body pressed into hers. She could feel his arousal against her and urged her hips against him.

'Laurie,' he gazed down at her urgently. 'We shouldn't do this.'

She closed her eyes, wanting to shut his eyes out. In the dark they were inky pools of insistence trying to instil sense into her but her libido didn't want to listen.

'Laurie,' he whispered again, a hint of desperation in his voice, his forehead dropping to hers. She felt the touch and for a moment they both stilled, connected in a moment of silence. She was conscious of the warmth and weight of his body draped over hers, like a protective blanket, surrounding her.

His warmth drew her in; she didn't want to relinquish it. She savoured the touch of his forehead against hers, holding on to the moment of closeness. They stayed like that until both their hearts stopped pounding, their breathing easing.

'Please don't leave me.'

He kissed her again on her nose this time and slid to one side, taking her with him, one arm sliding under her. He just held her, neither of them saying a word. Surprisingly, exhausted perhaps by the storm of tears, she felt herself relax and could feel herself dozing off, cocooned in Cam's arms.

She woke to a dual feeling of elation and dread and squeezed her eyes more tightly shut as if that might stop her from facing the day and the consequences of last night. What had she done?

Kissing Cam had been sublime and oh so wrong. She still felt little shivers of wanton pleasure scuttle down her back at the thought of those teasing kisses, his mobile lips and strong, hard body.

There was no movement beside her and she inched an eye open to take a look at Cam. Her heart stuttered for a moment as the memories resurfaced brilliant and golden in her head. He looked absolutely glorious, lying abandoned in sleep, the black curls spread across the pillow, his arm thrown up behind his head. Like her own personal fallen angel. Lust snaked in the pit of her stomach as she drank in the sight of him, which she immediately tamped down with a fervent sense of shame.

Now was not the time to admit to the fierce and dazzling

224

attraction that she'd felt from the moment she'd seen him in the church. Then, she had the protection of impossibility. A man like that wouldn't enter her sphere. Now, everything had changed and she couldn't deny the sizzle of fascination.

Never in her life had she been tempted to be unfaithful to Robert. Not even considered it. Never even thought she could be capable of it. And here she was the morning after almost being unfaithful, clutching an illicit well of happiness. If Cam hadn't put the brakes on … well, she knew exactly what would have happened.

Shame washed over her as she thought of Robert. She really had to make a decision about him. If she genuinely cared about him, the sort of stick with forever feelings, then she wouldn't be in bed with another man. Certainly not kissing another man, with so much enjoyment.

'If you think any louder, you'll take the roof off,' observed Cam and she started as she realised his green eyes were studying her, the usual amused look on his face.

Shyness gagged her and a deep blush rose up her chest suffusing her face with a rosy glow. Great, she probably looked like a complete idiot. Cam probably did this sort of thing on a regular basis, no wonder he looked so bloody relaxed. Mr I-Can-Have-Any-Woman-I-Want.

She had no idea of post one-night-kissing etiquette, because this was surely what it was, but Cam looked well-versed in it. The only thing she could do was act as casually as he was and pretend it was nothing out of the ordinary. She didn't want him to see her lack of sophistication. She'd just brazen it out. Pretend this was perfectly normal and she could handle it.

'You blush rather beautifully,' he said huskily stretching, turning on his side and lifting himself up onto his elbow.

Unable to help herself she stared at him, mesmerised by the promise and sleepy desire in those raw green eyes and the slow smile as he took in her flushed face and mussed hair. God she probably looked a complete sight, puffy-eyed with make up everywhere.

Unable to say anything she couldn't pull her eyes away from his. 'You OK?'

She nodded, swallowing hard. She could do this. Act grown up. Worldly. He probably did this all the time. It was new territory for her. Spontaneous wasn't part of her vocabulary. Normally everything was planned. The first time she and Robert had spent the night together, it had been planned weeks in advance. A company do with a hotel room thrown in. She winced at the memory of Robert's formality, asking if she'd mind sharing a hotel room. That was despite going out for six months and even then they hadn't had sex. And here she was having known Cam less than a week and if it hadn't have been for him, she would have quite happily shagged the living daylights out of him. She quite liked the phrase. Truth was, she still felt horny just looking at him.

It was just chemistry. Raging hormones leading her astray.

What would it be like to have sex with Cam? The insistent thought needled its way into her head. This might be the only chance she ever got to find out. Which would she regret more, sleeping with him or not sleeping with him?

His chest was lightly dusted in hair, his muscles defined. His skin deeply tanned. Further down his lean stomach a happy trail led downwards. Her mouth went dry and she blushed as she realised he was watching her intently.

The sensible thing would be to turn back the sheets, stand up and nonchalantly walk across the room to the bathroom, with the words, 'I'm going to take a shower,' instead she leaned in towards him and softly planted her lips on his.

He was a bad person. A really bad person. Taking advantage of Laurie when she was clearly confused and unhappy. Last night he'd tried really hard to do the right thing. He hadn't meant to kiss her and still wasn't sure where the instinct that propelled him into it had come from. The despair in her voice had sounded so wounded; he couldn't not reach out to her, to soothe, to help.

226

The catch in her voice as she tried to hold back the sob had been heart-breaking and twisted his gut in a way that he hadn't felt for a long time. He wanted to hold her, wanted to help her. He'd only meant to reassure her, remind her that she was a special person, that she shouldn't define herself by her mother and sister's standards.

Her tongue's insistent demand had pulled a totally unexpected response from him. The desire he felt was different from anything else he'd felt before. Was that because it was tinged with guilt? Normally the women he slept with knew the score, divorced and not looking to commit anytime soon. Laurie's sweetness, the shy hesitancy in that early kiss which then became all woman had thrown him.

This morning was different. The stirring in his groin at the first sight of her this morning turned into a raging hard-on. Laurie felt soft and warm, smelt fragrant. This time he didn't think he could stop. This time he didn't want to.

Hell, yeah, he was a bad person but with Laurie's soft hands stroking her way downwards, he couldn't stop his hips lifting or his hands smoothing across her nipples which were eager and ready for his attention. He kissed her with a groan. No doubt about it, he was on his way straight to hell.

Her hair, where her head nestled into his collar bone, smelt of flowers and she felt soft and pliant. So did he. At some point the sex had tipped the needy, passionate and hungry scale. Did she feel like him? Wrung out and sated, bone-deep relaxed and incredibly content. She hadn't said anything ... well not coherent, for the last half hour. Who'd have thought she'd got such a throaty purr on her? He smirked to himself. Laurie was full of surprises but he thought perhaps she'd surprised herself more.

He heard her sigh. Uh-nuh. Here it came? The regrets and guilt. Neither of them had given a thought to good old Robert.

She turned in his arms and looked up at him, her eyes sleepy

227

but with a very wicked twinkle in them. A hidden tiger.

'Wow,' she grinned at him. 'I'm …' she wrinkled her brow and he could almost see the thought processes, as her facial expressions flitted through a series of phases. What was he going to get? Doubts? Embarrassment?

He should have known better. She had an amazing capacity to surprise him.

He got honesty.

'Wow. That was … I know I shouldn't say this. I should be all sophisticated and cool about this but … you know I don't do this sort of thing … well, like ever. You're very good.' She gave him a cheeky grin and he was amused by how pleased she was with herself. 'Plenty of practice, I guess. Me not so much but … well that was a whole new ball …' she giggled at her unintended innuendo, '… game.' She sighed again. 'I wondered what all the fuss was about. Thought maybe it was me. You know … being frigid.' She winced. 'Robert … God I shouldn't really be mentioning him now, should I? But … that's what he said once. So I never feel I can say no, even if I don't you know … really feel like it … which is probably why it's not … you know.' She stopped and he realised embarrassment fuelled her sudden chattiness. 'But that was …' She gave him a candid look, and then her gaze slid in blatant approval down his torso. Her expressive face had desire stamped all over it. '… Amazing. Is it … sorry you wouldn't know … I wanted to say is it always like that?'

He laid a finger on her lips to stop her and couldn't help the temptation to stroke her lips and dip his finger into her mouth. Immediately her tongue touched the pad of his forefinger igniting a flame of desire that shot to his groin.

His hand smoothed the skin along her cheekbone. 'No Laurie, it's not always like that … in fact, it's almost never like that.'

'Really?' Her eyes lit up and he kissed her, suddenly wanting to put it to the test. He covered her warm skin with his body as her hands circled his, one hand snaking down his back.

'Do you know you have the most delicious butt?' she muttered and then gave herself up to his kisses.

She was still grinning from ear to ear like an overactive Cheshire Cat.

'Feeling pleased with yourself?' he teased as he emerged from the shower, towelling his hair dry, wrapped in nothing but a towel around his waist.

God he was absolutely gorgeous and she was a complete goner. Excitement fizzed through her veins and she firmly tamped down the 'what have I done' thoughts. She could do regret later. Somewhere in the heat of it all, she'd decided to abandon all her principles and go with the flow of lust rampaging through her veins. She felt like a born-again virgin. As if she'd only just discovered sex and it was a lot more fabulous than she'd thought possible.

And here in this completely over-the-top house ... none of this was real, Leighton Buzzard, the library, Robert ... it all seemed so far away. Another life. Here she was so far removed from her reality that she conveniently ignored any of the guilty feelings waiting at the barricades.

Breakfast was ... well weird. Obviously the cool people didn't do breakfast. So it was just her and Cam. After the intimacy they'd shared in the bedroom, she was relieved that he treated her exactly the same as he had done before. No touches or kisses. Back to normal again. Just ... friends she guessed, which suited her fine. The sex had been amazing and she was quite, she grinned to herself, satisfied with that. Parts of her tingled that hadn't ever tingled before.

The dining room with its vast table reminded her of a stretch limo. It was so long, it could seat all the statesmen of Europe. White damask cloths lined the table with regular intervals of posies of yellow and white tulips. Sideboards at either end of the room were weighed down with silver salvers of charcuterie and cheese, fruit, rolls and croissant. The extravagant buffet wouldn't have been out of place at a five star hotel and Laurie found herself wondering if it was always like this.

'Quite a spread,' murmured Cam helping himself to black coffee and a healthy portion of Weetabix.

Looking at the delicious selection of salamis, meats and cheese along with the mouth-watering array of bread rolls, she wondered if it would be rude to help herself and make up sandwiches to take in the car … Oh God that was exactly the sort of thing that Robert would do. And he was being shelved to the very back of her mind as a problem to solve another day. Her new motto, Carpe diem. Time for her to seize the day. Exactly as Miles would have wanted her to.

She should ask Celeste to have her cook prepare a packed lunch when they left tomorrow. That was the way things round here were probably done, and no doubt it would arrive in a proper wicker hamper complete with wine and crystal glasses. The sort that should be stored on the running board of one's car.

'So where do you think everyone is?' She looked at the long table. It was too wide to sit opposite Cam. It felt as if they were in a hotel rather than someone's home. No host, no other guests, no sign of anyone. She would sit next to him, even though being near him made her skin buzz.

'I think we're unfashionably early … its only 8.30.'

'Yeah, I guess this lot don't have to worry about getting to work on time.' She smiled to make it clear it didn't bother her and then realised, actually it didn't. She really didn't care about these people and what they thought of her. She couldn't help the grin that split her face. The thought liberated her.

Cam looked puzzled for a second and then shrugged.

'You think they're any happier than you?'

Odd choice of words. Why hadn't he simply asked if she thought they were happy?

'What do you mean 'any happier'? I'm fine. I'm happy.' She

sounded shrill now. Defensive. He'd spoilt the mood.

Cam's face looked guarded for a moment. 'I didn't mean you were … unhappy, just that …' His Weetabix suddenly commanded an awful lot of attention.

She stared at him suspiciously, feeling tension gathering in her chest. 'So I'm not unhappy but you think I'm 'un' something.'

Cam sighed and wriggled in his seat like a fish caught on a hook.

'Maybe I'm talking out of turn but … I actually … I don't think you are happy.'

Laurie bristled. He didn't know her. Just because they'd had … she didn't want to go there, how dare he presume he suddenly knew her?

'Of course I'm happy … why shouldn't I be? I've got everything I want. A home, a job I enjoy, a boyfriend, engaged to be …'

Shit, she hadn't meant to say that.

Cam raised an eyebrow. Laurie coloured immediately. So she was a bad person, sleeping with him but that didn't add up to being unhappy. Besides everything was different now. Today was a clean slate. A fresh start and every other cliché she could summon.

'What I meant was … I am … I'm happy.' She glared at him. 'Just because I'm not doing cartwheels all the time and singing "oh what a beautiful morning" doesn't mean I'm not happy. Or content. I am happy.' She pinched her mouth closed tamping down her fury at his supposition.

Cam stared at her for a long moment and she looked down to fiddle with the tail of her croissant. When she looked back up, he still looked at her and now she felt like that fish wriggling on the hook, unable to get off. Stuck under the probing stare which seemed to look right through her.

Her mouth curled in petulance and even though it was being childish she couldn't stop herself.

'Define happiness then, Mr I'm-an-expert-all-of-sudden.'

Cam's lips curved into a sad smile. 'I can't put it into words but I know when I see it, and when I look in your eyes, it's not there.'

'Really?' She raised an eyebrow and looked directly into his eyes.

He flushed. 'Aside from ...'

Cam embarrassed? It was kind of cute. Then his expression turned grave and suddenly she felt very small.

'I think we're probably best off agreeing to disagree,' she snapped, gulping back a large slug of tea. 'I'm going for a walk.'

Chapter 20

The garden opened out before her, with a path leading down to the right of the house to what looked like orchards, a walled kitchen garden to the left and in front of her a series of formal terraces which unfolded from the back of the house, trimmed with box hedges and ornate beds of flowers around statues. At the bottom in a large symmetrical and pristine lawn sprouted a marble fountain with intricate streams of water dancing in the distance.

She chose the formal garden, drawn by the tumble of water and the knowledge that from there she would get a good view of the house.

Everything was immaculate and perfect. Each hedge trimmed to precision, identical in height and width. She had visions of an army of gardeners furnished with rulers and nail scissors, drilled to prune with precision.

She couldn't imagine Celeste or Siena gardening or attacking a lawn with an ancient Flymo, its electrical lead taped together because they'd run over it so many times and cut the cable. She smiled to herself. Lawn mowing wasn't her forte, but she'd spent some happy times in the garden with Dad. Following his instructions as she weeded his beloved vegetable patch, watching him laugh when he realised she'd pulled up all the carrot seedlings because she thought they were weeds. How could she forget how he'd proudly cooked his first batch of home grown veg? Roast chicken, roast potatoes and fresh broccoli from the garden and ... the odd curled-up things that floated in the gravy. As they'd cut into the tiny florets, they'd released hundreds of tiny caterpillars which had been boiled alive.

Dad branched out into tomatoes after that. Smiling to herself she walked along the path heading towards the fountain. They'd had to go into chutney production because they'd had so many. There were still some damn jars of chutney in the cupboard which had to be at least five years old. They were never going to get eaten and despite Robert's impatience with the amount of shelf space they took up, she couldn't bring herself to throw them away.

Her dad had been one in a million, even if he'd overlooked buying her girl's clothes and signing her up for ballet lessons.

Fine spray danced on the morning air as the powerful streams of water shot upward, firing a million tiny droplets which caught the sun and shimmered with rainbow colours. Her face tingled at the touch of the cold mist of water but instead of drawing back, she went forward, tilting her head and relishing the feeling of freshness against warm skin.

The thunder of the water roared, thousands of gallons pumping upwards, flurries and jets dancing in a finely choreographed routine. Her ears reverberated with the steady rush of the jets and the pitter-patter of droplets bouncing the choppy surface. So many noises, so much movement. She wanted to hold out her hands and embrace the morning. Do a twirl for the sheer enjoyment.

The fountain was surrounded by stone benches, each supported by carved scrolls. She chose one that faced the house and sat down, the sun warm on her back, and studied the formal symmetry of the building with its windows identical in shape, evenly spaced across the wall and each of the panes of glass parallel like bars.

Cam's words of last night came back to her. A gilded prison.

Time stopped for a moment, as if fractured. She blinked hard trying to clear her head. Cam. Dad. Miles. Celeste. Robert. Everything felt off kilter, like a globe falling off its axis.

Fighting against a sense of panic, she closed her eyes. It made things worse. Then when she opened her eyes, it was like a kaleidoscope settling with a completely new view bringing with it a brilliant shaft of sunlight penetrating and illuminating the dark corners.

Her head ached from the revelations that flooded through.

Growing up here would have been very different, looking at Siena's life; if she was honest, she probably would hate it.

The only person that had limited her horizons was herself but that had been her choice. She was free in a way Siena would never be.

She had independence. A home, albeit modest, but hers.

With so much focus on what her mother hadn't given her, she'd missed seeing what her father had given her.

He had instilled the right principles and set the road map. Some of her choices had been stubborn because she wanted to prove a point. Like not going to university … for all the wrong reasons. At the time, she thought she'd been showing fidelity and loyalty to her dad. Proving she wasn't like her mother. Wanting to stay close to her father. What'd she'd done was close herself to opportunities.

Clever old Miles. He'd seen it all so clearly and had left her this journey.

She stared down at the engagement ring.

Which brought her to Robert. She lodged her chin in her hands and hunched over her knees. Robert. She looked at the ring again. The emeralds and the setting were ugly. She hated it. Recalling his proposal, she winced with embarrassment. Why hadn't she been braver? Dad would have asked, 'Are you sure?' Thrown up considerations and questions.

She didn't want to marry Robert, she didn't even want to live with him any more … her eyes had been opened to a wider world that she wanted to explore without Robert … cramping her style.

When had she started going through life without asking any

questions? Accepting things? It was as if she'd been sleepwalking through life ever since her mother had left. Not precisely happy but not unhappy. Cam had got it so right.

And like Sleeping Beauty she'd been awakened by a kiss … she touched her lips … and what a kiss. She bit her lip. Cam. She owed him an apology.

A sigh escaped her as she let herself relive this morning. The warm slide of Cam's body over hers, his scent, and the unbearable ache between her thighs that he'd stroked away.

It was just sex, but it had felt so good. She hadn't felt that good in … well, forever.

Feeling she'd conquered a particularly difficult mountain, she sat on the bench and contemplated her surroundings, thinking hard about the possibilities of the future. She stayed there for an hour, basking in the sun and her new found knowledge.

'Cam?'

Laurie's voice was hesitant behind him and he ducked out from under the bonnet and turned round. Her face was flushed and she looked as if she'd made some amazing discovery, her hands moving at her sides with restless energy. Despite his good intention to ease back on things with her, desire shot through him as it brought to mind her beneath him in the bed just hours ago, pink and breathless, the same hands clenching and unclenching at the sheets with unspoken ecstasy.

He swallowed hard, the image irresistibly sexy, and nodded, unable to speak.

'You were right.'

'What?' He was still trying to get a grip on stamping down the idea of pressing her up against the bonnet of the car.

'You were right?'

Was this a trick question? What was he right about? Men were never right.

Again he just nodded slowly, hoping she'd illuminate … and

quickly.

'I'm not happy … or rather I haven't been. What is it that they say … I've only been living half a life …' she gave him a mischievous grin, 'whoever "they" might be?'

'Well that's good to know, so what are you going to do about it?'

The question was supposed to be serious but when it came out, it was laced with innuendo.

A sly smile hovered around her lips and she met his gaze directly, her eyes filled with sultry promise. It was no good, in two strides he crossed to her, cupped her face and slid his thumbs along her cheek bones and slowly lowered his mouth, making his intent quite clear.

She watched him, holding his gaze with soul searing intensity. It was unbelievably sexy and his groin tightened in immediate response. He took his time tasting and teasing her lips, before opening her mouth and deepening the kiss. Her tongue met his and he pulled her closer to him, pressing her lithe body against his.

When they finally drew back, breathless, he held onto her, tucking her head beneath his chin, hugging her close and savouring the feel of her gentle curves against him.

'I want to leave today.' Her breath whispered against his neck.

'Today?' Taking her chin in his hand, he lifted her face. Her expression was sombre. 'Don't you want to stay? I thought you'd want to … you know spend some more time with Celeste and your sister.'

'No,' she said as if she'd made an important decision. 'I'm done here … although I need to go and say goodbye properly to Siena.'

'Really?' The thud of her heart beat against his chest, strong and steady as if to reinforce the certainty of her decision.

'Yup. I'm definitely ready to move on. Besides we have a schedule. I've got to call Ron at some point to let him know when to meet us in Maranello.'

'We've got a full two weeks to get there if we want. You don't need to worry about that.'

'I'm not worried. I just don't want to leave too much to do at the end.'

'I'll make sure you get there within the time-frame, don't you worry.' He kissed her again, ignoring his own niggle of unease. Too much rested on the outcome to miss the deadline.

Siena's face crumpled and she looked just like a little girl. Poor kid was so young for her age.

'But you've only just got here? Can't you stay a bit longer?' Her limpid eyes filled with tears that punched Laurie straight in the gut.

'Not this time but I'd really love it if you came to see me. Come and stay in England. You can show me where to shop in London. You probably know better than I do.'

Laurie suspected that just spending time together, watching films and eating chocolate like normal young women might be enough for Siena.

Siena brightened. 'Yes, we can go to Harvey Nicks. And see the London Eye and Buckingham Palace and Lady Di's dresses at Kensington and I must go back to the costume gallery at the V and A.'

The latter surprised Laurie and then she remembered Siena saying she'd wanted to go to St Martins. Maybe her sister had been more serious than she'd given her credit for.

'There'll always be a bed for you, if you ever want to come and stay.'

'Really?'

'Of course. In fact … there's a …room, it's yours whenever you want it.' It had been Siena's bedroom before.

'That would be so lovely … Where's your phone?'

Laurie handed it over and Siena quickly punched in her number.

'Snapchat me a picture of the house … my bedroom.'

Laurie laughed. The minute she got home, she'd be painting and decorating that room. Maybe there might even be a short local fashion course Siena could enrol on.

She lunged forward and gave Siena a fierce hug. 'I'm sorry.' She should have been a better sister but there was still time to change things. Her sister hugged her back.

'Make sure you text me.' Siena waved her iPhone. 'And Facebook me. You are on Facebook aren't you?'

Laurie rolled her eyes and wrinkled her nose. 'I wasn't but I will be … if I must.'

'You must, you must. It's brilliant. I've got 535 friends.' She looked hesitant again. 'Are you sure you want me to come?'

'It should have been your house too …' Laurie winced. That was probably a bit crass, reminding Siena their father hadn't left her anything.

'Why?' Siena shrugged. 'It's not as if he was my father.'

A strange numbness settled on Laurie's skin as if she wouldn't be able to feel anything she touched. 'Yes, he was.' She felt sad that Siena didn't acknowledge him as such.

Siena's pretty face crumpled into a confused frown. 'Not really Laurie, I think of Georges as my father.'

Laurie nodded too shocked at the revelation to say anymore. 'Oh, of course.' She made a show of checking her phone to see Siena's number there. It was a shame that she hadn't ever known her real father and what a lovely man he'd been. He would have had a positive influence on Siena, she was sure.

They departed with little fanfare, in fact no one was there to see the little Ferrari take its leave and speed down the drive spitting gravel as it went.

He was surprised that Laurie had insisted on leaving so promptly, he was sure she would have waited to see her mother but with a stubbornness he'd not seen before, she held firm and insisted that she was fine with leaving word with the butler that she was going and to let her mother know.

She was softer where Siena was concerned and had slipped away, he supposed to her room, to bid her goodbye, although he wasn't sure as she hadn't say a word about it. In fact there was definite tension once again around her eyes.

'Watch the paintwork, honey.'

'Screw the paintwork. Screw everything. Do you know what, to hell with the lot of them?'

He laid a hand on her wrist.

'Stop at the gates.'

She slowed to a halt and looked at him.

'There's no screwing the paintwork,' he said. 'What's wrong? What did Siena say?'

'She doesn't think of Dad as her father.'

'That's sad. What did you say?'

'I couldn't say much, not when I was just about to leave. I needed to get out of there.'

He could understand why. The family dynamics were enough to mess up anyone's head. Good job Laurie was so level headed.

'Just see that visit as laying the first brick. Building the foundations of a relationship with your sister and telling her more about her real dad. Rome wasn't built in a day and all that.'

He leaned over and placed a gentle kiss on her lips, wanting to chase away her troubled expression. As their mouths touched he felt the frisson of electricity sizzle between them.

She gave him a faint smile. 'Are you trying to distract me?'

'Yup; easily done too.'

'You just kiss well.'

He grinned. 'Are we going to get this show on the road or not?'

Straightening in the seat she fired up the engine, pulled away and quickly notched up the speed. The way she drove certainly seemed to have changed.

He knew what it was; great sex did that, made you feel invincible. Made you feel warm towards that other human. Made you wonder if you could live without them or whether you wanted to … and that was the slippery slope. He barely knew Laurie, and who'd have thought the chemistry would be this explosive but that's all it was. She was not his type … any more than he was hers. This was just post-coital glow … and would soon wear off. But damn it was good to see her happy, especially after their conversation this morning.

He wasn't sure what had happened but a few of her demons appeared to have been resolved.

The car moved like a dream, as Laurie whipped through the gear changes with confident aggression. Gone was the diffidence, as if she were asking the car to respond to her. Now, she drove with verve, demanding a response from the car, like a jockey on board a stallion making it clear who was in charge.

And wouldn't that be something in bed. Christ he'd turned into a bloody sex maniac. Couldn't get it out of his damn brain. Even that sizzling kiss before they'd set off had left him aching. What the hell was wrong with him?

It was difficult to take his eyes off her. Being a passenger normally sucked but his shoulder was glad of the rest and Laurie's enjoyment of driving was infectious. A broad smile teased her lips as if enjoying a secret joke. With her hand loose on the gear stick, responsive to the car's every need, she seemed completely unselfconscious, driving intuitively in a way he'd seen few other drivers achieve. She'd been taught well.

'Let me know when you want a break. It's going to be a long day.'

She flashed him a smile which hit him straight in the gut. 'Itching to get your hands back on the steering wheel already? I've only been driving for half an hour.'

'I can think of other places I'd like them to be,' he drawled.

Her knuckles tightened on the steering wheel. 'How long do you think it will take us to get to Basel?'

Only a saint could resist teasing her some more, especially with the delightful blush staining her cheeks. Her indrawn breath had not gone unnoticed.

'Why? Did you want to take a break before then?'

With a roll of her eyes, she shook her head and rather than

241

answer, with a sure confident burst of speed overtook two cars on the straight stretch they'd finally hit.

The sudden force pushed him back into his seat as the engine revs roared.

'No,' she shouted grinning at him in delight. 'I was just wondering whether we'd hit any motorway? If I get stuck behind any more Sunday drivers, we won't get to Davos this week let alone tonight.'

'Just take it steady.' He groaned. 'You've turned into a speed demon.'

'You spoil all my fun,' she said with an endearing pout. Funny and cute rather than petulant like Sylvie used to do.

'I don't think so,' he teased and then regretted it when he saw her swallow and moisten her lips, rubbing the lower plump lip over the top several times. Just like she had this morning when … This train of thought had to stop, it was killing him.

'Today's our longest trip but one of the easiest. Fast roads most of the way. Luckily the scenery is pretty spectacular. The Swiss are amazing road engineers, although as you're driving, you keep your eyes on the road.'

In response she stuck out her tongue.

'In another mile or so, we hit the E60 cross into Switzerland and then its dual carriageway and motorway all the way to Zurich. We'll need to stop in Basel—'

'To send a postcard by any chance?'

'Yup. And elevenses. Basel to Zurich is just over an hour if the traffic's OK and then another two hours on to Davos and then ten minutes up to Monstein. Probably about four and half hours' driving today in total.'

'What about the Vignette thingy? I remember Ron saying we needed one to get through all the tolls in Switzerland.'

'Already done. Ron sorted it out and sent it to me before we left. See that.' He pointed to the small square on the windscreen. 'That's our magic ticket.'

A sign announced the start of dual carriageway and already Laurie was tensing like a tiger ready to pounce. She'd definitely got the buzz.

'Sit back, enjoy the ride then and pass us a jelly baby.' With a roar of the engine, the car burst forward and they streamed down the outside lane. Relaxing completely was out of the question, after all it was a serious machine but he had to admit Laurie drove with real flair and he could *almost* trust her to look after her ladyship.

'Don't get a ticket?'

She just laughed and burned off a couple of Mercedes and BMW's who'd been hogging the fast lane.

'You won't be able to do this when you sell the car.'

She shrugged. 'Who says I'm going to sell. I might decide to keep it.'

'Yeah right, I can just see you driving around Leighton Buzzard in this.' His tone was light but inside a curl of panic rose in his stomach. She wasn't serious. That would be a disaster. No it was just the moment talking. They were away from home, away from the everyday. He lapsed into silence and took in the scenery. This was his only chance to ever own a car quite like this one, these days Ferraris with this type of pedigree were all way beyond his price range. Miles guaranteeing the sale price on this one to him was an unmissable opportunity. She had to sell the car.

The morning sped past and he let Laurie do most of the driving; it was only as they started to leave the suburbs of Zurich that he raised a hand.

'Can you slow down a little?'

Laurie looked in the rear view mirror on the dashboard. He'd noticed she always got slightly anxious whenever they passed a police car. 'It's fine, you're not speeding. I just want to listen a minute.'

'Listen to—'

'Shh,' he admonished, cocking his head towards the front of the car and listening intently.

Laurie reduced the speed. 'Is this all right?'

'Sh.'

'Sorry,' she whispered and maintained a steady speed and he almost laughed out loud at her comical focused expression. Leaning slightly forward over the steering wheel, she looked like an anxious hen, worrying about her chick. Every few seconds she'd glance at him and then whip her head back to concentrate on the road. Her concern was rather cute.

Cam groaned.

'What?' whispered Laurie.

With a shake of his head, he pulled a face and stroked his chin. 'Can you hear that?'

'Hear what?' Her eyes widened and she hunched even more over the steering wheel towards the engine.

Holding up one finger, he said, 'Listen.'

'I can't hear anything?' she whispered again, her face agonised by her inability to hear.

He ignored the twinge of guilt that flickered.

Distracted, she'd begun to decrease acceleration. As the revs fell, the car protested. 'Shit.' She fumbled for the gears, to change down.

'Careful,' he snapped, telling himself it was in a good cause. Laurie would still get a good price for the car, even if it wasn't a fraction of its real value. But like she said, she'd never expected to receive anything from Miles.

'Sorry,' she squeaked. 'Was that me or the car?'

'You. Concentrate, Laurie. It's not a Ford Fiesta, you know.'

With a cheeky grin, she ignored his sharp tone and poked her tongue out at him. 'Like you've ever driven a Ford Fiesta. I bet your Mum pushed you around in a Maclaren buggy … geddit. So what was your first car? Surely you didn't start with anything like this?'

'It was a little Triumph Hillman owned by the old boy next door to us. He'd kept it in the garage for years and asked Mum if I fancied helping him get it back on the road. I was only fourteen but car mad already. Me and Bill spent hours on it. He gave it to me on my seventeenth birthday.'

'Oh, that's lovely.'

Cam laughed. 'Yeah and the payback was whenever he got drunk down the local pub I had to go pick the old coot up.' And she'd distracted him once more.

'There. Can you hear it?'

Laurie listened. 'No.'

'Just a slight …' Now he'd done it, what? It needed to sound serious enough but not too serious. 'Knocking.'

'Is that bad? Should I stop?'

'Only if it gets worse. When we stop I'll check the oil levels. Take a quick look under the bonnet.'

'What could it be?'

'A car like this? Could be anything. Modern cars are all computerised. Lots of warning lights on the dash. You plug them into a diagnostic and it tells you what's wrong.'

He pointed to the pared down dashboard. 'This, you have to strip down. You need to know engines. Ferraris. Don't worry. It's fine. It might hold us up, but I know what I'm doing.' He paused, wondering how thick he dared lay it on. Laurie wasn't stupid but she was a bit of worrier. 'Of course if you were on your own, it would be a different story. An ordinary garage wouldn't have a clue. You'd need a specialist. And then you can be talking thousands in labour. Especially if a part's gone.'

He was reasonably sure that she wouldn't have a clue whether he was bullshitting her or not. 'You can't get new parts. I remember a mate of mine. Stranded in Milan for weeks … and that was in Italy.'

'Do you think you could fix … whatever it is?' Laurie's knuckles had gone white where she was gripping the steering wheel.

He tutted. 'I could, yes, but then I've been working with this car for years.'

The rest of the trip passed in relative silence as Laurie concentrated hard on her driving. Watching the rev counter, checking the oil and water gauges, and slowing periodically to listen to the engine. As her anxiety mounted, so did his guilt.

Laurie fell in love with the pretty mountain village of Monstein as soon as they wound their way through the tiny streets to the hotel Ron had booked them into, although that could be the relief of getting out of the car. These last few hours had been quite stressful, worrying that there might be something wrong with the engine; plus as fun as it was to drive, the Ferrari was definitely built for speed rather than comfort. Although she suspected, like Cam, she'd rather die than admit it.

Despite his offering and her concern about the engine, she'd driven most of the day. He'd been favouring his shoulder for the last day or so, rubbing it when they stopped and stretching his neck away in the opposite direction.

The Alpine style façade of the hotel with its window boxes spilling over with bright red Geraniums looked perfect, exactly like the mountain chalets in all the pictures she'd ever seen. Even the reception looked as if every last fixture and fitting had been made from rustic wood and the receptionist with her ruddy cheeks and flaxen plait looked like Heidi as she gave them a welcoming smile.

'Hi, I believe we have some rooms booked. Matthews and Browne?'

The smile slipped as the girl scanned her computer. 'I have a reservation for Herr and Frau Matthews,' she said apologetically, her accent very German. 'But nozing for Browne.'

With her pulse skittering, Laurie didn't dare look at Cam. What would he say? After this morning when she'd pretty much thrown herself at him, she'd decided that she would leave the next move to him. There'd been plenty of playful innuendo in the car throughout the day and she'd flirted back but nothing had been said, pretty rubbish really considering they were both grown adults. Adult enough to jump each other's bones this morning. Adult enough, from the low ache in her belly, to want a second round.

'I am very sorry but there are no other rooms. We are fully

246

booked. Summer hiking is very popular.'

Cam slid her a side-long look, giving absolutely nothing away in his expression. It unnerved her. Bloody hell, the big fat coward was leaving it to her. Did that mean he wanted to sleep with her again? Or was he worried she didn't want to? Or maybe he didn't and didn't want to hurt her feelings.

'Laurie?' Cam's voice was bland and reasonable. Still no bloody clues. Great, just pile on the pressure why don't you?

Bugger it, seize the moment. Hell yes, she wanted to sleep with him again. She'd thought about nothing else all bloody day. Rather than being sated by the explosion of passion this morning, it seemed to have fired her up.

'That will be fine, thank you.' She didn't look at Cam; instead she followed the girl to their room.

'This is getting to be a habit,' quipped Cam as he carried their bags into the room with a wicked twinkle in his eye.

All Laurie could do was blush. What would Robert say? She couldn't even claim innocence now. This time it was most definitely premeditated. The intimacy this morning had been spontaneous combustion. Flushing at the memory, she looked at Cam, catching his gaze full on. Sexual tension arced between them. It had been there all day, anticipatory and neither of them had had the courage to broach it.

Her face heated and her mouth went dry. In jeans and white shirt, rolled at the sleeves to reveal tanned skin and strong capable forearms, he was gorgeous and hers for the taking, if she wanted it. If she understood the rules. This wasn't for keeps. Strictly casual.

Her mind was already made up, although she wasn't sure if her mind had had any damn thing to do with it. Her hormones had jumped right in and taken charge.

'If you keep looking at me like that …' Cam growled.

With a sultry smile, she lifted her chin.

With two strides he filled the gap between them, grasped her shoulders and brought his lips down, their warmth immediately igniting heat flashing down to her core. God, help her but she wanted this man more than she'd wanted anything else in her life. Snaking her arms up around his neck, fingers delving into the long dark curls, she clung to him, kissing him back with fevered fervour.

'God, Laurie,' Cam groaned into her mouth, tightening his hold with one arm, the other sliding down to cup her bottom and pull her closer. Rubbing against him, giving into feeling, she pressed against the hard outline of his erection, both of them straining for more.

'Laurie.' Cam lifted his head. 'We shouldn't be—'

She didn't want to hear. Wouldn't hear.

'Laurie,' he tried again but she wouldn't let him. Desire drove hard and with her tongue she delved into his mouth, playing the aggressor, one hand slipping down to rub the length of him through his jeans.

'Jeez,' he whispered, straightening at her touch as if a thousand volts had shot through him. His low moan fired her blood. When his hand slid to her breast, she gave a feline smile and sank with elated triumph deeper into the kiss.

'Christ, woman. We haven't even unpacked the bags.'

They lay sprawled diagonally across the bed, clothes littering the floor and Laurie's head tucked on Cam's chest, his arm loose about her shoulder. Looking down the length of him, she couldn't believe she was sleeping with this Adonis and that sounded so juvenile but she'd never slept with anyone but Robert. When you lived with your dad, there wasn't that much opportunity and most boyfriends had melted away under his fierce inquisition.

Her blood fizzed just looking at Cam. The way he kissed, the way he teased her body – it was all so much better.

A giggle escaped her.

Cam grabbed her and rolled her on top of him, so she was looking down into his face.

'What are you laughing about? Not got complaints have you?'

he growled, his eyes alight with mischief.

Idly she rubbed one of his nipples, sighing at the sheer beauty of his smooth muscular chest. 'None whatsoever. I was just … happy, I've never …' It sounded so rubbish but she blurted it out anyway, her finger playing back and forth over the delicate skin, 'never had an orgasm. Well not … you know during proper sex.'

His hand topped hers, his breathing uneven again. 'Proper sex?' He raised an eyebrow. 'You're used to improper sex?' With a quick wolfish grin he asked, 'Want to show me?'

'Ha ha. You know what I mean!'

'Do I?'

'Yes,' she said severely, turning her hand to hold his, embarrassed by her admission. Sex with Cam was like drinking expensive champagne after a lifetime of Cava. Discovering a generous lover was a revelation. Taking his time, he played her body like a fine instrument, strumming and stroking until she vibrated with pleasure. Not in too much of a hurry, reaching his release with careful regard for hers.

He pulled her fingers to his mouth, sliding her index finger into his mouth, up and down.

Oh Lord, she could die a happy woman right at that moment.

Chapter 21

Who knew showering together could be so much … fun. It wasn't quite the word but it went a long way to covering it. There was no awkwardness, no shyness. For the first time in her life she didn't feel as if sex was something that should be tucked away in the dark. It was happy and silly and so much more. Her whole system buzzed with excitement and happiness.

'Ready?' asked Cam, holding out his hand.

She gave herself a last once-over in the mirror. In her new clothes, with her freshly washed hair which had fallen exactly into place as Marc had promised, she looked OK. Certainly good enough that no one would wonder why a good-looking guy like Cam was hanging around with her. Of course, he had his usual white shirt and jeans on and still managed to look edible.

'Thank God for that, because I'm bloody starving.' Right on cue his stomach rumbled. 'You're insatiable, woman.' He picked up their bags and gave the room a once-over, checking for anything they'd forgotten.

'It wasn't my fault we missed dinner,' she said indignantly, following him out of the room.

'Whose fault was it then?' His over-the-top leer made her giggle. She never giggled but it seemed to have become a new habit in the last twelve hours.

The innocent smile she tried out failed miserably and he leaned in for quick kiss which started to deepen.

She pulled away. 'Breakfast.'

The beep of her phone made them both stop. She glanced down. A text from Robert. Switching off her phone, she shoved it into her bag.

Cam's mouth firmed and a look of pain crossed his face. Guilt flooded her, they really needed to talk. Cam had tried. Despite her dismissing him as a playboy at first, her assessment had been totally wrong. It wouldn't be completely accurate to say she'd done all the running, but she'd certainly headed him off rather effectively every time he tried to raise the subject.

He had nothing to worry about, although she suspected that he didn't feel right about her being unfaithful with him, for all his sophisticated veneer.

'I've decided to break things off with Robert. It's over.'

Cam's jaw tightened and his gut twisted. Damn. The coffee he'd just sipped turned sour in his mouth.

'Sure that's a good idea?' He hid the crash of adrenaline that hit his system.

Her eyes widened. 'Yeah,' she answered in a tone that said, 'are you stupid?'

Damn. Damn. Damn. He shouldn't have got himself in this mess. Sleeping with her … no, he had no regrets. Fragrant rose teased the air, bringing with it the sensation of that satin smooth skin just under her delicate jaw line and the memory of tracing the fine bones of her face with his lips. No regrets for that.

'It's just … hell Laurie, I really like you …'

Her eyes narrowed, even to his own ears this was sounding clumsy.

'No, seriously,' he grabbed her hand but she shook it off, her eyes looking wounded. See this was why he should have left well alone. This sounded like the, I've ditched the boyfriend for you speech.

251

Laurie was the last person he wanted to hurt.

'Laurie just listen a moment. It's been amazing, but ... I'm not the answer,' he said, and leant over gently touching her face. When had he got all noble? Resisting the temptation to kiss that lush mouth, tease from her the tiny sighs. Damn it would be so easy just to kiss her.

Pretend, have fun for the rest of the ride and then sayonara.

And that was without factoring in the car. The car. Buggering hell, see that's what sex did, especially mind blowing sex. Short-circuited the synapses. How could he have forgotten? Dropping everything to drive across Europe because he wanted this car. Only the condition of Miles' will would ever give him the opportunity to own one of this value. When Laurie sold the car, he could buy it at the price Miles had paid for it. It was an offer no one in their right mind would ever refuse. The price of Ferraris had gone sky high in recent years. He sobered for a moment. The will hadn't said anything about screwing her.

'The answer?' As she said it, her body language gave off a dozen warning signals. Folded arms, rigid shoulders, curled lip.

One false move and he was going to be up to his neck in quicksand and he hadn't a clue what he'd said wrong. Who was he kidding? He *was* up to his neck and there was no going back. He had the serious hots for Laurie, hell, he liked her ... *a lot*. But he couldn't sell her a pup. Make promises that he didn't know he could keep.

'Laurie, you can't throw what you've got with Robert away, because we might or might not have something going. I really like you.' Crap – that sounded crap. 'I admit the sex is...' he swallowed, remembering the sweetness of her body and the honesty of her response, 'incredible but ... I can't give you what you want.'

He couldn't do it to her; she was the type of girl that would want more. He could see it now, the rest of the trip cosied up together, sleeping together ... *that* he could handle, her hand tucked in his as he drove, sharing bottles of Italian vino on the descent down to Maranello. But then she'd expect forever, to settle down. He'd already tried that with Sylvie, and what a disaster it turned out to be.

'I shouldn't have taken advantage of you. Despite what you think of yourself, you are a beautiful and very sexy woman, and,' he shrugged, he'd been seduced by a lot more sophisticated women and it had never been like it had with her, 'it sounds cheesy, but it was special.'

'You arrogant prick.' Laurie's low voice spiked upwards, filled with venom, striking at him like a viper.

He felt as if he'd been punched and for a moment, sat open-mouthed, metaphorically winded.

She pushed her chair back, tossing her hair back. The rich red highlights caught by the morning sunlight along with her angry stare reminded him of Medusa. 'It's not about you,' she hissed. 'Or Robert. It's about me.'

She loomed over him. 'Me.' She stabbed herself in the chest with her thumb, glorious and furious at the same time.

'I don't need you, or him, or my mother, or Miles pulling the strings. Sod the lot of you.' She snatched the keys from the table in front of him and stormed off.

The rumble of the Ferrari's engine sparked a tiny moment of unease and then he relaxed. Laurie was no drama queen. Yeah she was mad at this moment, but she'd calm down and realise what he was saying made sense.

The flap of the tyres on the cobbles had him tensing. OK, so she was good and mad. This was just bravado. She wasn't really going anywhere, just making her point.

The tail-lights disappeared round the corner as he took another sip of his coffee. Whoops. Not his finest hour but she'd be back. He could guarantee it. Nodding to himself, he looked at his watch and made a rough calculation. Give it ten minutes. Tops. She'd get to the outskirts of town, see the road signs with just how far it still was to Italy, come to her senses and come back. Sense and Laurie went together.

Although he had to admit her sudden outburst had shocked the hell out of him. Raw passion he'd seen, but behind closed doors. What had happened to sensible, buttoned-up Laurie?

He settled back in his chair and picked up a newspaper. It was all in French and his linguistic skills certainly weren't up to translating large chunks, but he didn't want Laurie to see anything but indifference on his face. He watched the passers-by, his attention caught by an anxious mother and her recalcitrant toddler who did not want to get into his buggy. The two finally compromised, he clutching the metal frame while she wheeled forward slowly. They left to the chime of the clock tower in the market square.

Cam looked at his watch. It had been twenty minutes. So she was being stubborn this morning, was she? Nothing he couldn't handle. He called the waiter over and ordered a second coffee. She wasn't to know that he had no intention of drinking it but if she turned up now, she'd get the message that he knew she'd be back. Two could play at her game.

When it got to half past and his second coffee had been drained, he started to scan the road more regularly, waiting for her to return. Things always took longer than you thought they would, he reminded himself. She'd probably only just got as far as the outskirts of town, and might have got lost trying to find her way back again. He listened out for the roar of the Ferrari's engine. How stupid – that would always be a give-away. He'd hear her coming. He crossed his legs and smiled to himself. He'd pretend to be miles away when she finally did turn up. Her face would be full of indignation and ire, blue eyes flashing with irritation. His imagination ran away with itself and an image of plump pink lips, slightly open, came to the fore. His groin tightened in response, remembering the tiny mewling noise she made when he touched her just as she climaxed. God, he was rock solid. He took a mouthful of cold coffee and tried to think about the car. He should have

254

checked the oil this morning. Looked at the tyre pressure.

After nearly an hour, he began to worry. He checked his phone. No calls. Surely she'd have called if there'd been a problem. But not if she was unconscious or dead. In an accident. He sat up pushing the coffee cup aside with an abrupt flick of his hand. Shit, what if she'd had an accident?

Damn it, he had to call her.

There was no answer, it just clicked straight to voicemail. That raised more questions. Was her phone switched off? Had it been damaged or destroyed? Was she trying to call him?

Where was she? Trying to programme the sat nav to come back? What if someone had hijacked her and the car? The car was worth a fortune. It wasn't exactly surreptitious. Anyone along their route could have spotted it and decided to follow them.

He looked at his watch again. Only a minute had elapsed but his mind had gone a hundred miles an hour. When had his imagination become so fertile? There were a million simple explanations and just as many equally horrific possibilities. The coffee in his stomach roiled and for a moment he felt sick. He tried her phone again but still it went straight to her voicemail asking him to leave a message.

With a terse message, he slammed the phone down on the table and looked at it balefully for a moment before snatching it up again. He stabbed out a text message.

Where are you? Get in touch so I know you're safe.

He went back to the hotel after an hour. There'd been no message, no nothing. Where the hell was she?

He logged onto the internet on his laptop. He looked at the map and today's itinerary.

Shit, had she really called his bluff and left him? Surely not? She wouldn't attempt the rest of the trip on her own. Not this leg. Please not this leg.

255

He studied the map more closely, calculating. Driving at their usual pace … shit, shit, shit … he traced the route with his finger. His eyes narrowed and goose-bumps rose on his forearms and he stilled.

She wouldn't. Would she? Blood rushed in his ears as the map went blurry. The Stelvio Pass, one of the most challenging pieces of road in the whole of Europe, possibly the world.

He grabbed his phone and tried her number again. Still no answer but then that was hardly surprising. There probably wasn't much of a signal up there in the mountains.

He slumped on the bed. What now?

He half-laughed at himself. She had some guts. Served him right but she'd left him stranded in Europe with no transport.

The spectacular scenery was unavoidable but she kept her eyes firmly on the road, enjoying the freedom of having the car to herself and determined to hold the stupid tears at bay. She could rev, change gear and if she messed up a gear change, there was no one there to see. Especially not Cam. It felt liberating. Before the roads began to climb and get really challenging, she let the engine roar and sped along well past the speed limit. Would Cam approve or disapprove? Thankfully traffic was light, so she didn't have to worry about anyone else on the road … or what Cam might say.

The crystal blue of the sky seemed to go on for ever up here in the mountains and with the window wound down, she could breathe in the fresh air which almost tasted sharp it was so clear.

Leaning back into the seat she felt like she'd got into the groove. For the first time, listening to the noisy throb of the engine and the slight rattle coming from the driver's door, the little list of the steering wheel, it felt like it was her car. She got it. She understood what Cam felt about this car. And why did the bloody man keep intruding in her thoughts?

Shit, she'd lost her temper. She never did that. Ever. Biting her lip, she thought of Cam's face. She hadn't intended to leave him

256

stranded ... but she'd been so mad. Running on instinct, she'd climbed into the car and driven. And driven. And driven. Until there was no turning back.

Tears blurred her eyes. She had to stop, she couldn't keep on driving. Not like this.

Stopping at a roadside café, the type Cam would have immediately approved of, she grabbed a cup of espresso. She needed her wits about her.

The first couple of sips of coffee helped stabilise the tears which still threatened to well up. Gazing at the mountains looming above, lush and verdant with green, she sighed.

She'd fallen in love with the Ferrari and quite possibly and totally stupidly Cam.

The car she could explain, she adored the way it made her feel, how it drove and what it symbolized. Out in the tiny car park, she could see people taking a second look, prowling round its sleek lines and inspecting every design feature.

Bursting with pride, she grinned, watching the scene. Sod Cam, behind the wheel she was invincible, she could drive for ever. Her and the car, a partnership. It was her freedom and her future and like the panorama around her, had endless opportunities and directions.

Cam wasn't so easy. Sublime sex had muddied the waters. Those pin-up looks had pulled her in to start with but there was so much more. Kind, easy going, his perception, that ability to look at the bigger picture, his hands on her body. OK so that was just chemistry ... but in just a few short days, he'd made her feel more than she thought she could ever be. Just thinking about him ... made her heart feel as if it might burst.

But he obviously didn't care that much. Checking her phone again, her heart pinched in disappointment. No call or text. Probably glad to disentangle himself so easily. He'd made it pretty clear he was running scared of any kind of commitment. Arrogant git. Commitment was the last thing she wanted right now.

Abruptly she put down the coffee cup, she didn't want it. She'd rather get back on the road. Normally she and Cam would take at least an hours' break, today she just wanted to keep on driving. Keep on driving forever. Get as far away from Cam and everyone else as possible. Just look out for number one for a change.

Grabbing the keys, she abandoned the coffee and threw herself back into the leather bucket seat, blasting out of the car park with all the finesse of a boy racer. *Tough*, she thought, accelerating hard and roaring past a Lamborghini.

During the long slow climb up along the mountain ranges, her mind had been so preoccupied, she'd failed to notice how busy the road had got or how the clouds had closed in. Weird. Suddenly there seemed to be lots of other high performance cars, motorbikes with serious engines that buzzed like super bees and road cyclists. The severity of warning of the road signs seemed to have ramped up significantly and ominously. Some sixth sense sent adrenaline racing through her system. It felt as if she were on a fairground ride she knew she wouldn't like but it was too late to get off.

Stelvio National Park, read the sign. It rang bells. What had Cam said when they were heading to Honfleur. Forty-eight hairpin bends.

At the crest of the hill, she gripped the steering wheel, ready as she rounded the bend. Beyond it the hillside fell away below, the road a grey ribbon of terrifying looking twists and turns that went on and on.

'Oh fuck,' she whispered. The first hair-pin bend was on her and she was wrestling with the steering wheel trying not to look at the drop below.

Chapter 22

Cam paid the taxi driver and walked over to the squat white building hauling his leather bag onto his shoulder. He gave a grim smile. Madam was going to get one hell of a surprise, he thought as he nodded to the guy in the office there.

'Monsieur Matthews?'

'Yep, is Patrice here?'

'Oui.' The man pointed out through the open door.

He could just make out Patrice over on the other side of the field. 'Hey.'

'Hey mate, how's it going? You owe me big time for this.'

'I figured I might. Got the flight plan logged?'

'Yep. Although the weather's not looking great in the mountains this morning.'

Cam shrugged. 'Worst comes to the worst, we'll just take the short route. But if we can I'd like to follow.'

'So this chick has … what, stolen your car?' Patrice's craggy face twisted in unholy glee. 'Liking her style. No one gets one over on old Camshaft.'

Cam rolled his eyes and gave Patrice the finger.

'It's her car. I was babysitting.'

'Not doing too great a job, then.'

'Yeah, I got that. All I need you to do is fly the route, so I can

259

spot her and make sure she's OK.'

'You mean make sure she hasn't put any scratches on the bodywork.'

Cam frowned. OK, that had crossed his mind but the bigger worry was that Laurie would lose her nerve half way down the hairpins. He closed his eyes. Shit. He hated that bloody road. Although she'd proved herself as a driver, she wasn't that experienced and this road was one hell of a challenge for a novice.

'I just want to make sure she hasn't driven off the road.'

'What you gonna do if she has?'

The knot in his stomach tightened.

'This ain't the cavalry. You're not expecting me to land down there?'

Cam twisted his mouth wryly. Not Patrice, no. Not without remuneration. This flight was costing a fortune as it was. He was one mercenary sod. But Cam would make him if he had to. With his bare hands. His fists clenched under his thighs.

What would he do if he spotted the silver splash of crumpled metal dashed down on the rocks of the mountainside, the image of which had been fixed in his head for the last few hours? The only thing keeping him calm was the fact that faced with all those hair-pin bends she was sensible enough to take them slow. Yeah, Laurie didn't take risks. Or at least she didn't used to. And hopefully the traffic would be heavy enough to prevent her opening up too much. This time of year the SS38 was a tourist mecca, no knowing how many bikes and motorbikes she'd encounter.

The chopper took off, wheeling away from the mountains before settling back on course. Cam gave the thumbs up to Patrice, even though his stomach felt as if it had taken flight too. Thank God for having good connections. He'd been this way many a time to Italy, although the route Miles had suggested wouldn't have been his first choice. There were other equally impressive mountain passes with a lot less traffic on them, although the Stelvio pass was the one everyone talked about. It made for a good story. He hated it with damn good reason. If the weather was on your side, for an experienced driver, it was easy enough. Try it before the pass closed for the winter and it could be treacherous. He'd been caught one nightmare time and he'd never done it since. That's when he'd smashed up his shoulder and a perfectly good car. Which Miles knew, damn him. That had been the clincher. Miles had known there was no way Cam would let Laurie attempt the pass on her own, without an experienced driver.

Shame Miles hadn't known his niece as well as he thought he had.

Cam looked down at the roads below. At least the weather was on his side. He was hoping they'd spot her before she hit the pass, overtake her and then he could flag her down. With luck he might spot her on a coffee break. She might have stopped. Then again, it was Laurie. She got the job done. All he could do was pray she'd made it in one piece.

Think positive. With good weather in the mountains, he could catch up with her and be back in the Ferrari with her this evening.

Below them the road snaked back on itself and looking down he could see the cars, although there was no sign of the little silver roadster.

Patrice handed him a pair of binoculars and spoke to him through the headphones.

'Any sign of your chickadee?'

'No and she's not my chickadee, she's … just a job.' And God would strike him down for the lie.

'So …'

'I don't mix business with pleasure,' growled Cam as if saying it out loud made it true. Laurie shouldn't have been a whole heap of trouble and he couldn't believe that he was now chasing her across bloody Italy. This was supposed to be an easy job, escorting her to Italy. And it would have been if he hadn't gone and messed up by sleeping with her and … caring for her.

The chopper ate up the miles, being able to fly directly as

opposed to zig-zagging back on itself like the road below.

There was no sign of the Ferrari, although there were plenty of other high performance sports cars, along with chains of cyclists and speedy, black ant motor-bikers zipping along leaning at terrifying angles into the bends. God, it was like petrol head central. Of course it was. Down to him, he'd have insisted they got up with the dawn and headed out as soon as the sun rose to get ahead on the road.

'Gonna have to return to base soon, Cam,' shouted Patrice.

'One more loop,' he yelled back above the ferocious whirl of blades above them.

Shit, where the hell was she? Had she chickened out? Changed her mind? Had he missed her? Had she turned back to come get him? What if she were driving back to England? No surely not. He tried to put himself in Laurie's head. No, she wasn't a quitter. He smiled in spite of himself. Actually she was pretty darned determined. No, there was no way this road would beat her.

He gave Patrice a wave.

'Can you head to Bormio?'

'Yeah but I can't land there.'

'Doesn't matter. I just want to make sure she got there in one piece.'

'You think she's already there.'

'Well she's not gone over the side anywhere, so I'll assume the best.'

Of course she was already there. She had to be. She just had to be.

Her head rested on the steering wheel. Every muscle in her body felt so taut that any second now something could go ping and she'd collapse like a puppet without strings. Forcing herself to move, she opened the car door and swung her legs out, hanging on to the frame to haul herself upright. Jelly had substituted knees and her legs felt as spindly as spaghetti, rather appropriate now she'd crossed the border into Italy. She gazed back up the mountain, at the grey zigzags cutting into the green mountainside. Good lord, had she really just driven down there? With an oomph she sagged against the car, wide-eyed and trembling at the achievement while feeling shattered and slightly sick.

Other drivers crossed to her, pumped her hand, patted her on the back and admired the car. A couple of men made low-grade flirtatious overtures but it was all very good natured and part of the general air of camaraderie.

Like a bubble swelling, she felt the elation grow and grow. This was quite something. Her mouth stretched into a mile wide grin. She'd really done it. One of the most difficult drives in the world and she, Lauren Browne, had done it. All by herself.

'Woohooo,' she screamed to the open car park and punched the air. She'd done it. Who'd have thought it?

A smattering of applause rocked around her but she was too pumped to feel embarrassed.

Stuff Cameron. Stuff Robert. Stuff her mother. She didn't need any of them.

Sinking to the floor beside the car, she stared up at the hillside, waiting until normal service resumed in her legs and then she straightened up still grinning at the awesome view.

She was on the home stretch now. Not far to Maranello at all. She could be there in four hours if she put her foot down.

Five minutes later, he was ready to bloody kill her when he got hold of her, however for now it was enough to know she was safe. A circuit over the medieval town of Bormio confirmed that Laurie had indeed made it one piece. You couldn't miss the shape of the car or the admiring crowd around it.

For the first time that day, Cam was able to stop the constant tapping of his right knee. Tomorrow, he'd hire a car and catch up with her in Maranello … and then tan her hide and kiss her senseless.

'OK. You want to head back?' yelled Patrice above the

reverberations of the helicopter blades.

'Yeah. All good.'

Chapter 23

His shoulders rigid with tension, Cam checked into the Hotel Candide.

Scooping up the keys to his room, he asked, 'And can you tell me what room Miss Browne is in? I'm supposed to be meeting her here.'

The pretty Italian receptionist smiled at him as if she'd put two and two together and made a romantic four. He maintained his pleasant smile. If she guessed what he really wanted to do to Laurie, there was no way she'd give him her room number. Her polished pink nails tap tapped over the keyboard and her smile faded.

'I'm sorry sir, we have no one by that name staying here.' Her face was questioning, still trying to please.

'Are you sure?' With a head start on him, she should have been here yesterday. Had she used another name? Checked into a different hotel? Maybe this one was full when she arrived, although he looked around the lobby and thought that unlikely.

'No one by that name is registered here at the moment.'

He thought for a moment. Had she been and gone? No, not without Ron verifying that she'd indeed made it. Ron. That was it. She was supposed to phone him a day before she expected to arrive so he could fly out and meet them.

'Has a Mr Ron Leversedge checked in?'

Her face brightened. 'He's not here yet but I took a reservation for him earlier today. He will be arriving the day after tomorrow.'

The day after? What the hell was going on? And where was Laurie? She should have been here by now. Bormio was only half a day's drive away. How could he have got here before her, unless she got lost on the way; but not with the sat nav, surely?

Taking the keys, he went up to his room. At least Ron's imminent arrival meant she'd been in touch with him – so the bloody woman was alive at least. He might get some sleep tonight. Now the main problem was getting to her before Ron did.

His shoulder hurt like crazy and all he wanted was a shower, a lie-down to get the kinks out of his back and to put a heat pack on it. The tiny hire car had been a pile of shite on wheels. Served him right for being so tight, although the choice at the car rental place had been limited. Coaxing a people carrier down the pass hadn't been very appealing.

As he stripped off, he checked his phone again. Reception was patchy in the mountains. Even if Laurie had texted him, he might not have received it. The thought hadn't stopped him checking a dozen times an hour. Where the hell was she?

He turned the shower on full and waited a moment before stepping in. The warm flow eased the headache pulsing at his temples. What if she'd been car-jacked? Kidnapped? Water cascaded down his aching back. That car was worth millions on the open market.

Only lucky bastards like him could hope to buy one at a fraction of its worth, providing she got it here in one piece.

He held his face up to the shower and let the jets hit full on, hoping it would wash away the insidious worry. She had to be somewhere.

No one who knew cars would try stealing the Ferrari. They'd know it would be virtually impossible to sell. High performance babes like that only got stolen to order and even then it would be impossible for an owner to pass it off as anything else. But idiots might try. Idiots who didn't know its real worth. He closed his eyes. The sort who were desperate. Jacked up on drink or drugs. What would they do with Laurie?

Getting out of the shower, he towelled himself vigorously, taking his frustration out on his damp skin, leaving his shoulders almost raw.

Maybe he should contact the police. Report her missing? If she hadn't checked in by nightfall, he would call the local police first thing in the morning. He hated this feeling of indecision.

She swirled the red wine around her mouth, savouring it. The half bottle had been expensive but worth it. The wine list looked so interesting it was tempting to stay here for a few days and work her way through it. Pushing her plate away to the side, she opened up the map. She'd decided to stay overnight in Bormio at the foot of the pass which was teeming with cyclists, campervans and other sports cars. There was a good natured, happy atmosphere about the place and at first it looked like she might not find a room because it was so busy. Luckily the quaint looking Hotel Cormori was far enough out of town to deter most tourists and provided safe parking in the enclosed private car park.

Warmed by the red wine and relaxed after a hard day's driving, she dreamily considered the map. If she put her foot down and drove all day, she could be in Maranello tomorrow evening and then what? Home?

Suddenly the lukewarm summer of home seemed another life away and Italy felt vibrant, exciting and busy. Her entire life had been spent driving through without stopping to experience it properly. The heavy accents and singsong voices of Italy were familiar and yet unfamiliar, the rapid rise and fall of excitable words entrancing. The incomprehensible words on the signs around the hotel and the town were alien. In France she had enough knowledge of the language to recognise a fair proportion of the words; here everything seemed completely strange … and she loved it – the feeling of anonymity, the ability to look around this restaurant and be an observer.

Before her like a plate of delicacies, the map offered Lake Como, Lake Garda, Parma, Milan, Turin, even Venice. They were all there … just for the taking. There was nothing to stop her driving to any of them. She had the money sitting in her pocket. A ball of illicit pleasure burned in the pit of her stomach.

With a sudden grin she made up her mind. She could do whatever she wanted. Responsible to no one but herself; with a pang she thought of Cam.

Then she stomped hard on that thought. OK, she missed him which was all the more reason to ignore his phone calls and texts. He was out of bounds, Mr Never Never and he'd made it completely clear he was not Mr Commitment, or even Mr Vaguely-Interested-In-The-Short-Term. Stupid man. Did he think she was too dumb to realise that? It had been a given the minute she kissed him. She'd known the score, apparently he hadn't.

Knackered by the drive and lulled into a warm haze of happiness by the excellent wine, she left the dining room and went straight up to her room to find her phone blinking furiously with a slew of new messages. It was tempting to ignore it.

Please just let me know you're OK. I'm worried about you.
Cam

Shit, he knew how to make her feel guilty. Now that she'd come through all those hair-pin bends, it was understandable why anyone might worry. Not that it had bothered him before. Pursing her lips, she hesitated but honesty made her admit she should let him know she was fine. Part of her wanted to crow that she'd made it to the other side of the Stelvio Pass and she was more than fine. Quickly she texted,

Alive and well.

The message failed and she realised that she barely had a signal. Oh well, it would do Mr I'm-Not-The-Right-Man-For-You good to worry a bit longer. Show him she was quite capable of looking after herself.

Unable to help herself she flicked through the photos on her phone. The best one, him in white shirt and faded denims, black curls dancing across his cheekbone, made her pause. He'd been kind that day … he'd been kind every day.

Sighing she threw herself on the bed. Robert and she were over that was for sure. It wasn't about being unfaithful … although that was bad enough. Everything had changed, thanks to Miles. Had he known what was hiding inside her? What she was capable of?

Now she thought back to the last time she'd seen him. Holding his hand at the hospice. It all made sense. He'd wanted her to see that although her mother had failed her, Laurie had failed herself by playing it safe. She'd missed out on so much because she'd been too scared to risk her emotions or challenge herself. Canny old Miles had seen it.

It was enough to put her off ever returning to England but tomorrow was a whole new day and she was off to Lake Garda.

Chapter 24

She took another bite of ice cream, enjoying the cold on her tongue and lifting her face to bask in the hot sunshine. Rich vanilla flavour swirled in her mouth as she walked along the path skirting the lake. No doubt about it, Riva Del Garda had to be one of the prettiest spots in Europe. Sunlight danced on tiny crested waves as the wind rippled across the water, like rhinestones winking joyfully.

It was the first time in her life she'd ever had the luxury of such solitude. In the last two days, she hadn't felt lonely once. It was liberating to feel so happy in her own company. She'd never lived on her own. Robert had moved in as soon as her father had died. At the time, with grief a constant, Robert's presence had helped. Looking back there'd never been a conscious decision that he should move in. Only now did it occur to her that something that important should have been considered. It just seemed to happen and then it became a fait accompli.

She stared out over the lake, watching tiny boats speed along the surface, zig-zagging to and fro like frantic ants in a hurry to go nowhere. Would she have settled down with him so quickly if Dad hadn't died when he did? Somehow she doubted it. Shading her eyes with one hand, she gazed out over the blue of the lake stretching beyond her vision. Mountains surrounded the picturesque resort like monolithic guardians charged with ensuring the peace and serenity of the inhabitants. Robert had been like those mountains, something solid to keep her anchored when her world crumbled and Dad's death hit so hard. And like them he had remained solid and immoveable. A sense of regret pierced her, a spear of sharp awareness, prising the truth to the surface. She didn't want immoveable any more. Life was waiting for her. She had so much living to do. And Miles in his cock-eyed way had seen that.

A shaft of sunlight broke past the shadow of the mountain, illuminating a brilliant patch of waterfront below, bringing colours and shapes in bright relief. She took it as a sign and turned back towards the hotel.

Booking another two nights felt horribly decadent, but that probably had more to do with the extortionate amount the hotel would cost each night. What was the point of coming to Lake Garda if you didn't book into a hotel that overlooked the lake?

The hotel's roof terrace offered such a wonderful, distracting view of the lake, she'd barely read a word since she'd arrived. Yesterday morning she'd had a deliciously long lie-in, until the brilliant sunshine had urged her to explore. Armed with a hotel packed lunch (she was getting used to the high life, before this it wouldn't have occurred to her to ask for one to be made up) she'd left at ten and then spent a thoroughly enjoyable day, walking round the lake, exploring the town, stopping whenever she felt like it, for the tiny potent cups of espresso which she'd developed an addiction to. The caffeine hit had made her a bit buzzy, and she'd almost given in and phoned Cam to tell him where she was. Luckily she thought better of it.

Today the weather forecast had predicted a storm, so with a newly bought swimming costume, she booked herself in for a day at the hotel's Spa. It was daft but she felt a little bit nervous. She'd never been to one before and the one in the hotel promised all sorts of treats. She'd booked the day's beauty package which, although eye-wateringly expensive, offered the best value and helped her justify the huge cost. It promised a long list of treatments which included a manicure, pedicure, eyebrow shape and a ton of other things she'd never heard of, but didn't like to ask. This was probably the sort of thing Celeste and Siena did all the time.

Thank heavens she had gone for the most expensive swimming costume, the Spa's sophisticated stylish atmosphere put her in mind of a sleek black jaguar who at any moment could turn on her. It wouldn't have tolerated a mere M&S costume that was for sure. Any moment now, an alarm could go off with a big neon arrow pointing at her lit up with the words, 'Imposter'.

The pool looked like a mountain cave with its obsidian black tiles and underwater lights giving the water a haunting mystical quality. She had three-quarters of an hour to kill before she was booked in for the first treatment. Flipping on her back, listening to the lap of the water around her, she gazed up at the midnight blue ceiling covered in zodiac symbols picked out in gold leaf, tiny lights arranged in appropriate constellations. Where would Cam be now? She couldn't help picture him here; sitting opposite on a table on the magical roof terrace upstairs, walking around the lake, all that long hair windswept and unruly, curls lashing his face, lying beside her on the crisp white linen sheets of the king-size bed in her room. She screwed up her eyes. Stop. Thinking. About. Cam.

She swam a couple of lengths, putting her all into a speedy crawl relishing the ache of her shoulders. Even as she hauled herself, arms shaking with the effort, a vision of Cam in briefs at the poolside popped into her head. Where would he be now? Waiting for her at Maranello? With Ron? She'd texted Ron, to tell him that she expected to be there in two days' time. Looking at the map, she thought that a day of driving would get her there, so she had another one here. And she didn't have to stay in Riva Del Garda, she could go off in *her* car and do some exploring on some of those hair-raising roads.

And now it was time for her first treatment. Wrapping herself in the thick, rich towelling dressing gown, she headed to the Spa reception for her appointment.

Laurie batted her new eyelashes at herself in the mirror and grinned at the effect. No more mascara. She liked the idea of that. And her nails, scarlet red, a colour she normally would have shied away from. Her toes were painted the same colour but with a little row of diamante along the perimeter of the cuticle. Eyebrows shaped. Skin exfoliated, moisturised, buffed and polished.

She felt like … not a new woman, but an absolutely knackered one. Who knew lying around all day could be so exhausting? She'd been primped and pampered by a team of young Italian women who spoke in husky broken English and looked as if they went through this daily regimen before breakfast.

Her eyes strayed to the clock. Six thirty and she was all dressed up. In honour of her shiny new nails, she'd put on the red jersey dress, ignoring the pang that Cam wasn't here to see it. It hugged her figure, the light silky material swishing around her legs as she walked.

Too early for dinner. Snatching up her bag and stuffing her Kindle into it, she decided to go down to the bar.

Who'd have thought she'd end up in a bar overlooking a fabulous lake in brilliant sunshine with a Spritzer in one hand and a book in the other? On her own!

She chose and ate her meal, occasionally glancing at her book but more often people-watching. Even after the meal, a Spaghetti Vongole with tiny juicy clams and a strawberry sorbet, she didn't hurry from the table. She ordered a second white wine and took her time sipping it slowly and gazing out over the view. The exorbitant room rate was worth every euro just to sit and enjoy this view.

Should she stay another day? There was plenty to do. She could go on a boat trip or take a hiking trip to see the Alpine flowers. Tomorrow the weather forecast was much better and she'd take a walk up to the Venetian fortress, The Bastion, just above the town.

She was in no hurry to go anywhere just now. Uncle Miles would have approved.

Entering the hotel lobby, in search of a cold beer at the bar, he heard the English voice speaking loud and slow emphasizing consonants. 'An. English girl. Driving. A Ferrari.' He signalled driving with his hands.

Cam shook his head. Arse. Didn't he realise Ferrari was an Italian word? Even if Cam hadn't recognised him from the funeral, he'd have known who he was. Had Laurie contacted him? He sidled closer to try and listen in to the conversation.

'Are. You. Sure. She's. Not. He-re.' His voice increased in volume. 'Laurie. Browne. Can you check again?'

Cam strained to hear, his throat tightening. The pang in his stomach was probably hunger reminding him he ought to eat but he needed to hear Laurie was OK first.

The receptionist replied in flawless English and the definite bite made Cam smile for the first time in twenty-four hours.

'Sir, the lady is definitely not here. I have already checked as another gentleman was asking for her as well. She has not checked in here and furthermore, she hasn't reserved a room.'

Cam ducked his head, hoping she wouldn't give him away. He didn't want to have to confess to Robert that Laurie had gone AWOL. Not when he should have been looking after her. Looking after her instead of getting into her pants and messing with her life.

Robert's shoulders slumped, reminding Cam of a sulky teenager, making him feel doubly guilty.

'Great. So what am I supposed to do? She's supposed to be here.'

The Italian girl's face was impassive. 'Did you want to book a room, sir?'

'What? Me?' Robert sounded annoyed. 'No, the room's for my girl-fr— fiancée.'

'So you wish to reserve a room for her.'

'Yes.'

'So when will she be arriving and do you want a single room or a double.'

'I don't know when she's arriving.' Cam winced at Robert's

274

sarcastic tone. 'But I can book for her now and I'll stay in it 'til she arrives.'

Cam almost laughed out loud.

'Sir we can't do that. If you are going to check in it will have to be in your name and we will need your passport and credit card details.'

'That's ridiculous,' snapped Robert, the tips of his ears turning red. 'What if I'd made the reservation over the telephone in my fiancée's name? The room would be booked in her name then, wouldn't it?'

'We would still need your card details.'

Robert shook his head. 'I'm not handing that over.'

'I'm sorry sir, but its policy for us to take your credit card details. We don't charge anything on it until you check out.'

'I don't believe it. The room is for my girlfriend, that's why I'm here. It's not down to me to incur expenses on her behalf.'

Cam clenched his jaw. The dickhead. He felt his hands fist fighting the temptation to deck Robert. Surely Laurie didn't put up with this crap?

The receptionist wasn't taking any. Her mouth firmed. 'I'm sorry, sir,' she said, sounding about as unapologetic as it got, 'That's policy. I can get the manager for you if you'd like to discuss it further. Otherwise I can direct you to another hotel.'

Robert snorted rudely. Cam shook his head in embarrassment to be the same nationality. The idiot sounded like a horse.

He heard the slap of plastic on the wooden desk as Robert begrudgingly pulled something from his wallet. 'So how much is the cheapest room you have?'

'400 Euros per night for a double.'

'400 Euros! You're joking, right?'

The girl stared gravely at Robert, not budging an inch.

Sulkily he pushed his card over to hers, muttering. 'Daylight bloody robbery.'

Which Cam thought was a bit a rich, considering the tight git had no intention of paying for the room. For a moment he hoped Laurie didn't turn up.

He shook his head in disbelief and leaving Robert still muttering, he strode over to the bar and ordered a Peroni.

Taking two strong swallows, he heaved out a sigh before putting the glass down and staring into it. What a wanker. Laurie could do a hell of a lot better than him.

And then a voice jeered in his head. What? Like you?

He rubbed his eyes, suddenly feeling knackered. Why would Laurie want anything to do with him? After his choice little speech back in Monstein. He'd proved himself as big an arse as Robert. An arrogant arse. No wonder she'd taken off the way she had.

She was the least needy woman he'd ever met and hadn't she proved that in spades, leaving him stranded, in a car worth millions and taking on one of the most difficult drives in the world.

A self-deprecating laugh escaped him. He was the dickhead. Who said, "You only love her when you let her go"? He'd mistaken suffocation for commitment. Sylvie had been incapable of leading an independent life.

Part of the attraction he felt for Laurie, apart from the spine tingling sex, was her ability to be herself and take responsibility for herself. In fact, he grinned to himself, sexual demands aside, she hadn't asked a thing of him.

Damn. He just needed to talk to her and get rid of that idiot Robert. Once she arrived, Cam would be making sure that she left with him.

Mind you, Robert might bring things to a head by himself; the desk clerk looked as if she might take the handy letter opener and slice it through Robert's ribs. It would save everybody a lot of trouble.

He scowled into his beer and hauled his phone out of his pocket for the umpteenth time that hour. Still nothing from her.

Finishing his beer, he ordered a second and settled into his seat. From here he could see the lobby and keep an eye out for Laurie's arrival.

Chapter 25

With great reluctance, she tucked her bag into the boot and took one last look at the lake. Time to head back to real life, whatever that held. The last three days had been cathartic. Giving her time to reassess and look forward.

She took a deep breath, lifted her shoulders and climbed into the car. Maranello, here she came. This morning was cool with the promise of another gorgeous day and a good reason to get an early start.

The car ate up the miles along the shore, last glimpses of the lake teasing her as she wound her way south. She'd probably make it by late afternoon. She kept a steady pace, conscious of the local speed limits. A man in a Fiat got quite irate behind her, virtually tagging her bumper desperate to urge her to go faster. Finally, frustration overtook him and he roared past waving his fist on a dangerous bend. She shrugged, having learned at the very outset that this car brought out the worst in some people. It didn't mean she had to drive like an idiot.

A straight long stretch of road, however, saw her notching up the speed, enjoying the purr of the engine. Too late she saw the police car sitting in the layby as she flew past. Glancing at the speedometer, her pulse pushed 100 beats a minute. 80km. That was legal on this road wasn't it? She glanced in her rear view mirror.

Damn the police car had pulled out. Breathe, she told herself. Just breathe. You haven't done anything wrong … well not that was immediately obvious to the police. She was pretty sure she'd been within the limit. Maybe they were just following her to make sure she stuck to it. Coming to a bend, she stretched out a shaky hand, alarmed to find she could hardly change gear for the banging of her heart against her ribs. As she slowed down, she saw the police car tucked in right behind her.

For a moment she slowed even further. But that would look like she'd got something to hide. Driving this slowly might shout guilty conscience. Grateful she could hide behind her sunglasses, she carried on driving hoping that the policeman would get some other emergency call, but no such luck.

The road stretched on. It was the main route, so there was little hope of losing her tail. Surely they would have pulled her over by now if they thought she'd done anything wrong.

There were two of them in the car, both wearing sunglasses so she couldn't see their expressions. They were clearly talking. Sweat trickled down her back, running between her shoulder blades. She could feel herself sticking to the leather seat. There were probably huge sweat rings under her arms. If only there was some place to turn off – a village to stop in but the road rolled on between wide open meadows sloping away down to stunning views which she didn't dare do more than glance at.

She almost missed the sign for the layby coming up in 3km. Thank you God. She'd stop here. Hopefully they'd keep going. She could stay here a while. Make it an early lunch with the water and fruit she had with her. That would give them plenty of time to get well ahead.

It was a relief to see that the layby had a large viewing area with plenty of car parking spaces. She indicated and pulled off smoothly, praying the police car would roar off on down the road.

It didn't. Instead it pulled slowly in behind her.

There were very few cars about, so she had the pick of spaces.

Going to the far side, she drove into a space. To her horror the police car pulled in alongside.

Shit. She closed her eyes. It wasn't as if she hadn't known the risk. The chance of being stopped had always been there. It wasn't exactly a car you'd miss. Keep calm. That's all she needed to do. They might not even ask to see her licence. She wiped her palms on her linen trousers.

And what if they did? She could play ignorant. Say she'd lost her licence. Or that it had been stolen. Italy was notorious for pick-pockets.

She took a deep breath. Her worst fear had been realised, and it didn't seem quite so bad. She'd just have to get on with it. What could they do? Arrest her? Throw her in jail? It wasn't the end of the world. She'd had a good run so far.

She waited as the policeman got out of the car and approached her window.

'Buon giorno, Signorina,' he grinned, pulling off his traffic cop sunglasses, with a wide smile.

'Buon giorno.' She swallowed hard, her voice a little rusty but gave him a cautious smile.

His eyes registered surprise.

'You're English.'

She nodded even though it was a statement rather than a question.

'A beautiful car and a beautiful lady.' His eyes roved over the car, like a lover measuring up vital statistics. He touched the bonnet reverently.

A flush of heat rushed through her. A Ferrari fan.

Opening the door, she got out of the car and left the door open in invitation to him.

'Would you like a look?'

As his eyes lit up with that unmistakable look of Ferrari fervour, Laurie felt light-headed.

He peered in the driver's door at the dashboard, admired the interior and then took a walk around the car.

'Where are you headed?' His heavily accented English had a definite American twang.

'Maranello,' she said proudly and patted the bonnet hoping he wouldn't notice her shaking legs. 'Taking her home.'

He nodded approvingly. 'What year is she?'

'1962, GT ….'

He nodded again. 'Nice, very nice.'

She found herself saying, 'Do you want to sit inside?'

He beamed, waved his colleague over and squeezed himself into the seat behind the wheel.

The other policeman was younger but equally enthusiastic. The two of them chattered in rapid Italian, examining the car from every angle.

Twenty minutes later, she was on first name terms with both of them and they'd exhausted all their questions. She'd taken pictures of both of them sitting in the car with their mobiles. Georgio, the younger policeman withdrew his head from the interior of the car as if it cost him to do so, while Pedro shook Laurie's hand. 'Grazie. Grazie. Va bene. You drive carefully.'

As she sank back into the leather seat, Pedro leaned into the window and miming as he spoke, said, 'Drive carefully now, Signorina. Keep the doors locked when you're in the city.'

As she pulled out onto the road, she let out a huge sigh of relief. Only one more leg of the journey … and no one had yet realised that she didn't have a full driving licence.

The rest of the journey passed uneventfully and as she left the mountains and the roads flattened out, they became more clogged. As she neared her final destination, the scenery became more industrialised.

The sat nav guided her into Maranello which after the mountains and lakes was a rather unremarkable town.

Ron arrived after Cam had downed his fourth Peroni. The solicitor looked a little faded around the edges as if the journey had taken it out of him. Cam rose immediately and went out to greet him and take his bag from him.

'Cam, how are you?' Ron shook his hand with vigour, happy to relinquish his small carry-on suitcase, a mischievous grin displacing the weary lines around his mouth for a moment. Cam suspected he was a lot older than he'd first thought. Probably over seventy, rather than under.

'Great, thanks.'

'And Laurie?' Ron asked eagerly.

Cam's heart sank. Shit, the beer had fuzzed his thinking. Of course Ron would assume she'd arrived.

'It's a long story. Why don't we get you checked in? You've probably had a long day. Have you eaten?'

Ron didn't look the least bit fazed. 'Food, now that's a wonderful idea. I'm not fond of budget airline catering; it's worse than service station fare.'

Cam harboured, in equal measure, an overwhelming desire to ask if Laurie had been in contact and a dread that Ron would tell him no and he'd come to find out where she was because her call was overdue. Did he know where she was?

Ron seemed in no hurry and Cam's thumbnail had been nibbled raw by the time they were ensconced in the hotel restaurant with their orders placed.

'So Cam, how's the journey been?'

'The journey has been fine … until … damn it Ron, have you heard from Laurie?'

Ron raised his eyebrows.

'I've lost her.' Cam's voice cracked as he said it. 'I've no idea where she is, whether she's OK. Christ, anything could have happened to her. She's not answering her phone. She's not called.'

'I see,' said Ron, his solemn expression belied by the wicked twinkle in his faded blue eyes.

'You know where she is?' His voice growled.

Ron's mouth curved into something that looked distinctly like a smirk and for a moment Cam was very tempted to throttle him. His temper seemed to be on a very short thread at the moment.

'She's fine. Phoned me to tell me she would be here tomorrow evening.'

'She's safe then,' said Cam bitterly. So Laurie had seen fit to contact Ron but couldn't even respond to a text begging her to let him know she was OK.

Ron leaned forward and patted his arm. 'She phoned to tell me she had decided to take a few days on her own and expects to be here tomorrow evening ...' he grinned, 'unless, her words, "she gets diverted".' He chuckled. 'Chip off the old block, that one. Miles would be delighted.'

'What?' Cam bit out. 'You think Miles would be delighted ... that an inexperienced driver, his own niece, has taken his most prized car down one of the most challenging roads in the world ...' His eyes blazed as he looked at Ron's complacent expression. 'What if she'd gone over the edge? Lost control? It's no car for a novice. She could have been ...' The terror that he'd held at bay for the last two days threatened to swamp him. He closed his eyes. Bloody Miles and his sidekick, playing God.

'Cam,' Ron interjected, 'Miles taught her well. Even at fourteen, she was a natural. He knew what he was doing. I tried to talk him out of playing God, but he was my very dear friend and he would have gone elsewhere to another solicitor to get what he wanted. All I could do was make sure what he wanted was water-tight. You knew Miles better than anyone.'

'Stubborn old goat.' Cam could picture him so clearly it made his throat ache. 'Yeah I can imagine, he wouldn't leave it.'

'I didn't necessarily approve of what he was doing. He was desperate to right wrongs. He felt bad about what his sister did to Laurie. This was his attempt to make up. While Laurie's father was alive, he wanted nothing to do with Miles. Blamed Miles for introducing Celeste to Georges.' Ron shook his head. 'If it hadn't been him, it would have been someone else. He was replaced by Harvieu who was richer. Presumably you've met her now. That one always wanted more.'

Miles' intentions might have been altruistic but Cam had seen at first hand the emotional blow that Laurie had taken. He wasn't sure she appreciated Miles' attempts to get her to reconnect with her mother. Without knowing it, his old friend had been cruel and thoughtless and he, Cam, was about to make things a lot worse. He should have been honest with Laurie. Should have told her the final part of the will.

As if he'd read his thoughts Ron asked, 'Have you told her the terms of selling the car?'

Cam's eyelids felt heavy, weighed down with guilt. 'No. There was never the right moment.' It didn't seem right to tell the older man that they'd been sleeping together.

He'd planned to tell Laurie. He really had but then they'd slept together and that had changed everything. He should have told her before that. Sleeping with her muddied the water. What if she thought he'd slept with her for the car? When she finally bloody turned up, he needed to talk to her.

As he made his way back from the bar carrying a brandy for himself and a Cointreau for Ron, he noticed Robert on the far side of the room. With his head bobbing like an overeager terrier scenting prey, it was clear he'd recognised them. Damn, no avoiding him now. Cam's lip curled as Robert made a beeline to the table.

'Thought it was you. You're the driver guy.' His head swivelled with great drama to Ron, 'And you're the solicitor. I spoke to you the other day. You,' he said with great accusation, 'told me she'd be here. Where is she? And where's the car?' Suspicion narrowed his mouth and Cam felt the dart of accusation. 'The receptionist said there was no one with a Ferrari here. What's happened to them?'

'Laurie wanted to take a few days on her own, driving the car before she came here.'

Robert smiled nastily. 'I don't think so.'

Cam gave into the desire to needle the idiot. 'Why's that?'

'She doesn't drive.' He folded his arms as if to punctuate his smug statement.

Cam shrugged and took a long swallow of his brandy, waiting until the burn in his stomach had dissipated. 'She did the last time I saw her.'

Robert shook his head, clearly unconvinced. 'Laurie never drives.'

'Well that's changed.'

'She can't drive …' Robert grew an inch or two as he straightened as if to deliver the killer blow, '… she doesn't have a driving licence. Only a provisional. She's not allowed to drive outside of the UK. So where is she?'

Cam digested the news in silent amazement and then started to laugh as all the pieces of the jigsaw popped into place. No wonder she'd been so keen not to drive at first. Laurie I-wouldn't-dream-of-taking-a-risk had changed her spots.

'It's not funny, you know. Are you telling me she's on her own with a very valuable car? Anything could happen!'

'What, to Laurie or the car?' Cam didn't even fight to disguise his dislike.

'Either.'

Ron who clearly didn't do conflict, which seemed strange given his profession, interrupted. 'Mr Evans, don't worry. I have been in touch with Laurie. She's perfectly safe. She decided to make the most of the trip and spend a couple of days in Lake Garda. Bit of a holiday. She phoned the library to get an extension.'

'Lake Garda?' Robert and Cam's voices harmonised in disbelief.

'That's ridiculous. Laurie wouldn't do that. She wouldn't take a holiday without me. We're creosoting the fence.'

'Well, well,' grinned Cam. 'Good for her.' He ignored Robert and turned to Ron. 'I'll kill her when I get hold of her. Left me kicking my heels in Monstein.' He chuckled as he remembered how convinced he was that she'd be back at any second. What an

284

arrogant prick. And she taught him a lesson. She'd gone off on her own, driven down the Stelvio pass and then taken off. The lady had balls.

'She's absolutely fine. Found a very nice hotel in Riva Del Garda. Enjoyed herself I think.' Ron seemed unperturbed by both their reactions.

'In a hotel?' Robert sounded outraged.

'Where else would you have her stay?' asked Cam with lazy amusement. 'In a stable?'

'Don't be ridiculous.' It seemed to be Robert's favourite word. 'We always stay in B&Bs, much better value.'

'Yet … here you are.'

Robert's mouth resembled a prune. 'This is business, besides Laurie … well you know. Once she's sold the car …'

Cam bit down the irritation that stirred in his gut at Robert's assumption even though the car was as good as sold. Today he'd sorted out all the finance and he'd be able to hand over a banker's draft the minute Laurie arrived. The official handover of the car had to take place at the Ferrari museum, where they were expecting her. Thank God Miles had put it all in writing. It would have been awful if the museum had made a counter offer for the car.

In just a few … hours … days … whenever Laurie deigned to turn up, the car would be his. He'd dreamt of this for years and now it was so close …his hand stilled on his brandy glass. Where was the elation? The fizz of excitement he should be feeling? This was the culmination of the trip and he felt … nothing. If anything, slightly numb. He picked up his glass and took a thoughtful sip. It was probably because he'd been worrying about Laurie's safety. All this time, she'd been living it up in Lake Garda while he'd been picturing all sorts of scenarios. Yeah, once his brain had absorbed it all and he saw the car again, that buzz would be back.

Chapter 26

It felt as if a daddy-long-legs had taken up residence inside her chest and she nearly gave in to the temptation to drive past the hotel. All eyes swivelled her way as the sound of the engine echoed around the hotel entrance. A couple of people stopped to stare and the concierge almost tripped over his own feet in his hurry to open the driver's door. When he realised she was female, his surprise quickly turned to appraisal before he returned a grin of approval. With a torrent of Italian, he welcomed her before she said, 'Inglese.' He nodded and then unleashed a flood of questions in perfect English. Of course they were probably quite used to guests turning up here in Ferraris although none of them were quite in this lady's league. Laurie almost patted the long low slung bonnet.

As if she'd been doing it all her life, she handed him the keys and walked into the hotel. She enjoyed every step she took across the cool marble-floored foyer.

Several heads turned as she walked by, as if they wanted to know more about the woman who owned the vintage Ferrari. Behind her sunglasses her eyes twinkled. Quite a few open looks of admiration followed her, although she didn't fool herself they meant anything; it was more about the car, but it helped that she looked the part in her smart white linen trousers, kitten heels, the lime green cardie and scarf.

For a moment she felt like she was in someone else's life and with the feeling came a starburst of awareness. It was as if she'd spent her whole life indoors and had just stepped out into the sunlight, been dazzled by it at first but now didn't want to go back inside ever again. Almost overcome with the thought she had to steady herself at the wide mahogany check in desk. Her smile took over her face and the small dark Italian receptionist smiled broadly back in response.

'Good afternoon. Can I help you?' she asked.

How did they always know you were English?

'Good afternoon.' She sounded calm and collected, at complete odds with how the revelation had rocked her. 'I'd like to check in. I called earlier. Laurie Browne.'

'Ah, yes Miss Browne. You're a very popular signorina,' said the receptionist with a quizzical smile.

Laurie returned the smile wondering what that meant as she went through the formalities of registration, trying to tamp down the churning excitement in her stomach.

She remained impassive in the lift, down the corridor and only when she'd tipped the bellboy and closed the door, did she let out the squeal of excitement.

The first room, a suite no less, had floor to ceiling windows overlooking the town, leading to a large balcony. Two grey velvet sofas faced each other separated by a glass table, each piled with cushions in white and pale gold. Matching silk drapes framed the window billowing onto the floor, where they pooled like a golden waterfall.

She grinned to herself. This really was her life now, not someone else's. She wasn't ever leaving the sunshine again. Time to text Ron. She couldn't wait to tell him what she'd decided.

Then, she'd check the rest of the suite out.

Satisfied with the huge double bed with crisp white cotton sheets and slightly repelled by the over ornate bathroom of onyx and gold plated taps … the Italians she'd discovered did love their bathrooms … she unpacked, still delighting in the new clothes as she hung up the perfect capsule wardrobe. Perhaps she could go to Paris once a year to visit her personal shopper. And didn't that sound something; sadly her new outlook wasn't necessarily matched by her income, but if she saved up she could make it an annual trip. As soon as she got home she was going to have to find a new job pronto.

The peremptory knock at the door startled her. Ron had responded quickly to her text even though he'd not replied. He must have come straight up.

It didn't occur to her until she'd begun to open the door that the loud rap had been far more forceful and demanding than she'd have expected from the mild-mannered solicitor.

Her hand froze but it was too late.

'Cam.' Her stomach fizzed at the sight of him and an involuntary smile broke out. His tan had deepened, accentuating the deep green of his eyes. A wave of longing almost felled her. He was even more gorgeous in the flesh than her constant memories. God she'd missed him.

The feeling, it appeared, was not reciprocated, not from the way his mouth narrowed in a firm slash and the air of menace he carried with each step over the threshold. He didn't return the smile and she took a wary step back.

'Where the hell have you been?' Cam's growl made her swallow.
'I … did text …'

Cam raised an eyebrow. Shit, he was right. He'd deserved more than that.

'Sorry,' she said in a quiet voice.

Cam took a step forward and she reversed up another step, although she lifted her chin. Now was not the time to back down. OK, she'd been a bit inconsiderate … but he'd been an arrogant git. She didn't owe him anything … he'd been paid by Miles for the trip. Hadn't he? Unease flickered in her mind. He'd always been quite evasive about that.

For a moment she really did think he might throttle her as something like fury blazed in his eyes. She licked her lips in a vain attempt to dispel the sudden dryness of her mouth and couldn't pull her gaze away from his.

For a charged moment they stared at each other, then with a single stride Cam hauled her into his arms, a firm hand behind her head as he brought his lips straight down on hers with a groan.

Like a match to a fuse, the touch of them ignited all the fluttery feelings in her stomach and she wrapped her arms around his neck, returning everything with the kiss.

The warm, mobile mouth searched hers, firm and insistent, and intent on taking, and all she could do was give back. It felt like she couldn't get enough of him, as if she was trying to breathe and still couldn't get air into her lungs.

When his mouth finally stilled, he sighed, making her heart sing.

'I'm going,' he kissed her again, 'to kill you,' and nuzzled at her neck. 'I've aged ten years, worrying about you.'

Guilt kicked like a physical punch to the stomach.

She plunged her hands into his hair and pulled his mouth back to hers. 'I'm sorry. I—'

The apology sank without a trace as he took control of her mouth again and she clung to him, knees weak.

Gradually the storm settled and resting her forehead against his, she savoured the sound of his ragged breathing and the closeness of his broad chest. She sighed.

'I should have let you know where I was. Guess I had to prove something, not just to you but me too. The time, I needed it … but it was inconsiderate … I was being stubborn.' She risked a quick glance. 'That needy comment …'

He shook his head, and grimaced and gave a half-laugh. 'Got that wrong didn't I? You're the least needy woman I've ever met. I was just too dumb to see it at the time.'

They both paused. Laurie wasn't sure where it left them. They liked each other. There was a strong attraction. In the past she would have left it, just let things drift without trying to define it. That's what had happened with Robert. Not once had she questioned the foundations of what they had. She'd been passive and let their relationship happen.

This time, she would define things and if it didn't work out – fine – but at least it would be on her terms. An active decision.

'Cam—'

'—Laurie.'

They pulled back from each other, suddenly awkward, but she had to say her piece. Now or never.

'Cam, I know you kind of freaked out when I said that I'd decided to finish with Robert, but it had nothing to do with you.'

'Ouch.' He rubbed his arm. 'That's my ego taking a bashing.'

'Look, I'm not … vastly experienced and I probably shouldn't have slept with you because … I just shouldn't.'

'I'm not so sure about that,' teased Cam.

Her lips twitched. 'Thing is … this whole trip has opened my eyes. I did sleep with you because I …' she couldn't help the blush that leapt into her cheeks, 'I fancied the pants off you.' With a quick grin, she gave him a deliberately lascivious look, revelling in the sense of power she felt. 'Still do. But I haven't ever really lived. Robert and I fell into a relationship, it wasn't planned or decided upon, it just happened. And that's what happened when I slept with you … it just happened. I don't want to fall into things anymore. I want to know what I want and act accordingly.' She stopped and sighed. 'God, that sounds prissy.'

Cam just smiled, his hands hooked in his jeans' pockets and she couldn't help her eyes straying to the noticeable bulge there. It made her feel a lot better and she grinned, her confidence back. 'I'm not even sure I want a long term relationship just now, or even commitment but,' she sobered and took a deep breath because this was where she took a chance, a risk, 'I'd like something with you.' There, she'd said it.

Cam blinked. 'What? No strings attached? Fling sort of thing.' He scowled. 'What about what I want?'

Laurie took an uncertain step back, wrong-footed by the suddenly serious expression on his face.

'You want my body, basically.' Cam looked pissed off.

She almost smiled but didn't dare, he reminded her of a small boy who'd had his favourite toy removed.

'That'd be nice,' she smirked, letting her gaze rove over his body watching his dilate even as his eyes narrowed. She'd riled him good and proper and it felt good. The feeling of control rocked through her.

'You are kidding?' He looked ready to throttle her.

Hiding a smile she said, 'No Cam, I want more than that but I don't know how much. I'd like to see what will happen. There's definite chemistry, we get on well … I'd like to see if there's more but I'm not expecting forever or anything like that.'

'What if I do?' His low growl turned her stomach over and for a moment she felt light-headed.

'Don't be daft. We hardly know each other.' She glanced at her watch as if that would tell her how much time they'd spent together. Although logically if you took the hours and minutes they'd spent together since they left England, it was a lot more than most couples did in their early stages of dating. 'Besides, I need to speak to Robert. I shouldn't have slept with you. I need to tell him it's over and I can't do it over the phone.'

Cam stilled. 'When was the last time you spoke to him?'

There was something he wasn't telling her, she could sense it from his sudden watchfulness. She'd been putting off contacting Robert using the poor signal in the mountains to help her justify delaying the inevitable. Or did he want to know whether she'd made the effort to contact Robert before him? Somehow she didn't think Cam was the jealous type.

'I texted him a couple of times but I haven't spoken to him since Paris.'

'You didn't invite him to meet you here?'

That didn't sound good. Laurie closed her eyes. 'He's here, isn't he?'

Cam nodded. 'Yup.'

'Oh God, how long has he been here?'

'Two days.'

'Shit.' She turned away and went over to the window. Facing Robert now was the last thing she wanted to do. He wouldn't approve at all. She sighed heavily.

'You know he's a dickhead.'

'I think you've said it before.'

'Yeah, well, just reiterating.'

Laurie could feel a pulse pinging in her forehead. Damn. Why did life have to go and get complicated? In Lake Garda, on her own without facing real people, it had all seemed so obvious and simple.

Robert was going to blow a gasket. She hadn't banked on him being around. Too late to disappear again now. She looked at her watch. Had Ron got her text yet? Which reminded her. 'How did you know I was here?'

'I bribed the girl on reception to let me know as soon as you checked in.' Cam grinned. 'Robert's been lurking in the lobby for two days straight now.' He laughed wickedly. 'He'll be livid he missed you.'

Laurie felt relieved that he had, which made the necessity of speaking to Ron all the more urgent. 'Do you know where Ron is? I thought you were him actually.'

'I had dinner with him last night. He said he'd got business at the Ferrari museum today. Something to do with Miles' estate.'

Damn. She really wanted to sort things out before she had to face Robert. Get it all sorted. She checked her phone. Ron's text confirmed what Cam had said. Ron was indeed at the Ferrari museum and suggested she meet him there at 3.00 p.m. in the car.

She showed Cam the text.

Cam merely grinned. 'Great, can I take you for lunch? There's a lovely restaurant just down the road, Miles recommended it. The Sil—'

'—Silver Fig,' she finished. It had been included in the dossier. Her stomach rumbled in agreement and Cam held out the crook of his arm.

'Just let me change, I'd like to put on a dress.'

'By the way ...'

She bit her lip at his tone, it didn't bode well.

'About this provisional licence ...'

Chapter 27

How had he ever thought she was needy? Cam could kick himself now. Chatting with great animation, as she sipped Pellegrino water, she told him about her run-in with the police.

'So how come you don't have a driving licence?'

Laurie's face clouded with sadness. He squeezed the hand he hadn't let go of since they'd sat down at the table. 'The day I was due to take my test, Dad had a heart attack.' She winced and he could see the pain in her eyes. 'After that, I just decided I didn't need to drive. I wasn't going to leave him. Not when he might die. Driving didn't seem that important.'

'After he died, Robert was always around and I never needed to drive, so there was no incentive to take a test. I could always drive with him because your provisional licence lasts for ages and then you can just keep renewing it. So I never got round to taking the test.' She pulled a face. 'It was one less risk to take in life.'

'So you decided to drive across Europe without a licence … that sounds pretty risky to me.'

'Yeah, well at first I had no intention of taking Miles' challenge. Then you … you were so bloody arrogant assuming that I couldn't possibly drive a car like that … which I knew damn well I could. Then after we went to the test track, it kind of got into my blood again. I figured I could get you to do most of the driving and if I drove when you were in the car, it would be all right.

'Only Robert looked it up on the internet … he didn't want me to go.'

'I bet he didn't.'

'Why do you say that?'

Her face shone with innocence and the quiet beauty he could now appreciate. 'I suspect, he knew once you had a taste of the big bad world, you would want more from life or that you might leave him behind in the slow lane.'

'That's …' She bit her lip as she considered his words. He felt unkind at being so brutal but it was true. She even looked different. Taller when she walked. Unafraid to look people in the eye. There was a sparkle about her which had been missing before. Yeah, the hair and the clothes had changed, but they were superficial. The change came from deep within. He would do anything to prevent that being snuffed out again. Even if he wasn't the one for her, he didn't want her to go back to what she'd been before.

He smiled to himself.

'What?' Laurie leaned forward. 'What's that for?' She touched his mouth, a gesture that a month ago, she'd never have initiated.

How did he tell her she was about to become very wealthy?

'Do you know the difference between a short wheel base and a long wheel base?' he asked.

She frowned, a dimple appearing in her cheek. 'That's what Robert asked me when I was in Paris.'

'Really?' The mercenary git. Robert had definitely been doing his homework.

'And yes, I do know actually …'

He waited a second, unsure whether she really did know how much the Ferrari was worth.

'A short wheel base is shorter and a long wheel base is longer.'

He leant over and kissed her. Adorable and completely innocent. He wondered how she would feel when she realised that she'd been driving the car without valid insurance all this time. He had a feeling she'd be horrified. That was one hell of a bigger risk than she'd have been prepared to take.

'Trust Miles to have some pomp and circumstance arranged.' As she turned onto the Via Enzo Ferrari, she spotted the stewards waiting.

'You know Miles …' Cam's voice trailed off. She touched his hand as she felt her own swift pierce of grief.

'He was one of a kind. I'll miss him, but he's given me so much back. This …' she paused, loath to use the clichéd phrase, 'trip has really been a journey for me.'

Cam squeezed her hand back. 'A good one though.'

'The best.'

'Can you hold onto that thought?'

His urgent tone made her turn to him. Worry lines erased the laughter around his eyes and a sombre expression had dimmed the usual vibrancy of his green eyes.

'What's wrong?'

He hesitated but just as he was about to say something, a loud cheer from outside the car erupted.

Blimey. There was a welcome committee, including a TV crew all waiting behind the huge chequered flag that was being waved enthusiastically by a diminutive man in a scarlet driving suit. The driveway was lined with Ferrari liveried drivers, the familiar black stallion etched on their breast pockets.

It would have been nice if Ron could have forewarned her. Good job she'd put her red dress on, although that was more for Cam's benefit. It might fool some people into thinking she'd prepared properly.

Actually, it wouldn't have mattered if she'd driven in stark naked. Every man's eyes were on the car and from the glazed expressions on their faces she expected them to collapse in a heap of drool at any second. No doubt about it, this car was a showstopper and if you were a Ferrari aficionado, it was like all your orgasms coming in one. Men would kill to get their hands on this baby. She patted the steering wheel. OK maybe kill was an exaggeration but she was pretty sure they'd go to great lengths.

As she brought the car to a halt just by a small podium, a loud cheer went up and she could see Ron on top of the podium, an A4 envelope in his hand, flanked by Robert.

Shit. Behind her sunglasses she closed her eyes a second. Served her right for putting off finding him in the hotel. Now it had come back to bite her, in full public view.

'This is it.' Cam gave her hand a final squeeze. 'You earned it all.'

With all eyes on her, she tensed her muscles, determined to get out of the car elegantly for once. She'd had enough damn practice over the last couple of weeks; it should be second nature by now.

With fluid ease she stepped out of the car and another cheer went up. Buoyed up by their good-natured enthusiasm, she waved, a little shyly at first and then broke into a broad grin as the overwhelming party spirit hit her like a physical wave of goodwill.

Grateful for her sunglasses she made her way onto the Podium. Robert stepped forward and flung his arms around her.

'Welcome back, Laurie.' He hugged her so hard she thought he might squeeze the last breath out of her. It meant she couldn't say anything but he was so pumped, he wouldn't have noticed. He almost bounced her up and down along with him as he jumped for joy. 'You did it. You did it. You did it. We're …Oh, Laurie you did it. You're amazing. We're made. We'll never have to work again.'

If it hadn't have been for Ron, she wasn't sure she'd have managed to extricate herself. Somehow the older man managed to intercede and separate them, firmly pushing Robert to the back of the podium. Thankfully the assembled crowd had gathered around the car and weren't the least interested in what was going on onstage. She glanced back. Cam leant against the back of the car watching her. She couldn't read the expression on his face. The blank contemplation made the hair on the back of her neck tingle. Despite the heat of the brilliant Italian morning sunshine, her hands suddenly seemed cold. The whole scene felt unreal and she felt separate from the volume of chatter.

'Laurie, lovely to see you.' Ron's smile had a touch of pride. 'You look wonderful, my dear. Absolutely wonderful. Miles would have been … so delighted. Well done for rising, not just rising but going beyond that and wholeheartedly meeting his challenge.' The weight of his words hit her hard. Tears gathered in her eyes and she had to swallow hard to hold them at bay.

Ron took her shoulders and kissed her on one cheek and then the other, just as Miles had always done. The import was clear, the kiss came from Miles.

She touched Ron's hand, conscious that this was as momentous for him as her. He probably missed Miles far more than she. They'd been chequers buddies for many years. 'Thanks Ron.'

'Now,' he squared his shoulders, which despite the heat, were still encased in his tweed jacket. 'To business.' He opened the envelope and she found Robert had sidled up to her. She stiffened as he threw an arm around her shoulder. If only she'd talked to him earlier. She wriggled away. 'Bit hot,' she murmured.

He winked at her. Relief at putting distance between them warred with dismay at the rush of knowledge that getting rid of Robert might be like trying to dislodge a limpet.

'Niece, if you are listening to this, then you have truly achieved the challenge. The Ferrari is now yours to do with what you will.' Ron paused here and looked at her. 'You have to decide whether you would like to keep it or sell it.' He looked very serious, almost as if it were life and death.

She guessed that to Miles, it would have been but it was immaterial. She'd already made up her mind what she was doing with the car. Robert had sidled closer again; she could feel his breath on her neck. Had he always exhibited this possessiveness? Or had she just not found it so irritating before? Now she couldn't get far enough away. Which made her a prize bitch. Even if she had fallen out of love, she ought to let him down gently.

'Have you any idea what this car is worth?' whispered Robert, nudging her in the ribs several times. 'It's a lot.'

Ron gave him a quelling look but it didn't stop Robert's fidgeting.

'At current market value,' Robert's face glowed with excitement, 'that car is worth millions. It is a Short Wheeled Base,' he said with a dreamy smile on his face.

Million what? Lire? Euros? Dollars? Surely not pounds because a car couldn't possibly be worth that.

Laurie looked at him in surprise. Robert knew nothing about cars.

'Millions of pounds … can you imagine.' His eyes looked as if they were about to pop out his head.

'Ahem,' interrupted Ron with a fierce glower at Robert, 'The documentation of ownership is all here. The car is yours,' he smiled gently at her. 'However, if you choose to sell the car—'

Robert snorted. 'Yeah, like you wouldn't.' He elbowed Laurie in the ribs again.

Laurie compressed her lips to hold in a laugh. Ron looked as if he'd like to squish Robert like a bug.

'There is one stipulation.' Ron referred back to the document and read out. 'If you decided to sell the Ferrari, in exchange for escorting you across Europe, first refusal must be given to Cameron Matthews …'

She glanced down at him with a smile, it seemed a fair reward for escorting her across Europe and making sure she got here safely.

'… at the price of £500,000.'

The gathered crowd gasped in perfect unison.

As if hitting an iceberg, her stomach lurched. Pins and needles hit her jawline and for a moment, Oh God, she thought she was going to faint. Her vision blurred before coming back into sharp focus on Cam. He stood, thumbs hooked through the loops in his jeans. The stance might have looked casual but she could tell every nerve-ending of his was alert.

Tension shimmered across the short distance between them.

She stared at him, her stomach feeling hollow.

She'd been so bloody stupid. Men would kill for this car. What was escorting a slightly stupid, unworldly librarian across Europe, throwing in a bit of sex to sweeten the deal? Nothing to a man like Cameron, who oozed sexual sophistication.

Ron returned to reading out loud, the formal words a merciful respite from having to think. 'The sale price to him is a substantial reduction in current market value.'

'Substantial!' wailed Robert in anguish, shooting a murderous glare at Cam. 'That's daylight robbery. It's … that's … you can't … it's worth millions. We'd be millionaires … multi-millionaires… I mean we'd have a million in the bank.'

Her face almost crumpled but she hung on, determined not to give Cam the satisfaction. Instead she gave him a look of total disdain and watched as he paled. Bastard.

To her surprise instead of backing away, he threw up his head, the black curls dancing in the sunlight like Medusa's snakes and scowled. He strode towards the podium. Shit, he looked furious. She took a step backwards.

'Don't you dare think that.' he hissed at her, almost nose to nose.

'Think what?' She spat. How dare he try to turn his back on her. 'That you used me to get the car you always wanted?'

'You don't think that.' he growled.

'Don't I?' Her nails scored her palms. 'Why else would you cross Europe? Out of the goodness of your heart?'

'I did it for Miles at first and then …' he paused and his gaze gentled. His eyes ranged over her face.

Her heart turned over and she so wanted to believe him. That he cared about her.

For a moment she softened and leaned towards him. But why hadn't he said anything? He'd had plenty of chance since she'd arrived in Maranello. He'd never said a word. Would she have believed him anyway?

'You did it to get the car.' Robert sounded horribly smug. 'You could sell it tomorrow for double what you paid for it. One trillion per cent profit.'

Cam gave him a disgusted look. 'You fool. It's not about money.'

No, she knew that. Cam wasn't interested in the money. He just wanted the car, of course he did. The pain in her heart, it really did feel like something was breaking, because she understood, oh she understood to the depth of her soul, exactly how he felt.

The Ferrari, a beautiful beguiling devil with the power to steal a soul, sat just beneath the podium. Sleek, beautiful … hers.

Of course Cam wanted the car. How could she blame him? Cars like this were impossibly rare. The opportunity to own one would never come along again. No, she pressed her lips together hard, she couldn't blame him at all.

Beside her Robert shrugged and muttered.

She stared down at the Ferrari. She could survive this. So Cam didn't want her, she would get over it. Robert didn't want her either. Not her. He might think he did but he just wanted what she represented to him. Security. And she knew now, security had to come from within. You had to feel secure within yourself.

She turned to Ron. 'I think that's everything, isn't it?'

'Yes, my dear. The car is yours. There is one last thing …'

'Yes?'

'Miles wanted to know what you planned to do next.'

She looked straight at Ron, her head held high.

'That's easy.' Her look around took in Cam and then Robert and then rested happily on the car. 'I'm going to keep her.'

Chapter 28

Cam's head whipped up. Instead of disappointment or anger, his eyes burned with admiration. They were so close she could see the slight nod as if of approval that he made. Her heart faltered for a second as their eyes held the connection.

'Are you mad?' Robert managed to squeeze his way in front of Laurie, oblivious to the charged chemistry arcing between them.

'You can't keep the car. Be sensible, Laurie.' Robert planted his hands firmly on his hips. 'I can see the romance, the allure. You've just had a lovely holiday. Nice time. It's like when you buy Ouzo – when you get it back it tastes rank.'

Actually she rather liked Ouzo but it probably wasn't helpful to say so just now.

She sighed. 'It's not about the now. It's about so much more.' How could she possibly explain to him? She'd shifted up a gear and left him behind. It sounded so callous and heartless but he was part of the problem. She couldn't go back.

'What more? It's an expensive car you don't need. We need a bigger house, a better lifestyle. We could have all that.'

'That's just material things, they don't make you happy.'

'Don't you think that's a bit fucking hypocritical? It doesn't get much more material than a multi-million pound Ferrari.'

'Miles wanted me to have it, I know he did. He taught me to

love life again. I don't expect you to understand.'

'Love life! What the fuck are you on about?' He grabbed Laurie's shoulders, pushing Cam out of the way. 'Millions of pounds! You can buy other cars with that. Another fucking Ferrari for all I care. We can have a big fancy wedding, like you wanted. It'll hardly put a dent in the money. Laurie, what are you thinking?'

Robert's panicked expression pulled her back to reality. She looked at him as if seeing him for the first time. Desperation was written all over his face, from the pugnacious tilt of the weak chin – why hadn't she noticed that before – to the anxious blinking of his eyes and the tension lines across his high forehead. He clutched her harder, his fingers sinking into her collar bones.

'Robert.' She wriggled, trying to get out of the hold. He just held on tighter.

'You can't do this to me.'

'I'm not doing anything to you.'

'You selfish cow.'

Cam grabbed Robert's arm, his angry stance making him looker bigger and dangerous.

'Touch her again and I'll flatten you.'

He shook Cam off with angry scowl, reminding Laurie of a pesky wasp, but he did let go of her shoulders. 'Butt out buster. Bet you've shagged her, haven't you? I know your type. Anything in a skirt.'

He caught sight of Laurie's instant blush.

'Bloody hell, you have as well.' His face contorted into an ugly sneer. 'You fool. He's a player. What's he going to see in you? Plain Jane. Flat-chested. No sex-appeal. He's played you. And you fell for it. Well I can tell you now, if you keep the car, we're finished.'

'I warned you.' Cam's voice, low and deadly serious, was all the notice given before he socked Robert in the jaw.

He went down onto his knees.

Laurie's eyes widened and she let out a horrified gasp. 'Cam!'

He shrugged. 'I'm not sorry. No one talks to you like that.'

Her face overheated, furious at Robert's insults and shocked by Cam's defence of her.

Robert swayed on his knees, rubbing his jaw and shooting Cam evil looks. He rounded on her. 'Christ, I've stuck by you all this time. Since your dad died. I could have got a better job. But no I stayed in Leighton to be with you. Mum said I could do better. You owe me.'

Owed him? Something slipped and loosened in her chest. Rage bubbled at the back of her throat and vitriolic words threatened to spill out in her defence. He wasn't worth it. Mortification washed over her. What a fool. Accepting Robert's domineering crap all this time. Because it was easier than being on her own?

'I don't owe you anything, Robert.' She stood tall, staring him down. 'You've lived in my house rent free for the last two years. I think that's ample compensation.' She could have said a lot more, the flat-chested remark still stung, but she didn't need to. She was the better person.

'We'll see. Don't expect me to come crawling back when you're all alone. He's,' Robert pointed to Cam, 'going to dump you now that you won't give him his precious car. You're going to be a laughing stock.'

Robert stomped down the steps of the podium and as he got to the bottom he looked back. 'By the way. You owe me for the flights and the hotel room. I'll send you a bill.'

'Don't bother, take it out of this month's rent.' She was proud of how calm and cool her voice sounded. If she'd responded to his venomous tones with bitchiness, she might have broken down.

Cam stepped forward. 'You OK?'

She levelled a dangerous look at him. 'Let's just say it's been an eye-opening morning. Ron, I'd really like to get out of here.'

Cam caught her arm. 'Wait, I didn't …'

'Didn't what? Sleep with me to get the car? Who are you trying to convince, Cam? Yourself or me?' She shook him off.

304

'Do you need a moment dear?' Ron's kind face blurred.

Sod it, she wasn't going to cry now. She felt like shit inside but no one needed to know that. She'd get over Cam and as for Robert, all she could feel was sadness that she'd been so dumb and needy that she'd mistaken companionship for love.

'Your uncle would have been so proud of you.' Ron beamed and thrust the envelope into her hand, as he pulled out a hanky to dab at his eyes.

'Really?' She wasn't so sure about that.

'Oh, yes. Miles really wanted to help you. He knew you weren't happy. It worried him greatly. He spent a great deal of time talking about you. I have to say I wasn't sure about his methods and after that little debacle I'm still not. Upsetting for you, my dear.'

'Yes, but life goes on … and Miles has given me a lot to think about.' Her life would never be the same again.

'All part of his plan.'

'Miles' plan?' Her voice rose an octave in disbelief. 'He couldn't have …' Of course he could. The sneaky old devil was nobody's fool.

'He wanted you to rediscover the happiness of your youth. It was a great regret he didn't insist to your father you continued to visit. Celeste upset him terribly with her treatment of you. He never forgave her, you know.'

'So why did he insist on me visiting the Chateau?'

'It was important that you came to your own understanding. Learned you hadn't missed out at all.'

'Wasn't that taking quite a gamble?'

Ron snorted. 'Miles' life was one long gamble.'

She thought of the horses and the cars and the wives. 'True; he didn't always come out on top though.'

'I know. Which is why I did try and talk him out of it,' Ron smiled ruefully, 'but Miles … you know.'

She nodded.

'Testament, really, to how well he knew you. I think you were

305

the daughter he never had.'

'Yeah I've inherited his extravagant taste in cars.' she grinned. She had no idea how the hell she'd afford to run the car. Could she even afford the insurance? All Robert's incandescent objections came back to her.

Cam had simply nodded and walked away as if accepting defeat.

'So you are going to keep it?' asked Ron as they got into the Ferrari.

She sighed, starting up the engine. It was easier now Robert and Cam weren't hanging on her every word. 'Yep. I know I can't really afford it but …' she shot Ron a mischievous look, 'I love it. It came to me last night, the first time I heard the engine with Uncle Miles. I was seven. In the paddock at his house. I heard that rumble and went running over to see it. I asked him if there was a dragon under the bonnet.' She smiled at the memory and could feel that initial excitement as her young mind wondered at what could possibly make such a mighty roar. 'Typical Miles; he didn't disillusion me.' He'd bent down and whispered in her ear. She still remembered the words now.

'That's why Laurie, you are the smartest little girl. No one else knows it's a dragon. It's our secret.'

The moment had cemented their friendship and forever confirmed the magical status of the car. As she got older and learned more about the mechanics of the engine, she knew there wasn't really a dragon under the bonnet but on more fanciful days, she liked to imagine there might be.

'He told me the story. He also told me that the light went out in you as you got older. As one tragedy hit you after another.'

Laurie turned. 'I never thought of them as tragedies. Parents separate. Parents die. You just have to get on with it. Be practical.'

'Miles thought you became too practical. He worried terribly that you'd settled … not for second best … but just settled for what was there. He wanted more for you.'

She sighed. 'And he's given it to me. It's not just the car. My

306

eyes have been opened during this trip. There's so much I could do. Sell the house. Go to Uni. Try to get a job with something to do with wine.'

'That sounds exciting. Miles said you had an amazing palate.'

'Probably because he brought me up on Chateauneuf du Pape. It's spoilt me for anything else.' Something that had been idling at the back of her mind popped into the forefront, unleashing a stream of conscious thought, which made her blurt out, 'The Comte has invited me back to spend some time with him, learning more about how the wine is made.'

Ron raised an eyebrow and took his time before he opened his mouth to comment on her sudden random statement, as if he'd pondered the possibilities.

'Will you go?'

Laurie paused. At the time the Comte made the offer, she hadn't even considered it. 'Yes, I think I probably will.'

It was an opportunity she couldn't let pass by.

'I'm afraid there's something else I need to tell you. You probably don't need to worry about selling your house.'

The length of his pause made her suspicious. What did he mean? She glanced over at him.

'Miles has left you the remainder of his estate.'

The engine roared in protest as she mismanaged a gear change and dropped from fourth to second.

Chapter 29

Cam shoved his things into the canvas bag. By the time he'd cadged a lift back to the hotel, Laurie and Ron had departed for the airport and he was in time to see the car being boxed up to be freighted back to England.

He tormented himself by standing and watching the Ferrari being loaded into the container, revisiting images of Laurie at the wheel, her hair mussed by the wind, her face alight with joy; that moment he spotted the car in Bormio and realised she'd made it and the overwhelming relief when she'd turned up here. The clang of the doors of the container interrupted his reverie, and he looked up to see them close tight, shutting the car into the dark.

For the first time in his life, he had no idea of what he was going to do next. There were jobs out there, at least three messages on his phone offering employment, but he didn't fancy any of them. He had five hundred grand burning a hole in his pocket. He could go anywhere, do anything and he had no desire to do a darn thing.

He shoved his hands in his pockets and found an unfamiliar edge. He pulled out the worn postcard, picked up a lifetime ago when Laurie had abandoned him. Laurie had chosen it in the tabac next to the hotel, having disdained the hotel selection, which she'd deemed too cheesy. How a postcard was anything but cheesy he didn't know. He tapped the postcard thoughtfully against his cheek and then strode into the hotel with renewed purpose. He knew exactly what he was going to do.

They'd arrived back to Heathrow's grey skies a week ago to be picked up by a driver thankfully organised by Ron. Laurie wouldn't have been able to cope with public transport. The events of those few weeks had caught up with her during the flight home and by the time they got into the taxi for the hour and a half drive, she'd a killer headache befitting of the emotionally induced hangover. All she'd wanted to do was get home, although the thought was ruined by the knowledge that once at home, she'd have to face Robert again.

When the car had pulled up outside her terraced home, Laurie looked at it anew. The house looked tired, as if old people lived there instead of two young people who should be at the peak of their lives. She'd made no move to get out.

'Will you be all right?' asked Ron as they sat in the back of the car.

She nodded. 'Just a bit reluctant to go in. I … don't know what Robert will do. He doesn't have anywhere else to go. I feel bad kicking him out … especially …' she thought of Merryview. At least she had somewhere else to go, although it wasn't home … yet.

'I can arrange it, if you like.' She wondered for a moment if Ron had read her mind. It had been so tempting. Just to run away. Horribly appealing. Let Robert come, take his things away. Leave in his own time. She wouldn't have to face him again. It seemed so cowardly; she'd shared her life with him for the last two years and now she just wanted him gone.

Instead she'd said, even though every nerve screamed against it, 'No, I'll stay here. I need to sort things out with Robert.'

'There will be a lot of paperwork relating to Miles' will. There's a lot going through probate at the moment and you need to sign things. Why don't you give my secretary a ring and arrange an appointment for next week? But if you need anything in the meantime, you will call me, won't you?'

'Yes.'

'Promise?' Ron gave her a stern look.

'I will, honest. Thank you.' She leaned over and kissed his papery cheek. 'Thanks for everything. I'll see you next week.'

She unlocked the front door, waved Ron off. The chill in the air struck her. Coming home had been a big mistake. She stood rooted by the door, the cold of the metal letter box at her hip. The dark hallway with its dated lino flooring seemed a million times smaller and pokier than she remembered. The pictures lining the walls were coated in dust and when she looked at them, not one held any significance. They were just pictures.

In the lounge the table of pictures looked accusingly at her. None of them had been updated in years. The one of her dad had bleached with age and sunlight. The weak light did the drab room no favours. Everything about it looked ordinary. She thought of the Comte's cosy salon, how Marie had filled it with cushions and knick-knacks. Her sewing basket, china thimbles and antique scissors. Nothing in this room gave any clues about the inhabitants of the house. It was as if the house had been encapsulated when her dad died and she'd done nothing with it ever since. It mirrored her lack of emotional development in recent years. She surveyed the room grimly. Well that was all about to change. She'd learn to live here before she did anything about Merryview. Make this home first.

In two days, she managed to make a huge dent in her savings, although with Miles' money she need never worry again. Thanks to Ikea, her lounge now looked more contemporary, with new furniture, a lick of paint as well as lots of brightly coloured cushions and throws, pretty lamps and framed postcards everywhere. Lugging that little lot back from Bletchley on the bus had been quite a challenge but she was delighted with the results. Hanging the brightly coloured postcards in groups gave her a huge sense of satisfaction, although something stirred at the back of her mind.

Even though Merryview would be hers, moving in straight away didn't feel right, even to avoid Robert. It would have been swapping one shelter for another … she needed to stay here and make it her home.

And a home for Siena should she ever want one. With freshly painted pale grey walls, white bedding and grey and silver cushions, Laurie was rather pleased with how her sister's room had turned out. Siena had shown her delight with a flurry of effusive texts and booked a flight to visit for a weekend at the end of August.

Robert turned up on Saturday. Even though she'd been expecting him, her heart banged uncomfortably against her ribs when the knock on the door came.

'Hello Robert.'

'Laurie.'

'I've got all your things ready.' She'd packed his clothes neatly into suitcases and boxed up all the CDs and DVDs. It seemed easier to give them all to him, rather than risk him picking a fight over ownership. A clean break was all she wanted.

Robert smiled grimly. 'You think it's that easy just to chuck me out.'

He didn't scare her, she told herself. 'It's my house.'

'Yes but we've been living here together as common law partners.'

'That's just a myth, it doesn't exist in law.'

'Sure about that, are you? Not what my solicitor is saying.'

She smiled. He had just given himself away. Living with someone gave you a certain insight. Robert wouldn't consult a solicitor in a million years. If he'd just come in and said he hadn't got anywhere to go or would she give him time to find somewhere else, she might have suggested he stay in the spare room.

'Robert you don't have a leg to stand on. We shared the bills but you didn't make any other contribution.'

'I think I deserve some kind of compensation. In lieu of a notice period. Landlords can't get rid of tenants just like that.'

'Is that all it comes down to? Money? We lived together. You wanted to get married.'

'Well you seem to have money to burn if you turn down half a mill.' An agonised expression contorted his face. 'How could you?' he moaned. 'It's criminal. You should contest the will. Your uncle was barking. That car is worth a fortune.'

He would never understand. And she didn't think she could ever explain it to him.

'I really am sorry Robert. It was just the right thing to do and … I know what Miles wanted me to do.'

'He's dead; he's not going to care.'

'Yeah, but I'm not.'

Puzzlement filled Robert's face. 'You've changed. My mother was right. You didn't know that, did you? She didn't want us to get married. Kept warning me against it.'

No wonder he'd been so keen for a quickie ceremony in the registry office and only after Miles had died.

'You're making a big mistake. You'll regret it.'

He didn't have the grace to look sad about it. She might as well have just taken away his favourite toy.

'Robert I'm sorry. But it really is over. I've packed all your things but if there's anything I've forgotten let me know.' She was trying to be nice but it was hard. 'I'll leave you to it, can you leave the keys?'

Turning her back on him felt risky, she could almost feel his pent up anger about to burst out but she didn't want to stand over him as he collected everything up. She headed into the kitchen and stood looking out of the window at the neat garden. It hadn't all been bad and she was as much to blame for accepting the status quo.

Robert came into the kitchen a little while later and stood awkwardly.

'That's that then. Hope you're proud of yourself.'

'Of course I'm not proud that it's ending like this,' she rounded on him. 'I feel sad and disappointed.'

'Really?' He raised a disbelieving eyebrow. 'You could still stop it. Sell the car. We could buy a house. Start a family. We wouldn't have to work. You could do whatever you wanted. Not look for another crappy job like the one at the library. We were good together, Laurie. We can be again. I can forgive you for having an affair. Loads of people do. I can see that you were dazzled by him.'

She shook her head, grateful that he didn't know about the rest of Miles' inheritance. He'd never leave. He still didn't get it. 'I can't go back.'

'You mean you won't.' He slammed his fist against the door making her jump.

It would have been easy to say sorry again but she'd done enough of that.

'No, I won't.' She turned her back on him and looked out the window again, so that he wouldn't see the tears that began to spill down her cheeks. Being cruel didn't come naturally but with Robert there could be no half measure.

She heard the door slam and then began to cry in earnest.

Decorating the lounge and Siena's room had started a small storm and now she wanted to make this house her home. Confirmation of her redundancy had come while she was away, so she was officially finished at the library and with time to fill, she started making various enquiries about wine courses and jobs in the industry, in between planning the redecoration of the rest of the house.

Ron called sooner than she expected, although his message wasn't very encouraging. 'Laurie, we have a problem. Please can you come and see me as soon as possible.' His urgent tone had her worried and it didn't help that when she called him back, his secretary created a slot for her that afternoon and she sounded equally anxious. What could have rattled them so much?

The large map of Europe on the wall was now surrounded by familiar looking postcards. She crossed to take a closer look, smiling as she did, feeling rather proud. There was her route. The postcard she'd bought on the Champs Elysées for an extortionate amount, the pretty scene of Honfleur right at the start of the journey, the perilous hair-pins of Bormio, a pretty mountain village on the N35 and one of the Comte's postcards from his winery. She tracked the highlighted route, taking a quick dive into the spill of memories. She could almost feel the warmth of the sun, hear the roar of the Ferrari and smell Cam's verbena aftershave.

Her throat closed and she swallowed, determined to ignore the twinge of grief that shot through her. It took too much effort to fight the memories and she let herself slip back, muscular thighs clad in tatty jeans alongside her in the car, the mischievous twinkle in the sea green eyes and the mobile mouth so quick to smile. She almost bowed under with the physical ache. She missed him.

Lemon verbena still teased the air and she closed her eyes, wishing the scent wasn't so evocative. She could almost imagine he was here.

Staring hard at the map she tried to steady herself. She couldn't fall apart in front of Ron. She traced the route again. There were positives. Lots of positives, she had to hang on to those. Her mouth twisted in rueful amusement. How could she ever forget Cam's face when she'd driven off and left him in …?

The breath caught in her throat. Holy shit! In her mind's eye she could see his amused disbelief that she wouldn't leave him and on the table … the postcard she was meant to post. The pin on the map with its string led to a blank patch on the wall.

Shit, shit, shit. Ron had been quite explicit. To prove she'd completed the journey she had to send a postcard from every designated point.

Heaving air into her lungs suddenly seemed impossible and then it was too much. Her ribcage worked frantically and her breathing pattern tied itself in knots. Panic started to rise and she blinked hard.

No wonder Ron wanted to see her.

Damn. After everything she'd forfeited the car. And lost Cam – not that having him was ever likely. Maybe if she had sold him the car, they might have stayed friends.

'Laurie,' Ron's worried face appeared from his office. 'Glad you could come. Sorry to have alarmed you but I think we might be all right.'

'Really?' She followed him into his office. The smell of lemon verbena was stronger here. Her skin prickled and she looked round, half hoping that Cam might appear from behind the door.

She sank into the chair leaden with the weight of defeat, wishing she could turn the clock back. She would have let Cam have the car. He deserved it far more than she did. He'd had life-long love of the Ferrari. She'd just had a week.

Ah well it was all about to be taken away.

'Robert has been stirring up trouble. But,' Ron looked slightly less grave, 'there might be a solution, although I'm not very happy about it.'

She sat up straighter. 'Robert?' Where did he come into things? He couldn't possibly know about the missing postcard unless Cam had told him.

The room swam for a moment and she closed her eyes trying to get some relief form the rush of thoughts filling her head. No, that just wasn't possible. Cam might be pissed off that she didn't put the car up for sale, but he wasn't vindictive. She knew him well enough to know that. He might have slept with her to get the car but he'd never made any promises.

'Robert has gone to the police.' Ron shook his head in a dear-dear-dear fashion. 'He really is a most unpleasant young man.'

'Do the police need to be involved? I mean I guess I just hand the car back. Is it a criminal offence?'

'Unfortunately the police do rather take a dim view of driving without a licence.'

'What?' Laurie couldn't keep up.

'I'm sorry, my dear, but your erstwhile young friend has taken it upon himself to avail the police of the information that you were driving in Europe without a full licence.'

315

She sagged with relief. 'Not the car then?'

'The car? Well if you get a driving ban you won't be able to drive it. You could lose your licence for up to six months.'

'I thought …' she paused. No point lying now, Ron would notice eventually. 'There's a postcard missing.'

Ron beamed. 'I wasn't worried about that, the vagaries of Italian post mean they've been arriving in a most peculiar order. The last one arrived today. But about this driving offence.'

Laurie jumped to her feet, feeling as if she might burst. Fireworks erupted in her stomach, starburst of joy fizzing through her. 'Can I see the postcard?'

'What?' The elderly solicitor looked at her over his glasses. 'We do seem to be at cross purposes today.'

'Please Ron,' she bit her lip, fearful that she'd got her hopes up.

All the time he rifled through his desk, she wanted to shout he loves me, he loves me not.

At last he handed over the card, considerably the worse for wear, folded and creased as if it had been in a pocket for some time. She flipped it over. On the back in a flowing scrawl Cam's writing simply said, 'Enjoy the car, you deserve it. Love Cam x'

She collapsed into the fabric tub chair clutching the card, her hands shaking. She lifted tear-filled eyes to Ron.

'I need you to draw up some papers for me.'

Chapter 30

Even a week after getting home, following the journey back from Italy that had taken forever, he still felt shattered. His shoulder hadn't recovered from the hell of driving a Fiat 500 over the Stelvio Pass not once but twice in a week. If he ever saw one of the wind-up cars again, it would be too soon.

The conversation with Nick hadn't been anywhere near as bad as the accusing look in Laurie's eyes. Cam's mind seemed to be stuck in some never-ending TV loop where he kept replaying various scenes of his time with Laurie. It didn't seem possible to get through a day without an image of her smile, the toss of her honey ponytail or her hands on the steering wheel seeping into his head and leaving a residue of longing. How could those brief flashes cause such acute pain?

He took in a deep staggered breath, closing his eyes in an attempt to blot out another interminable day.

And now some bugger was revving an engine right outside his bloody window at nine fifteen in the morning. Coming slowly to consciousness, the sound bored into his head. Hold on. The familiar tick over. The distinctive growl.

He threw himself out of bed and crossed to his window. Laurie's silver Ferrari sat beneath it. Pulling on jeans and the nearest T-shirt and hopping as he tried to yank on deck shoes, he got to the front door just as a manila envelope popped through the letterbox. Stepping over it, he threw open the door.

Laurie glanced back, guilt written all over her face, caught in the act of opening the garden gate.

'Where the hell do you think you're going?'

In two strides he caught up with her and grabbed her. There was no way he was letting her get away this time.

Her mouth dropped open in a little 'o' of surprise and taking complete advantage he swooped to kiss naked, pink lips. Her waist felt tiny as he pulled her towards him, definitely a few pounds lighter than he'd last seen her. The seeming fragility gentled his kiss as he teased her mouth open, touching the delicate skin inside with his tongue, needing to coax her in. The stiffness in her back began to recede bit by bit as her arms crept around his neck, her mouth moving beneath his.

Pushing one hand into her hair, the back of her neck felt silky and precious as he sank into the softness of her pliant body.

She took a shaky breath as he pulled back. Wide eyes, the pupils enormous, stared back at him and a dazed smile touched her lips.

'Hi,' he said, sliding his thumb across her cheekbone.

In the morning sunlight, almost ready to flee, she reminded him of a shy fawn. Not Laurie at all and he hated that he'd made her uncertain with him. 'I messed up. I'm a bloke. We do dumb things.'

Tears shimmered in her eyes. 'You did a wonderful thing. You went back to Monstein.'

He tried to look nonchalant as if it had been no big deal. 'Yeah.'

'You posted the card.'

'Yeah.'

She reached out and touched his face. 'Rescuing me?'

'Yeah.' He smiled and caught her hand kissing her palm. 'Thought it was time someone took care of you.'

He looked over at the car, pulling a quizzical face. 'Want to tell me what this is all about?'

Her feet suddenly seemed awfully interesting.

'I got it wrong. If all you cared about was the car, you wouldn't have gone back to post the card. I'm sorry.'

'I love it when women say they're wrong,' grinned Cam. 'Apology accepted. You can say sorry all over again over breakfast.'

'Oy, are you coming or what?' An indignant man stepped out of a beaten up Mondeo just behind the Ferrari. 'I've got a pick up at 10 at the station. If you don't get a move on I'll be late.'

'Gosh, sorry. I completely forgot.' Laurie fumbled in her handbag and produced her purse. 'How much do I owe you? I'm going to stay a while. Here.' She thrust a twenty at him.

He took it, grumbling about time-wasters, got back in his car and made a noisy and showy U-turn to mark his exit.

Cam stood stock still and looked from Laurie to the Ferrari and back again.

'What are you doing here?' he asked quietly.

She sighed as if she'd just been busted, which he had a feeling she had.

'Let's go inside. We can talk—'

'Uh nuh. Tell me now.'

'Don't make a big deal now. You wanted the Ferrari. I'm giving it to you. I don't want the money. I want you to have it. You love it. You deserve it. I'll never appreciate it quite the way you will. Besides if it breaks down I'd only have to come to you to get it fixed. You just have to promise to let me drive it every now and then.'

He opened his mouth but the enormity of what she was suggesting floored him. 'Laurie, I … can't.'

She put a finger up to his lips, the soft touch igniting a spark low in his belly. 'You can.'

Eyes glinting with mischief, she flashed him a self-confident cocky smile. It suited her, she looked like a woman at peace with herself. For the first time she glowed with happiness, as if she'd been released and set free.

He put a firm hand over hers. 'I can't accept it.'

'Too late. Ron's done all the paperwork and transferred

ownership. Done deal.'

She grabbed his hand. 'Come on, I'll tell you all about it over breakfast.'

She sat on his lap as they shared slices of toast. He didn't want to let her go in a hurry. He was still laughing at her blasé comment that she could afford to let one piffling little Ferrari go now that she owned four other Ferraris, a Lamborghini, an Aston Martin and a sex on wheels, E-type jag that might just be her new favourite.

'And if you think that, you definitely don't deserve the Ferrari,' he told her. 'So what are you going to do with all these cars, the wine cellar and the house?'

She worried her lip. 'You might think I'm mad … but when we were staying with the Comte it got me thinking about furthering my knowledge of wine. Maybe trying to work in the industry. Miles' cellar is quite something. Then there's the cars and he owns the track. I thought … well maybe a bed and breakfast for wine and car enthusiasts. They come and stay, taste wines and the next day drive the cars on the track.'

He stared at her, stunned.

'That's a brilliant idea.'

She sat up straighter. 'I thought so too.'

'Of course if you had the GT250 California Spyder that would be the crown jewel in your collection.' He leaned back and looked up at her.

'I was hoping that you might let me have it now and then on loan.'

He shook his head. 'Not a chance.'

Her face fell.

'I'd want to make it a bit more of a permanent arrangement than that.'

Her throat convulsed as if she'd swallowed hard and she raised her eyes to his, a question in them.

'I thought you didn't do permanency? Or commitment? Or

320

needy women?'

He tightened his hold on her. 'You.' He kissed her lips. 'Are.' Another kiss. 'The least needy woman I've ever met. When you drove off, I was so convinced you'd be back.'

She smirked.

'When I flew over the Stel—'

'—Flew?'

He ducked his head, trying to hide the expression on his face. 'Hired a helicopter to make sure you hadn't gone over the edge.' The moment felt right and his eyes held hers, his heart softening. 'Must be love.'

Her whole face softened.

'I love you Laurie. I've missed you.'

She sighed. 'Any man that hires a helicopter … must be love.'

She nestled into him and he held her, savouring the moment until he felt her shaking beneath him. God, was she crying? He eased her away to look at her face to find she was sniggering.

'What?' He asked trying to be indignant.

'I hope that helicopter cost you a small fortune.'

He pulled a face. 'It cost more in pride. I was so relieved when I spotted the car in Bormio, safe and sound. I planned to read the riot act to you about leaving me high and dry and then I was going to apologise for over-reacting.

'But you buggered off, without a word. Left me stewing for days before sauntering into the hotel without a care in the bloody world and hire yourself the Presidential, bloody, suite.'

'Nope, needy does not come into it.'

As Cam disappeared to shower she sat at the table, her fingers dotting the crumbs on the surface, ignoring the temptation to pinch herself. Cam's sheepish expression when he'd confessed about the helicopter had been so adorable. She didn't need any promises from him about the future or permanence. She was happy enough with the now. Truly happy. Thanks to Miles she'd shifted up a gear and learnt enough about herself to let herself be happy. Now that she was in the driving seat, life looked pretty wonderful.